Also by Kyell Gold

Argaea
Volle
Pendant of Fortune
The Prisoner's Release and Other Stories
Shadow of the Father
Weasel Presents

Out of Position
Out of Position
Isolation Play
Divisions
Uncovered
Over Time

Dangerous Spirits
Green Fairy
Red Devil
Black Angel

Other Books
Waterways
Bridges
Science Friction
Winter Games
The Mysterious Affair of Giles
Dude, Where's My Fox?
Losing my Religion
In the Doghouse of Justice
The Silver Circle
X (editor)

Black Angel

by Kyell Gold

This is a work of fiction. All characters and events portrayed within
are fictitious.

BLACK ANGEL

The poem quoted in Chapter 23 is "I Sigh For the Land of Cypress and
Pine," by Samuel Henry Dickson.

Published by Sofawolf Press
St. Paul, Minnesota
http://www.sofawolf.com

ISBN 978-1-936689-53-8
Printed in the United States of America
First trade paperback edition: March 2016
Second Printing: June 2019

Cover and interior art by Rukis

For Beth.

Hope I did okay.

Contents

Chapter 1

Hi. I'm Meg. I'm nineteen, and I'm fucked up.

That's not a big secret, by the way. Pretty much anyone who knew me from about fifteen to now would tell you the same thing. Only back then I thought it was a good kind of fucked up. Like I was just tired of taking everybody's shit, and that's why I basically didn't talk to anyone, painted my fur black, and got three piercings in one ear, one in the other, one over my eye and two in my nose. Richfield High School would sure as shootin' tell you I was fucked up, based on the three times I went to the principal so he could remind me that "guns and violence aren't an answer." Course, otters have the lowest rate of violent crime of any of the major species in this country and you can look that shit up on the Internet, only Mr. Bradkowski couldn't be bothered, so that's about as much weight as you should give his opinion.

About the only friends I made in high school were a black wolf named Sol and a red fox named Alexei, an exchange student from Siberia. They know I'm fucked up, too, only get this: Sol had a couple weird dreams and thought a ghost was talking to him. He told me that the absinthe I got from my best friend Athos gave him those dreams, which was ridiculous if you know Athos—I mean, if anyone *could* do something like that, it'd be him, but he never *would* without telling me.

The stress turned Sol's eyes bright green—something else he said came from "his ghost." He settled down the summer after we graduated, when he and Alexei and I moved into an apartment in Vidalia, about an hour and a half away (not nearly far enough, if you ask me). Then Alexei couldn't get it together. His sister was back in Siberia with their abusive parents, and he had a crush on some guy here who some other guy wanted to bone (boys are so uncomplicated). He insisted on trying to summon Sol's imaginary ghost to help him out, and he dragged me into it because I could get a summoning ritual from Athos. The ritual was completely bogus, but he thought it worked, so between that and his stress he started having these dreams about another ghost, not Sol's. Then he ran away downtown and a Siberian bum followed him back, and...and Alexei went into shock. When he woke up, he claimed that the bum had been *his* ghost.

So you see, my two best friends didn't have shit to say to me about being fucked up. Even Athos, who'd been a reliable fellow skeptic, started believing that shit because he was here for Alexei's breakdown. Oh, we all still got along well enough. After Alexei's ghost deal, they stopped talking about ghosts around me, and I never talked about my shit with them. Everybody stayed happy that way.

Still, in the three weeks since then, I blamed them for the creepy feeling I'd get walking down to the café, or on my way out of the pool, or just sitting alone in my room at night. Vidalia is a fucking sauna in August, so I have to choose between suffocating all night or listening to the construction out behind our apartment building. Usually I leave the window open, because that way I can sit on the windowsill and smoke a joint. If I don't blow the smoke out the window, my long-nosed roommates will wrinkle their noses the next morning, making sure I see it.

So I was looking forward to getting back to normal that Friday morning when Sol's parents showed up to take him to college, because they were also going to take Alexei to his interview for a visa to stay in this country. I was going to have the apartment to myself for three days, and hopefully with the Goosebumps club away, I wasn't going to have any more of those over-the-shoulder creepy feelings.

I lay in bed as the murmur of conversation outside washed over my ears. Sooner or later I was going to have to go out there, to say good-bye to Sol if nothing else. But I knew his parents didn't think much of me even when they thought we were dating, much less now that we were living together and not dating.

So I lay on the futon mattress—no frame; I like being closer to the floor—and checked my e-mail. Two more requests had come in for me to draw them in a fantasy setting, one riding a unicorn and the other battling pirates on a ship. It was fine; easy stuff, even if I might sprain my eyes from rolling them so hard. I replied letting them know it'd be a hundred bucks each and then went over in my head the drawings I had to get done this week. I'd started two and they'd be done quickly, and then I had one more, a boar who'd been referred by a couple friends and wanted to be an astronaut. Sure, whatever runs your motor. I'd have to do some research on spacesuits to get the details right, but that's what the Internet is for.

Then I pulled out my phone and looked at ScentBook to see if anyone there had recommended me to their friends, but nobody had. Eve and Alain from the coffee shop had gone out to a movie with Eve's girlfriend; a guy I'd drawn as a wizard last month was visiting his parents with his boyfriend; the usual blah blah of people's lives. Athos hadn't posted, but then, he did about as often as I did.

I dropped the phone next to my computer keyboard on the up-side-down milk crate. The voices outside were louder now. I figured I couldn't put it off much longer.

One old sweatshirt and a pair of black pants later, I cracked the door to my room open. All the wolves must have been in Sol's room, because Alexei sat by himself on our couch. The red fox had his tail curled into his lap and his paw on the bright new suitcase beside the couch, ears perked toward the bedroom he shared with Sol, but when I poked my head out of my room, the big black ears flicked my way, and his muzzle followed a moment later.

"Good morning," he said in his Siberian-accented voice. His English kept getting better—every week or so he'd drop a new word I hadn't heard him use before—but he kept the accent. Partly I think it was because his friend Liza and his boss Vlad were Siberian, but I think, too, he didn't *want* to lose the accent.

"Morning." I slipped through and shut the door behind me. Our living/dining room was not quite spotless, but the effects of Sol's frantic two days of cleaning did show: the scuzzy lime-green carpet was mostly clear of fur except for small pockets of red and black that collected in the corners; the only marks on the dining room table were the scuffs and scrapes that couldn't be scrubbed out; the appliances likewise; and even the kitchen floor practically sparkled in the morning light from the little living room window. Mostly what I noticed was that the smells of cooking oil, soy sauce, and fish from dinner had been replaced with a light, fresh pine. "Did Sol keep cleaning after I went to bed?"

Alexei grinned at me, showing his long canines. "He was still cleaning when I fell asleep."

I couldn't see into their bedroom from this angle even though it was cracked open. Indistinct voices made their way through the plywood, just distorted enough to jumble the words. "Did they say anything about it?"

He shook his head, his grin fading a bit. "They said the apartment was 'cute.' They were pleased that we have two beds. They asked if your room has a pool. Now they are arguing about Niki."

"Christ." Did I mention Sol has a painting of his "ghost"? "Can't imagine why his dad doesn't want him taking a picture of a nude guy to college with him. Idiot."

"It is not…" Alexei clicked his tongue. "Sexual?"

"Maybe not, but it is sexy. And unless he's planning on coming out from day one, it's not the kind of thing he should have. It's not like Charleton is up by Port City or Freestone, or out in Yerba."

"You think Niki is sexy?" He tilted his head.

We didn't talk about what was sexy very often, he and I—nor Sol and I, for that matter, though Sol and Alexei could go on for hours about some guy in a movie or at a ballgame. They knew I was friends-and-maybe-more with Athos, but I stayed quiet and private about it so they wouldn't suspect that I had no idea what sexy even *was* to me—let alone what my relationship to Athos was or could become. Sol respected that, but the fox, bright-eyed and curious, often probed in subtle ways.

Now I leaned against the wall next to the bathroom door, tail wedged against the molding, and mock-glared at him. "I think the painting is intended to be sexy."

Alexei leaned back against the couch and nodded. "This is what Sol's father says."

I crossed to the dining room/kitchen and sat down at the table. "I ain't gonna take his side too often, but this time he's right."

"Will your parents come up to visit?"

I shot a look at him, but he just had that smile he always did. "What, this weekend? No."

"Anytime." He rubbed his paw along the sofa's armrest. "That time your mother called, I think she wanted to come up."

"Yeah, well, I'm not stopping them." That wasn't strictly true, but I knew they were so sensitive about giving me my space that they'd never come up unless I asked. To head off Alexei's next question, I tilted my head toward their bedroom. "What else are they saying?"

The fox scowled, but focused his ears forward. "Arguing about the painting still," he said in a low voice.

He'd barely finished the sentence before I heard Sol snap, "Fine." The door swung open and he stomped out carrying his own suitcase. When he saw me, he paused, then kept on going to the front door, where he dropped the suitcase and slumped, all six feet of him, against the wall. His black tail curled tightly around his leg and he dropped his muzzle to stare down at his paws.

"Hey," he said in a low voice as his parents came out of the bedroom. "Alexei, you'll take care of Niki, won't you?"

"Of course." Alexei stood.

Now Sol's bright green eyes flicked to me. "And you'll take care of Alexei, right?"

"He can take care of himself," I said before Alexei could object. "He's got Mike now."

Sol's eyes flicked to a point over my shoulder as his mother cleared her throat. "Good morning, Meg," she said. "You look nice today."

"She doesn't paint her fur first thing in the morning," Sol chimed in with a little smirk at me.

His mother ignored him. "I saw your mother at the store the other day."

That I hadn't expected. I turned and met the eyes of the short grey wolf; she was about my height, both of us dwarfed next to Sol's big thug of a father. "Didn't know you guys shopped at 'Nature's Fish,'" I said.

She coughed. "It was at the pharmacy."

Figures Mom'd be getting drugs. I didn't say anything, and after a minute Mrs. Wrightson went on. "I told her we'd be coming here to pick up Sol, and she asked me to see how you're doing. And to tell you to give her a call."

"Yeah," I muttered. "I will."

"She said you're going to art school in September?"

"That's her plan," I said without emphasizing "her."

"You got everything?" Sol's father said to him, cutting across our conversation.

His mother kept talking to me. "That's great," she said with a beaming smile. "Art school sounds like so much fun. Is there one around here?"

"Yeah," Sol said to his father.

"Yeah," I said to his mother at the same time. "The Art Institute of Vidalia." All the really good art schools were up north; the Institute was a cookie-cutter artist factory designed to churn out a bunch of people who could all draw exactly the same way. But my parents didn't know the difference, and they liked it better if I lied about going to a school close to home.

"At least you'll stay in the area. And…" She paused, and with all her Southern gentility, asked delicately about my job situation. "You're…doing all right?"

Sol and Alexei both flicked their ears around to listen to my answer. Fortunately, I had the same lie I'd told Mom at the ready. "I'm being thrifty with the money they gave me, and Sol and Alexei are picking up a little more of the rent since I do the cooking."

"Meg sells stuff on AuctionThis," Sol blurted out. "She goes to flea markets. She's got a really good eye for it."

He and Alexei both thought I dealt drugs for money, but he'd never broken out that story in front of me. "That's right," I said. "You'd be amazed what some people will pay for other people's garbage."

"I kept it as short as I could"

Alexei hid a smile and turned away, tail flicking. Sol's mother said, with either sincerity or an excellent facsimile, "That's just super. I'm glad you can support yourself."

"We'd better get going." Sol's father looked up from checking his phone. "Traffic looks bad on 16."

"Hey," Sol said behind me, and he tapped me on the shoulder so I turned. I thought at first he was going to rescue me from his mother, but he said, "Get on ScentBook already so I can keep in touch with you."

"It's just for canids," I said. "What a stupid fucking name."

All of the wolves in the room flattened their ears, and I remembered too late that I probably shouldn't curse in front of Sol's parents. Oh well. Their problem.

"It's for everyone now," Sol said patiently, probably because he didn't want to call me the name he did the last time I sounded off about ScentBook.

"That ain't a selling point. You want me to get on so Marcia and Allison can make stupid comments on my profile? Who from high school is so fu—fuh-riggin' important that I need to give them another way to rag on me?"

His green eyes flashed. "There's me."

"Yeah, well. Use e-mail like a normal person." I pointed. "Alexei doesn't use ScentBook."

"I am going to," the fox said with a treacherous smile.

I shook my head. "Fine, then Alexei can post updates. Now let's get the good-byes over with before your parents shove you out the door."

His mother, behind me, said, "There's no rush," but his father hefted the large suitcase and set it next to Sol's at the door.

"All right," Sol said. "But stay in touch." He reached out with both arms.

I sighed, letting him see my annoyance, but he didn't give a crap. So I stepped into the hug and kept it as short as I could. "Don't go fucking changing in college," I whispered into his ear, hopefully low enough that his parents wouldn't hear.

"I'm gonna miss you too," he said, and he was grinning as he stepped back.

Alexei stepped toward me then, and I swatted him away. "You I'm gonna see in three days," I said as he laughed. "Kick ass on that interview."

Sol's mother clucked, but his father didn't seem to care. "Come on," he said.

"It was nice to see you, Meg," Mrs. Wrightson said as the guys all picked up the bags. "Are you going to have any company over while the boys are gone?"

Even other people's mothers couldn't stop asking me about my dating life. "No," I said. "No guests."

I couldn't tell whether that pleased or worried her. She gave me a small smile and said, "Call your mother, all right?"

"Sure," I said. I kept my paw up as the four of them filed out the front door. Sol gave me one look back, his green eyes bright in the dim hallway. I watched them walk away, tails still except for Alexei's long wagging white-tipped one, and then the four of them were just silhouettes against the sunlight of the glass door at the front of the building. I stepped back into the apartment and let the door close.

"Finally." I exhaled. The apartment, slightly crowded with three people, felt palatial with just me.

First thing I did was check that their fan was blowing out so the apartment wouldn't get stuffy. It was, and that was all I'd intended to do in that room, but I stopped to look at Sol's bed. His dresser was closed, so I couldn't see it was empty; the desk he and Alexei shared still had Alexei's stuff on it; his bed, though, was bare of the dark blue sheets and missing its pillow. He really was gone.

Maybe I would set up another ScentBook account, with my real name this time, only to talk to Sol and Alexei. I could ignore everyone else if I had to. And then my eyes drifted up to Sol's painting.

It was a pretty good painting, Sol's obsession with it aside. The composition and color in the park scene was really nice; the bright fall colors complemented the fox's reddish fur. He was nude, but his back was to the viewer, and you couldn't even really tell he was male except that a hundred years ago, nobody was painting flat-chested vixens. Also, his hips weren't quite wide enough, although you could've put that down to the artist being more comfortable with leaves and trees than foxes. His tail flowed like the way vixens' tails were traditionally painted, slimmer and longer and more curvy than their male counterparts' tails, but again, that might've been the artist saying something about his subject.

Sol thought that he knew the painter, a black rat named Henri Trounoir who'd at least existed, according to the Internet. His subject, the fox rising from the stone bench with his head turned over his shoulder to show one bright green eye, was not documented anywhere on the Internet. In fact, this painting was not credited to Trounoir either, but Sol had dreamed about it and was convinced that the fox in the painting was

Niki, a gay Siberian fox who'd somehow befriended him despite being dead for a hundred years.

I hadn't seen the painting since Alexei brought it into my room to try to summon Niki, and then I hadn't been paying a lot of attention to it. I had to give it to the artist, though: he'd captured something in the subject and the pose that made you linger, watch the painting to see if the fox would continue to rise. That kind of suspended motion was something I wasn't good at yet. I could do relatively decent pinups, but this—no matter what I thought of the subject—was art.

My fur prickled slightly and I started to turn to see if someone was watching me through the window. Aw, no. There was nobody outside, and I was not going to get that creepy feeling again, not with the boys gone. I stomped out of the room and shut the door, and then opened it again, feeling like an idiot. What, closing the door so the ghost couldn't get out? Was I fucking fifteen years old again?

I hurried back to my room. The second thing I wanted to do was get all the liquor out of my closet where Sol had insisted I shove it in case his parents went around opening cupboards. I grabbed the bottles without looking and brought them out to the kitchen, and only when I'd set them on the counter did I look down and see the blackberry brandy bottle.

Dammit. My first instinct was to put it back in the closet. Then I told myself that I wasn't going to let the prickling of my fur scare me into shoving this thing in the closet where it had stayed for months. With Sol and Alexei gone, it could be in the regular liquor cabinet. Let's be honest, with as much as those two drank, they wouldn't notice if I kept all the bottles in my closet, and they certainly didn't know what this one meant or why I'd never opened it.

At least looking at this bottle didn't provoke the feeling of being watched that Sol's painting had, and that was a relief because I didn't want to have to smoke a joint this early in the day, empty apartment or no. I shoved it behind the others in the liquor cabinet and closed the door. Part of me gave a mental fist pump at having beaten the specters of my mind, but another part of me said, *Are you sure you just didn't want it in your room anymore?*

That part of me could go to hell. I'd spent almost four years getting it drilled into my head that ghosts aren't real, and even being off the antidepressants didn't change that basic fact. I smacked my paw against the cabinet door and stalked back to my room to get dressed.

Chapter 2

Creepy feeling or no, I wanted to get down to the café. I had those commissions to work on and a personal project I wanted to start. Seeing Sol and Alexei run off to the next part of their lives had spurred me to be productive, and besides, if I got done quickly, I could run over to the pool afterwards.

Like I said, Vidalia in summer is a sauna. I got used to wearing shorts around Midland in the summer, but up here I found a couple skirts that didn't look completely stupid, and they kept me a lot cooler. With Sol and Alexei gone, I didn't have to worry about keeping up an image, so I threw on a skirt and a black t-shirt with a white skull design, grabbed my portfolio bag, and headed for the door.

The air always takes a second to adjust to even when you've lived in the South your whole life: wet and hot, it coats your throat and lungs with every labored breath until you adjust and forget to notice it. The concrete pavements rippled with heat, and sometimes I walked across the dusty grass yard if it was late in the day. But in the morning, it wasn't so bad.

Our big brick apartment building and all the others were set back from the street, leaving room for people to walk on the sidewalk without looking right in the ground-floor windows. Not that a lot of people walked up and down our street; it wasn't on the way to anywhere, except between places so far apart you'd be better off taking the bus. There was the Riverwalk area six long blocks west, the bus station a mile north, and a shitty strip mall on the other side of the expressway to the south. To the east sprawled more low-story crumbling brick apartments and then a big fenced-off industrial thing that Sol and Alexei hated the smell of. Fortunately, you couldn't smell it from our place when the wind blew from the river, which was most of the time.

That morning, a light breeze tickled my nose as I headed west. I passed a couple doorways where bums were waking up, then the construction site that my window looked onto. On the next block, the buildings looked nicer: marble and limestone accents glowed in the sun against the brick, and in another block I walked under the twittering of birds in the shade of small trees, looking to my right up staircases to ornate doors and front windows of the old row houses. A huge TV sat behind a window displaying the sticker of an alarm company; another window was decorated to look like an aquarium, with fish stickers, seaweed on the bottom, and even a sticker mimicking the surface of the water along the top. Otters, probably. We're dumb that way sometimes.

One more block and I saw rainbow flags over doorways, pride stickers on cars, the occasional same-sex couple walking together, sometimes holding paws. They usually smiled at me when we passed, like everyone else did here in Vidalia (if I went out without my fur color), but their smiles felt more genuine to me, like they thought I was one of them. How they thought they'd figured that out when I didn't even know was beyond me.

Traffic picked up here, and it was around this point that I could see the stone railing along the river up ahead. I never actually made it all the way to the river, though, because the Café LaCroix was right here. This block, full of precious little shops that people couldn't shut up about, teemed with crowds at any time of the day, but morning was better because the shops didn't open until ten.

The Café LaCroix opened at six, and they had a decent staff, a mean espresso bar, and, most importantly, air conditioning. Even better, if I got in before ten, I always found a table where I could spread out my art and work. I wove through the empty tables on the patio out front and pushed the door open, into the coffee-scented cool air.

"Hey, Meg!" Eve raised a paw from where she was polishing the counter. She'd tinted her raccoon mask light blue today and was wearing a powder-blue t-shirt above her apron with a cartoon sword from some TV show I didn't watch. "What's your poison?"

I scanned the twenty or so tables and picked one near the end of the counter, against the wall. "Black coffee, dark roast today, please. How was the movie?"

"Shitty." Eve kept her voice low enough that the other customers couldn't hear it. "Usual patriarchal fucknuts. Supposed to have a 'strong female character' but all she did was shoot a guy halfway through the film and then Big Hat Macho Lion got to save her ass—and squeeze it—half a dozen more times."

"Why'd you even go?"

"Alain wanted to see Big Hat Macho Lion's butt." Eve snorted. "For revenge we're going to make him see 'Por Su Corazón' on Sunday." She brought me a steaming cup of coffee in a bright white ceramic cup.

I let the aroma waft around me and sat down at my table, set the coffee down, and spread my pages out. "Cool, tell me how it is."

Eve walked around the counter and looked down at my table. "Working on the Art Institute thing today?"

"Nah, commissions again." I hoped she'd let it go, but there were no customers, so she stayed at my end of the counter.

"Did you finish it up at home? It's due in a week, isn't it?"

I pulled out a half-finished commission I was doing for Corra. I expected the rat to be in around noon like always with her girlfriends, and I wanted to show her the progress I'd made. "I've got it under control. Got to pay the rent."

"Show me before you send it, wouldya?"

"Yeah, sure." I glanced at the counter. "Hey, you have a customer."

She patted me on the shoulder and hurried back. "And I've already got a mom," I muttered under my breath.

Eve's great most of the time. I tried to put it out of my mind while I did some sketches in my warm-up book. I sketched the marten at the counter waiting for his coffee, I sketched the bicycle propped against the big patio window and the muskrat it belonged to reading the paper. I sketched the bookcase and the plant on top, a form I'd done so many times I could probably do it with my eyes closed. For variety, I sketched the plant as a monster with eyes and teeth. Maybe one of the wizards I was drawing could be fighting it.

Even though I'd been drawing like this for a couple months now, I still wasn't quite used to getting such a pleasurable rush from sketching. Transitioning from antidepressants to pot had opened up a lot of doors for me, the biggest one being the confidence and excitement over moving out on my own. But drawing was another one. Under the blue pills, art was a shallow, boring exercise. When I'd finally quit the pills (ramping down, kids, don't quit cold turkey), a week or two later I was chatting with Athos online and got the unfamiliar urge to draw. Unfamiliar, I mean, not because I hadn't been drawing. I knew I was good at it so I drew a lot for practice. But I'd rarely had the drive to draw something on my own.

That led to Athos telling me about one of the people in his office who paid for illustrations of his (terrible) horror stories, and from him I found a client who wanted a picture of himself as a vampire, and all along I was engaged with the drawings, enjoying them, pushing myself to get better every time.

My parents nudged me to apply to the Art Institute, which they'd seen on TV, and I went along with it so they wouldn't worry about my future. In truth, I had no ambition to go to school. Rediscovering art had been an unexpected windfall and I didn't want to commit to years of art school if two months in I was going to relapse into art-as-mechanical-exercise mode. If I wasn't, I sure as hell wasn't going to go to a shitty Art Institute.

That left open the question of what I did want to do. I could do commissions for a while, but especially with Sol moving on to college and Alexei moving on with his boyfriend, I was feeling left behind. So I'd decided to get back into a comic story I'd made up years ago. With the apartment empty this weekend, I thought I might be able to work on it at home as well as the café, and maybe if I got a few good pages done, I could show Athos and see what he thought of it.

Sherine, a light, short weasel, had been clearing tables and chatting with Bellie, a raccoon who worked at the Burger Bar down the street. She made her way over to my table as I was finishing up a quick sketch of the pronghorn now at the counter. "That was fast," she said, glancing down at the sketches. "You just sat down."

"They're warm-ups," I said, glancing up to add a few last touches. "They're shitty, but I'm about loosened up."

She plopped down in a chair next to me. "Did you already hear about last night's 'Angel Stories'?"

I shook my head. Sherine proceeded to fill me in on the adventures of Volstiel, the angel who had to perform good deeds on Earth to earn his re-admission to heaven. Funnily enough, the whole "angel" story didn't make me feel creepy. When it was contained in a TV show and people knew it was fake, it didn't bother me.

That last part, about knowing it was fake, wasn't a hundred percent with Sherine. After telling me the story of how Volstiel had reconciled two sisters who hadn't spoken in decades (I think it was something like that), she sighed and looked around the sleepy café. "If I could just meet a fallen angel," she said, and trailed off.

"What?" I said, putting away the warm-up book. "You'd want her to pick a lottery ticket for you? Or you'd try to sleep with her? Would whatsisname do a threesome with an angel?"

"He'd better," she grumbled.

I headed off that conversation quickly. "I hear heavenly fire stains are a bitch to get out of your clothes."

"Jesus!" She said it JAY-sus, which always made me grin. "Don't blaspheme."

"You're the one talking about fallen angels," I pointed out. "You know who the most famous fallen angel is, right?"

Sherine's whiskers flipped up as she screwed up her muzzle in distaste. "That's different," she said. "Anyway, how's your love life? Any motion in the ocean?"

"My two gay-boy roommates and I had a super-hot three-way last night before they both left today." I pulled the half-done commission to the top and stared at it. I had a couple hours left, and Corra wouldn't be in by then. I slid it back under the pile of blank pages. "I'm still sore."

The weasel snorted, and fortunately Eve called her to make another pot of coffee. "I don't like to think of you sitting all alone every night," she said as she got up and flounced back toward Bellie.

"I don't like to think of *not* being alone," I murmured to myself, more to be contrary than because it was true. The blank paper stared back up at me as I worked out the beginning of the story I wanted to tell, which was not a commission nor the material for the Art Institute application. I could spare half an hour for it before getting to Corra's picture.

I'd been fifteen when I'd had the idea for the story about a muskrat who lived in the swamps outside New Kestle a hundred years ago, when the town was wild and voodoo priestesses were part of the town's life. Voodoo seemed like a pretty cool culture, and the most famous workers were female, so I was into it for a bit. Anyway, this muskrat wanted to be a voodoo priestess, but her family wanted her to marry. It was a dumb story when I wrote it, but I never really forgot it.

But Alain had hooked me up with some great indie comics in the last month and I kept seeing the muskrat's story spread out in panels like that. Over the last couple months, especially, I kept finding myself thinking about the different turns her story might take.

Her name was Marie-Belle. I could see the splash page in my head, her body diving toward the viewer, into the water…

Chapter 3

Marie-Belle glides through the water easily, avoiding the mangrove roots and brushing past the fronds that choke the waterways. They slip across her fur, across the oilskin bag on her back, whispered greetings in green languages. There are times when her passage through the dappled water is as hypnotic as a dream, and she arrives at her destination with no memory of choosing a path, only of emerald light and sienna shade and the ripples of life great and small, as though she had simply remained in one place while the swamp moved about her.

Today is not one of those days. Today she is conscious of her destination and the water is little more than a medium. Crawdads flicker and skitter through shadows; great catfish gape reproachfully at her in the seconds it takes to pass them. Above her, insects dabble the water, their touches like stars that twinkle and then fade. But Marie-Belle sees only ahead of her, the great cypress with the branches twisted like the decoration on a wrought-iron railing, then the deep abyss, always black as night, and finally the four regular logs, green and yellow and brown with colonies of algae that have lived there since her grandmother's grandfather sunk the logs with his own paws.

The pier he built has withstood hurricanes and wars, children and the lack of children. She swarms up the ladder, the humid air only a touch less thick than the water, drops her oilskin pack, and brushes excess water and algae from her fur. There is nobody around to see her nakedness, and even if there were, it would hardly matter unless it were a trader from New Kestle. She'd spent more time naked than clothed until several years ago, when she'd begun to show her womanhood, as her grandmother put it, or grew too old to run about like a savage heathen, as her aunt put it.

"Toutou!" she cries, bursting into the small cottage thick with the smell of a roux on the stove. "What am I to do?"

Her grandmother sets aside her embroidery and looks up, eyes twinkling in the sunlight from the window. "Goodness, kitling," she says. "You're to dry yourself, for one, and while you're doing that I'll put on the tea, and that's two, and then we'll sit down and talk about what's wrong, and that'll be three, and three is enough to worry about right now."

She pushes herself up from the wooden chair and makes her way to the stove, where she adds a kettle to the cast-iron pot bubbling there. Marie-Belle watches, her breathing slowing as she reaches for the thick cotton towel from the rack beside the door. She wants to tell her grandmother what is bothering her, but knows that once Toutou has set the order of things, they will be followed. First the drying, then the tea, then the talk. And the silence will not be denied; it holds the words she wants to say gently down while she rubs the towel across her fur. When she's put on the dress and smoothed down the fabric, her thin tail has ceased its flicking about and her words have calmed, presenting themselves in orderly rows to be spoken when called upon.

Toutou collects two chipped teacups from the cupboard and carries them to the table along with the canister of tea. "Now," she says, sitting down, "that's one and two."

Her smile, with the warmth of the air in the cottage and the familiar, homey smells of thick soup and wood fire, completes the small world in which nothing bad can happen. Marie-Belle places her paws on the table. "Aunt Eloise says we must leave the swamp."

Toutou's shrewd gaze does not waver. "She means to marry you to Pierre Guignac, no doubt."

"Yes!" Marie-Belle exhales and reaches out for a teacup, holding it in her paws even though it's empty and cold.

"Well, my dear, then you must decide what you will do."

"I want to stay in the swamp. I want to learn vodou with you!"

The kettle begins to burble, but Toutou ignores it. Her gaze flicks to the back wall, a collage of miniature portraits and decorative glass, small dolls like toys and small skeletons like dolls and intricate ironwork like the skeletons of fantastical creatures, the shrine to Ayida Wèyo at the center of it. The statue of the goddess sits before a mirror bordered by a wooden snake painted yellow with red and green and purple dots and patterns, and in front of her lie the glossy black coils of a rat snake, both head and tail hidden from view. Marie-Belle fancies that Toutou's gaze lingers on the goddess as she talks, though it is difficult to be sure what draws her attention on that noisy, beautiful back wall. "Why do you want to learn vodou? It is not such an easy thing, nor is it—"

"For everyone, I know, I know. But it is for me, I know it is."

"Hm-mh." Toutou braces herself with one clawlike paw and stands, walking to the stove. The kettle is silent when she stands, but by the time she reaches the table beside the stove, it hisses and spits like an angry wildcat. The old muskrat lifts it carefully and pours the boiling water into the white ceramic teapot. "Is it vodou you wish to pursue, or Pierre Guignac you wish to escape?"

The younger muskrat lowers her head. "Can it be both?"

"Oh, my dear, of course it is both. I am asking which is the stronger; that is all. Pierre is not so bad, is he? He carries himself well, his father is a respected plantation owner, and he will take over the business one day. It is a good match."

"For him."

"And what would you have in a husband, Marie-Belle? The dashing good looks of Clement Totin? It is easy enough to imagine his features upon whomever you marry when you need to."

Marie-Belle understands this last bit dimly and files it away for a time when it may be useful, but now it seems irrelevant to her situation. So she sets her teacup down and pushes it away as though her grandmother had suggested she fill it with swamp muck. "Clement tortures small creatures when he thinks nobody can see."

"The charm of Jean Burel? The fortune of his cousin Pascal?"

"Pascal is a pleasant simpleton, and Jean applies his charm equally to any girl he meets," Marie-Belle says archly. "And besides, Isabelle is to marry him next year, which you very well know."

"Engagements may be broken." Toutou adds tea to the pot and stirs it. "If the will of both parties is strong enough."

"Everyone expects Jean to break it, anyway." The younger muskrat inhales, breathing in the warm herbal scent of the tea: blackberry and vanilla and lemon.

"Are there any males outside your species who have caught your eye, then?" Toutou covers the pot and rests a paw on it, though steam still escapes from it.

Marie-Belle looks down and does not answer. Toutou clucks and makes the lid of the teapot clink. "Are there females?" she says, and when the words bring Marie-Belle's head up, the older muskrat smiles a knowing smile.

"No." Prickles dance along Marie-Belle's fur. She looks back now, to Ayida Weyo's red curve of a smile.

"There is no shame in it," Toutou says equably, tracing a claw around the ceramic lid, following the cornflower pattern precisely. "Especially if you wish to become a vodou priestess, you may not want to create ties to a husband. There is little need when they are so easy to manipulate."

"With spells?"

Toutou chuckles. "You rarely need spells. But another female, priestess or no..."

"No," Marie-Belle says again. "There is nobody. I don't want anyone."

"Are you so certain?"

The young muskrat reaches out for her teacup. "I think the tea is ready."

"Another moment, dear." Her grandmother smiles. "Well, we can leave that question on the shelf for another day."

The cottage falls into silence save for the slow burble of the pot on the stove and the croaks of frogs outside. When Toutou does not speak again, Marie-Belle twists her fingers impatiently together. "You must help me!"

"I am helping you." The old muskrat's whiskers lift with a warm smile. She raises the teapot and pours, filling Marie-Belle's cup.

Blackberry and herbs tickle the young muskrat's nose again as the vapors curl upwards and then vanish. She takes the cup and holds it, staring down. "Are you going to read the leaves?"

"Now what purpose would that serve?" Toutou fills her own cup. "You know what awaits you in your future. In any case, that is superstition. The loa do not speak to us through tea leaves."

Marie-Belle exhales across the tea, cooling it. "Will you sing to them then?"

"Perhaps. When you tell me what you want."

The younger muskrat buries her nose in the teacup to hide her confusion. When Toutou asked her the same question over and over, it meant not that Toutou did not understand her answer, but that Marie-Belle herself did not understand the question.

She thought it had been clear that she does not want to marry Pierre. But what had Toutou said? She asked what Marie-Belle *wants*.

She wants to come study vodou. Was that not clear enough? She has seen Toutou prepare *gris-gris* and mix tonics and, once, dispense a cure-all. She has witnessed dances and songs to Ayida Wèyo and to Ogou Balanjo, for love and healing (though she has not heard these loa speaking to Toutou). She has been told of many wise pieces of advice dispensed to people seeking fortune and comfort. Maybe Toutou wants Marie-Belle to tell her what advice she would give herself, were she a vodou priestess.

What would she say to a young girl who wanted to run away from her family and study vodou? Toutou has said many times that the spirits will not talk to everyone, that some are more receptive to seeing beyond the shadows that guard that world from this. Not all the spirits are good spirits, and a priestess needs the ability to talk her way out of trouble with the dark spirits as well as talk her way into the graces of the good ones.

"I know I haven't talked to any spirits yet," she says slowly. "To any of the loa. But I want to learn. And I'm good with people. Everyone says so. You said that a priestess must be able to talk to people as easily as to the loa."

"You are charming, it's true," Toutou says.

"And I can learn to talk to the spirits. You can teach me."

"My dear," and here Toutou's whiskered muzzle crinkles into a severe frown. "Vodou is not a lawn party."

"No," Marie-Belle says quickly, her mind racing. "I want to live as you do. I want to help people heal, find comfort, find fortune."

"And love?"

"And—and love." She feels again that strange shame inside her, like the flush of having eaten rotten fruit, but more diffuse, wider than her stomach.

Her answer seems to satisfy Toutou, though. The older muskrat leans back and sips her tea. "I won't deny the thought has crossed my mind that you might be a priestess." The words drip out with careful, measured consideration. "You must know that once you cross the shadows, you cannot return to a normal life. You may lose your family—your Aunt Eloise for certain. Be sure you are willing—"

"I am!" Marie-Belle raises her voice.

This pleases Toutou less. "Hm," she says severely, and the younger muskrat quails below her grandmother's knife-sharp gaze. After a moment that lasts for a dozen heartbeats (Marie-Belle's, which are very quick), Toutou goes on. "Come back in a week and we will see how your situation presents itself."

"A week!"

"During this week, you will listen for the spirits. Do not essay any conversation. Listen only."

"May I…" Marie-Belle glances toward the back of the cabin, toward the shrine and the black coils below it. "May I ask Sébastien?"

"He is asleep," Toutou says, "and besides, what would you ask him? Your task now is to open yourself, not to solve a question."

Marie-Belle finishes her tea and thinks about this as she shares the gossip of her family and friends with Toutou. Too soon, the sun reaches in through the window and taps her shoulder, and she rises to return to her family. But she feels warm and hopeful as she walks to the doorway. Toutou will give her a chance.

"Marie-Belle." Her grandmother stops her. She meets the older muskrat's eyes. "The dark spirits will not announce themselves with shadows and fangs. They come with words sweet as honey and breath as fresh as spring, and you must listen to them carefully. Know them, do not shun them. Even the dark has its uses."

"Yes, Toutou," she says, and kisses her grandmother's whiskers before walking out to the dock.

Listen, she thinks, and closes her eyes, standing still as a mangrove tree at midnight, not a whisker twitching. Faintly, she can smell the roux bubbling, she can hear the clink of the metal spoon on the pot. She can hear birds and water and wind, but there is nothing more, no voice of honey, no words of wisdom.

She opens her eyes and stares forward into the mist. "Listen, Meg," she says.

Chapter 4

I'd gone into a bit of a drawing trance, a feeling I was getting used to having when it felt like my pencil was just highlighting shapes that were already on the page. The comic had taken on a life of its own; a lot of it was just loose sketches, but I had panels and word balloons, I knew what Marie-Belle and her grandmother looked like in my head, I got caught up in that voodoo altar, and my pencil just flew over the paper. And then I got to that last panel and I saw the muskrat's face even before the lines appeared under my pencil. She was staring out at me and before I knew what I was doing, I'd written my name in the word balloon. She looked *real.*

My paw jerked away from the paper and smacked into my coffee cup, sending it to the floor. I jumped again at the crash and the splash of cold coffee on my feet.

"Hey, Meg, you okay?" Sherine looked up from a table up near the front window. Eve, behind the counter, was staring at me too.

"I'm...I'm fine." I had my paw over the thing I'd just drawn. "Sorry."

"Let me get that." The weasel hurried toward me with her towel in one paw.

I grabbed my eraser and hurried to expunge my name before she got close enough, but the page was the first thing she looked at. "That's really good," she said, and my erasing drew her attention to the faint lines I hadn't quite gotten rid of. "Hey, you named someone in your comic after yourself?" She laughed as she bent to wipe up the coffee.

"No!" I snapped, and worked the eraser harder. Bits of paper rolled and came away, the whole area growing ragged and grey.

"I thought I saw—"

"I made a mistake." I swallowed, trying to slow my heart down. Jesus Christ, what the fuck was that about?

Eve finished with her customer and came over with another coffee. "You okay, sweetie? What happened?"

"She was drawing a comic with herself in it," Sherine said.

"I'm fine." I squinted out at the patio, very aware of the comic page on the table that my eyes were avoiding, aware of the sour taste of old coffee in my mouth and the racing of my heart. "How long—what time is it?"

"Little past eleven." Eve frowned.

"I—" Shit. An hour and a half? I took the coffee she gave me and sipped it.

"Your paws are shaking." Eve took the coffee and set it down on the table. "Did you have breakfast?"

"Yeah, I…" I shook my head. "No."

"Well, that's the problem. Hold on."

Eve bustled back behind the counter while Sherine finished mopping up. "Never seen you get that into drawing," she said. "You didn't even drink your coffee."

"I was…I was inspired." I took a chance and looked down at the paper again. Marie-Belle's eyes stared at me. I made quick work of them with the eraser and drew them in so she was looking downward.

Bellie came over and put a paw on my shoulder, which normally I wasn't a fan of but it was steadying and comforting in this moment. And then she had to go and talk. "What happened here, hon? Get too excited? Not drawing anything naughty, are ya?"

Sherine gathered the fragments of my coffee mug in the coffee-stained towel. "I think she dozed off." She nodded down at the page. "That looked neat. Why'd you change it? Can I see the rest of it?"

"It wasn't right." I snapped the words out as fast as I could and shoved the pages into my portfolio, leaving the half-finished commission for Corra on the table.

"I want to see it too," Bellie put in, leaning over. She had a narrower muzzle than Eve and lighter eyes, and she kept her cheek ruffs swept back where Eve fluffed hers out.

Sherine held the towel in her paws, making no move to go throw it out. "It looked fine to me."

"Well, lots of things look fine to you," I said, looking back over my shoulder and then all around the café and back over my shoulder again. The interest in my spilled coffee had waned and the only people watching me were Sherine, Bellie, and Eve, coming back with a croissant. "Trust me, it wasn't."

"Eat this," the raccoon ordered, shoving the croissant into my paws. "What wasn't fine?"

"And what's that supposed to mean?" Sherine was keeping her voice down, but her needle-sharp teeth showed as she snapped back at me. "If you'd just unclench a bit, maybe *someone* would look fine to you, too."

"Sherine!" Eve pushed my paws toward me and her dark eyes stared at mine. "Eat. And you two, leave her alone. Shoo."

The weasel grumbled something that Alexei would have been able to hear, but my small ears only let me guess that she was saying, "She started it," as she walked away to throw out the coffee cup shards. Bellie gave me a smile and a squeeze on the shoulder before following.

I took a bite of the flaky pastry, mechanically. It tasted good, but it wasn't what I wanted. I wanted the floating, relaxed sensation that let me forget that I was paranoid about creepy shit in my life.

Eve watched me carefully. "Good?"

"Yeah." I nodded, took another bite. "It's good. Thanks."

"All right. You going to be okay?"

The half-finished commission looked up at me from the table. Beside the chair I'd been sitting in, my portfolio rested with a few white corners poking out of it. "I think I might head home. When Corra comes in, tell her I'm working on it."

"Finish that first," Eve ordered, and went back to the counter, where a fox in a short-sleeved pink shirt with a rainbow pin on the lapel was waiting.

I sat down again and dipped the croissant in the coffee before taking another bite. The air-conditioned café hummed with background music—Eve must have put something on while I was drawing—and outside, people walked by, talked, perked ears, wagged tails, smiled, frowned. Everyone in the café sat in front of a laptop or smartphone, except for Bellie, who was still talking to Sherine.

I thought I caught them looking at me, and then thought, fuck, Meg, you're being all paranoid. You got caught up in drawing, and you worked yourself into the comic because…because why? Because you were thinking about Sol and Alexei being gone and thinking about their "ghosts"? Because you hadn't eaten and you were hallucinating?

No. No, no, no. It wasn't a hallucination. It was just a freak thing and it's done now and you're going to be fine. Marie-Belle wasn't *talking*, you just got a little confused and drew something in the panel.

But I still wanted a joint.

∞

Okay, this is why I know ghosts aren't real.

I'd just turned fifteen. Mom, worried about my increasing isolation (her words), arranged a slumber party with my two closest friends, who weren't all that close: Margie, a bouncy otter, and Amelia, a more timid weasel.

I thought it was going to be tedious, and it was, but Margie and Amelia seemed to enjoy being over. They insisted on raiding the liquor cabinet, but then they were disappointed when all we could find was some fruity liqueurs. They made a game out of sneaking them back to my room even though I basically could've asked my mom and she'd have let us have them (I knew that wouldn't be "cool," though).

Because it was so close to Halloween, we decided to play this ghost game. I'm sure you know it—Athos showed me a bunch of different names, after, though I didn't tell him why I was interested. Bloody Mary is the most common one, but there's Candyman and Betty Browne. Margie wanted to call Drowned William, because the others need mirrors and for him, you just need water—like our house pool. Drowned William is supposed to have been an otter who died during the Civil War fighting for the South, and when you call his name five times looking down into the water, his spirit comes back and tells you how you're going to die.

It's bullshit, of course, but we did it and stared down into the water and Margie kept pointing at shadows and saying she heard whispers. I know my pool pretty well, but she really had me spooked. Amelia had it worse, though, and when Margie said that Drowned William told her Amelia was going to die in a plane crash, still a virgin, Amelia's voice got high and she told Margie she was done with it.

After that, of course they wanted to talk about boys, being fifteen-year-old normal girls. I didn't, because I didn't find boys all that interesting. In fact, the parts they found most interesting I really didn't like talking about.

So I kept quiet while they talked about who was cuter and then they started talking about where they let the boys put their paws and hands (depending on who it was). Margie had gotten her first season the previous month and was over it now, but talked in detail about how much more intense her attraction to all the boys had been. Amelia and I hadn't gotten one yet, but Amelia listened raptly to Margie and kept saying, "I can't wait." Me, I kept drinking to cover up my disinterest-bordering-on-discomfort, but when Margie said she wanted to let Bubba Porter put his fingers *down there*, even out of her season, I couldn't keep in the "Ew," and they both turned on me. Who did *I* like, then, if Bubba was so *gross*?

It wasn't that, it was that putting fingers there…anyone doing it, I just thought it was gross. But I tried not to say that, so they kept asking me which boy I thought was cute, which boy I would let touch me, and I said I didn't want any boy to touch me.

Then they got quiet and Amelia asked if I wanted a girl to touch me. Margie and I were floating in the pool in my room, then, and Amelia was sitting on the edge with her feet in the water, and when she asked that, Margie looked at me sharply and got out. Amelia pulled her legs up out of the water and they both sat cross-legged and stared at me.

I said I didn't want girls to touch me there either, and they sorta relaxed but then also got more intent. Margie asked if I ever touched myself, and I said no, and Amelia asked if I knew it felt good, and I took another drink so I wouldn't have to answer. I was starting to feel all queasy inside. Then Margie actually put her paw inside her pants.

I only saw her rub for a bit before I looked away. I think Amelia was a little shocked, but she was more fascinated by my reaction. I asked Margie to stop, and Margie said it felt too good to stop, and then Amelia started doing it too.

I jumped out of the pool and yelled at them to stop it. I was mad at them for doing that in my room, I was mad at myself for feeling weird, and a minute later, when my mom swam in from the living room to ask if we were okay, I was mad at her for not having a shirt on and embarrassing me. I lay down beside the pool, and Margie and Amelia started whispering and I didn't even try to listen.

I did finish the rest of the booze, though. I thought it would put me to sleep. In retrospect, that was a mistake.

When I woke up, Margie and Amelia were asleep. The room was still dark and I didn't think I'd been asleep for very long. My parents were still watching a movie out in the living room; I could see the reflections shimmering in my pool, which connected to the living room under the wall, and I could hear the music. I knew which movie that was, that fuckin' *Across the Universe* movie that they watched like once a week now. Partly it was the lead actor, this British otter they thought was adorable, and partly it was all the music they liked, and partly it was all the love; that movie's lousy with it.

I got up in the middle of the night a lot around then, and usually I ended up laying there for an hour before going back to sleep. I'd fallen asleep at the edge of the pool, so I rolled over to get into bed, but when I did, everything wobbled and I felt kinda sick, so instead of crawling into my bed, I pulled myself over to the edge of the pool. Mom always said floating in the water helps settle a stomach, but I didn't want to get sick in my bed, not after last time, so I kinda waited there to see if I was going to heave up or not.

And I was staring down at the lights in the pool and I saw this shadow down there. Of course the first thing I thought about was Drowned William, but it looked like he had wings. I stared down as the lights all flickered around and then I heard him talking. He had a deep voice that was water-muffled even though it was in my head.

Meggie, Meggie, you want to know how you're going to die? I can tell you.

My mom used to call me Meggie when I was little.

"I saw this shadow down there"

You're going to die alone. You're worthless and broken, you'll never feel a lover's touch like your beautiful friends. And you're going to die with a heart full of pain, little Meggie, because everyone you care about, everyone who swims with you, they're all going to choke and cry and bleed and drown. And do you know why, Meggie?

There was something huge stuck in my throat.

It's because of you. You bring nothing but hurt.

I shook my head.

You want to help them, don't you? You want to save them, don't you? You want to spare them the life of pain and suffering?

Of course I did. What kind of question was that?

Then you have to go away. You know where the pills are, Meggie. Your mom's watching the movie. Listen, it's three songs from the end. You know where the pills are.

I did know. Mom kept sleeping pills by her bed. I stared down at Drowned William and two gleaming points of light appeared where I thought his eyes should be.

The only worthwhile thing you can do with your life is end it. You'll never give love, never know love, only hurt and pain.

And then he was nothing but flickers of light and dark. But it didn't matter. I knew where the pills were.

So yeah. I woke up in the hospital, and that's how I got left behind a year in high school and spent almost four years with Dr. Wallace, taking antidepressants and doing Internet research on alcohol- and stress-induced hallucinations. I know what Sol and Alexei think they saw, but look. I'm a fucking *expert.*

And since getting off the antidepressants, I hadn't seen or heard anything that couldn't be explained rationally. The pot helped calm me down if I started feeling edgy, and I'd smoked it whenever Sol or Alexei got weird about their "ghosts." It had been working great for me, kept my head level even when they went on babbling about a spirit world.

Lots of hallucinations come from loneliness, Dr. Wallace told me. I'd been rejected by my closest friends and was feeling bad about it, so I invented a vision to care about me, even in a negative way. Sol's trouble all started when he got demoted or kicked off the baseball team or something, and his dad started yelling at him and his brother was off in college. Alexei left his family behind and then left his foster family to come here. We all had loneliness issues and invented ghosts to deal with them. At least their ghosts didn't tell them to kill themselves, but I was keeping an eye out for them.

So that was probably all this was. My two friends had left that morning, and I was feeling lonely and vulnerable, so my imagination made the character I'd created talk to me. Nothing more.

∞

I shoved the last bit of the croissant into my mouth and fished a couple dollars out of my pocket to drop onto the table.

"Just a second," I heard Eve tell the puma in the red checked dress who'd been in line behind the fox. She hurried over to my table as I was sliding Corra's commission into the portfolio and settling the papers in it. "Don't worry about it," she said, picking up the dollars and pushing them into my paw.

"I'm paying for my food." I opened my fingers, but she caught the bills and reached around me to push them into my portfolio.

"I said, don't worry about it." She patted the paw that was gripping the portfolio handle. "It fell on the floor. I wasn't going to serve it anyway."

I searched her eyes. "Wait, really?"

She laughed. "As far as you know. Hey, why don't you come out with us to the bar tonight? Bring your roommates along for once."

"No, I—they're gone."

"All the more reason. Don't sit at home alone." The raccoon pointed out the window to the right. "You know where The Pickled Goose is, right?"

"Yeah."

"All right, then. Nine-thirty. Just come by, we'll have some drinks and chill."

"Fine," I lied, because she wasn't going to let me go until I agreed. I could just text her later, or tell her tomorrow morning that I was still feeling sick.

Sherine raised a paw to me as I left, and Bellie did too. A couple of the other regulars smiled at me as I pushed my way out into the thick heat, took a gasping wet breath, and started for home.

People kept bumping into me right and left. I tried to weave between them but felt like someone else was always right where I was trying to step. The smell of humid fur and sweat choked me; two blocks ahead, the haven of the quieter tree-lined streets beckoned. From every angle, the sun attacked me, reflected off cars and store windows right into my eyes, it seemed. If I kept my head down, I bumped into people, so I kept it up and squinted as best I could.

Only when I got into the shade of my building's stifling hallway did I feel any relief. The air wasn't cooler, but at least the sun wasn't beating down on me and the bugs weren't flying around. One lazy fly looped circles around the hallway light, and another—or maybe the same one, who gave a shit?—bobbed in front of my apartment door. Maybe it flew in when I opened the door, but I didn't care. I tossed my portfolio on the couch and hurried back to my bedroom, to the closet and the little peppermint tin.

And it was empty, nothing in it but a couple loose rolling papers and some pot-scented dust.

God *damn*. I smacked the lid down savagely and threw the tin back against the closet wall. I wasn't supposed to go meet my source again until next weekend. How had I already run out? It was Sol's fault, him and Alexei giving me the creeps, and I'd run through my whole stash in two weeks instead of three without realizing that those empty rolling papers weren't joints.

Great. Brilliant analysis, Professor Kinnick. You want to go on and explain how it's going to help you score some weed right now, when you need it?

I pulled out my phone. My parents' number showed up in "Missed Calls" and "Voicemail," and I ignored it, calling up the entry for Rachel. I texted her, *Can I see you this weekend instead of next?*

Then I opened my window and lay down on the bed. It was barely noon and already my day was fucked. Well, okay. I closed my eyes and felt the silence of the apartment around me. Through the open window, the sounds of Vidalia drifted in: voices, engines, the dull roar of an airplane overhead.

Listen, Meg.

God dammit. I stared at the ceiling. I couldn't stay in the apartment all day. The pool would be crowded, but fuck it. Swimming usually calmed me down a little, even counting getting hit on by the inevitable creepy guys who thought a lone female at the pool might as well be wearing a target on her crotch.

So I threw my stuff together, trying to ignore the quiet in the apartment. Sol and Alexei's door was open, so I couldn't even pretend they were in there. *They're at work*, I told myself. *They'll be back tonight*. And then: *try to be a little more pathetic, Meg, why don'tcha?*

But with my pool bag over my shoulder, I kept staring at Sol's empty room. If loneliness had been behind my hallucination, then what was my solution?

Work in process, I told myself. Athos offered friendship and wanted more, but I'd almost lost his friendship over Alexei's old bum-slash-ghost, and I didn't want to risk it again (though part of me, swimming under the surface of my thoughts, said, *you can't put it off much longer*). Bellie's constant flirting might offer a less risky alternative, but I didn't know if I was ready for any of it, was the problem. I didn't even know if I was gay or straight yet. Love might be nothing but a trick of the mind, but sex was definitely real, and living with two gay roommates had thrown into sharp relief the lack of interest I had in it, as compared to the general population.

I'd gotten used to that in high school; the antidepressants could mute my season, Dr. Wallace had explained delicately, and the Internet had shown me that they could also suppress *any* sex drive. Now I was waiting for that to come back, but after months, I wasn't exactly holding my breath.

"All right, Meg," I said, staring at Sol's empty bed. "Either start busting out the tears or get the fuck to the pool already. But don't stand here like a lump."

So I went to the pool. Not many otters there, because they mostly have pools in their houses, or they live in that big complex on the river and swim there. But about every other major species demographic was there: foxes, wolves, mice, rats, deer, squirrels, cougars, rabbits—a million goddamn rabbits—and even a few bobcats, playing against the water-hating stereotype. The pool blasted Neutra-Scent and today had added in a cut-grass smell that was supposed to make it feel like a backyard pool.

When you've been thinking about a story for a while, it's hard to get out of your head. Swimming made me think about those first few panels with Marie-Belle navigating the swamp, but I pushed that image out of my head and lost myself in the feel of water, the focus needed to avoid all the people splashing around, and the rhythm of exercise. I got in a few laps, fended off the creepy guy (today it was a groundhog who asked if my home pool was being cleaned), and found that being in a crowded, noisy, smelly room made me less worried about being watched because I *knew* I was being watched.

It didn't completely erase the shakiness from the morning, but at least I wasn't afraid of that comic by the time I got out.

Chapter 5

Rachel wrote back while I was at the fish market on the way home, saying that she was out, but had a friend who might have something and where would I be that night? I didn't want some drug-dealing stranger knowing where I lived, so I gave her the address of the Pickled Goose. Hey, I agreed to meet Eve there anyway and this would save me the trouble of making up an excuse to ditch.

The sun was setting as I arrived, lighting the Pickled Goose's old pub-style sign in bright red. The goose in the jar of green liquid looked pretty happy, and also looked recently painted, though I wouldn't have been surprised if the wood was authentically a hundred years old. The outside of the two-story building sure looked it: crumbling brick and old wrought-iron railings woven elaborately over the windows, a square roof with cherubic faces in relief around it that made me doubt that the building had originally been a drinking hall. I studied it for reference in case I wanted to draw something similar in Marie-Belle's comic, and then hurried through the door, putting the comic out of my mind.

I stepped onto an uneven dark wood floor crowded with tables and bodies. Around the edges, paintings on the ivory walls shone in the light of a bunch of ceiling lamps with faux-Tiffany shades. The volume of conversation probably would've made Alexei flatten his ears, but it didn't bother me as much as the density of people. I kept a close grip on my military surplus shoulder bag and pushed through the crowds of lesbians in sleeveless shirts, shorts and skirts, heels and boots. A vixen's tail brushed my leg, but when I turned, she wasn't looking at me, so it hadn't been flirty.

"Meg!"

Through the din, I heard Eve's voice and saw her brown paw lifted above the crowd. I could barely see her blue-tinted masked muzzle until I got closer, and then I saw her squeezed around a high table with Sherine and a mouse I didn't know. She and Sherine were dressed in fairly plain shirts, but the mouse's fur glittered with sparkles and a tasteful jewel winked in each of her ears. Her low-cut dress had a satiny collar thing and buttons that glimmered in the light. She seemed so out of place next to the two coffee-shop workers that I thought for a moment that the place was so crowded they'd had to share a bar table with a stranger.

"Hey y'all," I said as I came up to the table.

"Meg, this is Allison," Eve said, and as the mouse extended a paw whose claws shone as if they were lit up, the raccoon turned to her. "Meg's an artist at the café."

"Enchanted," Allison said with a smile.

I took her paw. "Nice to meet you." Her fingers felt cool and damp, which was weird in the warm bar until I saw the condensation on her tall iced drink. "Is it just you guys?" I couldn't catch any individual scents in this haze.

Sherine grinned as I slid into an empty chair beside her. "Willa's around, and Bellie's sitting there." She pointed to the chair I'd just sat down in. "She went off to the bathroom."

Great. Bellie. I shrugged my shoulder against the memory of her paw on it. "Yeah, well, now she's sitting there." I moved the cocktail napkin next to the last empty spot at the table. "Aren't the rats here?"

"Not everyone comes here every night," Eve said. "We don't really see the rats outside the coffee shop much."

"They go to film nights and poetry readings." Sherine said.

Allison wanted to know who the rats were, so Eve told her about Yolene, Gret, and Corra, while Sherine asked me if I'd had dinner. I told her I'd made fish, and breathed on her to prove it, at which point she waved her little paw in front of her sharp muzzle and said, "We need to get you a drink."

"She's not old enough," Eve said from across the table.

"Yeah, I'm used to drinking at home alone," I said to play it off for laughs, and Sherine did laugh.

"That's really not healthy." Allison's frown didn't go with her sparkles and jewels.

"I can see why you two are together," I said, pointing at Eve. "She's my coffee-shop mom already. It was a joke."

So Eve bought me a club soda and Sherine let me tip a bit of her vodka gimlet into it, which made Eve and Allison frown, but I pointed out that it was barely enough for me to taste, let alone get drunk on. Bellie came back from the bathroom and didn't comment about me taking her seat, just slid in beside me. We talked about Allison's job for a bit: she supervised an IT group and she had a boss who respected her, but she still had to fight for everything, being a lady in the computer field. "It's such a boys' club, even now," she complained.

It sounded to me like the kind of job I would cut off my hand rather than take, but I wasn't drunk enough to sound off to a stranger. When Eve and Allison went to the bathroom, though, I told Sherine that it sounded miserable.

"She makes three times what we do," the weasel said, finishing off her drink. "Bellie, you want something?"

The raccoon lifted her martini glass and sipped the pink drink. "I'm good," she drawled, stretching the "I" out into a long "aaaah."

Sherine turned to me. "You want another club soda?"

I looked down at my glass, then at her and Bellie. "If you get me something stronger, I promise I won't tell."

The weasel's eyes sparkled. "Just don't get drunk. Eve'll rip my ears off if she finds out."

"Something mellow." I took a crumpled ten out of my shoulder bag.

"Keep it, starving artist." Sherine grinned and disappeared to the bar. Bellie shook her head. "*One* drink," she said.

"Promise." I made the cross-my-heart gesture and didn't tell her that I'd had a rum and Coke with dinner.

"Hey, would you come with me over there?" Bellie nodded across the bar, below a "We Can Do It!" feminist poster. "There's an arctic fox who looks pretty cute and I could use a backup."

Shit. I thought I knew what this was about, but Bellie wasn't going to say it flat out. "Take Sherine. She doesn't have to tell them she has a boyfriend."

Bellie shook her head. "Sherine's a lousy backup. She wants to pull everyone into the conversation. Don't tell her I said that."

"Yeah." I shook my head and looked over toward the poster again. I could just see a gleam of white fur, a tossed head and small pointed ears. "I'm pretty sure I suck at it too. Have you talked to me at all?"

"Oh, you'll be fine." She patted my shoulder, and a little to my surprise, the touch didn't make me as uncomfortable as I'd been anticipating. "Just, you know, find one of the gals with her you like and talk to her."

"I don't like any of the gals with her."

"Meg." Bellie gave me that patronizing smile. Jesus, maybe Marie-Belle should have some friends in her story who thought they knew best, who told her she should get married to that guy no matter what she told them she wanted. "That's sweet of you."

What? Then I processed her smile—not patronizing; she thought I meant I didn't like any of the other girls because I liked *her*. "I didn't—I mean, I'm not ready to go talk to random girls. I'm still—I'm figuring things out." I really hate being put on the spot.

"What's there to figure out? You just gotta get out there—"

Everyone was staring at me. "I'm not ready yet."

"—but how will you meet the right person if you shut everyone out?"

"Because the right person won't be hanging out in—in this place." I might be a lesbian—I mean, I liked all these people and felt comfortable with them—but that didn't mean I wanted to pick up a girl in a bar.

Eve and Allison came back from the bathroom as I said that, and Eve said, "Bellie, leave Meg alone."

"I'm trying to get her not to hide her light under a bushel."

The feeling of being under glass came back in force then, the spotlight on me and eyes glittering all around the room. The loud conversations seemed to recede. *What would you have in a husband, Marie-Belle?* I shoved that memory away. "I don't need more people."

Bellie reached out one brown paw across the table. "You're at the café all day and you almost never come out with us..."

"I have roommates."

"Oh, yes." She drew her paw back. "Your two gay roommates who never come down to the gay neighborhood."

"They're in the VLGA," I muttered. "Well, they were. And there's Liza." I looked around as though even if Alexei's gay ermine friend were here, she'd remember me.

"Look, Meg's life is her own business," Eve said. She sorta kinda knew that I used to take antidepressants and that I'd stopped.

"Thank you." I turned from one raccoon to the other.

And if Eve had stopped there, it would've been fine. "But Meg, sometimes you don't know you're ready until you try."

"I'm not going to be..." I flattened a paw on the table. Where the fuck was Sherine? My heart was pounding again. "Whatever happened to meeting someone you like? Does everyone just hook up in bars now?"

They all stared at me, and I put a paw to my face, forgetting for a moment that I didn't have my black fur color in. Their faces rippled in the dim light, and for a moment I was fifteen again, sitting in a still room with a voice echoing in my head.

You're broken, you'll never feel the touch of a lover like your beautiful friends.

Shit. The room blurred and my stomach churned. I gripped the edge of the table and dimly heard Bellie and Eve saying soft, padded words at me. None of them broke through the shock of the memory I'd locked away with drink and drugs for years. "I told you to leave me alone," I said, with no idea how loudly I was saying it.

A glass clunked down in front of me. "What's the matter?" Sherine asked.

"She's probably sick from the vodka," Allison said.

"It's not the fucking vodka," I said, and to prove the point, I grabbed the drink Sherine had given me and tipped it to my lips. Fizzy lime and vodka poured over my tongue, the lovely sour burn of it numbing my mouth, and I held it there until the glass was nothing but ice and a crumpled slice of lime.

The four of them stayed silent as I dropped the glass to the table with a loud crack. "Okay? I'm fine. Just stop trying to set me up."

"Did you give her alcohol?" Eve demanded of Sherine.

Bellie pushed her chair back from the table and walked away, I assumed to go chase her vixen by herself. The vodka unclenched some of my insides, but it didn't help with the formless anger, not just at Bellie, but at the whole table, at the whole bar, this place that was supposed to be for people to get together and have a good time, and it was really nothing more than a veiled meat market. All the lesbians mocked the straight girls who went to bars to get picked up and then they did the exact same thing.

"She likes you," Sherine said softly, ignoring Eve's question.

"I like her too, when she's not trying to make me into what she wants me to be."

"That's not..." The weasel turned to Eve.

"Look, I need to do this by myself," I said.

"At some point you have to stop thinking and start doing." Sherine sounded earnest. "I know growing up around here it's hard to get rid of all that crap society saddles you with, but here you can go ahead and listen to that little voice inside you."

I almost got up and left, but Sherine's words froze me to the spot for a moment, and by the time that was over I'd had time to realize that she didn't know what she'd said. So I brought the glass to my nose again, tipped an ice cube into my mouth, and inhaled lime. "You know, as much as I'd love to sit here and discuss all my sexual issues, I think I'd rather do something more fun like jam this plastic stirrer into my eye."

"I think Sherine is saying that this is a safe space for you to talk." Allison chimed in, and then Eve touched her shoulder and she stopped.

The weasel had already been encouraged, though. "Right. Like, when you get your season, do you find yourself thinking more about guys or girls?"

"No."

Allison raised a finger. "Some people don't really feel their seasons. This one girlfriend of mine—"

"Hey, you might be bi," Sherine cut in. "On 'Angel Stories' last month—"

"Fucking hell," I said.

Eve shook her head. "Leave her be."

"I might be asexual, too." I couldn't resist tossing that in, mostly to prove that I'd read up on my different sexualities.

"What?" Sherine's little nose wrinkled and her eyebrows furrowed. "That's not a thing, is it?"

Eve cleared her throat. "Allison, you were telling us about that guy who tried to dry his laptop with an industrial heat gun?"

Allison took the cue and launched into a story of a melted keyboard, while I checked my phone. There was nothing, so I texted Rachel that I was here and were there any updates? And then I sat quietly and listened.

Sitting quietly wasn't as easy as I'd hoped, though. I kept fidgeting, and while I wasn't going to get Sherine in trouble for getting me another drink, I kept thinking I heard that voice behind me, or I would close my eyes and see Marie-Belle looking at me. One joint would get rid of all that, I knew, if only I could get my paws on one. Pot's not addictive, but the calm semi-high state it puts you in can be, especially when the world is trying to shake you up.

Willa, a pronghorn from the West Coast, swung by with a gazelle in a male-cut collared shirt she'd picked up. She'd apparently already shown the gazelle the picture I'd done of her as a nature goddess, because the gazelle told me my art was terrific.

I was still too disoriented to think properly, by which I mean "offer to do work if someone says they like my art," but fortunately Eve told her that I do commissions and she should come by the coffee shop most weekday mornings to find me. "Yeah," I managed. "I'd love to do something for you."

My phone buzzed then with a text, and I grabbed at it, praying it was Rachel and good news. I got one out of two.

Rachel: Sorry, friend is out.

Normally, I'd have stayed around to chat with Eve, especially with Alexei and Sol away. But I didn't want to have another drink here and have the room go weird again, and I didn't want to stay here without having another drink. So I told everyone that I was sorry, I felt bad, I was going to head home. Sherine asked if I needed a ride and I said I was fine, but Eve insisted she could take me in her car until Sherine forestalled her. The weasel took my arm and said, "You guys stay here. I'll take care of her and be right back."

So I let Sherine walk me out. In the warm night outside, I breathed in and felt better. I could hear myself think, for one thing, and for another, I hadn't realized how much I'd gotten used to the smell of a room full of humid, horny people until I was breathing in clean air. "Want to walk for a bit?" Sherine asked.

"I'm not drunk," I said. "I'm fine. I can walk home. It's like eight blocks." I waved in the direction of my apartment, but didn't start walking there.

"I'll tell Bellie you're sorry," she said.

"Don't tell her that." The raw anger hadn't gone, just simmered below the surface. "I'm not."

"Meg…"

"If you tell her I'm sorry, then next time she's gonna be doing the same fucking thing. Tell her I don't want to be set up, tell her I'm very happy being alone."

Reflections of the streetlights glimmered in Sherine's eyes. "Those aren't the same thing," she said.

"Oh, stop quoting Angel Stories at me." I meant to say it sort of amiably-jokey, like I did with Sol and Alexei, but jagged edges still spilled through and Sherine's ears went back. "Look," I said, "I won't give you the whole 'love is an illusion' speech."

"I remember being nineteen." Her smile came back a little. "It wasn't that long ago."

"So you remember what it was like when everyone wanted to tell you what to do instead of letting you work it out on your own time?"

She laughed. "Sort of. I didn't have a lot of friends trying to help me out."

"Lucky."

"People can help if you let them." She laid a paw on my wrist. "This is a really confusing time, I know."

I shook my head. It would be bad enough if being nineteen was all there was to it. On top of that there was four years of antidepressants and then there was whatever hangup I'd had before that, the unexpected burst of shame/fear that night with Margie and Amelia. "Trust me," I said. "I've got two gay roommates who can't shut up about the guys they're attracted to. I've got a male friend who wants to be more than friends. I've got Bellie hitting on me every other day. I'm good with people."

"But," Sherine said, "it doesn't sound like all those people are helping. And Bellie isn't hitting on you…exactly…"

I took another breath of the humid air and felt the lick of the river in it. Part of me wanted to run in that direction, throw off the skirt and shirt and dive into the water. All otters are like that; we have that instinct, that drive. It seemed like everyone else had this other drive, to pair up and have sex. I hadn't felt it yet; did that mean I never would? Should I be looking for boys, or girls, or not at all? I didn't bear uncertainty well at the best of times, which this was not.

"Look," I said, "I'm not trying to stop her from her never-ending quest for someone else to make her complete. Just tell her to leave me out of it."

She rolled her eyes and pushed me. "Go on home. Just one thing…"

"What?" I folded my arms.

"Come out with us again sometime. I promise Bellie will behave and we'll have a nice time."

"Yeah, alright." It wasn't anything like a real commitment and it would get me off this street and home sooner than having an argument about it. I did like Eve and Sherine, and honestly, when Bellie wasn't trying to make me admit that I was a lesbian, I liked her too. There were at least four other coffee shops in the neighborhood and there was a reason I went to La Croix.

As nice as it was that Sherine had reached out, I was still on edge waiting for the world to blur again, for that voice to swim back into my memory, for Marie-Belle's drawn whiskered muzzle to appear around the next corner. I'd taken a while to decline Sherine's invitation to walk me home because part of me thought that at least with her company, I might not spend the walk jumping at shadows, listening for voices to come out of the quiet. In the end, I was more worried that I would jump at shadows in front of her.

People think I like the night-time because it's dark and quiet and lonely, but I like being the dark, quiet, lonely one. It's less fun when the whole world is the same way. So I hurried down the blocks, past the trees where the birds had settled in for the night and the row houses glowing with the blue light of TV, past the construction site now growling with activity, huge mechanized monsters taking jerky bites of the ground in one area, lifting thick iron bars like matchsticks in others; blazing klieg lights throwing harsh, angular shadows around the sidewalk; the faint yells of the workers like the screams of bystanders in a Godzilla movie. I stopped to peer through the fence, wondering what could be taking shape out of the dirt, but they had only started laying girders, and apart from the familiar rectangular shape of a foundation, I could get no secrets from their movement. It distracted me until I watched the flow of shadows and thought I saw—no. No. I squeezed my eyes shut and backed away from the fence, then hurried on. I needed to get something to mellow my mind, and all the way home I had been trying to think who I could call for some pot, now twice as necessary to shore up the bulwarks in my psyche.

Rachel was out. Sol had only just gotten to college. It'd be nice to hear his voice again, and I might call him later to do that, but he wouldn't have hooked up with anyone there, and what would he do, FedEx something to me? Likewise Alexei was staying in his hotel until Mike got out there tomorrow to pick him up. Eve and Sherine wouldn't have gotten me anything, though I was sure they knew how, and Alain might have, but I didn't really want to impose on a newish friendship unless I was way more desperate.

My parents for sure had weed and would bring it up to me, but then I'd have to get into the whole Art Institute thing with them, and I didn't want to answer the same litany of questions about where my life was going. Also they would want to know why Rachel had flaked on me, which would lead to me telling them that I'd run out ahead of schedule, and one of the things we'd agreed on when I moved out was that I'd be responsible with my medication. Admitting how fast I'd gone through it would open up a whole raft of other questions I didn't want to answer.

That left one option before I went begging around Riverwalk for pot. I took out my phone as I got to my building and pulled up Athos's number. I stared at it all the way into the apartment and then set the phone down on the table as I poured myself a glass of rum from the cupboard, avoiding looking at the bottle behind it.

I could handle Athos better than my parents. The problem was that if I asked him for weed, he would have to come down and deliver it in person, and since it was Friday night, he'd be able to stay the weekend, especially if he heard I was alone. In fact, coming hundreds of miles from Port City, it'd be rude of me to make him turn right around and go back. Part of me wanted the company, and part of me was still back in the bar telling Sherine and Bellie that I didn't want to be with anyone. Inviting Athos into my empty apartment was not exactly a smart move—not that I didn't trust him, but having him here along with weed and alcohol and whatever might give him the wrong idea, or at least an idea I wasn't sure I shared. Yet.

But…I heard Sherine again: *Stop thinking and start doing.*

The rum warmed my stomach better than the vodka had done, or maybe I'd just been so tightly wound in that pickup bar that I'd needed more than one drink. I dangled the glass in one paw and walked over to the window of my bedroom. With the window closed, the noises of the work going on outside filtered through as a mysterious rumbling growl punctuated by barks of words that might as well be in a different language. Enough light came through to illuminate my room, and as I stood there, one of the big kliegs shifted around, silhouetting a tall crane in a burst of light.

I squinted and shielded my eyes but stayed where I was. The crane swung around in the light, and I was caught with it as it lowered another girder to the structure slowly taking shape. Daring, I stepped closer to the window. Maybe they could see me if they looked. Another swallow of rum, and I didn't care so much. The glass was warm beneath my fingers, and I felt as though I were looking into an aquarium, or looking out from one into the real world.

The world didn't blur. No more voices stretched out from my memory to reacquaint themselves with me. So maybe I didn't need weed. Maybe I just needed judicious applications of alcohol. I could take a flask of rum to the coffee shop, could get another couple liters of rum from the liquor store later, and that'd last me through the week. I wasn't going to freak out from dreams the way Sol and Alexei had. Dreams were all they were, dreams and memories, and they couldn't hurt me if I didn't let them.

Listen, Meg.

The voice, the echo was fainter now. I was stressed over Sol and Alexei leaving, I was missing my weed, and my imagination was overworked again. That's all it was. I'd heard that from my parents, from Dr. Wallace, from my own conscious mind more times than I could count.

Athos's name was still on the screen, the little phone icon waiting patiently. I closed the window shade and finished the rum, then turned off my phone.

Chapter 6

Hannah stirred awake, the dream still echoing in her head. Outside her window, the sun caught the lake, and for a moment she saw the shadow of a large machine in front of the light and a sharp, sweet taste filled her muzzle. Then the shadow was gone and Angeline was holding out a glass of water. Hannah drank, the memory of the rum fading, and looked out the window.

Immaculate Lake was as beautiful as Hannah had heard, sparkling outside like a diamond necklace God had placed amid the bright green trees. She rested her short muzzle against the window of the coach while her father and mother stepped down, taking in the azure of the lake, the luminous chain of reflections, and then the hundred or so people gathered on the lawn.

More than half were otters, clustered in large groups by the lake's edge, many with goblets in their paws that sparkled like the lake. Muskrats and beavers made up most of the rest, and Hannah saw her father's friend Adam, a jovial wolverine, entertaining a crowd of otters. All the males wore crisp black jackets over spotless white shirts with upturned stiff collars, and all the ladies wore long, flowing gowns of light pastel colors, a field of flowers amid the black shadows of thick trees.

"Hannah," a soft voice said behind her, "Come along."

When she turned, Angeline rose, and the older otter looked past Hannah with a smile. "It's lovely, isn't it?" she said in that same soft voice. "You see, Mother told you it would be worth the trip."

"It is." Hannah stood from the plush seat, sweeping the pale blue train of her dress around her thick tail. Angeline, in a plainer saffron dress, stepped back to allow Hannah to move forward.

When they emerged from the cool coach into the suffocating heat of the summer day, Hannah gasped. "I thought it would be cooler. Did we not go north?"

Angeline smiled and extended a paw to Hannah with a small accordion fan in it. "We did, but not very far."

"We were in the coach for hours." Hannah took the fan and waved it in front of her muzzle. Small panels on the fan hummed as they cooled the air that rushed over her nose and whiskers. "Ah. Thank you."

"We traveled many hours east, but only a short way north." Angeline straightened Hannah's dress and adjusted her collar and cuffs.

"I see." She looked longingly at the cool water. "Will we be able to swim in the lake?"

"Of course, once the wedding is over."

Hannah folded her arms. "I don't see why I must wait. The wedding won't start for an hour."

"You're no longer a child." Angeline laughed. "You may ask Mother, but I think she will say no."

Hannah pouted and turned back to the lawn, following her father and mother but looking to every side. A long bar stood to one side; she hadn't seen it from the coach. Behind it, a fox with bright red fur in a gleaming white uniform filled glasses and passed them to black-clad guests. She watched an otter bring two glasses back from the bar and give one to a lady in a light violet dress. "Look, Angeline," she said, pointing. "The Tidewaters are here. Where do you suppose Vanessa is?"

"Don't point." Angeline's voice chilled. "Come, I see Matthew Everett by the chairs. We should talk to him."

"I suppose," Hannah said, but she dawdled as much as she dared, looking around at the low hills that surrounded the lake, a patchwork of yellow dandelions and green grass bounded by thick elm forests and, nearer, clusters of crepe myrtle trees in full bloom, their papery flowers a violet that almost looked blue in the shadows. She walked to the edge of the lawn and pushed her white socks into the dirt.

"Hannah," Angeline said behind her. "Mind the path of thy feet."

"The point of the socks is to protect my feet," Hannah said, but she walked back to the grass until a white flower with five slightly rumpled petals caught her eye. The largest petal bore a yellow patch, and slender stamens rose from the center of the flower with a small fuzzy tip. "Anyway, I wanted to see the flowers," she said, inventing another reason for her digression.

The blooms smelled sweet and sugary. Bees hummed around them, but Hannah didn't bother about them, though Angeline warned her to be careful. They didn't bother her either, just droned on past with bright yellow patches on their legs as they hurried busily from flower to flower.

With the sugary scent in her nose, Hannah allowed Angeline to guide her to Matthew. He stood with a glass of some clear liquid in his paw, talking to an older otter whom Hannah recognized as Mr. Bluecrest, both of them looking down at the small notebook the older otter held. Angeline put a paw on Hannah's arm, as though Hannah needed to be reminded not to interrupt.

She stared across the lake as she waited, across the placid blue surface. "It is odd to see water so still," she murmured to Angeline. "It's like God's own pool."

"In a way." Angeline smiled tolerantly. "What do you think of the forest?"

Beyond the lake, high stands of trees rose, and rustling came across the water to Hannah's ears. Probably just birds, she thought, though there might be other large animals in them. Her father had taken her and Angeline to one of the forests around their home, but it was an hour away by boat, and he had warned her about the people who lived there. She had seen trails of smoke and heard the thunk of axes, and had wanted to meet the rabbits, or foxes, or perhaps other wolverines who spent their whole lives on land. Here, no sound of civilization emerged from the forest. "Do you suppose there are people living in it?"

"Living in it?" Angeline brought one white-gloved paw to her muzzle. "I should hope not. Why would you ask?"

"I only thought it might be polite for Mary's father to invite them to the wedding." Hannah had become adept at inventing reasons to engage with strangers.

"If there are people living there," Angeline said, "they should have the sense to stay away."

Perhaps people did live there. Hannah looked around the shores of the lake, but they were thick with rushes and weeds, and no path suggested itself. She sighed, and then a high voice called her name and she turned to see two young otters running in her direction.

"Hyperia!" a stern voice called behind them, and the taller otter in the lavender gown slowed, while the other, in bright turquoise, did not.

"How are you so late?" she asked, throwing her arms around Hannah.

"We stopped for breakfast and the armadillo asked Father to bless the restaurant, and then took ages saying thank you." Hannah smiled and hugged her friend, and whispered quickly to her, "I want to tell you something."

But at that moment Hyperia arrived, her companion Celestine hurrying behind her. Hyperia reached out to embrace Hannah and looked down, ignoring Celestine's fussing with her gown. "Where is Nephaline, Vanessa?"

"Oh…" Vanessa smoothed down her turquoise dress, looking very pleased with herself. "I told her I wanted a four-leafed clover to give to Mary. For luck, you know. She's still looking for it."

"She shouldn't leave your side," Angeline said, and Celestine nodded agreement.

Vanessa looked archly at the companions. "I'm hardly going to lose my virtue here on the lawn, am I?"

Hyperia gaped at the language, and Hannah had the presence of mind to pretend to look shocked. Angeline made a faint scolding noise, but Vanessa went on as though she'd said nothing unusual. "Doesn't everyone look lovely? It's even nicer than Amaranth's wedding was. Hyperia and I have been here for half an hour and we have been guessing who made everyone's dresses."

Clothing came in slightly below etiquette in Vanessa's list of most hated conversation topics. Hannah smiled at her friend's thinly veiled sarcasm. "It sounds lovely."

"In another year we'll all be getting married," Hyperia said. "We have to know whose designs we like."

"I don't know if I shall be married," Vanessa said.

Hyperia and Hannah stared at her as though she'd said she was planning to live on land. "But…" Hyperia said faintly.

"Don't talk nonsense," Angeline said. "You'll turn sixteen in a month. When do you plan to be married? When you're seventeen? Eighteen?"

"You're not part of my family," Vanessa retorted tartly. "I'll thank you to mind your family's business."

"Very well." Angeline took Hannah's arm. "Come, Hannah. Matthew is free now. We mustn't keep him waiting."

Indeed, the middle-aged otter had left Matthew standing with his paws clasped in front of him, and as Hannah looked over, Matthew was staring down at the cuff of his shirt. He looked up as Angeline said his name, and still looked distracted as his eyes met Hannah's.

She waited for him to greet her, and a moment later he said, "Good water, Hannah."

"Good water, Matthew," she said, conscious of Angeline's presence beside her. "How are you enjoying the gathering?"

Angeline nudged her; she'd forgotten to call Matthew "Mr. Everett." Hannah bit her lip. "Oh," Matthew said, unaware of the exchange, "it's a long way to travel, but…" He gestured toward a small group of older otters. "There's the opportunity to make connections for our business, and it's profitable to discuss matters in this more relaxed setting."

"I see," Hannah said. Matthew remained slightly distracted, so she asked, "Was your conversation with Mr. Bluecrest profitable?"

A sharper nudge from Angeline, and Hannah realized that the earlier one had been a warning to let Matthew guide the conversation, as this one was. *But he wasn't guiding it anywhere*, she protested silently.

Angeline must have seen her expression, because she spoke through the small piece Hannah wore in her ear. *"Let Matthew speak, and hold your peace. He may yet break off the engagement if you give him cause."*

Hannah subsided and stood obediently, but Matthew was looking down at his shirt cuff again. From this angle, Hannah couldn't see the display he was reading; she only knew it was a display because she and Vanessa had stolen a boy's shirt once and watched the glowing mysterious letters "BIOLOGIN NOT FOUND" scroll through the fabric. They'd been unable to make it do anything else, but boys could check weather forecasts and tides, waterball scores and company scores somehow (Hannah had heard the terms 'stocks' and 'shares,' but the boys reacted as though the companies were playing waterball games, so she still thought of them as scores); they could send messages and pictures to each other and even watch movies by themselves.

Not that Hannah wanted to see all of the moving pictures. Her father had described some of them for her: the ones made by the land-dwellers, even the ones who were good Christians, were often violent and strange. Rather than disturb her mind with such terrible things, he selected the ones made by water-dwelling folk with good morals so that Hannah could grow up properly.

Vanessa claimed to have watched one of the movies one night when her father'd had a little too much wine and fallen asleep with his display still running, but Hannah wasn't sure she believed her friend. Vanessa's father did drink, but Vanessa had also told Hannah that she'd swum from New Kestle to Hurricane Harbor in a day, that she'd seen a unicorn, and that the Jesus on the crucifix in their church had spoken to her. The idea that a movie would show fornication was almost as unbelievable as the idea that Vanessa would watch for longer than a minute.

Matthew continued to stare at his shirt cuff. Hannah waited patiently, though she did glance to the side to see Vanessa and Hyperia talking. Vanessa had told her some truths, too, like that time she promised they could drink alcohol without getting caught, or the time she'd shown Hannah that the Bible her father used had more verses than the one Hannah had been given. Angeline told her often that Vanessa was not a very suitable friend, and Vanessa's bold statement against marriage would be yet another brick in Angeline's argument. Hannah couldn't say why she wanted to spend more time with Vanessa than with any of her other friends, but she did, and as that was the only matter on which she defied Angeline, her companion allowed her that small freedom.

At length, Matthew looked up and said, "It's good to see you here. You look very pretty."

"Thank you." Hannah seized on the conversation. "You look very handsome as well."

"The business is going well." Matthew touched his shirt cuff. "I have a report due next week that's been worrying me."

Hannah knew how to respond to that. "I'm sure you'll do quite well. You needn't worry."

"It's a report to the president," he said, "So it's quite important."

Hannah gaped. Matthew was going to present a report to the President of the Sovereign Christian States, the stately otter she saw once or twice a year when he addressed the whole country? It seemed impossible that he was this calm about it. "Are you traveling to Millenport directly from the wedding?"

He frowned, his whiskers bunching out and his ears going down. "No," he said. "Why would I?"

Angeline came to her rescue. "*He means the president of his company.*"

Oh, of course. Hannah blinked at him and smiled. "You've mentioned traveling there for business before. I wondered if that was where your president lives."

"No, no, he's in New Kestle with the rest of the company." He looked amused, then dropped his eyes to his shirt cuff again.

It was going to be tedious to sit here and wait every time he wanted to check his display. Hannah shot a glance at Angeline, and her companion met her eyes with a steady gaze.

Through fifteen more tortured minutes, Hannah stood mostly silent while Matthew talked about his business and his younger brother, who was just starting with the company. Finally, he caught the eye of another business associate and excused himself.

Hannah exhaled. "He didn't even mention the wedding," she said.

Angeline brushed the shoulder of her dress. "He is waiting for his father and yours to arrange the date. Then you and your mother will plan the ceremony and he, like James Goodwright, will appear on the day."

"At least I can talk to Vanessa and Hyperia about it," Hannah said. "And Elly and Delilah."

"And me," Angeline said.

"Oh, of course." Hannah smiled and kissed the other otter on the nose. "Now, I should like to—"

But she would not get a chance to speak to Vanessa, because Mary's mother's voice came through Hannah's earpiece at that moment. "*Everybody please take your seats. We are ready to begin.*"

Hannah and Angeline found seats next to Hannah's mother, and they watched as Hannah's father took his place between the couple-to-be. During the following hour and a half, at pauses in the service, Angeline said things to Hannah like, "*Doesn't she look beautiful?*" and "*I know you'll look just as beautiful,*" and "*James went to Poplar to help clean up after the tornado last year, God bless him,*" meant to make her think about her own upcoming wedding. The rest of the time, during her father's readings, Hannah was supposed to be concentrating on God's word, but her mind kept turning back to the dream she wanted to tell Vanessa about. Her stomach rumbled, because she hadn't been able to eat much on the coach, but food was still at least two hours away.

The sun beat down on her and the air remained still. A haze of insects hovered over the lake, but the wands at the perimeter kept them away. On the opposite side of the lawn, one girl who looked to be a little older than Hannah, if not quite Matthew's age, wore a small brown hat with a brim. Nobody else wore a hat, and Hannah did not remember anyone wearing a hat at Amaranth's wedding a few months ago, though that one had been at the Great Salvation Dome in New Kestle, so perhaps nobody had feared the sun.

"Why is she wearing a hat?" Hannah whispered to her mother at the next break in the service, as Mary and James knelt to accept Hannah's father's blessing over them. "I would like to wear a hat. The sun is quite hot."

"Hush!" Her mother's whiskers splayed out and her eyes widened, and the grimace on her mouth frightened Hannah into silence. A moment later her mother had composed herself. "You look lovely without a hat, and the sun is God's, so we must bear its heat with good will."

Hannah nodded and lowered her eyes, but could not resist sliding a glance back toward the otter in the hat. What was so odd or terrible about it?

At last, at last, Mary and James were married, and the guests were allowed to rise. Mary's mother announced that the reception would take place on the lawn while the chairs were cleared—the fox servants were already bustling about, folding white chairs into thin sheets and loading them onto little self-driven carts—and that following the reception, there would be a swim in the lake and then dinner.

"Of course there will be a swim in the lake," Hannah's mother said when Hannah clapped her paws together and smiled at the announcement.

"When it's time, Angeline will collect the skirt from your gown and then you may swim in it."

They were talking with Mrs. Tettle, an otter with a halo of diamonds woven into the fur around her head, as she praised the dignity and eloquence with which Hannah's father had delivered the ceremony. Hannah knew she was important for some reason and knew she was supposed to remember why, but she couldn't, and she didn't want to ask Angeline. Mrs. Tettle had taken a breath, but before she could start in again, Hannah asked boldly, "May I have some sparkler?"

"Of course not. Not until your own wedding." Her mother did not even react with shock, though Angeline made a clucking noise on Hannah's other side.

Hannah hadn't expected her mother to say yes, but she wanted to ask to show that she was grown-up enough to be interested, and perhaps to get a taste later. "May I go talk to Vanessa?" she asked, and her mother waved her assent.

Angeline trailed Hannah around the lawn. "Why don't you ask Hyperia what she thought of the wedding?" the older otter said.

"Vanessa's my best friend." Hannah searched the party for the turquoise gown. It shouldn't be hard to spot.

"I doubt that Mr. Everett will approve of her company once you are married."

Hannah rolled her eyes at her companion's prim tone. "Then all the more reason I should spend time with her now."

She had wandered over by the lakeshore, and there she stopped with a smile. Vanessa was in the lake already, submerged down to her head. She waved, and now Hannah saw Vanessa's companion Nephaline on the shore, paws on her hips, no doubt speaking sternly into Vanessa's earpiece. But the swimming otter's smile reflected in white gleams from the water. "Come on in, it's lovely," Vanessa called.

"Don't go in, Hannah," Angeline said.

The rest of the wedding party milled about on the lawn. Nobody was really looking in Hannah's direction; they had congregated around the bar again, where the white-suited bartender fox was giving out thin, tall goblets filled with pale gold sparkler. "Take my skirt," Hannah said.

"I will not. You will wait until swimming is announced."

"If you don't take it," Hannah said, "I shall go in with the skirt on."

Angeline's lips tightened. "*You will be in trouble if you do.*"

Hannah took a step toward the water and looked back at Angeline. Her companion remained immobile, so Hannah pulled her white socks off and stepped into the water.

"Wait!" Angeline hurried forward. She tried to grasp Hannah's arm, but Hannah resisted, and in pulling out of the grip, her foot slipped on a wet rock and she slid backwards. Angeline let go, and Hannah fell all the way into the water with a very undignified splash.

Angeline glared at her from the shore, adopting the same pose as Vanessa's companion. "*Young lady, wait until I tell your mother.*"

"I shall tell her you wouldn't take my skirt," Hannah retorted, "and that is why it was ruined. I should unfasten it myself if I could work it." She kept afloat easily, bobbing in the lake, the cool water heavenly on her fur after all those hours in the relentless heat. The water smelled clean with a tinge of green that probably came from the algae collecting by the shore, and another earthy odor; no doubt she'd stirred up the muck when she'd slipped. Not quite as immaculate as its name when you got up close.

"*Your father will determine your punishment.*"

That thought passed like a shadow over Hannah's elation at being submerged in the lake. But it was done now; she was soaked and swimming, and Vanessa came up next to her to pull her along the shore. "Come on," she said, "let's get out of sight of the rest of them."

Their companions trailed them along the shore a little way, but stopped at the flowery hedge that bordered the lawn, the blue-violet crepe myrtle trees rising above them. The light perfume of the flowers wafted across the water. Angeline talked in Hannah's ear much of the way, and then went silent, simply watching along with Nephaline.

"Turn off your talker," Vanessa said.

"*Hannah, do not turn it off. If I cannot hear you, I cannot protect you.*"

She reached up to her ear and fiddled with the button that she was supposed to press only when she needed to use the necessary in private. "Five minutes," she said.

"What were you going to tell me?" Vanessa whispered, keeping her paw between them and their companions on the shore even though their talkers were off.

Hannah ducked her head below the water and re-emerged. The dream had been interesting enough to want to tell Vanessa about, but now in the moment, her ears flushed and her tongue wouldn't form the words. "I...I had this dream, but it felt really real. I was talking to someone, I think it was you and some other friends, and we were talking about going out on dates, but it wasn't with our fiancés."

Vanessa waited and then asked, with interest, "Who was it with?"

"With…" Hannah looked away. With her nose at the level of the water, the forest and hills became more imposing. She lifted her eyes to the thick, shadowy trees and breathed in the woodsy smell.

Shouts reached their ears at the same time as Angeline said, "*People have seen you. Hannah, come back now.*"

From the tilt of Vanessa's head, she must have gotten a similar message from Nephaline. She pushed her nose in close to Hannah's cheek and whispered, "Were we going out with other boys?"

Hannah gulped. Her heart beat faster and she reached out to Vanessa's shoulder to steady herself. "No, it was…"

"Hannah!"

Her mother's voice carried over the water, an unearthly shout that echoed and came back to her from the hills. Hannah met Vanessa's eyes. "We should go back," she said.

"It's okay." Vanessa smiled. Her nose brushed Hannah's cheek. "Tell me some other time." And as they turned, her tail slid along Hannah's dress.

Hannah swam back behind Vanessa. It had just been a silly dream. Why had it bothered her so much?

Chapter 7

I sat bolt upright in bed, convinced I was soaked through, heart still pounding. The dark room, as silent as when I'd gone to bed, still seemed to echo with the call from my dream, the name, "Hannah!"

I'd never dreamed that vividly before. The meds had given me some fucked up nightmares, but nothing that coherent, nothing with smell and dialogue and hunger in my stomach and the heat of sun and cool of water, that left me rubbing paws through my fur surprised that it wasn't still wet.

A dream like Alexei and Sol had had.

I made sure that I wasn't hallucinating something from my dream coming back to my bed, the way Sol had, but it didn't make me feel better when I didn't find anything. Alexei's dreams hadn't brought back anything except a ghost.

The good news is, my ghost is a fifteen-year-old otter girl, not a scary Russian soldier. I laughed at that and then clutched my sides, breathing hard, laughter turning shaky and hysterical. It was like I was listening to myself laugh and didn't have any control over it.

That cinched it. Whatever else it was going to bring, I had to get some weed, and Athos was my only real chance. I tried to breathe evenly to stop the giggling fit and managed to get it under control as I picked up my phone.

Two a.m. There was a chance he'd still be up, especially on a Friday night.

Hey, I texted, *can you get your paws on some weed?*

Second after agonizing second I waited. If he was asleep, I'd go out and find some coffee. There was a convenience store up toward the bus station that was twenty-four hours. But thankfully for my stomach and overall health, Athos responded quickly. *What kind?*

Mellow. Not super-high.

I walked over to the window, where I could still hear the machines outside when I got close to the glass. They were real, metal behemoths lumbering out there in the night, the sound comforting. My phone, clutched in my fingers, was real. The carpet below my feet was real. I slid the window up to breathe the warm night air and hear the machines more clearly, and then my phone chimed.

Can I call you?

Ah, fuck. I closed the window and turned the lamp on; the bright yellow glow made the room feel smaller and safer. Then I lay back on my bed. *Sure*, I texted.

He called before I could lower my paw to the bed. I thumbed the green "Accept" button and brought the phone to my ear. "Hey."

"Hi, Meg." His light, serious voice with the northern accent had recently annoyed me, but now it broke the silence of the apartment. "How are you?"

My paw picked at the sheets on the futon. "The roommates took off today, so I've been living the high life. You know how it goes. Wild parties, lines of coke, meth in the bathroom. Only I'm out of weed and the guests all want some."

"Heh." He chuckled. "I've got a friend who usually has some. How much do you need?"

"Not a lot. I'm going to see my friend next weekend. Couple grams, an eighth maybe."

"Shouldn't be a problem. Are you around all weekend?"

This was the part I'd known I was going to have to deal with: Athos was going to have to bring it in person. "You driving down?" I asked, to forestall the rest of the planning.

"Train. I can hop on in the morning and be there tomorrow night. That soon enough?"

"I don't really have a choice." I exhaled. "Thanks."

"So, uh." He typed on his keyboard in the background.

I knew what he was going to ask. "You can stay 'til you have to go back to work. Sol's room is empty; Alexei's not back until Sunday night. I'll call and ask him if it's okay."

"I can catch a plane on Monday, unless you need me to carry something back. If you're sure."

My last chance to back out. I thought of him staying there in the other room and that was better than it being empty. I wasn't going to run in there if I had another freaky dream—after the business with Alexei, Athos was going to tell me that Hannah was real and that she had a message for me or some shit like that—but at least I would know he was there, that someone was there.

It was a moot point anyway, because he was going to bring me pot and I wasn't going to have dreams or hear voices or draw pictures that talked to me. "Yeah," I said. "I'd like to see you."

"I'm looking forward to seeing you again, too." He started to say something else, probably about the last time we'd seen each other, then thought better of it. "So seriously, why do you need it so badly?"

I lay back and closed my eyes. "I told you, the party here's running out."

"It's a pretty quiet party." He didn't actually chuckle, but I could hear him restraining it.

"They're all mice. They party quiet."

He exhaled across the phone. "Meg, it's two in the morning. Why didn't you call me last night? Why do you need it at two in the morning?"

"It's medicinal."

"Right. For what condition is this?"

Fuck, if I didn't have this conversation now I was going to have it when he got here. Might as well get it over with. It'd be easier to get away with half-truths on the phone. "It's for withdrawal symptoms."

"Oh, I forgot about your heroin addiction."

"I'm serious," I said. "I was on antidepressants for a few years in high school."

That shut him up. "When I met you?"

"Uh-huh."

"Jesus Fox. I…I didn't know."

"Of course you didn't. I didn't tell you. How were you going to know?" I took a little pity on him. "Sol and Alexei don't know either." Sol kind of knew part of it, but not the drug part.

"Well, uh…I mean, you're off them now?"

"That's what 'withdrawal' means, right?" I sighed. "Look, it's no big thing. A bunch of the girls in my class were on them."

"Yeah, but…" I caught a scratching sound; he was rubbing his muzzle. "You never told me. You didn't seem depressed at all."

"That's why they're called *anti*-depressants."

"Heh. Yeah. Okay, so the pot helps with the withdrawal? I mean, how long have you been off?"

I weighed the truth and didn't see that it revealed anything I didn't want him to know. "Three or four months. Since about May."

"All right. I guess…right."

I took some satisfaction in having thrown him. "Hey, you want to give me a complex about it? I got a whole bunch of shit from my doctor about how it's totally normal and how if you break a leg you splint it up, so why not take something to splint up your body chemistry?"

"No, it's not that, I mean, I have a couple friends on them too, it's just…" He went quiet and I let him think it through. "You always seemed so together."

Except the last time we met. But there was a reason for that and I sure as fuck wasn't gonna tell him what it was now. One deep, dark secret at a time. "Thanks. I worked on the 'together' thing a lot."

He told me when his train was going to get in and I told him I would go meet him there, then he hung up to go track down his source. I didn't ask him what source he had that would be up at two in the morning; those big cities had all kinds of people living in them. Athos kept saying I should visit and I told him I wasn't up for that much weird in one place yet.

I set the phone back down and lay there staring up at the ceiling. I could still see the waterline, the trees and the rise of hills, the perfect lawn, the weird little science fictiony details of the dream and the other weird details, like blue crepe myrtle trees (the ones I'd grown up with back in Midland were pink or white or lavender). I never had much time for science fiction, not with the real world as fucked up as it is. Sure, I'd go see science fiction movies with Sol and Alexei, sometimes with my parents (they liked fantasy more, especially magical realism), but the movies I liked best were the big cartoonish ones and the literal cartoon ones: people putting their faith in superheroes to save the world, or reducing the world to brightly colored simple fairytales.

Restless, I turned to my computer so that I wouldn't have to lie there and either go back over the dream or, worse, go back to sleep. Thinking about escapes had reminded me of something I'd read a few months ago, so I did a couple searches on "antidepressant withdrawal."

There was the page I'd read: antidepressant withdrawal could cause anxiety, irritability (Sol would say "how would anyone tell?"), headaches, and vivid dreams. I stared at those last two words. Well, shit. Maybe the pot had just held off the other symptoms and this really was nothing but delayed withdrawal.

That didn't help my state of mind as much as I'd hoped it would. I mean, fuck, the whole reason I wanted to get off the meds was because I wanted to be *me*. If they were still screwing with my chemistry, then what was the point of anything?

I poked around the Internet to find something to occupy myself. After going through all of the current lists making the rounds ("Five Things You Won't Believe About Your Own Fur"), I was getting sleepy, but I was still determined to stay awake. Maybe I could search on Immaculate Lake, see if maybe I'd seen a photo of it somewhere and that was what I'd dreamed about…but when the results page for my search loaded, the image of a weasel with a white skull painted on his face grinned out at me.

Weird. The rest of the page was all about voodoo spirits and rituals. Bleary, I looked at the box. I'd typed in "voodoo."

I didn't remember typing that in. Shit, was this the kind of thing Sol and Alexei were talking about?

No. I was just tired, I'd been thinking about the comic, and I was going to type in a thing about my dream, but instead I'd typed in something else from my subconscious. It wasn't fucking ghosts or anything. It was going off my antidepressants and getting too wrapped up in creating a story. I'd thought Sol's problem was that he was spending too much time trying to live his story and not enough thinking about it to write it. Now here I was trying to make my own story up and I was spooking myself and typing weird shit into search engines. Time to shut off the computer and go back to sleep, and if I dreamed about that fucking lake again, well, I'd wake up and stay awake until Athos got here.

It would be good to see him again.

∞

I didn't go back to the lake and the wedding or anywhere else in my dreams, for that matter. When I woke up Saturday to a light drizzle and muted grey light—not as bright as the nighttime klieg lights—I had a minor headache and that was all. Headache: another symptom. Maybe all of Friday had been withdrawal weirdness, triggered by loneliness.

Athos texted me that he was on the train, and that in itself was enough for more relief, tempered by a little worry over what I'd say if he wanted to talk about his last visit or about our relationship. I toasted a couple slices of bread and then called Alexei because the apartment was so quiet.

"I have not yet heard about the interview," he said. "But Mike will be here in two hours."

"I guess being in Millenport with a friend is better than being in Millenport alone. But how do you think it went?"

Of course he was going to be optimistic; I just wanted to hear him say it. "The interviewer was very kind. Mike prepared me well and I think my answers pleased her." He paused. "She is a fox as well, so she treated me kindly."

"Best thing that could happen, getting a same-species interviewer. She wasn't fazed by the gay thing?"

"No. I had filed the paperwork." He coughed. "The worst part of it was that she made me talk about my family, and Cat's death."

"Ouch." It was still amazing to me that Alexei was able to do normal things like talk about his family, go to work…smile, even. But every so often he did get quiet, and Sol and I knew he was thinking about Caterina, and we left him alone.

"It was bad," he said. "But last night I dreamed…"

He'd said it quickly and then trailed off, like he'd just remembered who he was talking to. On Thursday, if he'd told me he'd dreamed about his sister, I would've let him tell me about the dream, and he would've kept it to himself if he thought it was more than a dream. But now, when he said that word, I flashed back to being an otter in a formal dress plunged into the cool water of an idyllic lake. So I acted as if he hadn't mentioned the dream. "If you were honest about it, then I'm sure it helped. If she saw how it hurt you…don't they count mental anguish in addition to physical danger?"

"Yes," he said, sounding slightly disappointed. "And Rozalina—she is the worker who helped me come to the States—she sent a message on my behalf. My father called her and abused her many times. So she can…" He pronounced the next word carefully. "Testify."

"Sounds hopeful. When will you know?"

"She said that because my visa expires soon, they will try to make their decision in two weeks at most. Perhaps before."

"Cool. Heard from Sol yet?"

"Yes. He is in his dorm. His roommate is a kangaroo and they both enjoy baseball. He sounded very busy."

Sol hadn't called me, but whatever. "Hope they get along."

"I am sure they will. Sol is a nice wolf."

"I don't think getting along with you means he can get along with anyone. You're pretty easygoing." When he didn't say anything, I said, "That's a compliment, sort of."

"Thank you." The fox laughed. "But remember that Sol also became your friend."

"This is a point. Wait, did you just insult me?"

"You are proud of not having very many friends, yes? Then it is not an insult."

He had me there. "Don't let anyone tell you that you don't belong in this country, fox-boy. Good luck and have a good weekend with Mike. Oh, forgot to tell you. Athos is coming down tonight. Mind if he stays in Sol's bed? Tomorrow night he can stay on the couch."

"He can stay in Sol's bed both nights," Alexei said. "There are spare sheets in our closet. I am glad he is coming down again. You have forgiven him?"

"Enough for now."

He chuckled softly. "So no ghost talk."

If he were here in the room, I would've given him the death glare, but that's probably why he felt brave enough to say it. I snapped out, "Fuck no," and then realized that he didn't know I'd been freaking out all yesterday, what with the comic and the weird dream.

"All right." Because it was Alexei, he didn't tell me to calm the fuck down the way Sol would've. "I will be careful."

There was a moment there when I almost said, "I had a weird dream." But Alexei was in Millenport and I was here, and I didn't want to have that conversation over the phone. Anyway, I told myself, what was he going to tell me? He'd insist it was real, that spirits were talking to me, or ancestors or something, even though the dream about Hannah had *clearly* been just a dream, my brain taking some "Pride and Prejudice" wedding with otters and adding weird science fiction touches to it: sleeve computers and tiny earpieces and paper fans with cooling units in them.

So I told Alexei when Athos was leaving, wished him a good weekend, and hung up. Then I went back to my room and dug up a few more episodes of "Disprovers" from the Internet, and watched the team of scientists and engineers take on myths and historical legends and try to re-create and either confirm or disprove them.

I should have been working on commissions, but when I picked up a pencil after lunch, I kept seeing Marie-Belle's face staring up out of the page at me. The rain had let up a bit, so I went out to the pool again, which was worse on Saturday. Fended off two different creepy guys and came back to the apartment at least feeling a little more refreshed and calm about the evening. No more dreams, no more voices, no more visions.

⟨∞⟩

Athos's train got in around sunset, the sky glowing orange with bright reddish streaks of clouds carrying off the last of the rain as I got off the bus at the train station. The train sat at the platform already, so I didn't have much time to worry about seeing Athos again.

When I spotted his sharp grey and russet muzzle over the long black cape, I grinned. All the other people in the station turned to look as they passed him, so he was easy to find, like an eddy in a stream. He saw me a moment later and returned my smile, his black-tipped tail brushing the hem of the cape as it wagged. When he reached me, he put out both paws and I clasped them, dark and narrow in my thicker brown ones. "It's good to see you," he said. "Thanks for inviting me down."

I had enough politeness and tact not to ask immediately for the weed; I wasn't going to smoke it in public anyway. "Thanks for coming," I said. "Though if you could have turned into a bat, it would probably have been faster."

He raised an eyebrow and swung a shoulder forward, making the cape flow and ripple. Under the cape, he wore a startlingly normal blue collared shirt and khaki pants. "Even a bat's wings get tired," he said.

"The bus leaves in twenty minutes," I said, and he picked up his duffel bag and followed me to the stop. "Just enough time to grab dinner at the burger place if you want."

"I was checking the restaurants," he said. "There's a nice country cooking place a short walk away. Supposed to have great peach pie. We could take a later bus."

I pointed ahead of us. "The burger place is right here and it's cheap and solid."

"You ever tried this other place? Carwin used to work there." When I didn't react to the name, he said, "The ferret? Season two of 'Top Chef'?"

"Oh!" I glanced in that direction. "He's not there now, though. Anyway, even if he was, we wouldn't get to see Chef Dickhead yelling at him as he adds coriander to the bouillabaisse."

"Well…" He glanced at the burger place, one of those bright-white-sign-with-big-red-plastic-letters kind of places that smells of charcoal and grease when you walk in. "All right. But before I go, you have to let me take you to a nice place."

Over dinner and on the bus, we talked about the train ride down, briefly about his job as a fact-checker for a Port City publisher on several magazines, and about my commissions. It wasn't until we were walking back to the apartment from the bus stop that he said, hesitantly, "I brought you the stuff. Have you been okay today?"

The air had cooled; the sky had darkened enough for the street lamps to flicker to life. I folded my arms and ran through the incidents in my head. "I've been fine. I had, you know, anxiety, irritability, headaches…" I listed off the symptoms from the web.

He gave me a sideways look, his eyes flashing in the reflection of the light above us. "Headaches that woke you up at two am?"

"Who says I was asleep?"

"Did you wait to call me until 2 am because you were worried I'd be out?"

"That was the point where I couldn't take any more of it."

We turned up the sidewalk and I got out my keys. On the front stoop, Athos turned while I was unlocking the door, staring out at the empty yard. I yanked the door open because I knew what he was thinking. "C'mon in," I said.

He followed slowly, but at least he didn't mention the old Siberian bum. I brought him into the apartment and locked the door behind us. "You'll be in Sol's bed. I'll help you make it up if you want. Just don't touch his goddamn picture."

"All right." He set his suitcase on the kitchen table, rummaged through it, and came out with a little plastic baggie.

"What do I owe you?" I asked, taking it, and then I saw the small crumbly squares in the bag. "Oh, this is…"

"Don't worry about it." He watched me turn the bag over in my paws. "Yeah, it's cookie squares. My friend didn't have any loose and he mostly deals with canids."

"You want one?" I opened the bag and offered it to him. "I mean, they're yours, really."

"They're yours," he said, "and sure."

He took one square in his fingers, and I reached in to take one too. It was barely larger than my fingertip. "Just one? They're tiny."

"Oh yeah." He laughed and leaned on the table. "Don't take two or you'll be useless."

"Cheers," I said, closing the bag and lifting the tiny cookie square. "Thanks again."

He raised his and put it on his tongue as I did the same. The taste of the herb definitely came through the sugary cookie as it dissolved on my tongue. I rolled it around in my muzzle and then swallowed.

When I smoked, I was used to feeling something pretty quickly, and Athos anticipated my question. "It takes a few minutes," he said.

"Okay. Let's make up your bed, then."

He followed me into Sol and Alexei's room, where we found the spare sheets and made up Sol's bed. He asked about Sol and I told him I hadn't heard from the woofer yet, him being all busy with getting settled at college.

As we left, Athos looked up at the picture of Sol's fox. As he had outside, he stayed quiet, but I could feel the wheels turning in his head. I walked out to the kitchen where I got a couple glasses of water, and after a moment he followed. I held one out to him and walked into my room.

The construction lights were on again, so I pulled the curtains shut. Athos looked at my futon and then slowly walked over and plopped down against the wall opposite it, cross-legged on the floor with his tail swept around his feet. "You got any music?" he asked.

There were a few bands on the computer that we both liked. I started up one album and sat back on the futon. "So," Athos said a moment later, "how bad were these headaches?"

"Bad enough that I called you at 2 am."

He nodded, dropping one paw to his tail. His large ears folded out to the side, and when I couldn't see their rounded tips, he reminded me more of Alexei. "All right. There's something else I wanted to ask you, too," he said.

"I'm still not feeling anything." I stretched my legs out in front of me, heels on the floor.

"I don't have to wait until you're high to ask."

I leaned back on my paws and nodded. "Go ahead."

"Well…" He hesitated. "I don't mind staying in Sol's room. There's a bed and all, I get that. I want to get that out of the way. But I like you a lot and I thought you liked me. And," he held up a paw. "I know what happened last time I was here."

Ah, shit. "I was pretty shaken up. You shouldn't have tried to hug me."

He smiled slightly. "Apology accepted." His tail tip flicked up and down. "So?"

"I do like you," I said. "I'm just not sure I like you like you like me."

He nodded. "But you're not gay."

"I don't know that either." I'd told him a couple years ago that I didn't fantasize about girls, which was true. He hadn't asked whether I fantasized about boys.

"You are hanging out with a lot of lesbians here, but you said they're just friends?"

"Their bars are better than regular bars."

He tilted his head. "And you're not at all curious?"

"Sure I'm curious."

"So you might be bi."

Athos and I had talked about dating in high school; several times I'd said online that if he were around we could've gone to the prom together, him in his cape and me in my black fur paint, and we would've had a great time. He'd said—once I turned eighteen—that he'd like to take me out, and at that point I started telling him I didn't know if I wanted to date at all. I was still on the pills then, though.

He went on. "From what you've told me, you haven't really tried anything. I understand that there's a lot of material out there on the Internet about sexuality, but—well, you know, I'm a big fan of verifying first-hand."

"The antidepressants messed with…a lot of stuff," I said, not really wanting to get into a discussion of female seasons and all. "Plus I'm not exactly swimming in opportunity."

His muzzle stretched into this slightly goofy grin, and then his eyes focused on me and the grin faltered. "I mean—I'm not saying—not with me, but—you know, just go out and do stuff…"

Of course I knew he did mean that I should do stuff with him; his splayed ears and whiskers going every which way told me that. I might've gotten annoyed at it, but I already knew where he wanted our relationship to go. Boys are nowhere near as complicated or subtle as they think they are.

If we did "do stuff," though, and it didn't work out…if it turned out I was gay, or that he wasn't the one who did it for me…then where would we be? I couldn't apologize my way out of that one. Our relationship would be a dead end street.

But it was okay. It'd be easy to avoid the issue and keep on going the way we had been. I knew it wasn't going to be a problem. And then I realized why I was so calm. "Hey, it's kicking in."

"Yeah, me too." His ears came back up; he stretched his legs out and pulled a USB keychain from his pocket. "Want to watch something? I brought a couple movies."

"Sure." I held a paw out for it and he tossed it across the room. I tried to figure out how to angle the monitor, but there wasn't a good way. Last time he was here we both sat on my bed and were cool—the first night, anyway, the night we got high together. "Why don't you come over here?"

The fox lifted his head, the orange patches on his muzzle catching the light of my lamp. "You sure?"

"Yeah."

He pushed himself to his feet and came over. My mattress was wedged against the corner, and I sat myself back in that corner, balancing on my tail. Athos came over to sit next to me, but not touching, leaning back against the wall. Up close, I could smell the sterile train air still in his clothes and his natural fox musk, softer than Alexei's, and it was a nice smell. For the first ten minutes the tension stayed at a distance, like I knew it was a tense situation but I didn't feel tense. He stayed still, and after that even the distant tension faded. Later, when his tail uncurled against my foot, we were both so mellow that I didn't care. The fur felt nice and he was smiling and I was smiling too.

It helped that the movie was dumb as shit, some pretentious art-house crap about the end of the world and the survivors trying to rescue the last people of some species so they didn't go extinct, or becoming like them so they're not forgotten or something. "In that situation," Athos said, "you're risking a few lives for what? More people you can't even have offspring with?"

"If they acted rationally, it'd be a very short movie," I said. "It'd be, 'hey, should we go see if there are any bears left?' 'No, let's stay here and survive.' The end."

"Also," he pointed at the guy on screen, "who cares if that guy's a ring-tail or a lemur? He's the only one!"

The mellow lasted until the movie ended, and then we sat on the futon and talked about life, about other movies by the same director (we'd liked his previous one), about whether Alexei and I would be okay living here without Sol contributing to the rent, about my business selling commissioned fantasy portraits. I told him about the La Croix and promised to take him in the morning. With the weed cookies, I could work on art without much risk, I thought.

Chapter 8

In the morning, Athos told me about some of the supernatural hokum he'd come across in his job. I could tell he was being careful to mention only the cases that he knew were fake, so we could laugh at them the way we used to. Once he glanced in at the bedroom, and I said, "Sol's picture didn't talk to you in the night, did it?"

He shook his head slowly. "No."

I said, "Good," and that was the end of it, for the moment.

Usually I didn't go to the Café on Sunday mornings, mostly because Alexei and Sol were around, but also because Sundays were big shopping days at Riverwalk and the intimate little café became annoyingly public. But Athos was going back on Monday and I'd already lost two days of work thanks to the Marie-Belle story. A couple people would start to get annoyed next week, and though I had enough money to cover rent this month, assuming I finished the two pictures I'd started, I didn't have a lot more in the bank.

Eve had the morning off, but the rest of the staff were all in. Sherine was clearing tables again, and Alain made drinks while the owner, a stout Geoffreys cat named Geoffrey ("A long line of Geoffreys comes down into me," he'd told me once with a wink), worked the register, a smoking pipe clenched between his teeth. He took it from his mouth and held it in a paw when he saw me approaching.

"It's my mistress of brushes," he said with his deep voice and warm smile. "Have you drowned a masterpiece for the walls of my coffin shop yet?"

"I'm behind on commissions," I said, sorting out that he meant "drawn" and "coffee shop."

"You must make time for the art of your soul as well, you know. So what do you want?"

He said it with a light, playful tone, but he stressed *want*, which confused me for a moment. But Athos was standing there, so I didn't want to ask if Geoffrey meant something else. "Coffee and whatever he's having."

Alain poked his long red muzzle over the pastry case, black ears perked. "Goodness, Meg, who is this?"

"This is Athos, my straight friend," I said.

The red fox laughed as Athos said hello with a sort of apologetic smile. "It's fine. My father's a grey fox, and I don't have enough daddy issues to be interested anyway. Pleasure to meet you. Any friend of Meg's and so on. What're you having?"

"Er." Athos looked up at the big chalkboard on the back wall. "Cinnamon latte?"

"If you like cinnamon, have you tried our Three Spice Latte? Cinnamon, cloves, vanilla. I know vanilla's only a spice with quotes around it, and the cloves are Christmassy, but lots of people like it."

"It's my first time here," Athos said, and then turned to me. "How is it?"

"It's good. I don't like lots of flavors in my coffee, but if you do, try it." Athos nodded, and Alain bowed to me. "*Mon plaisir.*"

He set about making the drinks, and I allowed Geoffrey to sell us on the pastries he had left that morning. Athos started to demur, but the cat held up a cinnamon roll and said in his deep silky voice, "My artist here doesn't indulge, but I can see that you have an appreciation for the finer of life's pleasures. I'll tell you, sir, you may take a later, lighter luncheon if you wish, but you will not regret whatever you give up for this cinnabar roll. It's sugar and spice balanced, rich pastry and light glaze, and why are you in Vidalia if not to sample her delights?"

Athos laughed. "All right, a cinnamon roll then, and one of whatever other pastry you recommend, only you have to describe it to me when you sell it."

Geoffrey laughed, and the armadillo behind us chuckled as well. "Take this banana bread, then," he said, pulling a slice out of the cabinet. "Not six hours ago it was ripe bananas, fine brown sugar, whole flour, and walnuts grown locally. This morning those ingredients gave up their solitude to create a carnival for the nose and tongue and even the eyes. Do you know how you can tell good banana bread?" We did not. "It has a glow about it. Some banana breads look flat; those you may pass by. Look at how this one changes when I move it under the light. That's the magic of this bakery."

"Magic?" Athos smiled, his whiskers lifting.

"A good banana bread is moist, and the moisture catches the light, but it will not be sticky. It must not glisten, but shine." Geoffrey gave the bread to Athos while I took the cinnamon roll and paid for the pastries. With my twenty percent "regular" discount, it was quite reasonable. "And maybe," Geoffrey said to me with a wink, "you will sample these delicacies and indulge yourself from time to time. A thin otter…" He shook his head mournfully.

"I'm a starving artist," I said. "It's part of my thing."

"Thank you so much," Athos said with a grin, though I wasn't sure if it was to me or the cat.

Geoffrey waved, and Alain held up a paw as well. "I'll get your drinks out to you, or Sherine will."

"He's a trip." Athos followed me to one of the few vacant tables in the café. "Looks like he could afford to lay off the cinnamon rolls, too. Or is it cinnabar?"

"That's how he talks. I only see him here once a week or so. Usually he comes in for coffee, but if it's busy, he works too."

"And he likes your art."

I nodded, and broke the cinnamon roll in half. "I think he's just being nice."

"Maybe, but why not draw him something?" He did the same with the banana bread. We swapped halves.

"I will someday. I need to get caught up with these commissions first. You know I need to do like ten of them a month to make rent and food." And booze and weed, but I left those as understood.

"You should make time to do something more for your future." He lifted the banana bread. "I don't know if this really is glowing or if I'm just seeing it because of how he talked about it."

"It's good banana bread," I said. "And I will, but I'm not going to have much of a future if I don't have a place to live."

"You could get help from…"

"My parents already gave me some money," I interrupted. "I don't want to ask for more."

"I was going to say, 'friends,' not your parents." He took a bite of the bread. "Wow, this is really good."

I hadn't seen Corra and her girlfriends when we came in, but the shadow of the little rat fell over our table before I could respond to Athos. "Hi, Meg. Missed you the other day."

"Hi, Corra. This is Athos." I introduced him because she was looking at him askance, the way a deer would look at a steak, I think. "He's a friend."

"Just a friend, or a 'friend'?" She had nearly as many piercings as I did, and her earrings dangled and clinked as she shook her head. Her light blue t-shirt was ripped at the collar, intentionally, I was sure, and she was chewing gum as she talked. Spearmint.

"He's a friend, that's all." I wanted to snap that it was none of her damn business, but the weight of my portfolio case against my leg reminded me that she was a customer and I needed to be at least somewhat polite, even if she wasn't.

"I'm visiting for the weekend." Athos extended a paw.

Corra eyed his paw, then reached out and laid her fingers across it, the minimum contact necessary. He held them briefly as she turned to me. "You said the art would be ready Friday."

"I know." I reached into the portfolio and pulled out her drawing and a few pencils. "It's partly done. I was going to work on it today and finish up."

I pushed aside the pastries to spread out the paper. I'd already sketched out Corra's figure and the warrior garb she'd wanted, which was similar to how I'd drawn her girlfriend Yolene. She pointed out places where she wanted changes, like wanting her breasts to be larger, which she was amusingly reticent about. She kept glancing at Athos and saying, "Just move this… out a little bit."

Finally, I said, "I got it. Bigger tits."

She went quiet, and then she said, "Yeah. Okay, Yolene and Gret and I are going to run down to Pret for a couple hours, but we'll be back."

Sherine came over with our drinks, and I had to take the drawing off the table again to make room for the cups. "I'll have it mostly done in a couple hours," I promised Corra, and she walked away without saying anything.

"Here you go," Sherine said. "Don't spill it this time. I'm running my tail off today."

"You spilled your coffee?" Athos grinned at me.

"Yeah, she fell asleep or something and woke up like this." The weasel flailed her arms. "Knocked the cup clean off the table."

"I'm fine," I grumbled, sipping the coffee, "and you're obviously not working so hard that you can't tell my friend stories about me accidentally knocking coffee over."

"Everyone spills shit," Sherine said, and turned to Athos. "She was touchy about it then, too. Ran out of the café right after."

"Really." Athos looked at me. "Well, I know she hates to be clumsy."

"She also hates to be talked about in the third person when she's sitting right there," I snapped.

"Enjoy your pastries." Sherine grinned at me, flicked her little tail, and hurried off to clear another table.

"You have a lot of friends here." Athos finished his half of the banana bread, curling his tongue around his muzzle to catch the crumbs. "Is Corra the one you went to the lesbian bar with?"

"That was Sherine. And Eve, but she's not here." I took another sip of coffee and broke off part of the bread to taste it. Damn. It was good, sweet and moist and full of flavor. I usually don't like nuts in pastries, but the walnuts were good too.

"When did you spill the coffee?" Athos asked casually.

"Friday, I think it was." I pretended I couldn't remember. "Yeah, it would've been Friday morning because Sol and Alexei were gone."

"Why'd you run out?"

I broke off another piece of bread and chewed it to stall. "Like you said, I was embarrassed. Why the third degree, shamus?"

Athos picked up the cinnamon roll delicately in his fingers. "Just curious. I mean, the spilled coffee stood out to Sherry—"

"Sherine."

"Sherine, then, enough that she mentioned it."

"She mentioned it because it happened a couple days ago."

He took a bite and chewed slowly while I finished my half of the bread. "I'm not trying to pry. But last time I was here, there were weird things happening, and now something made you call me at two in the morning and get me to spend all of Saturday on the train down here."

"Thanks." I took another weed cookie square from my portfolio and popped it into my mouth, both because I was going to try to draw and because I needed to mellow out to deal with Athos right now.

"Careful with that." He lowered his voice. "Canids can smell it."

"Alain is enveloped in coffee fumes and you won't tell anyone, will you?" I smiled.

He sighed. "Friday morning you spilled coffee, which I'm guessing you don't usually do."

"Right," I said. "I was anxious and irritable and I spilled my coffee. That's how I realized I needed to mellow out, and I went home and didn't have anything to do that with, and I thought I'd be okay, but then I started getting headaches and they woke me up in the middle of the night. Does that match all your facts, mister fact-checker?"

His ears flattened and he nodded slowly. "Like I said, I'm not trying to pry. Did you try ibuprofen?"

"What?"

"For the headaches."

"Oh." I took another drink of coffee and set it down to the side. "I don't think we have any in the house. Here." I pushed the other half of the cinnamon roll toward him. "You have that. I need to get going on this picture."

"It's delicious," he said, finishing his half.

"I'm sure." I pulled out Corra's commission.

Athos finished the cinnamon roll and took out his laptop to read something he was making occasional notes on. I filled in the lines on Corra's figure and started the rote work of making my fingers complete the design in my head for the background. This work didn't absorb me the way doing the comic had, where I felt like I was watching the story as my fingers raced to keep up, and while being more in control was comforting, I also missed the exhilaration of discovery.

Once the weed kicked in, I got that nice floating, disconnected feeling. I hardly noticed an hour had sped by until I scooted my chair to get a better angle and my portfolio bag toppled over. I was in the middle of working up a tree, so I let it go.

Athos's ears perked up. He slid to the floor and set his laptop on his chair. "I'll get that." He picked up the pages that had slid free and pulled one out to look at it. "This is really good. Is this a comic?"

He was holding one of the Marie-Belle pages, of course. I finished the tree and looked down. "Looks that way, doesn't it?"

"I didn't know you were working on a comic." His tail swished as he replaced the page and set the portfolio upright. "Can I have a look?"

"Maybe in a bit." Insulated by the pot, I felt more confident about drawing, and though Corra's piece was coming along well, I was bored of it. The smell of the banana bread and Geoffrey's flowery words belonged more to Marie-Belle's world; that was probably what turned my mind back to it. She would be going back to her family and trying to make her decision next, and even as I sketched out another tree that looked just like the first one, only different, I could see the clan of muskrats, the little town on the edge of the swamp, the old clapboard houses giving way to stately homes with wrought-iron railings and large front porches, big cypress trees drooping with moss. Not generic identical trees that…

I looked down. Next to the large generic oak tree, I'd drawn the outline of a cypress while I was daydreaming.

Athos was focused on his laptop, typing a few words. I erased the cypress and sketched out the tree again, but it's tough to get back momentum on a picture when you're bored of it. I got the tree done and sketches for where the rest of them were going to go, but I kept thinking of the cypresses and the muskrats and the houses. Corra would be cool anyway if I got a little done and finished it soon.

"What do you think?" I asked Athos, turning the picture around. "Enough progress?"

He glanced down. "For what?"

I rummaged in the portfolio for my pad of paper. "I want to work on something else."

"Did she want it finished?"

"Yeah, but it's a lot closer. Only got an hour or so."

He lowered his nose to inspect the paper. "Why not finish it now?"

"I don't want to." I brought the pad out. "You want to see more of the comic?"

"Sure."

So I gave him the pages I'd drawn, only hesitating over the last one, but I'd erased enough of the weirdness that it didn't show. Sure, I felt nervous about it, both because it was a story I was creating and because it had unnerved me two days before, but with the mellow attitude the cookie had given me, that anxiety felt silly. It was only lines on paper, and the story behind it was what was important. I could make the story in my head into harmless lines on paper and then Athos could see the safe version.

Cypress trees and elegant homes. I put my pencil to the paper.

Chapter 9

Cypress trees rustle in the breeze as Marie-Belle walks up to the porch. Here the symphony of insect drones and bird songs is muted background music, not a full-fledged chorus as it is in the green, thriving swamp. Even the dirt below her feet is dry, dust-covered pebbles skittering along the path around her every step.

At the wooden porch, she turns her head to listen. To her left, a broad field of sugar cane ends at a thick stand of cypress, around which bends the path along Marie-Belle has walked three miles from the mossy brown boards of her neighborhood. The roofs of three small brown cottages, where the workers live, poke up over the rustling cane leaves. To her right, more sugar fields and larger mansions, with elegant columned porches and elaborate iron railings around the upstairs balconies. Behind her is the spire of the church at the center of their small town, the one that stands taller than the simple red brick city hall and adjacent to the small one-room school she attended until she turned twelve. Here at the Guignacs' mansion, the paint on the elegantly carved columns is cracked in places, inexpertly patched in others. No balconies adorn the wall above the neatly shingled porch roof, though the Guignacs have purchased iron railings to display on the second-story windows, twisted into artistic repeating patterns.

Marie-Belle, to put off the moment when she must announce herself, crosses the porch to sit on the old swing there. It creaks under her weight, rocking slowly back and forth. When the creaking dies down, again Marie-Belle listens.

The language of the trees is foreign to her, the insects and birds too soft to distinguish, and her thoughts turn to the future. When she is old, perhaps she will sit on this swing. Perhaps the Guignacs' sugar plantation will have grown, and she will have children to watch the workers and trade the sugar. She will have a cool glass of tea next to her and a servant to take the empty glass away. That is what her Aunt Eloise sees in her future.

Heat comes to her dry fur even on the breeze, more real than her imagining. She is thirsty and a little hungry, though she ate two of her aunt's calas before she left. The spirits she is listening for remain silent as she envisions this future, and that, she thinks, is a sign.

The front door opens, revealing a slender mouse in a dirty apron. She sets her eyes on Marie-Belle and frowns. "Yes? What you doing on the Guignac's—oh, Marie-Belle, is that you?"

"Yes." Marie-Belle gets up, sending the porch swing rocking back. She smooths down her pretty blue dress and ignores the way it mats her fur underneath. "I'm sorry, Toc, I was just resting a little moment before coming inside."

"It's cooler inside and there's tea." Toquine smiles and holds the door for her. As Marie-Belle passes, the mouse says in a low voice, "What does your grandmother need this month?"

"Toutou?" Marie-Belle thinks. "She has plenty of sugar, but tea is always welcome, and tar-paper." She favors the mouse with her best smile. "And she is always pleased to see you."

"Armand and I would like another child," Toquine says with low, quick urgency. "She helped the last time…" And then she quiets as the door closes behind them.

The shade and breeze are cooler inside the house, but it is no less dry. Marie-Belle thinks of her little cottage and the water just outside of it; here the water all goes to feed the sugarcane, leaving the ground dry and parched.

Dry and parched also describes Mrs. Guignac, a muskrat perhaps an inch taller than Marie-Belle, today wearing a stiff white dress with a lacy collar below a bowl-shaped white straw hat garlanded with pale blue silk flowers. A pearl choker circles her neck and small pearl ear studs match it; below the choker dangles a golden cross. "My dear Marie-Belle!" She reaches out with both paws. "Thank you for coming over. Oh, you needn't feel underdressed. I dress up for the simplest occasions. Gérard tells me so all the time." After squeezing Marie-Belle's paws, Mrs. Guignac's fingers go to her pearl choker as if to reassure herself that it is still there. "I love wearing my pearls, and one can't wear them with a plain dress, can one?" She laughs shortly.

Marie-Belle brushes her paws down her best dress and says, "They are lovely."

"Oh, you shall have one as a wedding gift. It may not be two strands as this one is, but it will be of the very best pearls."

"Thank you." She curtsies awkwardly; it is a courtesy she has only learned last year.

"Toquine," Mrs. Guignac orders as the mouse returns with a tall glass of sweet tea dripping condensation down the sides, "go fetch Master Guignac and tell him that his fiancée is here."

"Yes'm." The mouse curtsies, more smoothly than Marie-Belle, and disappears into the shadowy hallway.

Her prospective mother-in-law takes Marie-Belle by the elbow and guides her into the small room off the kitchen, where three wooden chairs sit around a small table. Windows occupy two of the four walls from corner to corner; two are open to create a cross-breeze.

"Will your aunt be joining us?" Mrs. Guignac sits in front of one of the windows. "I have prepared the betrothal announcement for her inspection. It will appear in the papers in one month's time."

Marie-Belle, left without guidance, chooses the chair farthest from the older muskrat and presses both paws around the cool moisture of the glass. The tea is good, sweet and strong; they have no icebox out on the bayou, nor yet sugar unless Toutou brings some over. She gulps the tea before remembering that that is not polite, and then holds the glass, marveling at the cold seeping into her fingers. The betrothal announcement feels remote and strange to her, and she wishes her aunt were here to discuss it. "She is coming back here from doing family errands in town. She asked me to talk to Pierre," Marie-Belle says.

"Oh, of course. You are welcome to spend as much time here as you like. How lovely." She pauses and her fingers rise to her neck, hovering near the cross. "It is only your aunt coming, yes?"

Marie-Belle keeps her expression polite. "Yes."

Mrs. Guignac's features relax into a wide bucktoothed smile. "How lovely," she repeats. "I am delighted to get to know my future daughter-in-law. What occupies your time?"

"Oh, I…" Marie-Belle hesitates. "I gather herbs from the bayou and Aunt Eloise and I sell them in town."

"Have you learned sewing? Do you study your Bible?"

"I can sew a little." Marie-Belle is spared from describing the limited extent of her sewing skills by Pierre's arrival.

Marie-Belle's friends on the bayou describe Pierre as "handsome," and she can see that, she supposes. His sleek fur, a pleasing warm brown, shines when the sun falls on it. The thick white shirt he wears with all the buttons and pleats must be very uncomfortable, but he moves easily in it. His green and gold vest shows more color and life than many of the other eligible boys in the town of Benjamin, and so do his eyes. "Good day, Marie-Belle," he says in his low, soft voice.

"Good day, Pierre." She smiles, and then when he comes to stand next to her chair, she looks up, flustered.

He holds out a paw as though asking her to dance, and she places her paw in his, only remembering why as she stands. His warm paw brings her fingers to his lips and then releases them, and he takes the third chair around the table.

"Your fingers are cold," he says.

"Pierre!" His mother is incensed.

Marie-Belle smiles and holds up the glass of cold tea. "Ah," Pierre says, "of course."

He tells them that he has just been with his father and has been put in charge of repairing the stove over which the sugar is boiled, out in the back. Marie-Belle listens only a little, although Pierre is quite enthusiastic about it and she tries to be interested for his sake.

This will be her life if the spirits do not rescue her. She thinks of Ezuli, the female loa of hopes and dreams. She is most often represented as a wolf, but Toutou has told Marie-Belle that all female energy belongs to Ezuli when it comes to dreams, hopes, and beauty. Marie-Belle cares little for beauty, but she has dreams, and so she has been walking out under Ezuli's moon the last few nights in the hope of hearing the whispered words of the loa, but so far nothing has been forthcoming.

Again, Toutou's question echoes in her mind: *What do you want?* Marie-Belle has been asking herself that, but her inner self has been as silent as Ezuli. She knows only that this life, sitting in a stuffy room with the faint flutter of a breeze the only relief, listening to a conversation about sugar and markets and servants and politics (Pierre is now talking about his friend Jean-Gasquet who wishes to serve on the city council so that he may... something about planting, Marie-Belle thinks, but she has lost the train of the conversation), this life is not what she is meant for.

Toquine opens the door and sticks her little snout through it, rounded ears twitching, "Beg your pardon, madam, but Miss Eloise is here."

"Well, well!" Mrs. Guignac cries, standing from her chair. "Offer her some tea and show her in here."

Pierre stands as well, and looks around at the three chairs. He offers a paw to Marie-Belle. "Perhaps we should cede one of the seats to your aunt. Would you care to walk out to see the stove I shall be repairing?"

"Yes, of course." Marie-Belle rises. She and Pierre pass through the kitchen, greeting her aunt along the way, and then crowd through a narrow hallway to a back porch in considerably worse repair than the front porch. Paint is chipped and cracked, old buckets lie on their side amidst a pile of rags, and a broken chair—perhaps the fourth from the sun room—gathers dust in a shady corner.

If their house were in better repair, Marie-Belle thinks, they would not be marrying Pierre to some girl from the bayou. They would be seeking a match out in New Kestle, where there are many wealthier muskrat families. But by the same token, she could help this house, could bring the blessing of the spirits to it, and she could live well, much better than in the cottage on the bayou by some people's standards. She considers. Is that what she wants, to bind herself to this Pierre waiting to help her down the slanted steps of the porch? Or does she wish to help more people, and have the freedom to decide by herself whom to help?

Out there beyond the slow green waving of the sugarcane fields, the servants' cottage is closer, and another two behind it that were not visible from the front of the house. Two shapes sit on the porch of the farthest one, and though Marie-Belle's eyes cannot make out their species from here, she knows the Guignacs' workers. They are most likely Bolo the scraggly red fox with more claws on his fingers than teeth and Corzin the rat, blind in one eye but still quick enough to cultivate and harvest cane. Corzin has a cousin in town who has come to Toutou for help, though Marie-Belle does not know what with; Bolo and his family are Christian, but they live out in the bayou near Marie-Belle and the bayou people all watch out for each other.

Pierre takes her paw until she is back on the dry dirt, and they walk together through the sugarcane fields. The long-leafed cane is only as high as Marie-Belle's waist now; the plants will surpass her in height before the harvest. Here the drone of insects reaches her ears more strongly, though there are fewer birds, and the rustle of the cypress trees fades before the sussurations of the sugarcane leaves. Marie-Belle listens for a message from the cane, but the cultured plants only repeat the same soft lulling chorus over and over, as pretty and empty as the patterns in the wrought-iron railings.

At the second servants' cottage, the one nobody sits in front of, Pierre goes in without knocking or announcing himself. The four cots in the cottage are empty; perhaps he knew they would be. He goes to the stove and then stops with a short exclamation of disgust. "Oh."

From the top of the stove his fingers gingerly lift a burlap bag the size of his paw. The bones inside it click against each other. It is a *gris-gris*, perhaps one that Toutou prepared, perhaps one that another priestess made. "I'm sorry," Pierre says awkwardly, and with his other paw opens the grate of the stove and throws the charm inside. "We try to lead our workers to be good Christians, but these old practices still creep in."

He does not look at Marie-Belle as he says this. The room feels stuffy and close, only the droning of flies sounding over the soft sugarcane rustling outside. Marie-Belle thinks of all the things she could say, but if she defends vodou, will the Guignacs call off the engagement? Does Pierre expect her to agree with him? Does he know her grandmother's profession?

He keeps talking, like the drone of the cane. "I do not believe they would do anything so terrible as what happened down Pelican Harbor. Still."

Pelican Harbor: a small town some thirty miles away. Marie-Belle has not heard about what might have happened there, and does not want to know—not from Pierre, at any rate. Her betrothed does not look at her, and when she says nothing, he clears his throat and suggests they walk back to the house.

Once outside the cottage and back in the open air, he regains his garrulous manner. Dragonflies flit here and there ahead of the sound of his voice, and a white moth alights from the ground where Pierre steps. Marie-Belle follows its progress, listening with one ear to Pierre's story of the travel he will have to make in order to procure parts for the stove.

What do you want? Marie-Belle thinks of the moth. *Will you live your life here in the sugarcane fields? Or will you fly away? Is there another moth somewhere to take you away, or one that keeps you here?*

Pierre has asked her a question. She blinks and realizes that she does not know what he asked. "I'm sorry," she says with a nervous laugh. "I was watching the moth."

His smile is warm and easy. "It's all right," he says. "I asked what you would like to do this evening after you and your aunt have dinner with us."

"Oh." She looks around. "I very much like to take walks like this, especially under the moonlight."

"Then that is what we will do." He strides onward.

He is not so very bad, Marie-Belle thinks. If only she could pry him away from this plantation, from this life, he might be a pleasant companion.

But a vodou priestess has no companions, no ties.

What do you want?

Chapter 10

I stared down at the last panel. Again, without realizing what I was doing, I'd drawn Marie-Belle staring out at me, and even though I had managed to stop before writing my name in her word balloon, I knew the question was meant for me.

The pot hadn't worn off, either. It was like I was watching myself sitting there in the chair, staring down at the paper, thinking, *this is freaky*, and knowing I should be more freaked out by it, but with that distance that a good high gives you, I wasn't quite getting the emotional kick I had the last time. Part of me even wondered if it was the drug that had done it. *No, of course not*, I told myself, because I hadn't been high the last time it happened.

Nor the first.

That was the thought that got through the mellow haze, that dredged up panic and sent it flapping with great black wings through my mind.

"Are you okay?" Athos looked up from his laptop as I grabbed at my paper and shoved it into my portfolio. Now the mellow was completely gone and I was deep into paranoia.

"Hey." He tilted his head to look down. "It looked good."

"What did you see?" I held the portfolio shut with two fingers, so tightly they ached. I didn't trust myself to let it go even long enough to zip it closed.

He leaned back in the chair, ears splaying down at my harsh tone. Slowly, he closed his laptop. "I, uh, I saw a few muskrats, a younger pretty one and an older one, then a male one...and some cornfields..."

"Sugarcane," I said. "That's all?"

"The one muskrat was holding up a bag of something. Sugar?"

"No." My fingers pulsed as though Marie-Belle was in the bag trying to get out. I gritted my teeth, and the thought ran through my head that my front teeth were way too short, and then I realized that that was because they were mine and not a muskrat's. "I...I need to go home."

"All right." He said it mildly. "Are you okay?"

I shook my head reflexively and then, in the space between thought and word, said, "Fine. I'm fine."

He slipped his laptop back into its bag and stood up, and as I got up from my chair, my portfolio case banged the table and my coffee, so close to the edge, tipped right over.

Athos managed to catch the cup—on its side—so at least only coffee splashed the floor and the ceramic remained intact. He replaced it on the table and then held his paw up, coffee dripping from it.

"God," I said, "Not again."

"Could you get me a napkin?" He remained very polite.

"Yeah." My fingers stayed pressed around the top of my portfolio as I hurried back to the counter and grabbed a stack of napkins.

Sherine saw it and said, "Meg, you didn't spill your coffee again, did you?" When I didn't answer, she lost the amused expression. "Aw, hon, I'm sorry. Jus' teasing."

"It was an accident." I was still too shaky to make any kind of amusing remark about it.

"It's not a problem, hon," Sherine said as she pulled the table closer to the spill and put the chairs up on it. "I'll grab the mop."

Athos had taken the napkins from me and rubbed his paws dry, though even I could smell the coffee on them. "You want to wash those?" I asked.

"If you don't mind." He gave me his laptop bag to hold and went to the washroom.

I stood there clutching both bags and watching him go. *What do you want?* The phrase echoed in my head and I couldn't banish it, even by focusing on the things around me that were definitely real.

What the fuck was going on? I'd thought that the hallucinations were the product of withdrawal combined with the stress of being left alone. But here I was with a good friend, maybe my best friend, and pot to combat the withdrawal, and my mind was making up stories and pushing them into my consciousness harder than it ever had before. So hard, in fact, that my paws were shaking when I didn't focus on keeping them still. Marie-Belle had seemed so *real*—but I knew that that was a trap, better than (apparently) Alexei and Sol did.

Wait. The hallucinations hadn't technically started in the coffee shop. They'd started outside the apartment a few weeks ago, the night after Athos had made romantic overtures that I'd ignored. They were still on my mind when we ran outside and Alexei was fighting that bum. And there'd been some sort of reaching shadow…we all thought we saw it, and the bum seemed to be bigger at that point. And then Alexei fell, and the three of us rushed forward and we didn't see the guy run off. The lawn was dark. That was all it was.

We might've thought he'd gone transparent when Athos rang that bell, but it was possible for a group of people to experience the same hallucination.

We were all tired, it was late at night and the light was bad, and Alexei had been spooking us all with his ghost stories. That's what I told Athos after Alexei woke up, when we had that big fight that was only partly about the ghost. Sol and, I found, Athos, were susceptible to that kind of suggestion. I'd thought I wasn't, but what if I had been feeling stressed because Athos was pressuring me about our relationship, and vulnerable because I was off the antidepressants? What if that was the stress hitting me now?

I would have to figure things out, and sometime when I wasn't high, although my mellow was pretty much toast at this point, like my coffee spattered on the floor. The prospect of my mind going unreliable again was absolutely not fucking okay, and it seemed like it was not going to go away until I dealt with the underlying stress.

The thing I was *not* going to do for damn sure was go back on the antidepressants.

Sherine came back with the mop and stabbed at the coffee spill. "He's cute," she said. "Don't let Bellie see you with him."

"Guys and girls can be friends," I said.

"Sure." The weasel circled the spill and then pushed the mop at my feet. "I saw how he jumped up to take care of you. Total friend zone."

"We've had the discussion." I stepped back.

She pushed a napkin at me. "You've got some on your feet. And I'm sure you have. I'm sure you think that's the end of it. But you're nineteen and you don't know everything."

"I know Angel Stories aren't real," I said, and she made a little hmph noise and stalked away.

I dabbed at the coffee on my feet in silence, balancing awkwardly on one foot with the bags clutched in my other paw. Athos came back a second later and took his bag back. "You doing better?" he said.

"I'm fine." I gave him his bag back and he took my portfolio as well. At first I tried to keep it and then I figured I'd rather let him have it, so I let go.

Alain walked over to me with a coffee in a to go cup and pressed it into my paw. The red fox's smile reassured me a bit, and because of the species he reminded me of Alexei, who would be home tonight. "Drink that on the way home," he ordered me, "and it'll help. It's decaf, and I added a spritz of chocolate to sweeten it up a bit."

"Sherine is gonna kill you if you reward me for spilling my coffee." I took the cup anyway and breathed in its aroma.

"What she doesn't know." Alain winked and patted my paw, then looked at Athos. "Take care of her, will you?"

"It's not his job." My snap lacked its usual bite, because I was still scared and grateful for the coffee, and Athos just grinned and nodded to the red fox.

We were almost out when Corra interposed herself between us and the door. "Hey," she said. "You finish it?"

"Meg's not feeling well." Athos pulled me to the side, trying to get around her. "She'll finish up soon."

"It's two days late."

Christ, I knew it was a mistake to do a picture for her. I shook my head and gripped my coffee. "I'll give you your money back," I muttered, though I really didn't want to do that. I still had the other commission, the one for that boar. I could scrape together rent if I finished that one.

"I don't want my money. I want my picture."

"She'll be in touch," Athos said. "What do you want her to do, sit down and draw with a bucket to throw up into?"

Corra squinted at me. "She doesn't look that sick."

"I'm taking her home." Athos pulled me past Corra firmly, and the rat let us go, though she glared at me all the way until I was past her.

We hurried down the street, my coffee splashing against the plastic lid, and once we'd crossed the street and the café was left behind, I said, "I'm going to draw her with a huge overbite. Bitch."

"Can you get it done at home?"

"I guess, if Alexei isn't back yet."

Athos stayed quiet as we walked from the shopping area into the residential neighborhood, under the shade of the trees. "Why do you not want him to know?"

"Ah…" The distraction of this question helped me not think about my freaky art hallucination. "It just felt stupid. Drawing people's fantasies out like that, when I had this whole 'fuck people and their stupid invented lives' thing. I didn't want them to see some of the shit I was drawing."

"Lots of people have jobs they hate."

"I don't *hate* it. And I wasn't even doing that much early on. Like, initially it wasn't going to pay rent and I never expected it to. And I'm not that good."

"But you told me."

He was smiling, and I wanted to throw an arm around him and I wanted to walk faster, hurry my short legs away. Careful, I reminded myself. Don't stress. You'll figure this out. "I told you lots of things," I said. "Don't let it go to your head."

His ears perked up and his smile didn't vanish. "So will you tell me what just happened back there?"

"Maybe later." I regretted the words the instant I said them, because he kept the smile on and his tail swished from side to side.

"I liked the comic. What I saw of it. You draw very quickly."

"It's okay. It's just rough outlines." I glanced at the portfolio in his paw. Nothing was sliding out of it to curl around his fingers, no white ribbons of paper or green sugarcane leaves. The portfolio, his fingers, his striding legs, his smile (was that a concerned smile?), the brick sidewalk, the trees, the row houses, the birds and the sky, all were solidly, boringly real. No hallucinations crept out of them or lay atop them.

"It had a good flow. Would you mind if I take a look at it?"

"Jesus," I said.

"Sorry." His ears went down. "I guess it was something to do with the comic that bothered you?"

"You're too fucking smart for your own good." Now I wanted the portfolio back, in case he, I dunno, opened it up on the street and started talking to Marie-Belle about me—god dammit, why was I even thinking things like that? I swigged the coffee even though it was still hot and it burned my tongue.

Never compliment a fox on being smart, even in a snarky way. His ears came back up and he said, "All right, we don't have to talk about it now. How's the coffee?"

I didn't say much else to him on the way back to the apartment. Perhaps thinking I needed distraction (and he wasn't wrong about that either, damn him), he told me a story about his job, where last week he'd been correcting an article written by a supposed expert on colonial history about the number of people who moved from rural areas to the towns in the mid-1800s and how the information was right there a few clicks along the Internet.

"But you know that," he said. "Your comic was in Colonial times, right?"

"No. 1915," I said automatically.

He said something about the style of the houses and I replied that they were old houses, all the while thinking, how did I know the date that certainly? I knew it was about a hundred years ago, but then why didn't I answer "1912"? Or "a hundred years ago"?

By the time we got near the construction site, I was going round and round in my head and I wanted to lie down. The coffee was helping in the short term; I thought that probably in the long term it was making me more nervous and quickening my steps. Athos was telling me about his sister, a civil engineer in the Northeast who was going to be getting married early next year, as I opened the building's front door and hurried through to the apartment.

I held the door for him and then walked into my stuffy room and threw myself onto the futon, staring at the ceiling. Sorting out my relationship with Athos would take time, and it wasn't fair that my subconscious was putting all this pressure on me. Maybe I could find something stronger than pot to hold back the hallucinations while I worked on that.

Athos came into the room and sat next to the futon, cross-legged. "What's going on?" he said without preamble.

"What other drugs do you know—I mean, that you could get your paws on?" I didn't look at him.

"Nothing stronger than over-the-counter pharmacy, at least until you tell me what the hell is going *on*."

I turned at the edge in his voice to look at him. Sitting cross-legged on the floor, his wide, worried eyes were slightly above mine.

My gut twisted up even more. I didn't want to deal with his worry on top of everything else, but at the same time the temptation to share my distress kept my tongue in check, so I didn't tell him that it was none of his fucking business what was going on or that nothing was going on.

"Is it the withdrawal?" His eyes were as sharp as his teeth. "What is it? Panic attack? It seemed like something startled you."

"Panic attack." I seized on that. It was harmless enough and it didn't rely on anything else. Panic attacks just happened sometimes, they came without reason or warning, and so I wouldn't have to explain them.

He nodded and clasped his paws together. "Have you been having many of them?"

"Not when I had some weed." I closed my eyes and tried not to see Marie-Belle's face again.

"But this time it didn't help."

"I guess not."

His soft breathing reached my ears even over the sounds of the traffic outside. Finally he inhaled, and I knew from how long he'd waited that I wasn't going to like what he had to say.

"I hate to say it," he said, "but I think you should see a doctor."

I'd been right. "I don't need a doctor."

"Two panic attacks in three days? No, three—you spilled the coffee a few days ago, right? That was the same day you called me at two a.m., you told me."

"Maybe. I don't remember," I lied.

His fur rustled and I felt his movement on my whiskers, but he didn't approach too much closer. "Was it because the apartment was empty?" he asked softly.

"That's the only thing that changed." I didn't mind him knowing that. I didn't want him thinking I was worried about our relationship.

"Fear of abandonment." He kept going before I could interrupt, which I think he sensed I was going to. "It's nothing to be ashamed of. Your best friend is going off to college, and if Alexei's interview doesn't go well, he might have to leave too."

"He's going to be fine," I muttered.

"And if he does stay, he's got a boyfriend he's serious about."

That got me to open my eyes again and turn to meet his amber ones. "How do you know how serious he is about Mike?"

"We, ah, Alexei and I have been e-mailing some."

"Fuck. That little sneak. He never told me." I knew what they'd been talking about and had even guessed they might have talked about the ghost thing, but I hadn't thought they'd be getting friendly behind my back. Like talking about boyfriends and long-term plans kind of friendly.

Athos frowned. "No reason he should. We both knew that some of the things we were talking about would upset you."

"Yeah, but now it feels like you were talking behind my back."

He lifted a paw and extended it toward me, but stopped short of the bed. "Is it okay if I touch your arm?"

I didn't move. "Why?"

"Because it's a lot easier to reassure you that way."

His fingers hovered in the air. I didn't say anything, and he said, "If it bothers you, I won't."

"It's not that it bothers me." I was mostly afraid of how much I did want that comfort, and how certain I was that it was going to lead to him asking more contact than I wanted to give.

But I could always put that off, couldn't I? I could say: reassuring touch on the arm okay, intimate hugs not. Athos was a smart fox and after the last visit, I think I'd made it pretty clear where my boundaries were.

If it weren't for the comic and the dream—if all that was wrong was loneliness and the fight with Corra, say—then a touch on the arm would be okay. We'd done that before. And if my subconscious was sending me dreams about boring fiancés and terrible arranged marriages—well, honestly, the suspicion that my subconscious was trying to warn me away from

Athos was enough to get me to do the opposite. So I reached up and awkwardly took hold of his wrist.

(Seriously, my subconscious has not done me any fucking favors in the past. If I was Indiana Jane, my subconscious would be that Nazi torturer creep with the funky coat hanger.)

"You're sure…" His paw curled around to clasp my arm in return.

"I'll tell you the minute I'm not," I said. "So shut up."

He laughed softly, and said, "All right," and lowered our arms so they were resting on the futon together. "So look, ah. I, uh, I don't have to go back tomorrow."

"Alexei'll be back," I said. "I'll be fine."

"Right." He was experimenting with how tightly he could grip my arm, fingers squeezing lightly and then releasing, but he wasn't trying to stroke my fur or anything. "But I mean…I'm worried about you."

"Yeah, I'm worried about me, too."

He exhaled, with a little growl to his voice. "It's a long way for me to get back here if something happens. I trust Alexei, at least, to tell me, but still—"

"Wow," I said, turning my head to meet his eyes.

When I didn't go on, he said, "What?"

"I didn't know it was a Port City custom that when you hold someone's arm, you're married."

He let go, and with the absence of warmth against my fur came a rush of unfamiliar regret. Athos had always been fine with my sarcasm and the fact that he was turning away now with his ears flat and whiskers down, that he shoved his paw into his lap as though trying to warm it, and that he muttered, "Sorry," all were different from the way we usually interacted. They were different and I didn't like it. *Don't stress about it*, I told myself, but that's like saying "don't think about green apples."

"You aren't responsible for me," I said. "I got myself into this situation and I'll figure a way out of it."

"I'm not trying to be *responsible* for you." His breath hissed through his teeth, his arm still wedged in the crook of his knee. "I'm trying to help you."

"If I knew what you could do to help, I'd be doing it myself." I brought both my paws up to cover my face, exhaling through them, and the touch reminded me that I hadn't put on my fur color in days.

"I'm saying…" Athos's voice came from closer now. I cracked my fingers to peer at him. His ears had perked up again and he looked more determined than hurt. "You don't have to do everything yourself. Maybe you can't."

"I'm the only one I trust." The conversation was going quickly enough that I said it without thinking, and as soon as I heard the words I knew what his reaction would be.

First a flash of hurt, and a quick blink of the eyes. The ears flicked back and came forward again as he pushed the hurt away and replaced it with concern and determination. I didn't think he would touch me again, but he lifted his paw and draped it across my forearm below the elbow, where I'd bent it to cover my muzzle. "We've been friends for over three years. Trust me."

I didn't say anything, but I didn't tell him to move his paw. I stared up at the familiar brown of my fingers, too close to focus on, the fur and webbing between them, the smell of the pencil I'd been holding and of Athos's fur and the coffee all crowding together in my nose.

Slowly, I lowered my paws. He kept contact as my arms shifted and I rolled onto my side to look at him. "Just like that," I said. " 'Trust me' and that's that?"

"To be honest, I hoped you already did. I trusted you enough to come down here on short notice with illegal drugs."

"I appreciate that. Even if it didn't work." I noticed with a small pang that he used the past tense. When I thought about him going away, or about losing his trust, the shitty feelings from after our fight all bubbled up.

Here, with him close by and touching me, the uncertainties between us were harder to escape. But even though ghosts must have been on his mind—he'd referred to Alexei's episodes obliquely—he hadn't brought them up. He'd been respectful, pushing me to talk, but on my terms.

"God dammit." I pushed myself to a sitting position, and when he pulled his arm away, I grabbed his wrist and pulled it back.

He blinked at me and let his paw go limp as I held it. I took a breath. "Look. Some shit happened to me years ago. That's why I was on the anti-depressants. I got off them and things have been fine until..." Until the last time you were here. Until the Siberian ghost. "Until this weekend. But it might just be isolated incidents."

"Like flashbacks?" I could see the curiosity in his forward-cupped ears, the twitching of his whiskers.

"Sort of." I wrapped my fingers around the soft fur and delicate bones of his wrist. "I'm—I'm not ready to talk about what happened."

"You don't have to," he said quickly. "I mean, not with me. Maybe a therapist..."

I let go of his wrist and sat back. "No."

"All right." He stayed where he was and then reached out and I let him hold my paw. "But if you don't want therapy and pot isn't working—"

"No more 'mood stabilizers' either. They fuck up my—I can't draw when I'm on them."

The corner of his mouth curved upward just slightly. "You're not leaving me a lot of options."

"Welcome to my world." I breathed in and let the breath out slowly. "I don't know. I think my mind is fucking with me. Maybe I'm worried about being alone."

"You're not alone." He said it quickly, almost as soon as I'd gotten the word out, and his other paw took mine. The slits of his pupils focused on me and all amusement was gone. "I mean, there's me, but there's also Alexei and Sol, and your parents and your friends at the café. You're not alone."

"I know." The touch of his paws was good, warm, and welcome, and at the same time I felt the old familiar turmoil in my gut. What if paws led to hugs and hugs led to kisses and kisses led to more? In all my parents' movies, in all Sol's stories, the people who kissed and hugged yearned desperately to be with someone, and of all the turmoil of emotions, that was the one I didn't feel.

Besides that, I'd spent years deciding I didn't need anyone else. Relying on Athos felt like giving up some part of my strength.

Only I'd relied on him during all that so-called independent time. And I'd stuck with Sol, and later Alexei. So maybe my loner persona wasn't real, was nothing but a story I told myself.

"So…?" His eyes held mine.

I had no idea how he would be able to help me, especially if things got worse, if I saw—well, that hadn't happened yet. The question, I realized, wasn't what Athos could do to help. It was whether I would rather keep him in my life or not. And as much as there were things hovering over us that we had to avoid, on the whole I'd been miserable when he'd left. So that wasn't really a question.

"Yeah," I said. "I'd…appreciate your help."

He took a moment to digest that, and then he got a big goofy smile on him and lurched forward before he caught himself. "Sorry," he said. "It felt—never mind, I know—"

Again I didn't listen to any of the voices in my head. I grabbed him and hugged him, and thank god he stiffened enough that he didn't notice me stiffening as well. He relaxed quickly, and I tried to empty my mind and not think about anything.

I'm not great at that. He rested his muzzle on my shoulder and made some kind of contented noises, and I wanted to tell him to knock it the fuck off, but then I started wondering why I didn't want to make little baby noises. *Shut up*, I told myself, *this is part of figuring things out.*

After a moment he let go and leaned back, that smile still pushing his whiskers up and out, and his tail was wagging on top of that. "Thanks," he said. "I've kinda wanted to do that for a while."

"Yeah, I could feel that," I said, trying not to let on that my heart was pounding and I was itching to get off the bed. "Hey, Alexei's going to be home soon. I should put my paint back on."

"Why didn't you paint your fur down at the café?" he asked.

I shook my head. "I did the first time I went down, but everyone looked more…grown up, and it felt like a high school thing. Piercings are okay." I touched my ear and the weight of the silver in it. "But the face paint didn't feel right. Sol and Alexei know me that way, though, and I still like doing it."

He studied me and didn't say anything, until I said, "What?" and then he looked abashed.

"Oh, I was just trying to figure out what it means that you don't want to hide your face there and you do here."

"It's not hiding. It's making myself look different, that's all." He still didn't say anything, and so I said, "It's a part of me that's appropriate in one place and not another," trying to imitate his precise speech. "Like how you wouldn't wear your vampire cape to work."

His ears folded down and he looked away. "Okay," I said. "Bad example. Seriously, you wear it to work?"

"Not always. But if I don't call it a *vampire* cape…"

"Fine." I snorted and got off the futon. "I'm going to paint my fur. You can watch if you want."

He did, and we talked a little more while I painted, but it was mostly boring shit about the nature of panic attacks and more circular questions about why they might be occurring and whatever. It wasn't a helpful conversation, but it didn't make me edgy. And all the time I was thinking about the hug and wondering, if that's the price of his friendship, that's one I might be able to pay. It wasn't so bad, and if you leave aside the whole believing in ghosts thing, Athos wasn't a bad guy at all. One of the best I'd ever met, in fact.

Problem was, that made it doubly wrong for me to lead him on if I didn't feel attracted to him. It wasn't fair to either of us. But I didn't know if I was really maybe a lesbian, or just not attracted to him specifically, and I couldn't figure that out right now. So I just finished up and then turned and grinned at Athos. "How does it look?"

"Familiar." He smiled. "You missed a spot behind your ear here. May I?"

I inclined my head as he dipped two fingers delicately into the fur color and then rubbed them on my ear. The sensation felt ticklishly uncomfortable, and I wondered at his motivation. For foxes, I knew, ears were a sexual thing sometimes. Did he hope that I'd get turned on and kiss him?

If so, he was disappointed. I let him rub it in, endured the uneasiness, and when he took his fingers away I said, "Thanks."

He smiled that slightly goofy smile and asked if I wanted anything to drink. I wanted some rum, but I said, "Ginger ale," and let him pour it for me.

Chapter 11

Alexei and Mike came back that evening so excited and happy that I said, "You heard about the visa already?"

"No, no." The red fox beamed and closed the front door, his tail swishing. He was wearing one of the shirts that Mike had gotten him, a short-sleeved red check pattern thing with a collar hanging open around his fluffy chest ruff, and the big sheep was wearing the same kind of shirt, only blue and over a t-shirt instead of his bare chest. "In two weeks perhaps. Hello, Athos. It's good to see you again."

"Likewise. And you're Mike?" Athos stood and extended a paw to the big sheep.

Mike shook and then smiled at me. "Hi, Meg."

"Thanks for taking care of the fox," I said.

"Aw, it was my pleasure." He grinned down and put an arm around Alexei's shoulders.

"So why are you so bouncy?" I asked. "And you guys need a drink or anything?"

"Water," Mike said.

Alexei beamed at me, ears perked, teeth showing in his smile. "I'll get our drinks," he said. He disengaged from Mike and walked past me to the refrigerator. "And it was a very nice trip. That is why I am happy."

I raised an eyebrow, a wasted gesture because he couldn't see it bent over in the fridge, and Athos said, "That's good to hear. No incidents, then?"

"No," Mike said, and at that, Alexei turned from the fridge and caught his eye, and the two of them shared an embarrassed half-giggle. "Ah, no. I mean, almost, maybe, but…"

I pulled out a chair. "The two of you in a car together for hours. Why am I not surprised?"

So they protested that nothing happened, that they were just talking about football—soccer—and that Alexei was trying to explain the various Euro leagues to Mike, and…

They both got quiet, and then Mike said, "Well, he leaned over, and…"

"And I brushed him," Alexei said.

"We kinda, uh."

"It's all right." Alexei smiled at Mike's hesitation. "Meg and Athos are family."

"We kissed," the sheep said.

"Just for a moment." Alexei closed the fridge, a Coke in one paw, and moved to the cupboard. "And then another moment."

"I kinda lost track of the road. We drifted over to the edge."

I looked between them as they fell quiet. "That's it? You kissed and almost drove off the road?"

Alexei filled a glass from the sink. "It was enjoyably scary."

"Okay," I said. "So nothing happened on your trip."

"What about you?" The fox turned and walked over to Mike with the water. "What happened? You said Athos would not be coming down while we were away."

"I changed my mind."

Athos glanced at me and then said, "She's been having panic attacks."

"Hey!" I snapped.

Alexei set his drink down on the table, his smile gone. "What is a 'panic attack'?"

"It's..." Athos turned in his chair to look at me. "Well, you can tell him."

Fucking hell. I'd heard the term 'panic attack' around, like when my doctor had asked about them years ago, or when Alison Marcus claimed she was having one to get out of a test. I hadn't had the time to go look up on the Internet what a panic attack actually felt like. But I could make shit up. "You, uh, you feel like, you know when you're panicked about something? Really scared? And you get all tense and stuff? So it's kind of like that only there's nothing to really be scared about."

"Heart racing, shortness of breath," Athos supplied helpfully.

"Yeah, right."

Alexei frowned and stepped closer to me. "You had this 'panic attack' and then you called Athos?"

"I couldn't get weed anywhere else." I shoved the words at him, but although I saw his nose twitch, he didn't react.

"The weed, it helps with these attacks?"

I nodded. That much I was pretty sure of. Weed mellowed you out, and I thought I remembered one of my parents' friends out in Goldenwater, where it was legal, saying they used it for stress, which was kind of like panic attacks. "I ran out, and I'm not going to meet my friend until this Friday..."

Mike shifted, maybe uncomfortably, but I couldn't imagine him being unfamiliar with weed. "Anyway," I said, "Athos offered to come down, and it...it was nice to see him again."

"We talked a lot," Athos said, drawing Alexei's attention, "and it was a really nice visit."

"Oh?" Alexei turned, and the two of them looked at each other.

"All right," I said. "That's enough. No secret fox scheming behind my back. Mike, you staying for dinner or what? I don't have anything, so I need to run out anyway."

"We're going out for dinner," the sheep said. "But thanks for the offer."

"Would you two like to come with us?" Alexei asked.

Athos and I both made noises about how we didn't want to intrude, and both Alexei and Mike insisted that it wasn't going to be intruding, that it wasn't anything special. My main problem was that I didn't really feel up to going out around people again, but I did want to talk to Alexei, and Athos wanted to hang out with them. So I turned it around. "You guys don't want to get in your car again so soon," I said. "Why not let me go grab something at the market and I'll cook here?"

"We can't impose." Mike looked at Alexei, though.

"Oh, fuck that noise," I said. "It's the least I can do to thank you for all you're doing for fox-boy here."

The sheep winced very slightly. Oh, right. Alexei'd asked me to tone down the swearing around him. But he didn't comment on that, just said, "If you're sure…"

"Absolutely," I said, taking the 'fucking' out of the middle of it first. "I'll get some veggie options and chicken for the rest of us." Until I said it, I hadn't realized how much I wanted to do something nice and normal, with no dreams, no comics, no hallucinations.

"I'll come along," Athos said, and with that we headed out to the market.

Dinner was easy; I made the chicken in a skillet and steamed the veggies for Mike, though I made sure to ask him what kind of spices he liked. Typical Midwestern guy: he said, "Salt," and when I asked about soy sauce, he said, "I guess. I've only had it a couple times."

So I kept it simple, and soon enough we were all sitting around the table. Alexei told us about his interview in more detail, with Mike offering commentary about what particular things meant or didn't mean, and ending with an optimistic evaluation of the whole thing.

I found myself slightly optimistic as well, but not about Alexei's interview. I mean, I trusted Mike's thoughts on it because he had all that legal experience, but who knows what the fuck people's agenda is? The fox who interviewed him might be all for bringing more gay kids over here, especially from the oppressive shithole Alexei grew up in, but the fox's boss might be one of the closed-minded assholes who are all over the fucking place here. My friends in Riverwalk sometimes tell me about getting called names, and once the Pickled Goose had a rock thrown through the window.

It was getting better for sure, and for the most part the bigots left the gay people alone to have their part of town, but if I had to trust my life to someone, it sure wouldn't be in this part of the country if I could help it. Out in Goldenwater—the big cities there, anyway: Yerba and Crystal City—or up north by Freestone or Port City, that's where tolerance was doing a lot better and people let other people live their fucking lives. Here in Vidalia, the nearest big city was Millenport, the city where last year someone threw beer on a gay football player (but I mean, football fans, what do you expect?) and where they answered all the marriage equality marches in other states with a 'Traditional Pride' festival.

But still, there were people who could see past that, and people who were beginning to, like Sol's mom, and hopefully this fox was one of them. And all that aside, the reason I was optimistic was that Alexei and Mike were getting along real well.

With Sol gone, I was worried about Alexei and his friends, especially since he got kicked off the gay soccer team he was playing on with Mike, but he's apparently still in that group, even if he's not allowed to play soccer with them. I think. I'm not sure how that works, but he and Sol went out with them a bunch anyway. Now he'd have Mike to be besties with—maybe more—and that was good to see.

Alexei cleared the plates when we were done and then sat down again, giving me a serious look. "So," he said, "what is happening with these panic attacks?"

I glared at him. "It's under control," I said, "and it's not a big deal. Athos gave me some weed and I have enough to keep me going 'til Friday."

"But it didn't work this morning," Athos said, and I switched my glare over to him.

"Panic attacks can lead to hypertension and heart problems," Mike said.

"My heart is not the problem."

"For now." Alexei had both elbows on the table, leaning forward with concern.

I put my paws out and stared around at them. "I'm not going to the doctor," I said. "I'm going to keep self-medicating and the…attacks will go away."

Athos spoke across me to Alexei. "I think it was just the stress of everyone leaving, Sol going to college, life changes."

"I can handle my own life," I said.

Alexei answered me, at least. "You all helped me when I was having problems. And Mike was patient."

"Well, God, what you went through…" Mike trailed off. "It would've messed me up too, that's for sure."

"Having friends helped." Alexei gave me a meaningful stare. "I would not have made it through otherwise."

I wanted to keep us talking about Alexei and not me, so I said, "That's for sure. You wouldn't have a place to live, for one. For another, you wouldn't have anyone to come get you when you decide to sleep at the bus station."

If the reminder of that time bothered Alexei, he didn't let it show. Glow of his first real kiss with Mike, I guess—even if that kiss had almost gotten them into an accident. Also, his relentlessly cheerful nature had come back after that tough couple weeks, even though I still caught him sometimes looking off into space, or staring into the mirror.

"The bus station was not so bad," he said. "There was company, and coffee."

"Bus station coffee?" Mike leaned over. "Tell me you didn't drink any."

"I had to stay awake." Alexei stuck his tongue out. "It was like mud. Flavorless mud."

They laughed at that, and moved on to favorite coffee shops. Athos, of course, brought up the Café La Croix, and seemed surprised that neither Mike nor Alexei had been there. "Coffee's good, and it's in a gay neighborhood."

"What were you doing there, then?" Mike asked.

"Well…" Athos turned to me, ears askew. I couldn't very well give him the 'shut up' look in front of Alexei and Mike, so I stared back at him without talking. He gestured in my direction. "Meg took me."

Both Alexei and Mike looked at me with some surprise. I shrugged and spread my paws. "I don't get hassled by guys there, the coffee's good, and it's nearby."

"Do you get hassled by girls?" Mike wanted to know.

"Some. They mostly get the hint pretty quick."

I could see them wanting to ask the question and holding back. "Look, it's no big deal. You want to go sometime, I'll take you."

"I would like that," Alexei said quietly. His grin spread a little wider. "Now we begin to reveal the mystery of Meg's daytime journeys."

"It's a really boring mystery," I informed him. "You'd be better off focusing on the mystery of Who's Going To Go Out And Get Dessert."

Mike and Alexei volunteered, because I'd gotten dinner, which left Athos and I alone. "I'm sorry," he said right away, as I went to the sink to do the dishes. "I didn't know—I didn't mention the art, I know you didn't want them to know about that, but..."

"It's fine." I didn't turn around to look at him.

"I know you're trying to keep your worlds separate. I don't know if that's necessary. Alexei really cares about you."

"I'm feeling a lot of love." I scrubbed hard at the plates, getting the chicken grease off them.

He stood and came over. "Can I help?"

"You can dry." I nodded toward the dishtowel. "But you don't have to. We have a rack."

He took it and waited for me to be done with the first plates. "I was thinking maybe I could come down another weekend. If it's, ah, not at the last minute, I can book a flight."

And if I don't ask him to bring drugs. "That's expensive."

He laughed. "It's not so bad. What else do I have to spend money on?"

"Your supernatural research?"

That quieted him a bit. "I wouldn't mind sharing my notes, if you want to see them."

I stopped and mimed dropping the plate I was holding. "Really? Wow, what do I get if I hug you again?"

"A hug back." He play-snapped the towel at me. "I'm serious, though. I know I'm sort of weird about the book, but it's just..." He sighed. "I keep thinking of those people who had their research stolen, or who had their research mocked on the Internet before they got to present it fully. I think this is really important stuff."

"Well, plus you had to throw out most of it after the last time you were here."

He draped the towel over his shoulder. "Not all of it. I certainly added a few chapters, though."

Fuck. Somehow he'd tricked me into talking about Alexei's ghost. Maybe he hadn't done it on purpose, but he was a fox, after all. "I think I want another one of those cookies before I have this conversation."

His tail flicked. "So you're willing to have it?"

I took a breath. "If we can have the conversation without you pressing me to believe something I don't, and without you calling me stupid for not believing it."

He winced and folded his ears down. "I didn't say that, not exactly."

I went back to scrubbing the plate, giving him time to remember what he had said, exactly, and to feel a little bad about it. If he didn't recover quickly, I'd say something nice, but he spoke before I had to. "I'm sorry—again—about how that came out. You know it isn't what I meant."

"I know. We already said all this in e-mail."

"Yeah, but not…" He reached out and took my soapy paw. "Face to face."

I met his eyes, narrow pupils in a speckled sea of amber. He smiled so wide that for a moment, I worried he was going to lean forward for a kiss. But he didn't, just squeezed my paw and said, "Now we have."

"Yeah," I said. "Thanks. And thanks for the weed and all. You might not think it helped, but it really did."

"So when can I visit again? Couple weeks? A month?"

"Uh…let me check my crowded social calendar and I'll get back to you."

He nodded and let my paw drop. "I'll check airfares. What movies are coming out? We could go to one opening weekend."

After that, we talked about movies we were looking forward to, which was nice because it skirted the issue of him coming down again and the ever-closer day when I knew things would get a lot more complicated.

Alexei and Mike came back soon after we'd finished the dishes, and I pulled up an episode of "Top Chef" for us to watch on my laptop while eating the carrot cake they'd bought. And after that, Mike took the plates and Alexei asked if he could talk to me for a moment. So we left Athos in front of the computer to find a couple Internet videos he wanted to show us, and walked into the boys' room.

The fox closed the door, his ears perked. He smiled past me, up at the picture of Niki on the wall. "What is it?" I asked, ignoring his look.

"I am going to spend the night at Mike's," he said, and gestured toward the bed. "Athos can stay here."

"Oh. Congratulations?"

"Thank you." His tail curled and wagged behind him, and his eyes sparkled.

"Hey." I nudged him teasingly. "You're not doing this just to give me room with Athos, are you?"

He giggled and covered his muzzle with a paw. "It started like that. Mike said, do you think they want to be alone tonight, and I said that I thought you had had your time and did not want it, and he said that if you did, it would be okay for me to come stay with him. And then I asked if he *wanted* me to come stay with him, and he asked if I wanted to, and I said that I did if he did, and he said—"

"Right, I get the picture." I wanted to be annoyed, but Alexei was too damn happy. "Go, have your night with Mike."

He grabbed me by the shoulders and started to hug me, then stopped, his eyes so close to mine I could see the shine behind them. "Oh, fuck," I said, and hugged him. If I was going to hug Athos, I could hug Alexei, because at least then I didn't worry that it was going to lead to anything else.

He giggled again next to my ear. "I do not know if it will come to *that*," he said, and when I snorted and released him, his eyes were shining at least as bright as Athos's had been.

"Is it your first time?"

"Ah, it…" He folded his ears down, still smiling broadly as he nodded.

"Okay, well, uh…make sure you, uh…" I looked around the room. "Wow, you poor guy."

"What?" His ears perked again and the smile faded a little.

I shook my head. "Here you are with a good relationship and you're roommates with two people who are completely useless when it comes to advice about how to handle sex. I mean, I'm pretty sure Sol's not much more experienced than you are. Just the one almost-being-raped, which really doesn't count."

"It is all right." Alexei clasped his paws together, fairly bouncing on his feet, the smile back. "Mike and I will talk. He knows I am not experienced."

"Just be careful." I searched for any sex advice I'd heard over the years. "Don't do anything you don't want to do. Don't let him talk you into things. Um. Have your phone ready and call 9-1-1 if you have to."

Alexei laughed. "I said, I do not know if it will come to that. We might just…hug? Sit next to each other?"

I rolled my eyes. "You guys were kissing in the car. If you start cuddling, you're going to do more."

"Cuddling." He filed the word away. "Thank you for worrying. I promise I will not do anything stupid."

"Call me if you need to."

His smile danced in his eyes. "While I am waiting for the 9-1-1 people."

"Yeah." I shook my head. "Go on, git."

He started to go, and then paused. "There is one more thing," he said slowly. I waited, and he glanced toward the closed door. "You and Athos…I know you have said you are not…" I didn't help him out by supplying any words, because I knew the problem this time wasn't translation. Eventually he said, "Boyfriend and girlfriend."

"We're not."

He nodded. "It feels," he said cautiously, "like he thinks maybe you are close to that? But you are going to this gay café—but he does not think you are gay?"

There were questions in there beyond what Athos thought of me, but I ignored them the way I was trying to ignore my heart pounding a little faster. "We're talking. He doesn't think…I mean, he's concerned about me, and…"

The fox nodded, and then smiled again, but it was a comradely smile rather than a joyful one. "Do not do anything you don't want to. Don't let him talk you into things."

"I've got 9-1-1 on my phone, too." I walked up next to him and patted his shoulder. "And I can handle Athos."

"Hm." He grinned. "Should I give this advice to Athos too?"

"Go." I pushed him toward the door, and he laughed.

Athos had pulled up a couple videos to show us, a cartoon adventure and a parody of a vampire movie that had us all laughing—well, except me, though I put on a good pretense. I was thinking about Alexei's comments, about how his night out with Mike was going to leave me alone for one more night with the grey fox.

Not that I thought he was going to try anything, but we were definitely going down a path. For tonight, things would be okay; he'd stay in Sol's bed and he'd leave in the morning. Beyond that…I'd manage that when it came around.

Predictably, of course, when we'd said good-night to Alexei and Mike and watched them walk out of the apartment—well, practically skip out of the apartment together—Athos brought up the possibility of a return visit again.

"I'm not trying to push things with…with us," he said as we were cleaning up. "But I'd like to come back sooner rather than later, because I'm worried about you."

I picked up the laptop and brought it back into my room. "You don't have to worry," I said over my shoulder. "I'm managing these attacks just fine."

Athos followed me. "See, you are now, but these things typically don't just stay the same. They get worse. And what happens if you're here in the middle of the night and you have an attack and there's nobody around?"

"Alexei will be here."

"Not if he's over at Mike's."

I set the laptop down and stood with my back to the window. Outside, the construction had started up again and lights shone through the blinds. "I could get one of those MedicAlert bracelets."

He sighed and shook his head. "I don't mean I want to be here 24-7. I mean, I want to help you manage this."

"What if the panic attacks don't come back? What if it was just a temporary thing?"

"Then...then great." He tilted his head. "But why are you so worried about me coming back?"

Ah, fuck. "I'm worried that if you get your scent all over Sol's bed, he'll be upset at me."

He managed a slight smile. "I don't have to stay in his bed."

"For now, you do," I said.

"Right, right, I meant—" He gave a nervous laugh and rubbed his paws over his whiskers. "I slept on the floor in here before, or I can sleep on the couch."

"It's late," I said, "and you have to get up in the morning. I'll talk to you online about it, I promise. Okay?"

"Yeah." He stood there another moment, and then when he straightened his head, the light caught the backs of his eyes and shone out eerily. I'm used to canids from living with Sol and Alexei, but that eyeshine still freaked me the fuck out sometimes.

He wanted another hug, and I obliged, cutting it short before he could push things any farther. His tail swished, and in the wake of the hug, he said, "I'm glad I came down."

"I am too," I said, and it was true, although maybe not in quite the same way.

It should've been easy to get to sleep after the day I'd had, but I just lay on my side, staring up at the lights moving beyond the window. Thinking about sex stirred up my memory of Margie, her paw moving down her stomach...

The memory of that night persisted despite my best efforts to shut it out. I didn't like the feeling that those girls still had power over me, four years later. Ridiculous, too, to think that one night could affect me that much. It wasn't even as though they'd forced themselves on me, not like Sol still hating sheep because of his one asshole ex. But watching Margie finger herself was my only real sexual experience to date, as pathetic and horrible as that was to realize.

I turned over onto my stomach and buried my head in my pillow. Unbidden, the watery shadow rippled back into my memory. My heart raced and warm flushes blossomed on my skin, raising my thick fur.

You want to know how you're going to die, Meggie?

"Shut up!" The pillow muffled my words and the construction drowned them out. Athos, even with his fox ears, wouldn't hear.

Athos. I had his cookies somewhere in my bag here. I groped around the edge of the futon and had the plastic bag in my fingers before I remembered that if I ate one now, I wouldn't get high for twenty minutes at least, and then I probably wouldn't get to sleep for another hour. Sleep was what I needed now.

Booze was best for that, but that was out in the kitchen, and if I started clinking bottles around, then fox-eared, worry-minded Athos would absolutely come bolting out to see what was wrong.

Okay. I had relaxation exercises. I let go of the pot and bunched my fists into the pillow.

Listen, Meg. Marie-Belle's imagined voice, calmer. *What do you want?*

I breathed in, held the breath, exhaled. Inhale, hold, exhale. Marie-Belle's voice, strangely, helped calm me this time. My subconscious was a piece of shit, true, but at least in this case, Marie-Belle seemed to be fighting with the older, darker parts of it. I'd never had that happen before. I guess if we're continuing the Indiana Jane analogy, maybe Marie-Belle was the asshole archaeologist who at least wanted to preserve the same things.

Inhale, hold, exhale. I enumerated the things in my life that were real: Sol, Alexei, Athos. My laptop, my futon, my clothes. The Café, Eve, Sherine. My paper, my pencils. Slowly, my muscles unclenched.

Chapter 12

The pastor concluded the service with a ringing, "God's love be with you all," and remained on the lowest bough of the great cypress tree. Above them, the bells knotted into the upper branches pealed, and around Hannah, the water rippled with otters diving to swim out of the church.

"Come along, Hannah." Angeline put a paw on her shoulder.

"In a moment." She liked to look at the trunks of the big cypresses around her, to feel God's majesty in the way they rose and met far above her head. Even the bells were coated with a slick reflective sheen that made them nearly invisible. As lovely as the services here were, she liked the rarer moments of floating in the warm water by herself, when the smell of greenery could penetrate the scents of crowds of people, when birdsong and insect hum took the place of bells, when she could pretend that all the trees and their leaves and the sun and the sky existed to welcome her and that one day she might float up to them. Here, the surface of the water felt like a starting point, not a limit.

"Your mother has shopping to do. You shouldn't tarry."

"Oh, don't *tarry*, then," Hannah said. "Go along, I'll catch you up. You can tell me what shop she's in."

"Hannah…"

"Go *on*. What's going to happen to me in *church*?" Hannah dove before Angeline could answer, plunging through the water toward the roots of the nearest cypress. She knew Angeline could follow easily, but when she surfaced by the trunk, only a few otters remained in the church water, and Angeline was not one of them.

Hannah smoothed down her dress, watching the cloth flow in the water, and then turned around, placing her paws on the cypress. She drew her claws along the grooved wood at the thick bole, upward to where it narrowed. Where her paws stopped, her eyes took over, traveling upward to the fluffy green leaves like clouds around the trees.

"I swear those services get longer every day," Vanessa's voice said from behind a nearby tree.

"The weekday ones aren't so bad." Hannah lowered her voice, glancing toward the now-empty pulpit. "Sundays are…" She hesitated, one paw still on the cypress, aware that she was floating in the church itself.

"They're a chore." Vanessa sighed, coming around to float next to Hannah. "How was your trip back from the wedding?"

"Angeline read the Bible to me." They were nearly alone in the church now, although some people might still be swimming under the water.

"Poor dear." Vanessa smiled and reached out a paw, leaving it on Hannah's shoulder. Her voice dropped. "No time to read that little book I left you?"

The fingers on her shoulder tingled, warmed her even in the muggy air. She turned her head slightly and reached up to turn her microphone off. "I read it," she murmured. "I had a dream…"

"Oh?" Vanessa moved closer, her voice dropping more intimately.

Hannah squirmed pleasurably. "Not…not that kind. I dreamed I was hugging a boy, a fox of some kind, but I…" She looked around the now-empty church and whispered, "I didn't feel God's love at all."

"I told you."

"I know." She murmured low. "Just because it was in a dream doesn't mean anything, though." And the crumbs she'd thought were sticking to her fingers when she woke, the cookies that made her feel like she was in the water even when she wasn't, that had just been hysteria.

"Why a fox?" Vanessa's breath tickled her ear and the water stirred by her friend's motion came over in gentle waves. "To prove that even another race doesn't excite you?"

"I've never even met a fox," Hannah said, leaning into Vanessa. "Not properly."

"The fellow who got me that book is a red wolf." Vanessa's fingers trailed down the fur of her shoulder. "He's a trader. He comes to the bayou every so often."

Hannah had the strangest impulse to kiss her friend. Vanessa's whiskery muzzle was close, too. It would take just a little motion to do it. Of course, God forbad such things, but the book Vanessa had loaned her… "Is that the one from the north?"

"He goes to the Northern States, but he isn't from there. His name is Vilan. I'll…introduce you."

Vanessa's breaths stirred the warm, muggy air, curling around Hannah's ear, and the tickling raced through her, to her breasts and farther down. That was what Mary had haltingly said she felt when James touched her, near the end of her bridal shower when it was just the girls talking. Hyperia had cooed and Elly had said shyly that Terrence made her feel the same way. Hannah had stayed very quiet, and Vanessa had noticed.

"Maybe," Hannah said, excited and scared all at the same time, wanting to keep Vanesssa close but needing a distraction, "maybe he could bring something from the North. For my engagement party."

"You want forbidden books for your engagement?" Vanessa murmured the words, and now her head rested against Hannah's shoulder.

"Flowers, maybe." But Hannah giggled at the thought of the salacious book Vanessa had loaned her being given out to all of her friends. The giggling intensified the warm excitement.

An otter surfaced in the water of the church, right in the center. "Hannah!" Angeline called.

With a quick tumult of waves, Hannah and Vanessa separated. The commotion drew Angeline's attention. "What do you mean by turning your microphone off?" the older otter said as she swam over. "And what are *you* doing here?" she snapped at Vanessa. "Where is your companion?"

Vanessa waved a paw and spoke coldly. "She has the courtesy to leave me time to meditate upon God's word, unlike some other companions, it seems."

Angeline's eyes narrowed. "I shall speak to her about it. Hannah, you may contemplate God's word in the beauty of the dresses your mother wishes to buy. She has been waiting for almost five minutes. Come along now."

"You shouldn't let her order you about," Vanessa said.

"And you should keep your tongue in your head," Angeline snapped. "Do not imagine that your father's station will keep you safe from the consequences of your actions forever."

"Really?" Vanessa climbed the cypress root a little ways so that she could look down on Angeline. "Perhaps I'll have him buy you, and then we shall see about that."

The older otter's lips pressed tightly together. "Come, Hannah," she said. "Your mother is waiting."

Hannah pushed off from the root, raising a paw to Vanessa. "I'll see you tomorrow," she said.

Her friend smiled at her and brought two fingers to her lips quickly, an unmistakable gesture of a kiss.

Hannah's eyes widened, and she felt stirrings of that warmth in her again. For a tense second, she waited for Angeline to cry a protest, but her companion must be facing away. Daringly, swimming backwards, she brought her fingers to her lips and mimicked Vanessa's gesture.

A leaf stuck to her fingers, but it didn't matter. Her friend's smile shimmered with the reflections all around, and remained bright as Hannah swam across the warm water under the arched branches of the cypress cathedral.

Chapter 13

I woke with a noise in my throat and the smell of cypress in my nose. Looking up at the shadows cast on my ceiling, for a moment I thought I saw interlocked branches and near-invisible bells, and my futon swayed like water under me. I brought one paw out from under the blankets, and a small leaf fluttered from my fingers to the floor.

Oh, shit. *Shit.* Not cool.

I sat there staring at the edge of the futon beyond which the leaf had disappeared. My heart pounded like a drum, and the mattress rocked and swayed even worse. My fur stifled me, and the air felt muggy as a swamp.

"No," I said aloud. I pressed both paws to the futon and closed my eyes, taking in a slow breath. I did not believe that this shit was happening. My mind, already proven treacherous, was just fucking with me a little more. I'd listened to Sol's stories of things that came back from dreams and now I was remembering those and because I was having vivid med-with-drawal dreams, my mind had convinced me that a leaf had followed me back. I would look over the side of the futon and it wouldn't be there, because it had never been there, because I hadn't really seen it. Chemical imbalances in my brain produced auditory and visual hallucinations every now and then and it was just a thing that happened and then went away. I could manage it.

The futon stabilized slowly. There. I focused on my heart, did some of the breathing exercises that were supposed to be for meditation, but fuck that, whatever works. For a minute or two I worried that I was really, in some kind of karmic justice shitstorm, having a panic attack, because I could not get my heart to slow down. I was getting dizzy, and I kept wanting to lie on my back and float there looking up at the cypress church. There is no cypress church, I said to myself. There never was. You're having fucked up withdrawal dreams.

(*Five months late.*)

(Whatever, it could happen.)

(*And hallucinations about a muskrat.*)

(One thing at a fucking time, okay?)

Slowly, slowly, the branches faded. I was sitting in my room looking up at the stucco ceiling in the light coming in from the construction site outside, paws pressed into the cotton fabric of my solid futon. The racing of my blood slowed, the rushing in my ears died down, and the real world reasserted itself around me. The bass drum in my chest softened back to its normal, slow, unnoticeable beat.

I glanced again at the side of the futon, but not over it. I was going to go back to sleep. No, wait. Athos was probably asleep by now. I could go get some rum.

There was half a bottle left in the kitchen cupboard. I wouldn't finish it all tonight, just one glass to steady my nerves. I'd put the bottle back and closed the cupboard when the boys' bedroom door opened and Athos came out, rubbing his eyes. He was shirtless with a loose pair of boxers, his ears askew, chest and tail fur all ruffled.

"What's going on?"

I took a gulp of rum. It burned, but the burning faded. I waited for it to numb my nerves. "Couldn't sleep."

He eyed the glass, and I said, "I don't suppose it's any use pretending this is iced tea."

"I can smell it." His nose wrinkled. "You often drink to go to sleep?"

"I wouldn't say 'often,' but whenever I need to, I guess. It works."

He nodded, leaning against the wall of the kitchen about two feet from me. "How do you buy alcohol?"

The rum was starting to work. I took another gulp. "There's a store a few blocks that way." I nodded my head toward the front door. "My fake ID from high school works fine there."

"Doesn't seem very safe. For them, I mean."

I hadn't really thought of that. "I'm careful. I don't get falling-down drunk. I just need it to settle myself now and then."

"You want to be careful about that." He sighed and scratched behind one ear, then the other. "Sorry. I don't want to lecture you. It's just that I'm worried."

I finished the drink, then set the glass down. "It's the middle of the night. I'll take it at face value."

"Thanks." He smiled. "You going to be okay?"

"I'm fine." And I felt it, too. I was calm, I was starting to feel tired, and the dream was fading. Well, sort of. Not really like a real dream would. I was thinking about Hannah hugging a fox and feeling nothing, or dreaming that, and then about the way her body—my body, in the dream?—had lit up when Vanessa came close.

Was my subconscious trying to tell me that I might be gay? That just looking at girls might not be enough, that I should try getting close to them? Certainly, standing here looking at a half-naked boy, I wasn't feeling anything like those tingles and flashes of warmth, and I hadn't felt them even when he laid his paws on me.

But I'd never, strictly speaking, tried it with a girl. I'd hung out with all my lesbian friends, but that wasn't the same as being close to them, so close our whiskers brushed. It wasn't the same as hugging them as closely as I'd hugged Athos.

Good job, subconscious. Fuck you. If you think I'm gay then I'm pretty sure I'm not.

"All right," Athos said, and brought a paw to his muzzle to cover his yawn. "If you're all right, I'm going back to bed."

"I'll see you in the morning," I said.

When I stepped back into my room and closed the door behind me, I honestly didn't mean to look down at the side of my futon. But my eyes went there, the way they do sometimes.

The carpet was bare.

So I walked closer, knelt down beside the futon, and actually looked. No leaf.

Great. So it was all just mind tricks after all. Maybe it was the rum, but I actually felt relieved. Mind tricks I knew. Mind tricks I could deal with. The freaky dreams were new, the muskrat hallucinations were new, but at their core they were nothing I hadn't dealt with already.

⌇

I got up at way too fucking early-o'clock to ride with Athos to the airport, a very nice cab ride during which we didn't talk about my mid-night drinking or panic attacks and only briefly mentioned a followup visit. On the bus back I got a message from Alexei that he was going straight to work.

How was your night? I typed back.

It went very well.

He didn't use emoticons, like Sol did, and usually that was okay. Today I would've liked a big smiley or something. *Like, life-changing well? Or you got a good night's sleep?*

I did not get very much sleep. I will tell you tonight. A moment after that, he typed, *Mike was wonderful. Do not worry.*

So he'd gotten laid, or at least had fooled around. At least one person in our little pack-family was getting some. That reminded me of Sol, so on the walk back from the bus stop I dialed the woofer up.

"Hey Meg," he said. "Just getting ready for orientation."

"Orientation? When do classes start?"

"In two weeks. Hey, how's Alexei doing? He posted on ScentBook that he was back, but nothing else."

"Oh, he's good." I debated whether to spill the fox's secret and then thought, what the hell. "Spent the night at Mike's last night."

Sol went really quiet, and I thought I'd lost the connection. "Woofer?" He sounded quieter and a bit wary. "So he didn't come home?"

"He came home. Athos was down for the weekend, and—"

"Wait, Athos came down? When did that happen?"

"Saturday."

He made an exasperated "tchah," and said, "This is why you need to be on ScentBook."

"Why, so everyone can know what's going on in my life? I wouldn't have posted about that anyway." I crossed the street to our block and slowed, taking smaller steps. For once, it was a nice day, though the clouds that were keeping the temperature down also threatened rain later.

"So what happened? With Alexei, I mean. Is he okay?"

"He's fine. I'll let him tell you about it. Maybe he'll post pictures on ScentBook or something."

Sol snorted and then said, "I'll call him. So why'd Athos come down?"

"To keep me company."

"Things going well? You guys make good use of your alone time?"

"Bite your tongue." I leaned my head back and looked up at the sky, taking in a calming breath. "Sorry. I told you nothing's going on between us." Though that wasn't strictly true anymore, was it?

"Uh-huh. He comes down at the last minute to see you on a weekend when you're alone."

"I asked him to come down." I got so caught up in proving Sol wrong that I let that slip.

"Ah ha."

"Oh, fuck you, 'ah ha.' I asked him to come down to bring me weed, okay? I ran out."

That shut him up. So before he could get on my case about smoking, I said, "How's Charleton? Any cute boys?"

I'd hoped to embarrass him, but he got all excited. "I looked up the LGBT group on campus and they had a meeting on Friday. It was a welcome-back-slash-getting-to-know-you thing, where a lot of the upperclassmen came back early and a few of us freshmen showed up to meet them. It's mostly guys, and I talked to about five and I'm going to the thing this Friday, too."

"What thing?" I had no doubt Sol would be popular with the gay crowd at any college. Young, cute, athletic wolf? Sure.

"Oh, there's a cookout. Bret says it's a lot more chill than the orientation."

"Oh ho, there's a 'Bret.'"

I could see in my head his ears flattening, the abashed grin in his black muzzle. "He's a dingo, over here for college, and he's got this amazing accent. He loves baseball, too."

"And he likes you."

"Well, I dunno. Maybe. We'll see."

"What about whatsisname, Mitch? The bear?"

"Oh, uh. Well, we both knew that would end when I went to college."

"Really. Mitch knew that too, did he?"

He paused again and then sounded slightly petulant. "We talked about me going away. I'm sure he didn't expect us to keep seeing each other. He gave me a nice good-bye present."

"All right, all right, you manage your own love life." My slow steps had brought me to the apartment. I unlocked the front door.

"I gotta go anyway. Oh, hey, how's Niki?"

The door swung shut behind me. "I'm rolling my eyes. I'm telling you because you can't see me."

"Yeah, yeah. How is he?"

"Your picture is fine. It's still on the wall. Athos did not steal it, or drop it, or…or walk into it or anything."

Don't know why I said that last part. Just to taunt him maybe. He didn't rise to the bait. "Okay, thanks. Hey, thanks for calling. Sorry I've been busy, but glad you had company this weekend."

And then he hung up. I went into the apartment and checked the painting to make sure it really was okay, and there it was on the wall, the fox still getting up from the bench, the glass clear except for that thumbprint the framing place had left inside it. Sol didn't want to "risk" having it re-framed, as though someone in a Vidalia framing store would covet his painting enough to steal it, or as though they weren't professionals who handled hundreds of more valuable paintings—originals even, not giclees on canvas—every day. But whatever. We all had our weird things to believe in. I just wished Sol would let go of Niki, even a little.

He'd only been gone three days. It was hard to believe that. Alexei and I were going to be okay without him, I thought, but if this thing with Mike worked out, then Alexei would probably move out, and what would I do then?

I'd find another roommate. Maybe Sherine would want to live a little cheaper, if things with her boyfriend didn't get serious. Or maybe I'd just find a random person on the bulletin board at the café.

Which reminded me that I should probably get down there and draw today. I wouldn't work on the comic; I shouldn't have worked on it yesterday, for that matter. The end of the month was coming up and I needed to get Corra's and Chet's commissions done. Normally I wouldn't have worried about it, because I could do one a day without too much trouble, but the last few days had not been really good for my confidence in my drawing.

Maybe if I did something like Marie-Belle's story for my commissioners, it would suck them in, too. I could probably make a bundle off that, I mused as I gathered up my portfolio.

The Café La Croix wasn't terribly busy on Monday morning. None of the rats were in evidence, thank god, so I said good morning to Eve, got my coffee from Alain, and went off to draw in a corner.

Corra's commission. I pulled it out and stared down at the page. The tree sketches were still where I'd drawn them the day before, but even though I had one very nice oak tree there, I couldn't see oak where the sketch lines were. The cypress trees from my dream pressed their images around the lines, and every time I tried to draw them, the branches didn't look right or the clumps of leaves felt wrong.

After half an hour, I had a bunch of misshapen oak trees that looked like they'd been drawn by a ten-year-old from New Kestle who'd only ever seen cypress trees and vaguely knew how oaks were supposed to be different. I blew the eraser shavings off the paper and considered the figure. At least Corra herself looked all right. I could fill in detail and go back to the trees later. They weren't a big part of the picture; they'd just been how I'd envisioned it in my head, so it was hard getting past that.

I started doing detail on Corra's fur and outfit, as I'd already made her tits bigger and noted most of the other changes. What it needed was some sheen on the metal armor and fur detail on the places that were showing, and also her tail, which I hadn't done.

For a little while, I slipped into a drawing haze, but when I sat up to drink coffee and examine my work, I noticed a problem. The metal armor looked more like leather; my attempts to make it reflective weren't coming out so well. And I'd over-darkened her fur, too. Corra's a light brown rat, and I was shading her the dark brown of an otter.

Or a muskrat. I stared down and realized that I was giving her Marie-Belle's fur and some kind of weird compromise between metal armor and poor bayou clothes. Somehow the picture in my head that I was drawing had gotten messed up again. I sighed and picked up the eraser to lighten her fur and start over.

An hour later, I had at least managed to get her fur the right shade, but I still couldn't do anything with the armor. Everything I tried looked wrong. Her tail was almost as bad: I kept making it thicker and then it looked wrong for her, but when I redrew the lines closer together, it didn't look right to my brain. I'd erased it so many times that I worried I'd wear through the paper.

The café had picked up as eleven rolled around, people coming in for lunch breaks early, or coffee breaks late. When I was drawing, though, I barely noticed any of that stuff. I looked up when I took a sip of my rapidly cooling coffee, and it seemed that all the tables had filled up in moments.

Now that I wasn't lost in the drawing, the increased buzz of sound was a lot more noticeable. In the water, I'd be able to notice the movement better (though Hannah had been oblivious to Angeline's return—in my *dream*, I reminded myself), but even here in dry air, I could feel the increased pressure of the room filling with people.

And there, at a table by the window, was Corra. No, wait, it was Gret. I was pretty sure, anyway; those three are hard to tell apart, especially at a distance. Nearer to me, Bellie had come in and was rubbing a finger thoughtfully across her mask. As I watched her, she turned and caught my eye with a smile. So she'd forgiven me for the other night, I guessed.

Not enough to come over and say hi, and that was fine with me. I stared down at the drawing and sighed. Probably it'd be best to take off before Corra showed up.

But I'd no sooner dropped my pencils in the pencil case than a sharp voice over my shoulder said, "That doesn't look finished."

Dammit, she'd snuck up behind me when I wasn't paying attention. How long had she been standing there? I didn't think very long, but the coffee and crowd drowned out her smell. "It's not. I've been working on it all morning."

"It doesn't look it." She stared down. "My tail's too thick. And the armor's weird."

"I *know*."

She folded her arms. "Just forget about it. I don't want it anymore."

"That's not how it works."

Skinny fingers gestured at the drawing. "It's not working this way either."

"Look, you…you agreed to pay me a hundred fifty for this. You can't just back out."

"That doesn't look finished"

Her eyes glittered down. "You said it'd be done last week."

"It's barely a week over!" I didn't like sitting down when she was looming over me, as much as a five-foot-four rat girl can loom, but I didn't want to get up and turn this into a real fight, either. "I'll get it done."

"You've been working on it for three days and it barely looks any better. When's it going to be done? September?"

"It'll be…" Frustration gripped my throat, curled my paws into impotent fists. "Soon. I *promise*."

"I know what your promises mean." She lifted her head so that her voice projected over the coffee shop. "I don't *want it* anymore. It's a terrible picture and you're always late and you're rude, too."

I slapped a paw down on the paper. "I'm going to finish it," I said. "And you'll get it for a hundred-fifty when it's done."

By now, people were staring, not that I cared. From behind the counter, Eve and Alain gave me worried looks as they handled the customers, but I didn't even try to reassure them. I just wanted Corra to agree that in a couple more days she would have her precious commission. The temptation to say, "Fine, then," and tear it up right in front of her was getting harder to resist with every word she said.

"You can't make me pay you money for something I don't want." She stared down her nose at me.

Fuck it. I stood up. "I've already invested hours—days—in this picture. You can't just back out."

"If it's not what I wanted, I can."

I raised a finger. "Listen—"

A smooth voice approached. "Now, now, girls, what's the trouble? Let's not have a fight here."

Bellie, coming up with a big smile beneath her mask, slid around the table to stand between us. "There's no need to get loud," she said in her slow drawl. "Corra, honey, I know you didn't mean what you said about Meg."

"Look at this picture." Corra stabbed a finger down at the table. "*Look at it!* She did one for Gret in half the time and it was a million times better!"

"It's been a rough weekend," I said. "My best friend left for college."

"And she's been working on other things, too," Corra said. "Some comic-type thing."

"That's none of your business," I snapped.

"It is when my picture is late!"

"Why do you need it this week anyway?" I asked.

"That's none of *your* business."

Bellie held up her paws. "That really doesn't matter. Look, you two, can we compromise? Corra, what would you want fixed in the picture now? At a minimum?"

"It's all terrible." The rat tossed her head so that her piercings clinked, and glared at me.

I flicked my ears so my piercings clinked too, not that it made any difference. Bellie rested a paw on Corra's arm. "Just look. It's not that bad. It looks like you, see?"

Under Bellie's calming influence, Corra grudgingly dropped her eyes. "The tail's too thick," she said.

"Okay, sure, I see that." Bellie smiled at me and raised her eyebrows a little, just enough to tell me to be patient. "What else, hon?"

Corra gave a loud, exaggerated sigh. "The foot looks weird, there." She pointed at a bit that I thought was fine.

I started to say something, and then Bellie asked her what else, and as I looked at the foot again, I saw that probably she was mistaking a little rock I'd drawn in for part of the foot. I could make that clearer.

"I dunno," Corra said. "I guess the armor's okay."

"Okay. Meg, can you fix the tail and the foot right now?"

I swallowed back the retort that I'd been trying for hours. "Yeah."

"Okay. Corra, if she fixes those things, would you buy the picture?"

The rat still looked angry. "Well, I'm not giving her a hundred fifty for it."

"That's the price we agreed on," I said before Bellie could step in.

"All right, all right, don't let's get our fur all needly." Bellie turned to me. "Meg, it's late and it's not completely done, so you can give her a discount, right?"

I calculated what I would need to pay rent for the month, especially if I couldn't finish any of the three commissions I had left. "A hundred twenty-five?"

"Twenty-five dollars off?" Corra screeched. Again, heads that had gone back to their own business turned our way. "I'll give you fifty for it."

"Fifty? I can't—I spent hours on this!"

Bellie gripped my forearm. Holding us both, she said, "How about seventy-five? Corra, would you do that?"

The words felt as though they were being dragged out of her on a fishing line. Her eyes burned into mine. "I *guess*."

Bellie turned to me. "Meg, how's that?"

How was that? It sucked. It left me fifty bucks short of rent, which would be no problem if I could finish one more of the pieces I had to do this month, but I didn't know if I could do that, and I didn't know where else I could borrow money from.

But it was clear that I wasn't going to get any more out of Corra. So I said, "That works," with about the same enthusiasm Corra'd shown.

"All right. See, a good compromise is when both sides aren't happy."

"It'd be better if both sides were happy," Corra muttered.

"Then you wouldn't need me to make you talk. Now shake paws." We did so, reluctantly. Corra's paw felt spindly and dry and she let go of mine almost as soon as we'd made contact. "Corra, go sit with Gret. I'll sit with Meg and make sure she finishes."

"I don't need a babysitter," I snapped.

Bellie smiled sweetly. "It's my pleasure, darlin'," she said.

And that was that. So I took my pencils out again and sat back down at the table. Bellie fetched her coffee and bag and sat beside me. "I know you don't need someone to keep an eye on you," she said. "But I figured Corra would feel better if she thought someone was pushing you to stay focused."

"Yeah," I said, staring down at the tail on the picture.

"And this way I get to spend a little more time with you and watch you work."

She was smiling when I looked up. I managed an answering smile. "You don't have to wait until some bitch flips her shit. You could just come over and say hi."

She handled my foul language without batting a mascara-curled eyelash. "Well, I wasn't sure and I don't like to intrude."

She hadn't minded intruding so much at the bar, but maybe that was a different situation. She wasn't coming to watch me work there, after all. "All right. I hope this isn't too embarrassing for me."

I started to try to do that damn tail again, but before I'd drawn an inch of it, I realized I owed her something else. "Thanks," I said. "I really appreciate you coming over. That's seventy-five bucks I probably wouldn't have gotten."

"And she was yelling in the coffee shop about your reputation," Bellie said. "That's just not done."

That was something I hadn't even considered. Now I looked up from the table and saw Holi, a lion I'd drawn, unloading baked goods for the lunch rush from the bakery where he worked. Nearby, his brother's boyfriend Babe, a gazelle in a tight flowery silk shirt, sipped a latte and looked at the paper. Babe had talked to me about "getting serious" with my art, and was on my list to ask about commissions. I got a lot of my business from this café and Corra had been trying—deliberately, I thought—to ruin it. My fingers tightened around the pencil. "Yeah. Thanks for managing that, too. I could…I could do a drawing for you, no charge."

"Oh, there's no need." Bellie smiled. "I'm just glad of the chance to get to sit and watch for a bit."

"You can do that anytime," I said, though to be honest, I wasn't sure what effect that would have on my productivity.

"Anytime that other friend of yours isn't here?"

I bent to try the tail again. "Athos wouldn't mind." And then, as I was getting the curve of the tail meticulously right, I got the subtext in Bellie's tone. I thought about my dream and my worries about my sexuality. Bellie liked me, and I liked her well enough when she wasn't hitting on me, but what if I said that the flirting was okay, removed that objection entirely? Considered in that light, she was my most likely choice to date—if I was actually a lesbian.

So I said, "If you don't want a drawing, how about a drink?"

"I already have a coffee."

I looked up into her smile. She knew what I meant, but she was making sure, giving me an out. Smart and considerate; I appreciated that. "At the Pickled Goose, I mean."

"Well, dear, that'd be lovely. When would you like to meet up?"

I bent back to the drawing. "Tonight?"

"I'm working until ten, but after that would be fine. I don't have to be up until ten tomorrow."

"Great." I said it and then wondered what she meant. Was that an invitation to stay the night, or just a reassurance that we could stay out late and she wouldn't bail on me because of work? I chose to believe the latter, although I honestly wasn't sure what my own intentions were as regarded the night.

I got the tail done and fixed the foot, and while I was at it, I took a stab at the trees. Bellie's presence kept me from zoning out, which made everything a little longer and more tedious, but at least I was able to focus on the details.

Corra came over before she left, pronounced the picture acceptable with the single word, "Fine," and gave me a check for seventy-five. She walked away without any more words and though I didn't want to watch, I saw her bitching at Gret on the other side of the café.

"Don't watch them," Bellie said.

"Thanks again," I told her, packing up my things. "I couldn't have gotten this done without you."

"I'll see you tonight," she said with a smile. "And if you want to come to the Burger Bar for dinner, I'll give you a discount on your food."

"Might not be a bad idea, since I'm still short on rent money." I sighed. "You're there until ten?"

She gestured down her front. "Bright red apron and all. Come on by, sweetie. The food's good and I'll make sure we don't put on any of that new music."

"I don't think your customers would enjoy the kind of music I listen to." I picked up my portfolio.

Bellie winked. "You might be surprised. See you tonight, darlin'."

Chapter 14

What was I doing with Bellie? I thought about it all the way home. Maybe it was bad of me to lead her on. But that dream. If I really was gay and didn't want to admit it to myself, I'd rather explore that with her than go out to the Pickled Goose and pick up some random girl. Bellie would listen to me and if I had to bail out partway into the evening, she wouldn't be that upset at me.

And Athos and I were still, delicately, just friends. I could go to him and say, hey, turns out I am a lesbian, sorry. He'd be disappointed, but it would be good to have some certainty between us. Of course, he might decide he didn't want to keep being friends with me if the relationship wasn't going further, but…I hoped he'd stay.

So I texted Alexei and told him I was going out for dinner. He wrote back a little while later that he'd arranged to meet Liza and Alice and Zayda with Mike for a sort of informal VLGA dinner, and I resisted the urge to say, "I guess it's Lesbian Night for us," because I didn't want him to know what I was doing.

I tried to get working on the other commission that was almost overdue, the one for that boar, but even the urgency of knowing I needed money didn't help me get over my art block. I sat and doodled sketches for an hour and got nothing I could use. Even finishing off the rum didn't help quell my mounting sense of dread.

It would pass, it had to pass. I'd done a dozen commissions this summer and never had this problem. Art block happened but people got over it, and I would too. Maybe it was this comic, and I needed to get Marie-Belle out of my system. Maybe it was the disruption of Sol leaving and Athos's visit and my subconscious dredging up old terrors and new fears about the future. So hopefully tonight would be a step toward easing those.

When I got to the Burger Bar, it wasn't all that crowded. Monday nights aren't super busy down at Riverwalk in general. So I slid into a table, and then Bellie came over and told me to take a different one so I'd be in her section, and we walked over to a small table by the window.

The Burger Bar is a dark wooden room with a chalkboard menu on the back wall where the regular burgers and the specials are listed. I read down the list, and when Bellie came over, I told her the tuna burger sounded good.

"Figured that's what you'd go for," she said. "Want a side? I'd advise the onion rings instead of fries if you like onion. Otherwise get the coleslaw. Fries are meh." She made the accompanying "meh" gesture with her paw.

"Onion rings work." I leaned in. "Can you get me a beer?"

Her muzzle squinched up a little. "I would, but…"

"Don't worry about it." I leaned back against the chair. "Coke's fine."

"All right. I promise, hon, I would, but they're really strict and the manager checks sometimes."

"It's not a big deal." I wasn't sure I wanted alcohol anyway, not if we were going to be having drinks later.

While she was getting food, I looked around. A couple big TVs broadcast sports in the corners of the room, and the clientele I could see was mostly male. Smaller tables held gay couples, while two larger tables had raucous parties of friends or co-workers maybe. Mostly there were meat-eaters here, even though the menu showed a vegetarian selection tucked away in the lower right hand part of the back page.

A pair of male wolves, a fox couple, a bear and another otter, a spotted skunk with a striped skunk (what must their families think?), two more wolf couples. I watched some of them to see if I'd be attracted to them (nope) and then to see how they behaved with each other. Many of them looked like just friends. One couple—the grey wolf and black wolf—were probably on a date, both trying to look at the other between bites without being noticed. The two skunks were much more into each other, sitting on adjacent sides of the square table rather than across it, and as I watched, they switched plates halfway through their meal.

Alexei and Sol talked about seeing someone and feeling a spark, which I guess was code for getting aroused. That was what Alexei had with Mike, and what Sol kept having or not having with a bunch of guys. He'd only really felt it with Niki, maybe, which made him more fucked up than me.

Okay, maybe just on par.

But there were a few people I'd read stories from who said they didn't get turned on looking at people, or thinking about sex; they got turned on from emotional connections and getting to know people. They enjoyed sex, just didn't think about it whenever they saw someone attractive. But they did think about it in general, and I really didn't. Hell, what did I know, though?

(You're broken.)

Yeah, well, you're not real, I reminded the memory-voice.

Of course, I wasn't even emotionally into Bellie. But she was nice and I was pretty sure she'd treat me okay. I mean, everyone vouched for her, even if Eve sometimes rolled her eyes. Sherine and Bellie were pretty thick, and Sherine might have the wrong idea about a couple things, but she wouldn't let anything bad happen to me.

But now I was thinking about all the bad things that could happen, that had happened to people who'd gone out on dates. What if Bellie slipped me a roofie with the Coke? What if she tied me up and forced me to do… things? What if she became emotionally dependent on me and I couldn't go to the Café anymore because she'd always be there?

Maybe this whole thing was a mistake. I should tell her that I'd meet her for the drink but then I'd have to go home to work. Lower her expectations—of course, she didn't know I'd already decided to go home with her, so maybe I didn't have to say anything yet. And thinking about work reminded me that I wasn't currently able to work, so maybe changing things up would help.

I dropped my head into my paws. This was all leading me down a road where I was going to have to go back onto the drugs. If I couldn't do art anyway, then there was no point in avoiding them. They shut my subconscious up, and maybe if I went to that commercial art factory school my parents wanted me to, I could learn to draw shitty cookie-cutter art while my subconscious was tamped down and locked away. Plus, then I could blame my lack of sexual interest on them and I wouldn't have to go through these fumbling, stupid exercises.

And Athos, knowing we didn't have a future, would find some other girl who liked all the things we liked and who also liked sex.

All in all, that didn't sound like a great future. So maybe one awkward night of experimentation wasn't too much to gamble with.

On the other side, I hated awkwardness and I wasn't sure this was the only way out. Fuck, my mind was a pendulum tonight. There was alcohol at home; that was one thing. Also there were a few more of Athos's cookies. Just because they hadn't worked in the one case didn't mean they would never work again.

All right, fuck it. I was going—

"Here's your food, hon." Bellie plopped down a hot plate of tuna burger and onion rings in front of me.

The smell grabbed me and pushed me back down into the chair. Bellie asked if I needed anything else and I said I didn't, so she sped off to another table and I dug into the food.

The onion rings were great, hot and crispy. The tuna wasn't great, overcooked slightly and bland, but it was on a pretty chewy bun with some good pickled relish, so it was definitely edible. I polished off the burger quickly and then made the onion rings last as long as I could, even though that meant they dropped to room temperature by the time I was halfway done. I'd never come to this place and it was nice to have another cheap(ish) burger joint on my list.

Bellie came by a couple times to check on me and to let me know she'd be off soon. I nodded, the full stomach making me more agreeable to what was coming later—whatever that was going to be.

When her shift was almost over, she rang up my meal and gave me a pretty big discount. While I appreciated it, as we walked across to the bar I felt like I owed her even more.

At the Pickled Goose, we sat at a high table and Bellie got me a vodka gimlet. "Thanks," I said, sliding a twenty over to her. "I won't guzzle it this time."

"Didn't seem to affect you that much." She swirled her own drink, a gin and tonic. "I grew up in a small town too. I know what the parties there can be like."

"You're one up on me, then," I said. "I didn't get invited."

Bellie smiled. "Well, you're out of high school now. All that bullshit drama and parties and whatever."

"Were you popular?" I asked.

"Ha. Well, I dunno. I mean, you know what it takes for a girl to be popular in high school, right? I guess I was…moderately popular. Didn't really know what I wanted then."

"How did you figure it out?" Here was something that might be useful information.

She laughed and took a sip, then leaned in so she wouldn't have to yell over the music. "I just thought sex was supposed to be uncomfortable. Then I got to college and I met Lydia. She was really sexy, and she thought I was too, and it wasn't like anything I'd ever done before."

When I didn't say anything, she said, "You haven't gone to college, right?"

"Nope." I smiled and lifted my drink. "Am eighteen, though. Nineteen actually."

"Well, yeah, college is a great place to experiment. If you haven't done that…"

"I'm open to experimenting." I'd never tried flirting, but from the way she smiled, I guess I did okay.

"You never seemed it," she said.

I nodded and took a breath. "It's scary, y'know? I don't really have any feelings."

Bellie rested a brown paw on mine. "That happens to lots of girls. You don't let yourself have those feelings because you're ashamed of them."

That sounded almost plausible. At least close enough to several sites I'd read on the Internet for me to let down a little more of my guard. "Did you ever have slumber parties?"

She looked at me weird. I fidgeted with my glass. "With other girls, I mean."

"Yeah, sure." Her ears flicked. "But we didn't, you know, fool around."

It was my turn to lean in, because I didn't want to say this out loud, but now that I was going down this road I wanted to know the answer. It had been years. "Did any of your friends…I mean, did you talk about sex?"

"Sure. Like who was doing what with who?"

With *whom*. No, don't correct her. "Yeah. And…like, how you all felt about it?"

She nodded. "Didn't you have slumber parties?"

"Just once." Again, the truth slipped out.

Again, she gave me an odd look. "Didn't go well?"

Ha. Ha ha ha. Oh, Bellie, if you only knew. I finished off my drink, let the warmth settle and build. "I wasn't interested in all the sex talk. And… one of my friends started touching herself, and I wasn't ready for that at all."

"I guess I can understand that." She had a look like she wanted to go have that slumber party right that minute. Interestingly, too, she didn't seem surprised at what my 'friend' had done. "Some people are late bloomers when it comes to sex."

Late bloomer. Another phrase I'd seen a lot, along with: You just haven't met the right person. Give it time. You can't hurry love.

While I was pondering those phrases, she said, "You want another one?"

At first I thought she meant "another tired saying about sex." But then I saw her paw pointing to my empty glass. "Oh," I said. "No, I'm fine."

"So." Her eyes rose to meet mine. "Evening's over? I'm okay if it is. It's been a nice time and I got to know you a bit more."

I thought about it. Here was yet another out, yet another chance for me to discharge my obligation to Bellie without taking a chance. And then more and more days of not knowing. "Well," I said, "I could use one more drink, maybe."

She gave me a smile, and I went on. "What do you have at home?"

Chapter 15

Bellie lived in a small third-floor apartment that she shared with two other people, but she had her own bedroom and a balcony. One of her roommates, a coyote studying political science at Vidalia College, was home with her bedroom door cracked open. Bellie said she didn't like to be disturbed. The other roommate, an ibex, had her own friends and stayed out late most nights. Her bedroom door was closed, keeping silent in her absence.

Bellie's room, a touch larger than mine and much more decorated, also benefited from air conditioning and a window overlooking the river. She had the curtains drawn—"Keeps out the afternoon sun"—but pulled them back so I could see the reflections of moonlight on the water and the street lamps glowing like signposts along its dark, shimmering path.

"It's a lot prettier at night," I said.

Bellie put a paw around my side and leaned in close. She was about my height, so everything kind of lined up. I couldn't stop my immediate tensing up at the touch, but I did exhale and force myself to relax. She swished her tail across mine, and I let it happen. It wasn't all that bad, really. It just wasn't all that enjoyable. With Athos, at least, I had a lot of trust. I knew that our fight had shaken him at least as much as it had shaken me, and I knew he wasn't going to do anything that might screw us up again, not without a lot of warning and discussion.

Bellie I didn't know as well. I'd met her through Sherine barely a month ago, and though she was in the coffee shop a lot, our interactions had mostly been limited to her flirting with me. I had come here expecting her to be forward, so it didn't really do me much good to be nervous about it.

And yet I was anyway. Probably there was nothing I could do to prevent it. Short of anti-anxiety medication, which would've been a fabulous idea if I had brought one of Athos's cookies with me to eat or had had the foresight a couple weeks ago to go get a prescription for a drug I might need in case I got completely freaked out about my life and sexual orientation and needed to calm down while a female raccoon stroked my tail.

That's what she was doing by then, stroking my tail lightly with her fingers right at the base, and again, there wasn't anything specifically bad about it. It's just that my reaction wasn't, *hey that feels nice*, it was, *you know, you don't need to keep doing that.*

But I was smart enough to know what reaction someone expects when they're touching you intimately for the first time, and so I sort of draped my arm around her and tried poking at whatever part of her I could reach, the same way she was poking at me. It made her giggle, and at first I was paranoid that she was laughing at my lame attempts to imitate her, but then she moved my paw down and said, "I'm a bit ticklish around the ribs," and after that I rubbed her side and she didn't giggle so much.

We rubbed each other like that for a few minutes, with me bouncing between thankful that it wasn't going faster and wishing she'd get it the hell over with already. I had the feeling that I was in a kind of art trance, like with Marie-Belle's story, or the dream about Hannah, something that was going to move along fairly independent of me one way or another.

And finally, after a good fifteen minutes petting each other's whatever-we-could-reach, Bellie pulled me around to brush her stubby muzzle against my rounded one. I waited for the light in my chest to come on like it had in my dream, but everything stayed dark. So I was on my own.

Kissing was something I had no experience in, to put it charitably. I had seen it a million times in my parents' movies, and young me thought it was hysterical when some long-muzzled girl was trying to kiss a short-muzzled guy. Not that even same-species kisses were super graceful, but at least they managed to look like they knew what they were doing, like they had a sense of where things were going to line up.

As I got older, I realized that the funny dance with the tongues licking and the muzzles turned to expose whiskers and so on was how it was done. If you could get your lips together then something happened with the tongues that the movies let you see in quick, furtive shots that usually made teenaged me want to go rinse my mouth out with mouthwash. Someone else's tongue? In your mouth? What the fuck was that about? And yet the girls in high school asked the question in hushed whispers after being told about a kiss, and the question was one word: *tongue?* If the answer was yes, they squealed loudly and I cringed.

So I'd never kissed anyone like that, and when Bellie started licking my whiskers, I just kind of nuzzled back. I didn't want to say I wasn't into it and I didn't want to try doing it and fail spectacularly, so I went along with it even though I kept my tongue in my mouth. I mean, I didn't want to taste her, so why would I lick her?

After a little bit of her trying to kiss me and me half-responding, she pulled her head back. "Well, I guess you haven't done that a lot," she said. "Here, try..." She tried to position my muzzle.

"Uh," I said, pulling back from her grasping fingers, "you know, I'm, I'm okay."

"All right, hon." She smiled at me and dropped her paws to my shoulders. "I know you're nervous. You want to keep going?"

I swallowed back a couple expletives. I'd wanted to make this decision once and have it over with, and she was forcing me to make it over and over. The knowledge that this was considerate of her made me angry at myself as well. "If I didn't want to, I wouldn't be here."

Guess I didn't hide my annoyance all that well. Her ears flattened for a moment, and then she brought them up again. "I know the first time I did anything," she said, clearly forcing a smile, "with another girl, I mean, it was weird. So we can go slow, but I wanna make sure I'm not forcing you into anything you don't wanna do."

"You're not." I was trying not to grit my teeth. Did everyone go through this the first time they had sex? How did anyone ever manage it? My heart was pounding and I kept feeling like I wanted to run away. I would've thought I'd get used to her touching me by now, but every time she moved her paw, I jumped. She mistook it for nervousness and desire, and at least she was right on the first count.

"Why don't we sit down?" she said, and I thought that was a good idea, except that I'd forgotten that the only place to sit down in the bedroom was, duh, the bed.

So we got on the bed and her paws ventured to other places: sides, stomach, breasts. She lingered there, obviously thinking that was going to be the thing that turned me on, the gateway to my lesbianism or something. And I mean, at least in addition to the whole "what the fuck is this person doing touching my tits," there *was* a little bit of physical pleasure to it. I tried to focus on that, figuring at some point I'd lose the rest of the discomfort, the sense of being invaded.

Maybe that would've been true, but she kept changing things up, and I couldn't tell if it was because I wasn't reacting right or if this was just her "move," like we were in some fucking 90s sitcom, "The L Words" or something, and finally she grabbed my paw and put it on *her* tit.

That helped, only because it was a bit distracting. I mean, it felt like mine, but bigger, and so for a bit I focused on what was different about them. Then I imitated what she was doing, and got her to moan, so I guess that worked. If I viewed it as a game where I had to get her to moan while ignoring what she was doing to me, then it calmed me.

She noticed pretty quickly, though, that I wasn't joining in the moaning party, and that wasn't going to fly with her. So she pushed my paws away and said, "Sorry, let me focus on you."

"I'm fine," I said.

"This is what Janelle did with me." She gave me a big smile, pushed me on my back, and lifted my shirt.

My fur was dry because of the air conditioning in her apartment, but I couldn't very well say, "Not tonight, my fur is dry." Besides, she didn't really care so much. So I lay back and stared at the ceiling for, god, hours or something. Probably only ten or fifteen minutes. Bellie tried to work her magic on me, and while the physical part got maybe a little better, I couldn't get past the whole problem that I barely knew her and she was touching me more intimately than anyone except my parents had, pushing up my fur against the grain, scraping my skin with her claws.

But it wasn't even that, when it came down to it. The intimacy was awkward but it was only uncomfortable. She was touching with affection, clearly, in the hope that I'd enjoy it. I don't think she wanted me to be her girlfriend or anything; she just wanted to "wake me up."

I wrestled with whether to tell her to stop or wait for her to stop on her own, and right as I'd figured I would say something soon, she stopped, exhaled and rubbed a paw across her eyes, ruffling up the black fur of her mask. "Let me try something else."

Oh god, I thought. She went on, "When you masturbate, what do you do?"

I stared up. Her eyes gathered the reflections of the room's dim light and shone down at me. "I don't..." I stopped. "Feel comfortable..."

Bellie laughed. "Oh, come on. It's natural. Look." And she undid her pants.

Didn't you ever touch yourself? It feels good if you're normal.

"Margie," I said, and then caught myself. Fuck, Meg, keep it together. "Bellie, you don't have to do that."

"Who's Margie? Someone you think about?" She grinned at me, pointy muzzle and sharp little fangs, and pushed her pants down. Underneath her fur was matted and she ran her claws through to fluff it up the way I'd seen Sol and Alexei do. Not with those parts, but their arms and stuff.

"Not if I can help it." I squirmed, but she put a paw down on my stomach and ruffled my thicker fur, which didn't make me feel better but was clearly *supposed* to. Her arms weren't as thick as mine, but she felt stronger.

"Relax." Bellie laughed. "It's the same equipment you've got. So do you do this? Or this?"

I didn't really look at what her fingers were doing, letting them blur into a little dance of motion two feet from my eyes, black clawed fingers and greyish white fur. "Seriously, it's—I told you, I'm not—it's not something—"

"A lot of girls don't really know how to do it," she went on. "If you just do what feels good, though, you can't go wrong. I know it's easy to get screwed up by the church and people telling you God doesn't want you to feel good, especially around here." She closed her eyes, breathed in, then looked down at me. "But it's okay to feel good."

"I know." Refusing to look at her fingers meant I pretty much had to look at her face, the black mask stretching across tan fur, the eyes bright as they met mine.

Or her chest, which was rising and falling with more urgency now. She was getting herself off in front of me, which was fine and actually had been one of my best-case scenarios for the night, right after discovering that I really was a lesbian and wanted to have sex. Since that first one was off the table, "watching her masturbate" wouldn't be so bad.

Of course it wasn't going to be that easy. She panted harder, her chest heaving up and down, and with a quick, "Like this," she grabbed my fingers and pressed them where hers had been.

So that was my first sexual experience: lying on a bed getting a raccoon off while her ringed tail flicked all over the place and her moans filled the small room. I settled into a comfortable place of doing a favor for a friend, and once I found something that worked, it wasn't too hard to stick to it. She guided me once or twice and when it ended, it was almost exactly like in the movies and at the same time very much not. The only way I can think to describe it is that the theatrical aspects, the arched back and the moans and stuff, those were like the movies. The other stuff, the shaking and the loss of balance and the awkward curl of her tail and the scent I caught, those were unexpected.

If it weren't for the way her scent changed, I might have tried to fake it. I had always heard about people smelling like sex, and once or twice I'd smelled something on Sol or Alexei when they'd been alone in a room (and they'd always been self-conscious about it so I made sure to say, "Hey, I don't care if you whack it as long as I'm not in the room," to let them know I didn't care and also to see their ears go back). But Bellie's whole scent changed, and it came off her like a wave, all that satisfaction and relief blown toward me by the air conditioning, and I knew I would never be able to fake that.

She rubbed her paw through my dry stomach fur, a misty smile on her muzzle that included a bit of her tongue sticking out the front of her lips. "Thanks, sugar," she breathed finally. "That was pretty nice." Her paw moved down toward the top of my pants. "Now let's let you have some fun."

When you look back at moments like that, it's really easy to see what you should have done. All I could think at that moment was that I wanted to wash my paws off and go home. "I'm not a lesbian," I told her.

Her paw stopped, and the smile wavered. Her voice lost its dreamy quality. "You said you weren't sure."

"I am now." I didn't want to remove her paw from my stomach, but I would if she didn't do it herself. "I'm sorry. I'm just not."

The only sound in the room for a while was her heavy breathing, getting lighter. I stared at her arm, at the brown fur with streaks of grey and white, wondering whether she'd ever move it.

Then she did, abruptly. "Well," she said in a horrible bright voice, "can't blame a gal for trying."

I lay there with no idea what the hell to do. I wanted to put my shirt back on and go, but Bellie was still kneeling on the bed. She looked like she didn't know what to do, and I got annoyed that she'd put all of this hope into me being a lesbian. How the fuck was she supposed to know what was going on in my head when I didn't have a fucking clue myself?

"I told you I was still figuring things out," I said tightly.

"Then why stop now?" The false brightness remained in her voice as it got louder. "You haven't even tried anything."

Hadn't she just told me she remembered me saying I wasn't sure? How many times did I have to tell her that? "I tried watching you get yourself off, remember?" Another one of those sentences I'd regret later; in this case, "later" was about five seconds after I finished saying it.

"I see." With a quick motion, she got off the bed and pulled her pants up. "Then I suppose we're done here."

"If you're going to be pissy about it…" I found my shirt and started to pull it on, but I hadn't gotten more than my head through the collar when something soft smacked me in the face.

"Pissy?" Bellie yelled as the pillow dropped to the bed. "Pissy? I go out of my way to help you out and I bring you back here, and you call me 'pissy'? Get out of here, you little spoiled brat, just fuck off!"

The bright tone was gone, leaving only raw, scraping anger. At least she was being honest with me now, I guess. I yanked the shirt down and scrambled off the bed. "Help me out, right," I said. "You wanted another name on your recruitment clipboard. If you gave a shit about what I really think and feel you'd have asked me instead of just feeling me up, so save your self-pity."

"Get out!" She stood there, paws balled into fists, and her scent had changed again with her posture: now it was black, fierce, spreading. "I was trying to *help*! I was doing this for *you*!"

You know it feels good, right? What's wrong with you?

"Nothing's wrong with me!" I yelled, and ran out of the bedroom, past the other doors, past a startled coyote at the refrigerator, out into the hall, down the stairs, out into the street.

I ran the wrong way at first and found myself at the railing overlooking the river. In the darkness beyond the streetlights, the reflections of stars glowed and rippled in the water. My apartment was in the other direction, but before I turned, my attention was caught by a gap amidst the reflections, a stretch of water destitute of light. The shadow looked like a silhouette of a person, with great black wings spread out behind it.

You're broken.

It wasn't anything, of course, it wasn't the shadow of a dead otter talking to me. It was just the shadow thrown by a statue on the bridge, or a building. The only voice was in my memory.

Do you want to know how you're going to die, Meggie?

I shut my eyes, squeezed them until I saw flashes of light and my head hurt. *You're not real. You. Are. Not. Real. You're misplaced chemicals in my brain.*

You're going to die alone.

Even the echoes were unsettling, vibrations returning to me from the depths of the abyss. I didn't want to know what else might crawl out of the blackness. Dr. Wallace had given me pills and a lot of terrible advice, but one of the few actual helpful things he'd said (corroborated on the Internet) had been burned into my brain: if you feel the hallucinations coming back, hold onto what's real, and if you're out in public, get help from anyone.

So I scanned up and down the street and saw a pronghorn in a loose collared shirt leaning back against the railing, talking softly on his phone. The worry about going up to a stranger stood no chance against the thumping of my heart and the shadow encroaching on the edges of my awareness.

He put his phone down with a "hang on" to the speaker as he saw me approach. Concern lit his soft brown eyes. "Are you okay, darlin'?"

I looked down to his collared shirt, open to show his thick chest ruff and glittering gold chain. "I'm fine, for now, but can I ask you a favor?" He inclined his head and I took a breath. "Can you walk me away from the river?"

He turned his horned head back and forth, looking up and down the empty river walk. "Ex-girlfriend trouble?"

Bellie's mask flittered across my awareness and I let out a choked giggle. "I'm not a lesbian."

He raised his eyebrows. "Ex-boyfriend?"

"No. Just…I get…" Breathe. Tell him enough of the truth, but not all of it, because Jesus Christ. "I get panic attacks and I thought I was over them, but the water sort of triggers them sometimes, so I need someone to make sure I'm okay because I feel really edgy right now." Panic attacks were things normal people had. I didn't want to tell him, *I need someone around in case a voice whispers into my head and I do what it says without thinking.*

"Sure, darlin'." He brought the phone back to his ear and said, "I'm gonna take a quick walk. There's an otter girl here needs some help. Back in ten minutes." He listened to the reply. "Just down Main."

"Three blocks should be fine," I said.

He repeated that and then nodded. "I'll be careful."

"You'll be careful?" I said when he'd hung up.

Brown eyes regarded me gravely. "Jeff thinks you might be part of a gang. The shill, the girl in trouble, leading me to get robbed by your pals. An otter, getting panic attacks from water?"

My heart raced. "Yeah, it sounds crazy. If I wanted you to believe me, I'd have made up something better, now, wouldn't I?"

"Just so you know," he reached into his pocket and brought out his wallet, "I've got forty bucks on me and that's it."

"I don't want your money. Fuck, man." I took a step back.

He replaced the wallet. "Let's go, then."

I prepared to resist any attempt of his to touch me, but he kept only his eyes on me as we crossed the street and walked up through Riverwalk, past empty shops and raucous bars and crowds of people having too-loud conversations. As we walked, the weight of the shadow around my mind faded, my breathing slowed, and shame at having to ask for help grew at the back of my neck.

When we'd gotten to the edge of the shopping district, he eyed the townhouses and trees ahead, darkness punctuated by streetlights. "You live there?"

"Yeah." I gestured ahead. "I'm fine now. I'm pretty sure." The darkness there was just absence of light, nothing more.

"All right." He stuck his hands in his pockets. "Thanks for not leading me into a mugging."

"Yeah, thanks for…for not being a creep." I raised a paw and hurried away from him, into the quiet of the townhouses and trees, past them to where lights shone and machines clanked around the construction site, and back to the apartment. I couldn't believe I'd just walked up to a random guy and asked him to walk me three blocks. What the fuck was wrong with me, I couldn't walk three blocks by myself? Couldn't just walk away from the river?

And if he'd talked to you, Meggie, if he'd told you to climb the railing and jump into the river and go to the bottom and wait there, what then?

But he didn't, he wouldn't, he couldn't. He'd never actually been there at the river, despite the flare of memory. Fuck. If Bellie had planned to dredge up my childhood trauma, she couldn't have done a much better job of it.

As I closed the front door of the apartment, Alexei called out from his room, "How was your dinner?"

I didn't answer, just stalked across the dining room to my bedroom. I'd never before been so grateful that our apartment didn't have a pool. Then I remembered that I wanted to wash my paws. Were they still that bad? I lifted them to my nose and caught Bellie's scent. Yeah. Okay. Also they were shaking. I should probably do something about that.

I took a moment after patting my paws dry to breathe, to look at myself in the mirror. My body was still mine, and though there were places where Bellie's touch lingered, I could run my paws down my sides and over my breasts and feel that I was still myself, intact, and like a chalkboard eraser, the touch erased the memory, leaving a faded echo of raccoon paws behind.

When I came back out of the bathroom, paws pressed together, heart almost at a normal rate. Alexei was leaning in his doorway in a t-shirt and shorts, his red tail swishing slowly, ears up. "You are doing all right?"

My paws still felt damp. I rubbed them together. "I'm fine," I repeated, because the words came without any effort or thought, and because the catalog of things that weren't fine was too overwhelming to parse.

He peered at me, his ears cupped. "You look upset. Your tail is down and you are not looking at me."

His paws and feet were dark brown, not black. His ears were black, but not when they were facing me the way they were now. His fur was red and his scent was musky and he was solid and warm and real. I looked him in the eyes and said, "I'm fine."

His eyebrows rose and met in the middle. "I beg your pardon, but you do not seem 'fine.' If you do not want to talk about it, that is all right—"

"Just so you know, 'I'm fine' is code for 'I don't want to talk about it.'" That wasn't strictly true. I did want to talk about it, but there weren't many people in the world I could talk to. Alexei wasn't one of them. Athos wasn't even one of them.

When I moved toward my door, Alexei took a step forward. "One thing I have learned this summer is that it is better to talk about a thing than not. Your friends will understand. I did not think you would believe me, about Konstantin."

"I didn't," I reminded him. "I don't."

"No, but Sol did, and—and you saw that I was in trouble and you helped."

"I'm not sure I did, to be honest. You guys are both still all ghost-sick."

He glanced back at their room, reminding me of the portrait of Niki. "Sol is, perhaps. I am not. I have not had a dream of Konstantin since that night." His voice held a wistful note and it pissed me off.

"I thought you got rid of him." The crazy notion occurred to me that I might be able to exorcise my ghosts, if the ritual were something that had a psychological effect. Of course, that was ridiculous, I told myself. I would have to believe they were real in order to believe the exorcism would work. I couldn't just fool myself. It's like trying to tickle yourself. If you're expecting it, it doesn't work at all.

Alexei smiled and met my eyes. "Are you sure you wish to talk about this?"

"It's fine, fox-boy, just tell me."

"Well," he said, "Konstantin no longer wishes me to join him in the after-world. But he has told me he will still watch me and perhaps see me in dreams."

"Wow. Hey, aren't you worried about a homophobic make-believe ghost being upset at you popping your cherry with a big male ram?"

"Cherry?" He tilted his head.

"It's an expression. Never mind, it was…" I shook my head.

"Konstantin understands that my life is my own, and he watches only." Alexei clucked his tongue.

"That seems like a harmless enough psychosis," I said. "Congrats, at least one of us is doing all right."

He got the steepled eyebrows look of concern again and said, "Please, talk to someone. It need not be me."

"I'll be fine." And I was feeling better, here in my home with Alexei nearby and a relaxing cookie not ten feet away. "I'm going to call someone."

"Your parents?"

Alexei was like that, a fox who'd grown up with shitty, abusive parents who was always trying to get me and Sol to be closer to ours. But in this case, I think he was close to right. Mom and Dad knew about my creepy night, them and Dr. Wallace, but I sure as *hell* wasn't going to call *him*. Mom and Dad might tell me to go back to him, but I didn't have to listen to them.

"Yeah," I said. "I'll call them right now."

I didn't, though, not right away. First I went into my bag and found one of Athos's remaining cookies and chucked it in my mouth. Second I put on some music and paced the room for twenty minutes until I felt the pot kick in. Third I fell down on my bed and waited for it to kick in more, only it didn't, and I was still sort of shaking, so I took another cookie. Finally I felt okay enough to call my parents.

And then of course they didn't answer. I looked at the time as I hung up the phone—twelve-thirty in the morning. How had it gotten so late? Bellie and I had gone to the bar at ten when her shift was over, we'd only been there forty-five minutes at most, and then...then we'd been at her place for fucking ever. The pot helped me replay that whole miserable scene in my head in slow motion, until I fired up my computer and put on an episode of "Top Chef" to distract myself.

But wow, even though I'd seen this episode before, I couldn't follow it. The host, this smarmy ringtail, took forever to introduce the contestants, and I swear he switched languages at one point. And then one of the contestants looked like a rabbit, but she had blue fur?

My phone rang, and I picked it up. "Hello?"

"Meg?" My mother's voice, sleepy. "What's wrong?"

"Mom?"

"It's me, honey. What's wrong? You called us."

"I did?"

Her voice sharpened. "Are you all right?"

"I'm just stoned, Mom."

"All right." Relief. "Why did you call us?"

"I keep thinking about that night, about Margie and William. I'm fine, I just, I need you to tell me it's not real, that I'm not crazy."

"Oh, honey." She sounded worried again. "Did you see something again? I'll call Dr. Wallace's office for you. You can come down this weekend."

"No." Even in my increasingly dissociative state, I held on firmly to the things I knew I did not want. "No Dr. Wallace. He's a fucking creeper."

"He helped you."

"He drugged the shit out of me. And I think he wanted to rape me."

"Meg!"

"I'm sorry. I don't know why I said that. But no Wallace. I didn't *see* anything, I keep thinking about it is all. Just—just tell me I'm okay, Mom."

"You're fine. What you saw isn't real. You know that."

The words helped, a lot more than I thought they would. I don't know if it was just being high, but I really trusted her. "Okay."

"Is the pot helping?"

"Yeah."

She breathed across the phone. "Good. Can we come up and see you this weekend?"

"I really don't think so."

"We're worried about you. Isn't there a place around Vidalia you'd like to visit that we could take a drive to?"

I closed my eyes. The vision of a lake swam into my head, clean and pure with a forest along one bank. "Immaculate Lake," I said.

Mom hummed. "I don't know that one," she said. "But we'll look it up."

"I saw it in a dream." I opened my eyes and the ceiling stared down at me. "Seriously, Mom, I'm fine, you don't have to come up."

"We want to. You never answer our calls, and now you need us, so we're coming up."

And that was that. Really a typical conversation with Mom, which is why I tried to avoid them as much as possible. I dropped the phone over the side of the bed and the last thing I remember thinking was, *No matter what she says, I'm not going to that damn art school.*

Chapter 16

"We've only got three minutes left," Hannah whispered.

Vanessa's fingers teased inside Hannah's ear. "Hold still," the other otter hissed. "I can't get it attached if you keep moving."

"It tickles."

The sun emerged from a cloud, shining through branches and hanging garlands of moss into shimmering patches of white on the water that made Hannah squint and move her gaze up to where Vanessa's house rose before them, elegant ancient water oak logs held in place by a sophisticated invisible system of plastic connectors. The above-water part glistened in the sun, and below the water, the logs gleamed pristinely amid the green algae-covered foundations. Hannah stared at the logs and the intricate designs on them, calligraphic carvings of Bible verses that she knew well enough to identify by the initial flowery letter and the shapes of the words, even though she was too far to actually read them. The grand "T" in the shape of a cypress tree began the verse from Isaiah: "They shall not hunger or thirst; neither shall the heat nor sun smite them: for he that hath mercy on them shall lead them, even by the springs of water shall he guide them."

She read those words to herself as Vanessa's fingers tickled the inside of her ear and the implanted mechanism that allowed her to communicate with Angeline. "Are you sure this is going to work?"

"It worked for me," Vanessa replied, "and stop distracting me."

"But this Vilan person…"

"He's a red wolf."

"This red wolf, then." Hannah flinched as Vanessa's claws brushed her ear fur.

"Hold still!" Vanessa kicked herself closer, pressing Hannah into the trunk of the cypress tree. Branches above them quavered and trembled.

"I can do it myself." Hannah's protest subsided as she felt Vanessa's weight against her, the otter's arm pressing in on her breast. She thought again about her dream and the discomfort of having someone else touch her there, and how she felt none of that now, only excitement and a quickening of her breath and pulse.

"Almost got it." There was a very loud click and then the touch and the weight lifted from Hannah. "There."

Hannah reached up to touch her ear as Vanessa swam around in front of her, a big smile flaring her whiskers out. "Is it working?"

Vanessa came a little closer and put her paws on Hannah's shoulders. "Let's see." She touched her nose to Hannah's, and her breath came warm across Hannah's lips.

The echoes of Hannah's dream swirled through her thoughts like a chill current. "I..." She met Vanessa's eyes.

"Don't you want to try this?" Vanessa waited, her paws warm on Hannah's shoulders.

A cloud moved over the sun again, bringing a chill breeze between them. "I do," Hannah said. "I just had this weird dream."

But the dream had been with a raccoon, and Hannah had felt different, as though she were another person, not Hannah here with Vanessa.

"Dreams!" Vanessa laughed. "I've had dreams. They're nothing to be worried about. Tell me about it."

"It was silly," Hannah said. She reached out tentatively and put her paws on Vanessa's sides. Beneath the sheer wet fabric of the dress, her fingers closed around ribs and warm muscle.

Her friend smiled and moved closer, barely a paw's breadth separating their bodies now. "Tell me. I want to hear."

Hannah exhaled. "I was in a cold, dry apartment. I was there with a raccoon girl."

"Raccoons." Vanessa smiled. "The masks and the tails, right?"

"Her mask was cute," Hannah said. "I don't remember the tail so much, but it was pretty. But she was touching me..."

"Oh?" The smile grew across Vanessa's muzzle until Hannah thought she was looking at a reflection of herself at her happiest.

"But it wasn't—it wasn't like it is with us." Hannah breathed in. "It wasn't nice."

Vanessa frowned. "That's not a good dream."

"No. I was afraid, in the dream. Oh, not afraid, I suppose, but uncomfortable, like I didn't belong."

The reflection of happiest Hannah faded. "You belong," Vanessa said in an urgent whisper. "Don't let the dreams scare you. You belong here with me, and there's nothing wrong with us. Even when we're married, we can still see each other and give ourselves the pleasures of God we can't get from our husbands. Marie told me so, and Vilan says in the North, girls like us live openly and nobody says they have the Devil in them."

Like us. Hannah pulled the words close and held them to her heart even as they made her shiver.

Vanessa misinterpreted her shiver—or maybe she didn't. "Don't be afraid." She spoke as softly as the leaves above them. "You don't feel the touch of God when you look at boys, do you?" Hannah shook her head. Vanessa smiled and raised a paw from the water to place it on Hannah's breast.

Sparks, fire, a rapturous pleasure coursing through her. Hannah gasped, digging back against the cypress to steady herself, and her head tilted back. She looked up and up the great tree, its branches swaying slowly in the wind. Light filtered through the leaves, glowing softly. This must be what angels' wings sounded like.

"And now?" Vanessa's smile told Hannah that she already knew the answer.

"Uh-huh," Hannah gasped. She felt light and warm, as though she might glow and rise from the water to swim through air. This pleasure was what she'd been taught was God's gift, and if Vanessa's touch brought it to her, how could that be wrong?

Vanessa came closer, and now Hannah leaned forward eagerly to press their lips together, hot and wet, and she closed her eyes to better see the glow inside her. Vanessa's body pinned her to the tree and Hannah threw her arms around her friend, transported by the joy. God was great, God was good, and she understood that deep inside her in a way she never had before.

"Vanessa," she breathed when her friend pulled her head back, her smile brighter than the sun glinting in her eyes.

"Hannah!"

Angeline's voice knifed through the still air. Hannah and Vanessa froze. "What are you doing?" the older otter demanded, and the splash of hurried swimming filled the air.

The two otters separated, Hannah still breathing hard. Angeline was kicking up a froth in the water, approaching at unnatural speed. "I'm not doing anything," Hannah murmured.

"Turn your earpiece on this instant." The companion spoke clipped and cold, very unlike her normal speech.

Hannah reached up to disable the small device Vanessa had added, praying that the motion would escape notice, but as soon as Angeline arrived beside Hannah, her fingers pushed Hannah's head to one side and fluttered in her ear. It didn't tickle.

"Ow!" Hannah squirmed.

"There." With a snap that made Hannah wince, Angeline pulled the small mechanism free. She held it up in front of her, then turned her disdainful eyes on Vanessa. "Where did you get this?"

"The air crackled."

"I...I found it," Hannah said meekly, but Angeline did not so much as look at her.

"Where did you get it?" She shook it in the direction of Vanessa, who had retreated but was now holding her ground. "And how dare you touch my Hannah with it? She could have been infected, could have gotten ill..."

"There's no illness on them," Vanessa reached up to her own ear. Her voice was not quite as cold as Angeline's, but it was close. "And you are intruding on private property where you were specifically forbidden. Nephaline! Come here now. I need you."

"The safety of my charge overrides everything," Angeline replied. "I am not surprised you are unacquainted with that rule."

"I know it well," Vanessa said. "Hannah, were you in any danger?"

"No," Hannah said. "At least..." Vanessa's eyes drew out echoes of God's gift, and she trembled. "No, I was not in danger."

"You're clearly frightening Hannah." Angeline gripped Hannah's arm and attempted in vain to pull her away from the cypress trunk. "And Hannah, you may not have felt danger, but I have seen many of your family grow up, and I can recognize danger better than you can, especially to your soul."

Vanessa's eyes kept flicking toward the house, and then without warning she lunged at Angeline. "Don't hurt me!" she cried.

Angeline raised a paw to defend herself, gripping Vanessa's shoulder. Vanessa fell back and cried out, "Help! Help!"

The air crackled. Hannah only saw Vanessa fall free of Angeline's grip, down into the water, and she thought for a moment that her friend had been shot. She screamed, and only as she dove to help Vanessa did she see in a flash Angeline's arm held up against the bright sky, the paw dangling grotesquely limp from a smoking half-severed wrist.

Vanessa's arms reached out and clung to hers as Hannah surfaced, pulling her friend with her. "Are you hurt?" she half-sobbed.

"She's not hurt," Angeline snapped, too loudly.

"Vanessa, Vanessa!"

"I'm fine." Vanessa reached up and patted Hannah's shoulder. "Thank you for rescuing me."

Another voice rang across the water. "Release Vanessa now."

"Nephaline, it's me," Hannah called. She looked past Angeline and there was Vanessa's companion, a silver tube extending from her paw.

"It's all right, Neph," Vanessa said. "There's no more danger."

"Are you sure?" The silver tube retracted into the companion's paw, vanishing as quickly as a sun-sparkle on rippling water and leaving the paw perfectly ordinary-looking.

"I'm sure," Vanessa said.

Hannah, meanwhile, had turned to Angeline, who was examining her own ruined wrist and paw. Wires and a half-melted silver tube were visible below the fur. "Bother," Angeline said. "Come, Hannah. We must go to the shop for a repair. It will be charged to your family, Miss Holywater."

"Of course." Vanessa smiled at Hannah as Nephaline drew close to her, floating protectively between Vanessa and the other two. "Please give Mr. Morningdew my regards. Good-bye, Hannah. Thank you for the visit."

Hannah hesitated. "Good-bye," she said, trying to think of a way she could convey all the feelings she wanted to without Angeline or Nephaline hearing what she meant.

Hannah. Now! Angeline's voice snapped.

She jumped and followed her companion across the water. The only time she dared to turn, Vanessa had her head down, no doubt being lectured silently by Nephaline.

"I think you shall be forbidden from visiting the Holywaters until further notice," Angeline said abruptly as they got into their skimmer at the front of the house. It started automatically as they entered, and pulled out into the open water once their harnesses latched.

As they hummed away, Hannah looked back again at the house. Even though her friend was hidden from sight, she felt the same warm glow she'd felt a moment ago. She would send Vanessa a message when she got home. At least she could see her in church once a day and in finishing school three days a week, even if they couldn't talk much then.

"You shall never be completely sheltered from heretical ideas," Angeline went on. "The important thing is that you recognize them for what they are and do not fall prey to them. I am preparing a report for your father."

"Oh, no!" Hannah cried, and reached out to grasp Angeline's arm. As always, her companion was steady and firm. "Please don't tell Father. I—I know it was wrong, but she's my friend."

The skimmer made its way independently through the channels of the bayou, passing small aboveground houses and larger partly-submerged ones. Usually Hannah liked to look at all the different places people lived, how the grand, rich otter and muskrat and beaver families lived in tune with the water and how the raccoons and foxes and squirrels lived awkwardly over and around it, as though afraid of it. But now she saw only Vanessa's face and the face of her father, the fury of one of his sermons gripping him. When Angeline remained silent, Hannah said, "I know what Father will say. He'll say the Devil comes in pleasing guises. He'll tell me that the path of the righteous is rarely simple, that the clear, bright water often disguises dangers beneath. I—I know all that. I made a mistake, that's all. I didn't know what Vanessa intended when she took me back there."

That, at least, was true enough that she could put her heart into it. Angeline paused the skimmer at a clearing and turned to Hannah. Her eyes looked perfectly alive, unless they caught the sun at the right angle, and then the curve of the lenses behind them flashed crescents through the irises, as they did now. "Your father will ask why I had to replace my wrist."

"Not if you charge the Holywaters for it."

Hannah held her breath as Angeline considered. She was not so worried for herself; if her father gripped her shoulders and shouted the Lord's words at her, it was no more than she was used to. But if he were told, then Vanessa's parents would be told as well, and then Vanessa might be in the most serious trouble they'd yet been in—and that was saying something. Nephaline she was not worried about, because Vanessa had proven adept at handling her companion—a skill Hannah had tried to learn from her with middling success.

But now, Angeline studied her and then said finally, "While my wrist is being replaced, we will have a conversation about what happened. You will tell me everything, and I will decide whether you have learned enough."

"Yes, yes," Hannah said eagerly, and so she sat in a private office at the back of the repair shop and Angeline talked into her ear while Mr. Morningdew worked on her wrist. She told her companion an abridged version of what had happened, only that Vanessa had put the device into her ear and then had kissed her, that it had felt good but that Hannah knew it was wrong.

Why is it wrong? Angeline said, and Hannah had that answer ready too.

"Because God's gift binds male to female, and is the light that brings kits into the world. Two males or two females cannot bring kits forth, so whatever they feel cannot be God's gift, but the mimicry of the Devil. For the Devil has learned to disguise his temptations, like the red berries of the skimmia that look delicious but will kill if eaten."

What does that mean?

Here, Hannah was on shakier ground. "It means…it means that God's union is the family blessed by the church. And that I should be patient and wait for God's gift to show itself with Matthew." But it hadn't, not once, and the feelings with Vanessa had been so vital, so wonderful, that Hannah thought they could not possibly come from the Devil.

As she recited her lessons, though, doubt crept in. Was not the whole idea of mimicry to make something indistinguishable? She was no expert in temptation. What if Vanessa really was in danger of losing her soul? What if Hannah was, too?

And what have you learned?

This one was easy. "To trust the Bible and my father and you."

Instead of?

"My own experience. I am young and easily fooled."

She had spoken these words many times, and yet she had never really quite believed them. What all of her transgressions had in common was that she had known full well what she was doing at the time, though she pled ignorance and naïveté after the fact. If it had not been for the giddy flush she still felt from Vanessa's kiss, this part of the conversation would have been positively boring.

Angeline was quiet for several minutes, so Hannah said timidly, "How is your wrist?"

Mr. Morningdew will be done in another fifteen minutes. Sit quietly and meditate on Scripture.

Hannah pressed her paws together so that the fingers of one pressed into the webbing of the other and closed her eyes. Her breast tingled where Vanessa had touched it. She prayed to God for the wisdom to choose the right path.

Chapter 17

I didn't exactly wake up with a hangover, but it felt like I was dredging my mind out of mud the next morning. The first thing I did was stumble to the kitchen to get some water and then look to see if Sol or Alexei had left any instant coffee around. Fuck. I was going to have to go out.

It wasn't until I was staring at the cupboard that I really thought about the dream I'd had. It had remained stuck in my mind with the fixed clarity that the last couple Hannah dreams had, but I was too groggy to really process it. In a way, it felt like a movie I was watching rather than a dream my own subconscious had generated.

When I did poke at the memories, Hannah and Vanessa under the cypress getting caught by that companion otter-droid, and the stern religious scolding, well, I wondered briefly if I could file a complaint against my subconscious for abuse. I mean, shit, it wasn't enough it had punished me for fucking up the evening with Bellie by dredging up my number one all time least favorite memory? It had to feed me this shit on top of it all, not just replaying being interrupted but having the character in my dream *remember my evening* and show me up by enjoying a lesbian kiss?

Little Hannah, a rebel in just the right way, whose body responded the way mine was supposed to and who was willing to risk censure and who knew how to get around authority figures somewhat diplomatically. Hannah, who had someone she cared about who made her body feel right, who had an oppressive church to fight against in some future Christian cult, who was given my experiences as a dream to dismiss, who felt the "touch of God" when a girl she loved touched her, who didn't just feel uncomfortable and scared. Hannah, who said the right thing all the time and didn't blurt out that she wasn't a lesbian in the middle of getting felt up by another woman who, however clumsily, was only trying to help.

I didn't like Hannah very much right now. I resolved that Marie-Belle was not going to have any amorous scenes with Pierre in my comic, or if she did, she wasn't going to enjoy them. The decision felt so easy that I wasn't sure the alternative had ever been an option.

"What are you looking for?"

Alexei had opened his door so quietly that I'd barely noticed, or else I'd been so deep in my fucking head that my ears had cut off. "A clue," I grumbled. "Or coffee."

"We don't drink coffee here," he said. "Sol and I sometimes get it on the way to work."

"Yeah, I know. I thought I remembered seeing it…" Though now that I thought of it, I was picturing the cupboards at my parents' house. "Forget it. I'll go out."

"Do you want company?"

I squinted. His bedroom window limned his red fur with gold and I couldn't quite read his expression. "Don't you have to go to work? It's Tuesday, right, or did I sleep for four days?"

"It is Tuesday," he said agreeably, "but it is early. I can walk for coffee and still catch my bus."

"Okay. You need to shower?"

He shrugged. "I am clean and I move boxes all day. I will be ready in five minutes."

So I took him with me down toward Riverwalk, intending to hit one of the coffee shops that wasn't the Café La Croix. The company was nice because I hadn't seen him much and because getting him to talk about his evening with Mike was easy and let me take my mind off Bellie and Hannah.

"He cooked dinner," he said, "and he brought chicken for me though I said I didn't need it."

I let him go on about the roast chicken and the succotash and the dinner rolls while we walked past the construction site and into the quiet residential neighborhood. "Dinner was great, I get it," I said. "So how about after dinner?"

He laughed and bumped his shoulder against mine. "You have never asked about this kind of thing before."

"You've never done anything like this."

"No." He grinned at me through half-lidded, canny eyes. "But Sol has and he tells me you never ask."

Damn. "Maybe I'm just not interested in *his* sex life."

"I will not tell him."

I had little idea why I was asking. Partly it was probably because Sol was gone. But partly, too, it was the dream working on me. I wanted to know how healthy people pursued relationships. Was it like what Hannah had done in my dream? When I didn't care about sex or anything like that, it was easy to ignore. Now, even if I didn't want to *do* it, I needed to know *about* it.

So Alexei went on to describe in very vague terms how Mike had been gentle and considerate. "He asked me every time if I wanted to go on and finally I had to show him I did." He folded his ears back and ducked his muzzle, but the smile showed he was happy with what he'd done even if telling me was embarrassing.

"Good for you," I said. "So you enjoyed it, I guess. Did you go all the way?"

"Ah." He reached up and scratched his whiskers. "What is 'all the way'? We went, ah, to the end…"

"Was he, you know…" I tried to convey the concept of intercourse with gestures, and Alexei giggled and pushed my paws down.

"Not this time. He—"

"Hey! Meg!"

Both of us turned to see a pudgy boar jogging toward us. Shit.

"Hi, Chet," I said warily. He didn't look like he was running to give me a hug.

"You've been avoiding me." He glared as he got closer, huffing to a stop. His stocky frame filled out the WonderWolf t-shirt, leaving it hanging over his baggy jeans. His scent rolled over us, and though Alexei was too polite to turn away, he did wrinkle his nose. Chet smelled like he'd been running for an hour. I could only imagine how he smelled to Alexei.

"I've been busy. I had company in town—"

"So you got it done?"

"Not yet."

He snorted in disgust and tossed his head. His tusks showed; he was still panting from running and leaning in toward me. "I heard you gave Corra half off 'cause hers was late and it wasn't done."

"That was a special case."

"Oh yeah? I'm not special?"

"Jesus, Chet." He always leaned in close and talked a little too loudly, only today it was bothering me more than usual. I was also aware of Alexei's interest and the fact that this was the first he was hearing about my job. I shouldn't have come down here. I just wanted some company this morning.

"I want half off too." At least he kept his jaw shut now, his tusks just poking up over his upper lip. "Where's my picture?"

"I told you Monday," I said. "It's Tuesday now. Just—just back off."

"So let me see it."

"I don't have it on me." I took a step back to drain away some of the tension, but Chet stepped right into the space.

"Well, what are you doing then? Why aren't you working on it?"

And Alexei, of course, stepped up beside me.

"Hey," he said good-naturedly but with Siberian iron in his voice, "we are just going for coffee. You can talk to Meg another time."

Chet turned on him. "What are you, her boyfriend?"

"I am a friend." Alexei kept his mild tone. "So you can finish your conversation another time."

"Look, Chet," I said, "I'll message you when it's done."

He squinted at me, his attention drawn away from Alexei. "And I can have it for half price?"

"I can't do that." Damn it, I knew I shouldn't have given in to Corra. She'd probably posted it online or something and now all my commissioners would want half-price discounts if their pictures were late, which now all of them were because I couldn't draw anything without Marie-Belle getting involved, even when I was high.

Chet stepped in toward me again, and he wasn't being aggressive or anything, but his posture was aggressive and his tone was loud enough to draw the attention of a possum walking the other way. "You did it for her, so do it for me, too!"

Alexei stepped in front of me, and the iron in his voice was not as well hidden. "Come on, Meg," he said. "We need to get our coffee."

He shielded me as I walked forward, one eye on Chet. "I'll e-mail you," I said.

For a moment, I thought that would actually work. We got a few steps down the street and almost to the corner. But then Chet's lumbering clomps sounded on the bricks behind us and he said, "I want it for half price."

I turned and glared. "Then forget it," I said. "You pay full price or not at all."

"You bitch." He glared again. "Stuck up art-school dyke bitch."

"Fuck you. Now I'm not doing your picture at all. You happy?"

"Dyke bitch!" he yelled.

"Ha ha. Oh, I'm not that. Just ask around." And then I couldn't stop myself from laughing for real, 'cause otherwise the jangling barbed wire of tension coiled inside me was going to shred me.

Chet raised an arm and maybe there was a fist on the end of it. That was enough for Alexei. He put a paw out and snapped, "I think you had better leave us alone."

"Oh yeah?" Chet glared at him. "You going to make me?"

"Better watch out." I shouldn't be enjoying this at all, and I wasn't, much, despite the fact that I was still hiccupping laughs. Maybe a little. "He knocked a guy's tooth out last month."

Chet narrowed his eyes and huffed through his nostrils. "What, like a mouse or something?"

"Pine marten," Alexei said. "Tougher than you."

"Okay." I got myself under control and held Alexei back with a paw. "That's enough. You're not going to fight. Chet, get the fuck out of my face. We're done. You get nothing. You happy?"

"You promised!"

Alexei started forward again and I tightened my grip on his arm. "Yeah, and you promised not to be an asshole."

He bugged his eyes out. "What?"

"It's a societal contract. I'm sorry I didn't get your picture done on time. Life happens, shit happens, if you can't deal with that then you shouldn't be dealing with artists. So go draw it yourself or get someone else to do it or whatever. I don't care what you do anymore, but you don't come threatening me and my friends, so just fuck off, okay?"

"You bitch," he repeated.

"And if you follow us across the street I'm going to call the police and tell them you're harassing me. Got it?"

He got it when I took my phone out, though he didn't like it, and he stood there while we crossed. My heart was pounding and I didn't let go of Alexei until we got to the other side. "I am all right," he said quietly to me.

"Yeah." I nodded. "Give me a minute to catch up to you."

"We are both right here." He looked puzzled.

"I mean give me a minute to be all right, too."

"Ah." His sharp muzzle gave a quick nod and I saw him file that use of the expression away.

Halfway down the next block, I unclasped my fingers from his arm. I didn't want to look back to make sure Chet was still standing there, but I did anyway, and he was, staring after us resentfully. "Thanks for standing up for me," I said. "But I didn't really mind missing your other fight. You didn't need to reenact it."

He smiled. "He is not as tough as Kendall. It would not have been so dramatic."

I took a breath. "So you're probably wondering what he was talking about."

His slit-pupiled eyes met mine and his smile didn't diminish. "I will listen if you wish to tell me."

I didn't answer right away, figuring out how much I wanted to say, and he went on. "I assume it is not a sex thing, because it would not take so long to finish."

"What?" His ears were up and the corners of his mouth curved in a slight smile. "Are you making a joke?"

Now the ears folded back. "I am sorry. This is serious, this boar has upset you."

"No, no." Two doors down from us, a brown awning labeled "Coffee Time" fluttered in the breeze. "I didn't expect it, that's all. It was funny. Come on."

Coffees in our paws, we walked back toward the apartment. I told him about the art I did and the mostly-nice people I did it for. "I do not understand," he said.

"People want to see themselves as something else. It's fantasies, mostly dumb fantasies."

"I do not think it is dumb," he said, "but that is not what I meant. I meant to say I did not understand why you would not tell us."

"Yeah," I said, "I'm not sure I get that myself anymore. I started out doing a couple dumb pictures for money and I didn't know it was going to turn into anything more. Sol's been pushing me to do stuff with art and if I told him and then I didn't get any more work, he'd be bugging me to keep doing it..." Or to go to that shitty Art Institute.

The fox had kept his ears perked, listening, and when I trailed off, he said, "Is it a thing you enjoy?"

"Not right at the moment." I blew on my coffee. It was about cool enough to drink.

"If it was not for Chet."

"It's all right." If I told him I'd enjoyed it until a week ago, he'd ask me what had happened a week ago, and that was a fish I didn't want to scale right now.

He nodded. "So you wish to keep doing it?"

"That's all in the future. I don't know."

My tone was probably enough hint, because he started talking about his job and how he had been talking to Mike about careers he could pursue if he got his visa approved to stay in the States. "I might be able to go to the Vidalia Community College," he pronounced the name carefully, "in the evenings. I do not have enough money to go to college like Sol, although Mike says banks will lend money to students like me sometimes."

"Uh-huh." The prospect of Alexei spending all his evenings at community college didn't make me happy, but it'd be good for him. "Ah, shit."

He scanned the street ahead. "Is it Chet?"

"No. I just remembered I invited my parents up this weekend."

"Oh!" He brightened. "I will meet them?"

"Yeah, I guess. If you're around Saturday morning."

"Then I will be." He raised his coffee cup and sipped from it. "This is better than the convenience store."

"Not surprised." I took a drink of mine as well.

We'd gotten back to our street and the bus stop, where Alexei set down his coffee cup on the bench and turned to me with a serious look. "You will be all right?"

"Me? I'm fine. I'm going to stay in today."

"You should not let fear rule your life."

I rolled my eyes. "I'm not letting it rule my life. I'm just staying in today."

He patted me on the shoulder, which was the closest he'd get to hugging me unless I initiated it, which I didn't. "There is my bus," he said, gesturing down the street. He lifted the coffee. "Perhaps we can walk to coffee again in the morning?"

"Yeah, maybe," I said. "Don't know how often I'll be up this early."

And *that* reminded me of why I *was* up that early, on top of everything else Chet had pushed out of my mind. Hannah and her robot companion and her memory of my night: my mind shaming me for my failed lesbian evening. I waved to Alexei as he got on the bus and then headed back to the apartment, thinking about the dream because I couldn't not.

I'd read somewhere that everyone in your dreams is some aspect of you, so Hannah was definitely supposed to be me oppressed by something or another but fully a lesbian, just as that robot was my superego trying to rein in my lesbian desires and Vanessa was my id or something, tempting me, or maybe I was mixing up psychology there. But I wasn't sure where the robot companion had come from. I didn't read science fiction and rarely went to see those kinds of movies, though Sol liked them. There'd been a rash of them a few years back with intelligent robots, but it still felt like a foreign thing to have in my dreams.

So I drank my coffee and watched a couple episodes of "Top Chef," and then I decided to try working on commissions again. If I didn't get full price for these last two I had, and get them to agree to pay early if I finished early, I was going to be in deep, deep shit. As it was, I would have to beg for money from my parents to make rent, and the whole art school situation made that a stickier proposition.

All I could do now was draw, so I pulled out a blank paper and my pencils. One commission was for a gazelle and the other for a lion; I started with the gazelle because it was a simpler picture, just a guy on a dragon. The blank page came out and I put the drawing into my head and then visualized it on the page.

But when I touched the pencil to the paper, what I started drawing were the familiar gestures of a muskrat, the sketchy lines of swamp vegetation. What had been the dragon in my head turned into a sweep of lines across several poses, connecting the panels of a comic page.

Chapter 18

Part of the dowry for Marie-Belle is a small house on the edge of town, the ground firm, the water a good five hundred yards away. She and her aunt have been allowed into it for the first time and are cleaning it of the detritus left by its former occupants (Pierre's great-aunt and her daughter, who had both died of influenza three years before) and by its current occupants (rats, mice, and birds, and one fat, lazy ground squirrel, whom Marie-Belle shoos out with shouts of "sorry, little cousin, find another burrow").

But the windows are clear, scrubbed with newspaper, and the worst of the mildew has been sanded from the wood. The old wallpaper will do for now, and Marie-Belle sweeps a brush-broom across the wood floor while her aunt searches for cedar and lilies to sweeten the air.

When the last cloud of dust has been banished to the outside dirt, Marie-Belle reaches into the pocket of her skirt and takes out the packet of tea.

Chapter 19

No! Fucking hell. I shoved the paper aside and tried again, and again my fingers wouldn't make the lines I was trying to make.

Well, great. This was fucked up even for me. Previously I'd at least been interested in the story, but now here I was needing to work to earn the money to pay my fucking rent, and my problem had gotten worse. It was like I was

(possessed?)

No. That's not what I meant to say. I was highly delusional, or there was a disconnect between my brain and my fingers, or I was hallucinating—but a weird kind of hallucination that took over my imagination, controlled or diverted my thoughts into some story that my mind thought was important.

I'd never heard of this kind of thing happening. I'd read about artists going into trances, light or otherwise, and maybe that's what this was. Maybe they didn't report it as a mental illness because they thought that's how art got made.

Or it was like the religious people who had visions. That one made me laugh. Was Marie-Belle the muskrat going to turn out to be a prophet? Or some kind of goddess, and I was the prophet who'd been chosen to tell her story? I'd *made her up* four years ago and my mind was now obsessed with her because…because I was going back to that four-years-ago innocent otter girl who'd found comfort in a young muskrat's story for a brief time in art class? Because things were getting pretty fucking shaky in my world right now?

There was only one of Athos's cookies left. I was here, safe at home, and it really wasn't worth risking needing it later. Maybe if I drew out the comic, then I could get back to work on my commissions after. And besides, it was a lot better than thinking about how bad my life was going at the moment. I could stand to draw someone who was going to have it a lot worse soon.

I took the second page and started sketching in the lines.

Chapter 20

"There's more cleaning to be done." Aunt Eloise looks down at her suspiciously.

"Not so much, and you did say I could run an errand later." Marie-Belle holds the oilskin pouch in which she has placed the tea, turning it over in her paws.

Aunt Eloise straightens to her full five and a half-foot height, lowering her head to look down the length of her broad muzzle. "I thought you meant town, or to see your fiancé, but you are not looking toward town."

"I did not say town," Marie-Belle says.

"No, you did not. So where is it you have business? Where are you taking this pouch?"

Marie-Belle closes her paws around the oilskin and does not speak. Aunt Eloise reaches out. "Give it to me."

"It is not yours."

The paw remains before her, insistent, beckoning. Marie-Belle knows its lines, the claw broken last week, the few grey hairs and the configuration of pads, a unique constellation of four ovals. She holds stubbornly to the pouch. "I am to deliver this."

"To whom?" This time, when Marie-Belle does not answer, her aunt answers for her. "To my mother's crazy sister, yes? To the 'voodoo witch' living in the swamp like a filthy animal, the one whose name everyone whispers when they think of our family?"

Aunt Eloise's "everyone" is in fact a small collection of people that Marie-Belle could probably list by name. Bringing that up would not help the argument, so instead she says, "Toutou does good for many people."

"She encourages belief in evil spirits and performs unspeakable rituals with snakes and blood!"

"Toutou has never used blood! And Sébastien is a pet! I have held him!"

Aunt Eloise shudders and withdraws her paw. "You will not swim in the swamp or listen to fanciful rituals or hold horrible creatures any longer. You are to be Marie-Belle Guignac and there is no room for such things in the life of a respectable lady."

"I can be respectable and still visit Toutou," Marie-Belle insists.

"Oh, child, you have learned nothing. The first time you returned from the swamp, tongues would set the town ablaze with rumor. Why is the fiancée of Pierre Guignac going to a voodoo witch? What is wrong with him?" She shakes her head, her frown deepening. "The betrothal announcement has not appeared yet. The Guignacs can end the engagement, and this," she swept her arm to include the whole little cabin, "will all go away. We will be consigned to living in the swamp forever."

"I like the swamp."

Aunt Eloise's eyes blaze and she takes a half-step closer to loom more effectively over her niece. "Nobody *likes* the swamp. They tolerate it because that is the only place they are suffered to live. They swim in the mucky water and clean their fur and hope desperately for the day when they can buy their way to firm land and polite society. For us, that day is here."

"Then buy your way out," Marie-Belle says, "and I will go live with Toutou and you can leave off worrying about me."

"Stupid child," Aunt Eloise hisses. "You are this family's most valuable possession, and we are buying a new life with *you*. But you are a selfish girl. You would condemn your cousins Jerome and Deveu to live in the swamp forever, to marry only swamp girls. You would have Edouard and me die amid the thick marsh gasses without knowing what it is to walk into town and be greeted as equals."

"If you forbid me to visit Toutou," Marie-Belle says fiercely, "then I shall marry Pierre and I will make him let Toutou live in this cabin. Then you may either live with her or in the swamp, and I do not care which it would be."

She knows it is an empty threat, because Toutou will never leave the swamp, but perhaps Aunt Eloise is not thinking clearly or is caught up in Marie-Belle's confidence, because she shakes for a moment and then says, "Selfish girl!" and her paw lashes out to strike Marie-Belle across the muzzle.

Marie-Belle cries out and drops the oilskin pouch, and Aunt Eloise pounces on it. Marie-Belle grabs at her aunt's paws but cannot dislodge the grip, and the older muskrat yanks the pouch free, bringing it to her nose. "Tea," she sniffs. "Bergamot. Stolen, no doubt."

"It belongs to Toquine!" Marie-Belle lunges for the tea again.

Her aunt lifts it out of her reach. "Now it belongs to me," she says.

"You're a thief!" Aunt Eloise has done bad things before, but mostly with words, and Marie-Belle has grown used to ignoring them. This, though, she cannot simply forget.

"I am doing a service to the world. Go back and tell Toquine that her tea has been delivered to the Church and that we will pray for her. I doubt the Lord will answer such a wicked servant, but at least you will not be adding to her wickedness."

"She asked me to take it to Toutou and—" The nature of Toquine's request almost slips out, but Marie-Belle closes her muzzle in time.

The older muskrat shrugs. "So tell her it has been delivered to the voodoo witch. Whatever you tell her will make no difference."

"I won't lie to her." Marie-Belle keeps an eye on the pouch in case her aunt drops it or lowers it.

Aunt Eloise does neither. She holds the pouch up and says, "You were prepared to lie to her anyway."

"I was not!"

Her aunt's eye fixes her again. "In telling her that voodoo works, you are passing on the witch's lies. Knowing they are false—"

"They are not false!" The words erupt from her and drive her aunt back. "Toutou helps people and talks to the spirits and she does good and vodou works!"

It is exactly the kind of thing Toutou would never do. Marie-Belle knows this as soon as Aunt Eloise's expression closes like the shutters in hurricane season. She pushes past Marie-Belle into the cabin, and Toquine's tea disappears into one of her voluminous pockets. "You will not enter the swamp under any circumstances from this day forward," she says without looking back. "Now, go to town and bring back sugar. You will join me for tea this afternoon."

Her back turns. Marie-Belle pleads, but she may as well speak to the timbers of the house or the large, flat stone that is its doorstep, where she stands after the door has closed. The young muskrat shakes as the rage comes back to her, and for a moment she is tempted to pound at the flat wood until her aunt comes out and relents. But that would be fruitless. Better to wait for a calmer moment and then use reason.

So she walks down the path to town under the bright sun, the humid air taunting her with the water that is denied to her now. This path leads to the Guignac house: this is her future, walking this path back and forth, dirt crunching under her feet, the smell of dead grass and dry wood smoke in her nose, the dust of the town in her fur. The water cannot be so terrible as Aunt Eloise thinks it. Marie-Belle is certain that her mother would agree with her, because her mother always loved the water. She might not have followed Toutou's beliefs, but she loved the old recluse as well.

She can run away; she can always run away. But none of the spirits have spoken to her, and without their help, what life would she have as a vodou priestess? She would be no better than Aunt Eloise's vicious caricature of her great-aunt: a faker, a predator upon hopes and dreams.

"It's a rough life and a dry path, and no mistake about it."

"It's a rough life and a dry path"

The voice startles her from over her left shoulder. She starts, turns, and faces a tall weasel, taller than Aunt Eloise even, thin as a reed and dressed more elegantly than even Pierre Guignac in a smartly cut black jacket whose slender tails frame his natural one, black-tipped itself. Atop his white shirt is a black bowtie, and atop his sharp smiling muzzle is a shiny top hat, circled with an immaculate white band. Everything about him is spotless: his fur, the sleeves of his jacket, the cuffs of his pants, and even his feet. Bare like Marie-Belle's, they nonetheless show none of the dust of the path, as though they simply glide over it. His right paw holds the silver top of a black cane; his left flicks about his muzzle and suit, brushing back his whiskers and grooming his ears, careful of the cigarette whose smoke drifts up in languid ribbons.

"Begging your pardon, sir," Marie-Belle says, "I didn't smell you there."

"Nor do you now," the weasel replies lightly, his smile as fixed as the sun.

She lifts her nose, but it is true: no scent but hers and the world's fill her nose. And then she takes in a breath and all the smells invade her nose in a rush. She smells finely worked wood and varnish, echoes of ale and wine, tobacco smoke and sweat and frying oil. She smells old cardboard and new money, fresh cake and aged cheese, crawdads and catfish and calas.

What she does not smell is weasel. She looks up at him, and because she has just been thinking of them, she knows what he is, if not precisely which. "Good afternoon, Baron," she says, her heart quickening.

"Ah, now you know me." The weasel laughs, but it is not the kind of laugh that invites Marie-Belle to join in. He takes a step down the path, then another.

The young muskrat follows, trying not to display her eagerness. "I do, sir," she says. "Are you here to show me my calling?"

"Slowly, slowly!" He spreads his arms out along the path. "Take the time to enjoy the day. Look, the sun is out, the birds sing, and the flowers smell sweet. Up ahead there is dancing and singing and drink, there is gambling and gamboling and pipes and pipes. The town is not so bad, is it?"

Marie-Belle does not want to gainsay a loa, especially one of the Guédé, but if she agrees, will she be condemned to live there? And he seems so real. Is this how he appears to Toutou? "I like the swamp," she says tentatively.

"But of course you do!" he cries, skipping ahead. "Who could not? Gumbo gumbling in the pot, tea singing on the stove, okra frying in corn-meal that you can smell for miles…the wild bon-frères, the dancing…"

"Will you help me escape this marriage?" Marie-Belle hurries to catch up to him, intent, impatient.

"Escape? What interest have I in that?" The Baron feigns amazement, his eyebrows rising as the lips stretch back from his teeth in a wide grin.

"You…" Marie-Belle's brow lowers and her nose wrinkles. "But you help people. Toutou talks to you—well, your family—and you grant favors if people ask properly."

"Favors, oh, favors." The weasel waves at the air as though shooing away a slow, fat fly. "There is so much joy in life, we merely show people the way to it."

"What if joy is not what they seek?" She thinks of Toquine, whose tea is locked away behind the door. "What if they seek a child, or love, or… or freedom?"

"Children, love, freedom: why do you think they seek these things? Do you think they seek the squalling nights and soiled pants, the debts and worries that come with children? Do you think they seek the jealousy and responsibility of love, the complications of marrying two lives together? Do you suppose that when the slave asks for freedom, she wants the paralysis of choice, the weight of the world, the terror of failure? No, my girl, no. They think only of dandling their babe on their knee, laughing; they think of passionate kisses and the heat of the night; they think of the soaring of their heart as their feet tread the path of their choice." He looks down at her.

She scuffs her feet in the dust of the path as she walks. "Joy, then," she says. "You help?"

"Sometimes." He flashes white canines and the tip of the cigarette glows. "Sometimes there are joys other than those they think they want."

"How do you know?"

He throws his head back and laughs in a grand puff of smoke. "You don't! You must try! Dance the waltz, trot the fox, rhumba the samba, *pas le deux*. One may not be to your taste, one may hold your body like a lover's fur. Do you not like corn cakes? Have a beignet! Prefer pork to poule? Wine to ale? All of them are but spokes on the same wheel, and it goes around and around and around." His paw describes the arc of the imaginary wheel.

Marie-Belle takes a breath and stops in the path. The baron goes on a few more steps, and she fears she may be left behind. But then he stops and turns to face her, the sun behind him in the sky. "So," she says, "I have a friend who wishes a favor."

Brighter than the sun is the light dancing in his eyes. "And do you know how to ask?"

Chapter 21

This time it was not Marie-Belle staring at me from the last page, but the sharp, sun-backed face of the weasel. I'd drawn him in sharp contrasts, clear white in his eyes, deep black defining the outlines of his face until it looked almost like a skull. I didn't want to keep looking at him but I didn't want to look away, and if he weren't staring right at me, I would've said he looked fucking cool.

"Do you know how to ask?" the speech bubble said over his head, whatever the hell that was supposed to mean. I didn't care at this point. I was done trying to analyze messages from inside me, done trying to figure out why my brain was going into overdrive to fuck up my life. Trances and dreams and shadows and lesbians and parents, all that could seriously fuck me up if I let myself think about it. The important thing was that I'd gotten it out of my system for today and maybe now finally I could get down to business.

I grabbed another sheet of paper, but as I tried to draw, my paw shook. I gave it one more try, but the same thing happened, and then I realized that my stomach felt hollow.

Shit, what time—four in the afternoon? I'd drawn for five hours straight? Well, at least while I'd been drawing, I hadn't been freaking out about William or Bellie, past and present traumas.

As nice as that productivity was, it also meant I hadn't really eaten anything today. Should probably fix that.

I took some leftover fish from the fridge and didn't bother heating it up, just shoveled it onto a plate, grabbed a fork, and sat at the table. While I was eating, I pulled out my phone and saw a text from Athos: *Call me.*

Great. It had come in two hours ago and I'd missed it. I chewed the cold fish and stared at the words again. What the fuck could he want now? But it wasn't a message I could ignore; it was an imperative. And the more I stared at it, the more I realized that I kind of wanted to talk to him. I could ask him for advice on what to do with my parents. I could tell him with a laugh that I'm not a lesbian, although if I did that then he'd want to get closer to me…ah, shit. Why did everything come with fucking consequences?

Most importantly, I realized as I kept eating, I could ask him what to do about my rent. Once I got him to stop offering me money, he might actually have some advice on how to get through the next couple months while I figured out if I could keep on with the pot or if I needed to get some blue pills again.

(Spoiler: I am not getting the pills again. Not unless—nope. Just nope.)

So I called him when I'd finished, and he answered right away. "Aren't you at work right now?" I started with.

"I'm in a conference room. What happened with this boar guy?"

"What? How did you know about that? Oh, fuck." Goddamn that fox. "Look, I handled it, it's fine."

"I'm coming down this weekend."

Wow, what? "You are not. I don't need a bodyguard."

"Not just for that. I miss you." Before I could figure out what to say to *that*, he added, "and I just bought the ticket. Done."

"I told you, I handled it," I said. "The guy was bent out of shape and I told him where to go take a flying leap. He went away, problem solved, end of story."

"So that's another commission you lost. Have you gotten any new ones?" The silence stretched on until he said, "How are you going to make rent?"

"Yeah, funny, that wasn't on my mind at all. Thanks for reminding me."

His tone softened. "I can help you for a month," he said. "Maybe two."

"I'm not asking you for money." *Do you know how to ask?* Shut up, I told the echo.

"Oh. Then, uh, what—I mean, do you have a plan?"

I took a breath. "I want to earn the money. But I need ideas. Something I can do. You're smart."

"Thanks."

"So what do you think?"

He paused. "Have you thought about getting one of those job things everyone's talking about?"

"Ha ha. If I wanted jokes, I'd wait for Alexei to get home. Or call Sol. Or just turn on YouTube."

"I'm serious. Get a steady job."

I sighed and walked into the bedroom with the phone. "Want to put more than five seconds of thought into this?"

"See if that coffee shop is hiring—"

"Okay, first off, even if I could go get a job at the coffee house…" Whoops, let's leave out the part where I've alienated all my lesbian friends.

"Even if I wanted to, you know, sling coffee for a bunch of ungrateful shits like me, it'd take weeks to get hired and get that first paycheck, right? Or do jobs let you just walk in and get money now?"

"If you have a job," he said steadily, "you could get a loan against your first paycheck. Or what about that place Alexei works? They pay under the table. You could get cash right away."

I flopped down onto the bed. "Super. I could commute with fox-boy and stack boxes all day."

"It's money. You can't afford to be proud."

"Oh, fuck you I can't afford to be proud. I can afford whatever I want, and right now I don't want to stack boxes in a stuffy warehouse for eight hours to get paid shit. Alexei has to do it until his visa comes in, but you think he's going to stay there a second longer?"

"My point exactly. He does it because he has to. You would do it because you have to."

"Fine. We'll put that down as Plan Z. What else you got?"

"Well…" He hesitated. "What about a grant for your art or a patron or something?"

"Sure. Sounds great. You know any that pay out in two weeks?"

His teeth clacked together. "All right, why don't you tell me what you've already thought of so you can save me a little time?"

"The best idea I had was trying to find a bunch more people to do art for," I admitted. "Which was so shitty I figured I wouldn't even mention it."

"Hang on, hang on. Why can't you do that?"

"Well, I can't finish the ones I've got, so how is getting more work I can't do going to help?"

He got a little more excited. "No, no. You've got room, Corra and this boar guy are off your plate. So maybe you can get people to pay up front, just one or two of them."

"I don't exactly have the best reputation now," I pointed out, trying to avoid the real reason I couldn't take more commissions.

"So find people who don't know your reputation. There have to be a lot of people who want art out there, right? What about that re-creation group, the Medieval Life people?"

"I guess." I sat up in bed and powered on the computer.

"Check them out, and we can talk more this weekend."

"Yeah, okay." I typed, the phone against my ear.

"I'm gonna get back to work."

"Okay." But he didn't hang up, and a moment later I realized what he was waiting for. "Hey. Thanks."

"You're welcome. Sorry I can't be more help, but if I think of something else, I'll let you know."

I meant to go check out that Medieval Life site just to tell him I did, though I didn't know what I was going to do. Post on forums? "Random artist wants to draw you, needs money up front"? Sure, that doesn't sound shady at all. I hadn't finished putting my gallery up online, which I supposed I could do first, but that meant having to collect the scans of the pictures, and some of them were still raw and hadn't been cleaned up yet. So I'd have to do that, and then I'd have to put together the website, which also wasn't quite finished, and that meant I'd have to contact the web designer, and the whole process felt too big for me to deal with right then.

And anyway, I got distracted because one of the first things that popped up was that calendar reminder about the deadline for art school, which had been four days ago.

I cleared it right away—fucking thing—and then started thinking. If I applied, if I at least put something together I could show my parents, then maybe I could get a month of rent out of them. I didn't have to actually send the thing in (but I could, I could send it in late, ask for consideration anyway, because who the fuck expected artists to keep to a deadline?), but as long as I showed them I was trying, they'd help me out, and then next month I could say I hadn't gotten in.

Another month to get my shit together—I could do that. How much longer could this muskrat story go on? No, I'd fill out the art school application and show it to my parents this weekend…

Shit.

I called Athos back. "Hang on," he said, and I heard movement in the background, his hurried, "Excuse me," and then a door closing. "What?" he asked, panting.

"You can't come down this weekend."

"I told you, I bought the tickets." He was recovering his breath.

"My parents are coming up."

"So?" He didn't even hesitate. "I'll be glad to meet them. Have you told them about me?"

"No, I haven't fucking told them about you. I wouldn't have told them about Sol or Alexei except that they wanted to know who I was living with. I haven't told them about anything."

"Okay, then, you can tell them this weekend."

"Tell them what?"

"That I'm a…a friend. How about that? I mean, I've been down to visit you twice now. Has anyone else?"

"No," I said, before I realized that he was actually asking in addition to making a point. Sizing up the competition, if there was any, which he was pretty sure there wasn't, but just making sure, I guess. What a guy thing to do.

"Friends, then." He sounded pleased with himself. "Unless you've figured out something about yourself that you want to talk about."

"Like my lesbian tendencies?"

That punctured a little of his smugness, which might have been just my imagination anyway. "We can talk about that this weekend."

"In front of my parents?"

He sighed. "Would it be easier for you if I didn't come down?"

"Yes."

"Really? You don't want someone there to help you deal with your parents?"

I scooted back on the futon and sat with my back to the wall. "I can ask Alexei to hang out with me."

"Meg, I'll respect your boundaries, I swear. If you really don't want me there, I'll cancel the tickets. But I want to come down. Please say yes."

At least he was asking now. I was about to say no again, and then I thought, what if they don't go for the art school thing? Alexei was all well and good, but he was constantly trying to get me to talk to my parents, and how did I know he wouldn't take their side? Athos at least I could count on to be on my side, even if I told him the truth about the art school application.

"You'll back me up to my parents? No matter what?"

"Yes. Absolutely."

"Fine. All right, then."

I still felt uneasy about the weekend, but the prospect of having an ally perked me up. I might have to tell Athos about some of the other stuff, but at least if my parents got shitty with me, I'd have someone to defend me, someone with a steady job, someone they might listen to.

Shit. I'd have to remind him not to wear that cape.

⌒

I worried briefly that the art school application would fill up with muskrats, but apparently the ridiculous exercises they wanted you to do weren't artistic enough to trigger one of my trances. Reputable art schools asked for a portfolio, but these guys wanted you to draw the same ten things everyone else was drawing, presumably so they didn't have to exercise any kind of creative judgment when deciding who to admit. I drew the building, the bird, and the car, and was just starting on the people (the first was a big lion guy) when Alexei came home.

"Hey, fox," I called from my room.

"Hello," he said, and then I heard the shuffling of paper on the table. "What is this?"

In a flash, I remembered leaving Marie-Belle's comic on the table. "Just a project," I called, tossing the application aside and hurrying out. "It's nothing, I'll take it."

"It is good." He put down one page and studied another, but did not stop me as I gathered them all, holding out the one he was looking at so I could put it on the pile. "Someone pays you to do these?"

"No. Not really. I'm just…just doing them."

His eyes gleamed as they met mine. "There is a spirit in the comic."

"Yeah," I said.

"You tell a story about spirits now? I thought you did not believe." He grinned, teasing me, but there was something serious below his words, too.

"It's a story." I shoved the pages under my arm. "Make-believe. Not real. I was inspired by you and Sol."

He pointed a claw at the comic. "That spirit is not Siberian. It is also not Lutecian."

"My family's from New Kestle," I said. "That's where the spirit's from. Athos helped me research them. There's a lot of spiritual stuff there."

"He has not mentioned that to me."

God dammit. "I asked him not to. So don't say I told you, or he'll— he'll worry about why I asked him not to tell you and then told you myself."

The fox inclined his head, his ears perked forward. "Why did you tell me?"

"You found it on the table. I didn't 'tell' you."

"So why not tell Athos that?" His tail swished, and he still had that grin on his muzzle, the points of his canines showing.

"Why did you tell him about Chet?" I said.

The grin faltered, teeth disappearing under his lips. He lifted a paw to scratch the base of his ears. "I only sent a text over lunch. He asked me to tell him if anything strange happened."

"That wasn't strange!"

He lifted a paw, one finger held up. "It was a *little* strange."

"Only because you didn't know what I'd been doing for money." I knew already that this conversation wasn't going to have any kind of good ending, and probably my best bet was just to bail on it, but Alexei was so polite that it was hard to walk out on him.

"And I did not know if he knew."

"Fine," I said, "it doesn't matter, it's done, it's over. But thanks to you, he's coming down this weekend."

"Good!" The smile came back and his ears perked all the way up. "He can meet your parents."

☙

Monday night's episode at the river had not been a good sign, but with four days quiet since then, I felt more relaxed, more in control. Over the next three days, I tried to talk Athos out of coming down, unsuccessfully, and I tried to draw my remaining commissions with marginally more success. I could still draw—the Marie-Belle comic looked great, lots of energy even if the panels weren't finished—but I just couldn't be enthusiastic about any of the commissions. It wasn't like when I was on the pills; I knew what I wanted to do and that it would be cool, but I couldn't make myself work at it for more than fifteen or twenty minutes at a time.

I did venture down to the Café La Croix once, but stopped outside when I saw Sherine through a window. She stared at me and then turned away, so I knew the kind of reception I was likely to get. I went right back home without going in. At least there I had Alexei to talk to.

The fox seemed disappointed at my reluctance to discuss the spirits in the comic with him, but he did accompany me for coffee every morning. He asked me if I'd drawn more of Marie-Belle, but she left me alone, and by Friday I almost missed her. Diving into her story had been scary, but now it was far preferable to mine. I had ideas on how she handled the meeting with the Baron, and had even looked up the Barons so I would know how to draw him.

That was Friday, and the results gave me a bit of a shock. I knew about Baron Samedi from movies, but I didn't know the names of the other two Barons who were responsible for the world between the living and the dead in voodoo lore (part of the Guédé; confusingly, they were also referred to as three aspects of the same Baron). One was Baron Cimitière (Cemetery), and the other was Baron of the Cross—or, in Cajun, Baron La Croix.

Coincidence, of course. Had to be. I checked the online descriptions against my picture, which I'd drawn from my imagination, and there was no doubt. Baron Samedi wore a skull mask or skull paint over his face; Baron Cimitière wore a formal suit. I'd drawn Baron La Croix, who enjoyed culture and the many pleasures of life. Who shared a name with the Café where I'd done most of my drawing until this week.

Subconscious again. The name had stuck with me, and I'd seen the descriptions of the three Barons somewhere. Only this on top of Hannah's world and the other things supposedly based on books I'd read and forgotten was an awful lot of work for my subconscious to do. I'd been fascinated by voodoo when I thought up Marie-Belle's story, sure. But I hadn't really researched the voodoo gods or gone so far as to think she would actually talk to them (leaving aside that night after Sol had left when I'd looked up voodoo on the Internet for some reason). I'd imagined her running away to live with her grandmother, and that was the story's happy ending.

Still, somewhere in the research I must have looked up the Barons of the Guédé. And then I'd been attracted to the Café La Croix because of some hidden memory? Or else it was all a coincidence. Coincidences still happened, didn't they?

They did, but even I couldn't ignore the mounting strangeness in my life. The Marie-Belle story-trances, the Hannah dreams, the return of my water-shadow: all of them were combining to push me to something. What I didn't know was what. If I ran into Alexei's room sobbing that I believed him, if I clapped my paws and said, "I do believe in fairies," if I figured out my sexuality and relationship with Athos, if I reconciled with my parents, if I actually applied to the fucking art school, if I did two of those or three of them or all of them, would the dreams stop? Would the comic lose its compulsion?

I knew the answer to that, of course. There were only two ways this ordeal was going to end. The first was with me getting control over my mind and settling it down. The second was with the blue pills.

⚭

Friday evening when Athos arrived, Alexei walked with me to the bus station to meet his bus from the airport, and helped carry Athos's bags. The grey fox asked how I'd been, and I didn't tell him I hadn't been to the café all week because I figured we'd be hanging with my parents and it wouldn't come up. Alexei told him about the comic and he didn't ask about the commissions, talking instead about the latest "Top Chef" episode.

We played Uno that night and there were no spiritual manifestations. Athos slept in Sol's bed and I slept alone in mine, tossing and turning with worry over my parents' visit for about an hour. And once I finally got to sleep, of course that night I dreamt about Hannah again.

Chapter 22

Sixteen young female otters floated in the pool defined by the low ring of sedge, each one flanked by a companion. Facing them at the break in the ring, an older female otter directed them. "Paws below the water surface. Float effortlessly. Delilah, your head is too low in the water. Can't you feel it in your whiskers? Eloise, you're making ripples."

"Everybody makes ripples," Hannah hissed to Vanessa. The two of them were the oldest there; Honoria and their other friends had finished with the school months ago.

"Hush," Angeline ordered.

"I don't think your ripples are embarrassing at all," Vanessa said.

Nephaline shushed her as well, but the words had already had their intended effect. Hannah smiled and pressed her paws briefly to the warmth in her heart.

"Remember God's words: 'When thou passest through the waters, I will be with thee.' A lady always behaves properly under God's eye. Marie, ripples."

Hannah's gaze slid upward to the sun, which she knew wasn't God's eye, but which she always felt was watching her. Angeline's presence behind her tingled in Hannah's whiskers; her companion was always watching her even if God wasn't, more so after the incident at Vanessa's.

"Hannah! Ripples."

It was Angeline, not Mother Light, but her companion didn't use the internal voice. Hannah stilled her paws, slowing them to a speed that wouldn't disturb the water's surface. For the rest of the lesson, she tried to forget Vanessa and focus on reciting her favorite Psalm, the 34th,, as she'd learned it from childhood.

I will always thank the Lord.
I will never stop praising him.

"Hannah," Vanessa whispered.

Aware of Angeline behind her, Hannah went ahead with the psalm. She got through a few more lines as Mother Light swam by her, paused to worry about whether the old otter would make a remark, and resumed with a grateful sigh when she passed without a comment, on to Vanessa. "Look straight ahead," Mother Light told Vanessa. "Ears up."

The helpless call to Him and He answers.

It took her nearly the rest of the psalm before Mother Light dismissed them for that day.

The righteous call to the Lord and He listens; He rescues them from all their troubles.

Hannah wanted to finish the psalm, but Angeline was already pulling her away. As they passed Vanessa, Hannah's friend stretched out a paw below the water's surface but stayed silent. Hannah clasped her paw quickly, and when Vanessa withdrew hers, Hannah quickly closed her paw around the small device her friend had left floating there.

Angeline didn't suspect, or at least didn't say anything all the way home other than to remind Hannah of her duties for dinner and the meeting with her fiancé's family the next morning. Lovely, Hannah thought, another morning of floating perfectly still and saying nothing while they discuss wedding plans. At Mary's wedding, she had been somewhat excited about her own, but even that marginal excitement had faded with time.

And yet she still had to be involved in the planning, where "involved" meant that she listened and nodded her head while her mother and Matthew's mother talked about flowers and place settings and water fragrances and the previous weddings of the season. It was important that they do certain things better but not so much better that they seemed to be putting themselves above the others, and the nuances of this, while endlessly fascinating to the mothers, bored Hannah.

Over the last week, she had taken to imagining Vanessa while these discussions went on, but yesterday her mother had asked her opinion about the flower color and whether the dress they had commissioned was a certain shade of yellow or another shade, and Hannah, thinking of the color of Vanessa's eyes, had replied without thinking that the yellows were all the same and nobody cared anyway. It had taken only three seconds of shocked silence for her to realize that she should not have spoken so honestly. Her mother would never say anything to her in front of Mrs. Everett, but on the way home Hannah received a long lecture about her attitude, ending with an instruction to Angeline to make sure Hannah received extra instruction in etiquette.

And that was why Hannah had spent the entire morning with Mother Light with the girls two years younger than her before spending the afternoon with her peers. She was heartily sick of the school and wanted nothing more than to go to the sanctuary of her room when she got home, to climb out of the water and lie on her bed until it was time for her to help with dinner.

She had made it halfway across the wide living room when her father stepped out of his office, black robes draping his stocky form with the blue stole around his neck. "Hannah," he said. "Come in here."

This was not likely to be good news. She had only been in her father's office five times, four times when she had been punished for something more severe than her mother could handle and once when her father announced her engagement. Her paws found the edge of the soft living room fake-grass floor, and she pulled herself out of the water. Her dress's mechanics whirred to life, and a moment later she trailed a damp claw down the dry fabric, dropped Vanessa's device into a pocket, and walked forward.

A large golden cross dominated the room on one side. Below it, on a small table, a large Bible bound in plates of lapis lazuli lay open. In a display case next to it, smaller, more ornate crosses rested next to small chalices. Hannah knew that several of them were relics from the Great Church in the City of Crystal, brought here at the founding of God's country. One was a relic from the Holy Land, rescued from the Flood fifty years ago, but she didn't know which one.

Her father stood behind his desk, his muzzle underlit by the desk lamp, shutters drawn on the large window behind him. The only other light, from the living room behind her, faded, then vanished as the office door closed with a click.

He looked up at her, smoothing down his robes. "You have spent the day at Mother Light's school."

She waited until it was clear he was expecting a response, and then said, "Yes, sir."

"Are you making progress in correcting your behavioral issues?"

"Yes, sir."

This was not what he'd called her in to talk about. Her father thought that this would put her at ease, but she had heard him use this same technique with others: a few easy questions to relax his opponent, and then the real questions, quick and brutal as a summer storm.

"Good. Mrs. Everett has been asking whether we should postpone the wedding."

Again the pause. Hannah breathed in. "I only asked about a color. I know how to comport myself in public."

"Do you?" Her father stared until she lowered her head. "Angeline thinks that you are harboring rebellious thoughts about the wedding."

Hannah glanced reflexively behind her, but her companion had not accompanied her into the office. "I'm not," she said.

"Are you certain? Do you think perhaps that there is a better match somewhere? Someone more suited to your temperament?"

Hannah knew this was a trap and yet could not hold back the words. "Matthew—Master Everett—is fine."

"Fine." He repeated her word slowly, his drawl echoing around the room. "But you would prefer another match."

"There are other matches?" She tried to look innocent. She and Vanessa had run down the list of eligible bachelors in the community and had determined that Matthew Everett was among the most desirable, personal attributes aside. There were two others who perhaps would be considered better matches, if not equal, but she felt nothing for either of them.

Her father looked down at his desk. His claws tapped at his wrist. "Perhaps you would prefer that there be no wedding."

His tone was casual, but Hannah felt a sharp spike of alarm. The words hung in the air. Why would there be no wedding? Only if she were accepted into the service of the church, or given a teaching role; neither of those had ever been mentioned as options for her. "How could there be no wedding?" she asked disingenuously, to buy time. "What would I do?"

"There are positions in our church." Her father continued to look down at his wrist rather than at her. "Your enthusiasm for your new life with Master Everett does not appear evident to his mother, nor to yours, nor to Angeline."

"I was not aware that my enthusiasm was considered."

Then he did look up at her, and smiled. "My dear daughter, of course your enthusiasm is considered. If you have reservations about the wedding, if there is something about Master Everett that worries you, then you would be remiss if you did not share that with your parents."

That might have gotten her to speak, but the echoes of her latest dreams swung in her head. The presence of her dream-self parents loomed threatening, though they had not yet appeared in person in the dreams. Hannah had never had dreams like these and she was beginning to take their messages seriously. Slowly she shook her head. "There is nothing I can think of."

"So you feel the touch of God's gift?"

An electric thrill jolted her. Her father had never spoken of God's gift to her. Even her mother had only spoken of it twice, when discussing her engagement. She stammered now under her father's gaze. Here was the question, here was what he wanted, and she must answer properly. "I... Father, I..."

She trailed off while he waited. Presently he said, "You may speak of it to me without shame, Hannah. You know that it was I who assisted Father White with his sermon last week, in which he spoke of God's love for us and the ways in which He shows us how He means us to live our lives. God's gift is one of those: a lady should feel it for her betrothed, and that is how she knows God approves of their union. If God does not approve, then how can I?"

The light played tricks on his muzzle, highlighting parts of it and leaving others in a sepulchral shadow. For a moment, she had the impression of seeing a skull below her father's fur, and she shivered, but then her father's face returned. "Well," she began, "in truth, Father, I know that God's gift may not become apparent immediately...and Matthew is a good—will be a good husband..."

"So you do not feel it."

Slowly, Hannah shook her head from side to side. "Not...not in the time I have spent with him."

"I see." His paw moved slightly against his wrist. On the wall behind him, next to the shuttered window, an image flared to life.

Hannah gasped and took a step back. She'd seen that image before, the two naked female otters entwined, muzzles pressed together. It had fired her imagination in the privacy of her bed at night, had lingered in her memory during the day, especially when Vanessa was near. The image's caption came to her mind in a rush: *I will always love you, Suzie, no matter what they say.*

Seeing it now in her father's study with his eyes burning into hers, she felt as though she'd been stripped naked and made to stand out of the water in front of class. Her ears burned and yet she could not look down.

"Do you think," her father said with the same casual ease, "that your inability to feel God's touch has something to do with this?"

Hannah swallowed and could not form words. Her father went on, his voice still even and rich. "Where did you get this filth? Who has been filling your head with heresy and sin?"

He lingered over that last word, "sin," drawing it out and holding the final consonant as he held her fixed with his eyes. Still she could not form words, could barely even look away from the screen.

"Hannah!" He roared it, with all the force of his years of preaching.

She jumped and stared back at him. "Who?" he demanded.

She swallowed again and shook her head. "I...I found it..."

The image flickered and changed. Bright reds and oranges dominated, a lake of fire, dotted with the heads of otters, each one a grotesque horror. Bloody eye sockets on some, ragged patches of flesh where ears should be on others, blackened fur, some actually on fire, some dripping blood from the gaps where their teeth had been and you could see the gaps because all of them were screaming, screaming, and above them the slender-muzzled vulpine face, red and laughing, gazed down while small squirrel-imps pushed the otters down into the cauldron of flames.

Hannah stifled a gasp and stepped back. She knew this image too, had known it for decades in her books and her nightmares.

"You may yet save yourself from this fate!" her father roared. "These are the heretics and the thieves and the liars, these are the ones who turned their back on God. Would you cause your mother and I the pain of knowing that this is your fate?"

"No," she whispered. The otters on the wall screamed and screamed.

"Then who has corrupted your heart? Tell me and you may be delivered!"

Her mouth worked but no sound came out. Her father glared a moment longer, and then the image vanished and the desk lamp went out as well. The lines of light beyond the shutters glowed ghostly in the air. "Angeline," her father called in his normal voice.

The door opened, and the ghostly lines of light grew into a view of oak trees under a cloudy evening sky as the mechanical shutters folded themselves back with a soft whirring. "Yes, sir?" Angeline said behind Hannah.

"Angeline, who among Hannah's friends has provided her with forbidden books and twisted her mind against God?"

The weight of dread crushed Hannah's lungs, but she gasped out a name. "Amaranth," she said. Amaranth had been married a year and was expecting a kit. She would be safe.

"To my mind," Angeline said as if Hannah had not spoken, "it must be Vanessa Holywater."

"That is as I suspected," Hannah's father said. "I will speak to Mr. Holywater. I know he has had his own reservations about his daughter's mental health. Perhaps this will be the encouragement he needs to heal her."

"No!" Hannah cried. "It wasn't Vanessa! She's not sick, she's not!"

Angeline remained silent. Hannah's father sat down and called up a screen on his desk that Hannah could not see. "You may go," he said.

"Father—"

"Hannah." He spoke the word coldly, without any love. "You have been led astray, tempted near to disobedience. If your behavior does not improve with the removal of the temptation, I will be forced to conclude that you also suffer from a sickness, and then I will spare no time in curing you before your wedding."

Her heart fluttered. The way he'd said 'curing' gave the word a knife edge. Curing, healing, those couldn't be bad, could they? And yet if one were to be cured of something that wasn't a disease...could Hannah be cured of being an otter? Of being able to swim?

Angeline took her arm at the elbow. "Come," the older otter said.

This was the time to protest, to stand up for Vanessa, but what could she do? Her father would believe nothing she said. She turned, head bowed, and followed her companion out of the office. The golden cross gleamed as she left.

Chapter 23

I saw a golden cross as I forced my eyes open, and nearly fell off the futon. But it was only the sun through the window frame. I rubbed my eyes, and the knocking at the door that had woken me up came again.

"Meg," Athos's voice called softly. "Your parents are here."

I saw again the stark face of Hannah's father, his preacher's roar as he condemned her friend to re-education or whatever the hell bat-shit fundamentalist Christian future societies did with free thinkers. And Hannah had stood there and taken it—though I felt a little more sympathy for her, seeing the parents she had to deal with.

I threw the covers off me and hurried to the closet to grab clothes. I wasn't going to take whatever my parents were going to dish out. I was going to let them know that they couldn't control me, that they weren't going to send me to any fucking re-education art school.

Oh, shit, right. Those weren't *my* parents. I don't think I'd heard my dad raise his voice my entire life, not even the time I kicked him in the stomach (I was six and it was mostly an accident). As I calmed down from the dream and pulled a t-shirt over my head, my reality (such as it was) reasserted itself. I had to pretend I was applying so I could get them to give me one more month of rent money. In the morning light, with Mom and Dad standing outside my room, that felt horribly sleazy, and I almost abandoned that plan. Then I remembered that I was really low on options, so I grabbed the papers, folded them up, and shoved them into my jeans pocket. I didn't have to show them, but at least I'd have the option.

Hurrying out of my room, I saw Mom and Dad on the couch talking to Athos, who was sitting at the kitchen table, and Alexei, standing in the doorway to his room. I waved and mumbled, "Morning," and disappeared into the bathroom.

Once in, I freshened up and took a deep breath, staring at myself in the mirror. I could do this. A small black tin on the sink caught my eye, and I reached for it, opening it out of habit.

I hadn't really looked at myself much the last few days, and I found I wanted the black coloring. It went better with the silver piercings. So I scooped some out and rubbed it through the fur on my face, but when I was halfway done, I looked up and got a flashback to Hannah's father's face in my dream.

Fuck. My paws shook and I hurriedly filled in the remaining brown areas. That was better. I flashed myself a smile, white teeth in a black-furred muzzle, and went back outside.

Mom never made any effort to hide her disappointment in my fur coloring ("it isn't *ex*pressive, it's *de*pressive"). When I came out of the bathroom, she sighed and shook her head. Dad gave me his hazy smile. "There's our Meg," he said. "Ready for a trip to the lake?"

"I hope you're not going to swim," Mom said. "That stuff can't be good for the environment."

"I'm not going to dunk my head in the water, if that's what you mean," I said. "I can swim without getting my head wet." The image of Hannah floating in the water almost made me say, "without any ripples, even," but I caught myself in time.

"Do you wear that to the pool?"

"When I go."

"*When* you go?" Mom's eyes widened. "*When* you go? You go every day, don't you? You're getting enough swimming time?"

"Plenty." Telling the truth would create one more thing for her to bug me about, and I didn't need that.

"Every day?"

"Every day."

"All right." Mom sniffed. She turned to Athos and Alexei, the smile blooming again as she did. "Do you foxes have your swim trunks?"

"Oh," Alexei said, "I am not going with you. I have plans this weekend."

"He's going to spend time with his boyfriend," I told the parents.

"That's so nice," Dad said. He sounded like he was already stoned.

Mom added a, "So sweet," and then turned full on Athos. "But you do, don't you?"

"I didn't know," he started, and then looked at me. "Meg didn't tell me."

The parents both turned to me. Mom put her paws on her hips. "You invited him down and didn't tell him where we were going?"

"He invited himself down," and then I had to stop there because I didn't want to tell them why he'd invited himself down. "And I forgot. Come on, Mom, it was like two in the morning when we talked."

"You mentioned the lake like it was important to you." Mom leaned earnestly toward me. "You specified the name and everything. We had to look it up."

"What name?" I could barely even remember the conversation.

"Well, the name wasn't right. It's actually Inmaculada. You must have read about it in the article we found, in the Vidalia Times."

"Sure." Mom would love it if I told her I'd seen the lake in a dream. I was surprised they'd found a lake with a similar name so close, but then again, how many variations on "Immaculate Lake" did there have to be just in the South? "So how far away is it? Do we have to go now?"

"We have time for breakfast if you want. Of course, your father and I have already eaten, but I don't know if you two…I mean, I presume you just woke up…"

"We haven't had anything." Athos grinned at me, and I knew he and I were thinking the same thing: that Mom thought we'd slept together and had planned an elaborate charade to disguise that when they arrived.

"Oh, before we go." Dad took a baggie from his pocket and dropped it on the table. "You said you had a good supply, but this is some good stuff from my guy. Can't have too much, right?"

Athos and Alexei and I stared at the pot, and then I scooped it up and said, "Thanks," on the way to drop it back in my room. I'd been holding off on seeing Rachel until Athos's cookies ran out, and now I wouldn't have to.

After a quick breakfast, we got on our way in their car. The art school application pressed against my butt, a constant presence, but Dad just leaned against the window watching the scenery and Mom, driving, didn't ask about it right away.

She wanted to ask; I knew because she kept asking Athos what he did for a living. He told her about his fact-checking job and they chatted about that. I watched the city disappear outside the car window and rolling green hills take over from urban congestion. Scattered trees broke the farmland as Mom and Athos discussed the state of print journalism these days and then the recent political trouble somewhere or another. While they were doing that, I tried to get rid of the shakiness I felt whenever I thought about the last two weeks. *Hey,* I told myself, *last time things fell apart, you didn't have this much warning.* Somehow that didn't make me feel better.

The pressure was too much for Mom, of course, and when their conversation flagged, she turned from the wheel to look in the rear view mirror at me. "So Meg, how is the art school coming along?"

I shifted on the seat. "Fine."

Athos shot me a look, curious and warning. I replied with a quick shrug. Mom wasn't likely to have looked up anything on the school except maybe the deadline for applications, but it turned out she hadn't even gone that far. "When do you hear back from them? Did you already turn in your application? We didn't get anything about financial aid."

"I dunno," I said.

"I'm sure you'll get in." Dad was still staring out the window. I could see his dreamy smile reflected in the glass.

"Yeah, I'm just thrilled at the chance to learn how to draw exactly like all the other hacks they let in." Even though I hadn't actually applied, I couldn't help it. I told myself that if I didn't act sarcastic about it, they'd be suspicious, but really that was giving myself too much planning credit. The truth was I was too on edge to filter myself at all. You know how when you're reading a book that's like, about tornadoes, say, and because you're reading it you become hyper-aware of all the signs of tornadoes, like you'll look at a thundercloud and say, "That could become a funnel! The air's moist enough." Like you know what the hell you're talking about, like there's ever been a tornado within a hundred miles of your house. Well anyway, substitute "freaky voodoo gods" for funnel clouds and you get kind of where I was. I knew that Baron La Croix wasn't going to jump out in the road or appear between me and Athos in the back seat, but at the same time, I would catch shadows out of the corner of my eye as we whipped by them on the highway. I remembered Sol and Alexei talking about ghosts appearing to them and I had to remind myself sternly that they'd been hallucinating.

Which wasn't much comfort, honestly, because I was, too. What else could you call the Marie-Belle story? Okay, technically, I hadn't *hallucinated* in going on five years. But—going back to the tornado analogy—that was kind of like having your house flattened by a windstorm and saying, "At least it wasn't a tornado." Technically accurate. Realistically? Not much better.

My mother, with uncanny mom instincts, chose that moment to ask, "And the business with…you know, Dr. Wallace…how is that?"

Athos's ears shot up even though he tried to disguise it and look casual. At least Mom remained too afraid to mention William by name (I never asked, but I couldn't tell whether it was fear of reminding me of him or of calling him up herself). Even if Athos weren't there, she wouldn't have said the name. "It's fine, Mom," I said. "Like I told you on the phone. But thanks for bringing it up again."

"You sounded worried on the phone."

"It was two a.m.!"

"Not just about that. Meg, if you need to go back to—"

"Shut up stop talking!" I didn't look at Athos, but I could feel his eyes on me. "I told you, I'm not going back to Wallace."

"I didn't mean that. You're acting a little bit…"

"What? Crazy?" I snapped.

Dad stirred in his seat. "Hey," he said. "Let's calm down, everyone. We haven't seen you in a couple months."

I wished I'd had the guts to stop them from coming up. But I still needed rent money and when they weren't harassing me about art school or bringing up my sketchy past, I loved them. They'd taken care of me, and the whole art school thing was actually their lame attempt to encourage my talent. On the flip side, I couldn't forget that most of the last four years I'd known them, I'd been on the antidepressants. Our interactions had been muted except when I'd tried to slash through the numbing fog with sarcasm.

Athos cleared his throat. "So are you guys getting as tired of political commercials down here as I am up there?"

"We don't really watch much TV," Mom said, but Athos gamely kept that conversation going for another twenty minutes, while Dad and I stared out the same side of the car. When the conversation flagged, I could hear him humming, "All You Need Is Love," and I thought it was very charming and at the same time annoying as hell.

"Honey," Mom said to Dad when we finally exited the highway, "help me with the map." And while they struggled with directions, Athos edged across the seat toward me, resting a paw on my tail. I twitched it but let his paw stay there.

"I know about the antidepressants," he whispered. "You told me."

"I know." I tried to whisper back, knowing his ears would pick up pretty much whatever I said. "I just don't want to talk about it." And I inclined my head toward the front of the car, indicating *with them*.

"Ahh, yeah." He patted my tail and smiled. "I get it."

"This is so pretty," Dad said. We turned off the state road onto a smaller one. A fresh sign in blue read "Inmaculada Lake 5." Trees crowded thickly on either side of the road and the air turned from hot and full of car exhaust to green and moist. Birds skittered through the trees, and once Athos rolled down his window I could hear them twittering as well. "I sigh for the land of cypress and pine, where the Jessamine blooms, and the gay woodbine," Dad recited.

"There's no pine here," I pointed out, but nobody in the car paid attention.

He kept reciting the poem, with small breaks to say things like, "Left up here," or "Two miles to go."

We came up behind another car, a station wagon full of armadillos going about five on the dirt roads, so it took another fifteen minutes to cover that last mile and a half. We pulled off into a small parking lot and got out of the car as armadillo children spilled out of the wagon. They made enough noise for a hundred, but I counted five of them.

"Four," Athos said when I grumbled about the harried-looking parents.

"What?"

"Four. Armadillos always have four kits."

I looked again. "I'm sure there are five. Look." The parents were corralling them. "But—oh, you're right, one is larger than the others. Family friend maybe."

"Yeah." The armadillos chattered away as they walked by us, and we waved to the kits. By "we" there I mean Athos, because I kept my arms folded and glared at them. The parents carried a picnic basket and a cooler, struggling along behind their brood. I heard the father mutter something about the lake being worth it, and the mother saying it was supposed to be beautiful.

Finally Mom and Dad got their shit together and we followed the armadillo gang down the dirt path. I guess it'd been arranged so that you couldn't see the lake until you'd parked and came around on foot and it was supposed to be all breathtaking. And I did stop cold when we rounded the bend and saw it, but not because it was beautiful.

"You okay?" Athos touched my arm.

I swallowed. "You ever have déja vu?" I whispered.

"Déja vu is a phenomenon in the brain. It happens when you see something but haven't fully processed it yet…"

"Yeah. I'm okay." I took a breath and walked out onto the green clearing where I'd first dreamed of Hannah.

There was no mistaking it. The clearing was dotted with wildflowers rather than wedding chairs, and the grass was not manicured. But the curves of the lake shore and the rise of hills behind it, those were unmistakable. The trees were not quite as tall, and the forest spread farther around, but there could not be two lakes like that.

"You sure?" Athos kept a paw on my arm. "Did you eat a cookie this morning?"

"I'm…" I took a breath. "It was in the paper. I must have seen it before."

Mom came up beside us then. "Oh, the picture didn't do it justice. They said they've only just finished decontamination. You know there used to be a DeSantos plant up there and it drained right into the lake. This was a Superfund site thirty years ago and it was certified pure again last month. So nice to see civilization helping nature for once. This was a lovely idea, Meg."

The picture. I'd seen it online, I must have, and that had sparked the dream (How many things had I seen that my subconscious remembered and I didn't? Did I walk past pictures of lakes and voodoo arcana every day without knowing it?). But it had all been so vivid. Right over there was where her bus or coach had parked, here was where the wedding had happened, and over there was where she'd swum with Vanessa. There was the undergrowth, down there the crepe myrtle trees with their purple-blue blossoms, and across the lake was the forest where Hannah had pointed, asking if people lived there.

The older armadillo kit had heard us talk, and came over to us with her smartphone out. "You want to see what it looked like before?"

"Oh, was it terrible?" Mom came over to look. Dad continued to wander down to the lake side.

The armadillo held her phone up. There were paired pictures of the lake, a before and after shot. It had looked horrible before, foul and black water glistening with an oil sheen, the ground brown with patches of unnatural green and fungal black. Beside it was the lake as I was seeing it, healthy green all around, the water a clear, pure blue.

But the problem was that the pictures weren't from where I was standing right now, where I'd seen the lake in the dream. The pictures were taken from somewhere up on the left side of the lake, to judge by the hills. Maybe it had been taken from the factory site, although I couldn't see anything up there right now. The point was, neither picture fit this view. The crepe myrtle trees weren't in it.

So either I'd got one of those dumb Hollywood 3-D cameras in my head that could take a flat picture and rotate it accurately to show things that weren't pictured…

"Come on, Meg," Mom said.

…or I could ignore the problem for now. I let Athos keep his paw on my arm all the way down to where Dad was spreading out a blanket. And that turned out to be both a mistake and a blessing, because Mom said, "So how long have you two been going out?"

"Oh," Athos said. "Uh…"

"We're not going out," I supplied helpfully.

"You're not?" Mom was looking in my direction but I refused to look at her. "Well, at least you're sleeping together, right?" Her smile had a little smugness. "I was nineteen once too, you know."

Athos gaped, but I kept staring straight ahead. "Mom, I have a healthy and active sex life that may or may not include, um." I turned to Athos, realizing I didn't know what name he'd given her.

"Me," Athos said unhelpfully.

"Well, I hope it does," Mom said. "He's young and he's cute and he's very well-spoken."

Athos's ears flipped back in embarrassment and he smiled. "Er, thank you," he said. He was still holding my arm and I was still letting him, and it occurred to me that probably that wasn't helping Mom's perception, but at the moment I was actually feeling somewhat more stable from the touch and that was more important than Mom knowing I wasn't sleeping with him.

Also, if she thought I was sleeping with him, she might stop asking me about it. That alone would be worth the lie.

It didn't quite work out that way. She smiled back. "And you got your season?"

I thought Athos's ears were as flat as they could be, but they flattened back still further at that remark. He disengaged himself from my arm and coughed. "I'll just, ah, help your father get settled."

"He's adorable," Mom said as he hurried off. "I'm relieved, honestly."

"What?" I didn't bother to keep my voice low, even though Athos was just ten feet away with Dad. "You thought I'd end up with some lowlife from the wrong side of the tracks?"

"No, dear, that you got your season. Dr. Wallace told us the drugs might suppress it, you know, but it's been five months. I never went more than three between mine, nor did your grandmother."

"Oh my god, you and Grandma talked about that?"

"It's natural." Mom sighed. "That was always something that worried me about the drugs, that they suppressed so much. But it was worth it to see you happier."

Happier? Did she ever actually see me? "I'm still smoking pot, you know."

"Oh, Meg." She laughed. "Pot doesn't affect your season. Well…" She glanced past me at Dad. "Sometimes it can make it more intense, if you know what—"

"Hey!" I said loudly, turning to Athos and Dad. "You guys need any help?"

Mom gave me a smile, an "isn't it cute how embarrassed you are" expression, and then changed topics to the art school: what it would be like, whether I could live in the apartment or would have to move closer to the school, how big the classes were, and so on. Athos and Dad stayed a little way apart, talking quietly about movies, as best I could tell, but Athos did keep an ear perked to my conversation. When I stalled, he jumped in to tell Mom how much I'd been practicing my art, which I appreciated from a conversation-diverting standpoint, but which led predictably to Mom asking for examples of this wonderful practice, and ultimately I had to grab a ballpoint pen and sketch a picture of the lake.

I got a little bit of Marie-Belle, but I guess the lake was different enough, maybe because I was sketching from life, that I didn't get sucked into her story. I did get the attention of the armadillo kits, asking to see the picture, asking if I could draw them. Mom thought they were adorable, but it was all I could do to keep from smacking them. Eventually their parents called them over to eat and Dad brought out the containers of quinoa salad and tofu cubes.

After a completely unsatisfying lunch, we lay about and I added some finishing touches to the drawing. The sun blazed and the insects buzzed, and when we'd lain around enough, we changed into our suits and headed for the water. The otters did, anyway; Athos remained on the shore watching us swim despite a half-hearted attempt by Dad to get him to come in even without a suit. I was glad to see that Mom and Dad had both actually brought suits. I wouldn't have put it past them to dive naked into the lake even with the family of armadillos there.

I kept my head above water, as promised, and I would have even without Mom reminding me every two minutes. There was something uncomfortably restrained about not diving completely, besides the echoes of the dream with Hannah. I should've been able to lie back in the water and relax in the bright noon sun, but I was thinking too much about the lake and how I knew it, and when I successfully stopped myself from thinking about that, I worried about when to ask my parents about rent. I figured I'd do it on the way back, because then if there was awkwardness, it wouldn't last so long. The problem was that if I just considered that problem postponed, I was back to having to think about the lake again.

And then I turned to the side and found that I'd drifted toward the shore where Hannah and Vanessa had floated in my dream. My parents were farther toward the east side, where I'd guessed the factory used to be, and the armadillos were splashing around in the shallow end. But it wasn't sound that panicked me.

The crepe myrtle trees were in bloom, but their papery flowers even in the shadow looked purple to me, not blue. Maybe that's what was different about the lake from my dream, I thought, and then I looked below them. Not twenty feet from me, a small stand of white flowers with golden stamens and yellow patches on their petals bloomed under the brush at the side of the lake. Their scent drifted across the water to me and I remembered it from the dream, remembered experiencing it as Hannah.

I couldn't possibly have gotten that smell or seen those flowers from a photo. I couldn't have seen them here, and I knew Athos was going to say that it was just a trick of wiring in my brain but it wasn't. It wasn't a trick, it wasn't a hallucination, which meant that it was either a premonition or—

Or nothing. There was no other choice.

And the ripples of that realization cascaded back, dominoes tumbling through months and years of my life, until I realized that I was floating with my back to the shadows at the bottom of the pool—the lake.

My blood turned cold under my sun-warmed fur. I thrashed in the water and dove, my only thought to get back to the shore as soon as I could. My body knifed through the chilly clear water, eyes squeezed shut, and didn't stop until I hit pebbles and rolled out onto the shore. I scrambled to my feet, fell, and got up again.

By this time, Athos was coming toward me. I met him, wiping at my face, and I'd intended to hurry past him to the blanket, but he gripped my arm. "What happened? What's the matter?"

My breath came in cold, hard gulps, and I couldn't get words out. "I saw...shadow...lake..." Jesus, get your fucking shit together, Meg. "I mean, I...I didn't see..."

"Whoa." He put an arm around me even though he was fully clothed, and I didn't care. His clothes and his arm and his chest were warm and I leaned into them and breathed.

"What'd you see?" he asked softly.

I shook my head. "I got freaked out...the water...I can't explain it." I remembered my cover story. "Panic attack."

Those words got him to put his other arm around me. I didn't back away. "Okay, you're out now. Breathe. You're going to be okay." He paused and then went on carefully. "Do you know what triggered it?"

To avoid having to talk about it, I pushed the memory back and forced a giggle. "An otter afraid of the water. Ha. Ha ha. Fuck, I must look pretty terrible about now."

He exhaled across my shoulder, close enough on that side to look at me. "You look fine," he said softly.

The pressure of his embrace still felt good, but I was starting to remember that it shouldn't. It wasn't that it was sexual at all, it was—it was beyond the boundaries of our relationship. I let myself enjoy it for a few more long sun-warmed moments, and then said, "I think I want to lie down."

"You sure you're all right?"

"Yeah." I shook my head. "I'm…it was stupid."

Stupid. I'd panicked over a shadow in the lake I hadn't even seen, a thing that probably hadn't even been there. What didn't feel stupid, what kept pounding at my head as Athos let me go and I stretched out on the blanket, was what the smell of the flowers had meant.

Hold onto what's real, I'd learned. But if the smell wasn't real, then what was? The crepe myrtle? The lake? And if the smell was real, then what *else* was?

I didn't want to think about it. Eyes closed, I pressed my nose into the soft cotton blanket. The sun beat down on my back; water rose out of my fur as vapor into the air.

I might have dozed off, or maybe my mind just went blank, but I know I didn't hear Mom and Dad come out of the water until they were right on top of me and talking. "That water is so lovely. They did such a nice job cleaning it up. Meg, you were hardly in there for half an hour. It's not like you have a pool at home."

And Dad: "Did something bite you, honey?"

Mom again: "Your face looks terrible. I thought you weren't going to get the paint wet?"

Dad: "Hang on, I've got a paper towel."

"I'm fine," I grumbled, without moving. "Just wanted to get out."

"She saw something," Athos said. "But she seems all right now."

"Saw something?" Dad had a deep chuckle. His paw reached down to my muzzle with a paper towel, and I let him sponge the fur paint out. "Like oil? Maybe they didn't clean it up as good as they thought."

But Mom knew right away what he meant. "Saw something? Oh, honey, why didn't you tell me? I knew we should've called Dr. Wallace. I'm going to call him right now. Where's my phone?"

I rolled over as she rummaged through her clothes. "Not that," I snapped. When Mom poked her nose into my problems enough to make me angry, my chest and stomach burned. It was a familiar and unwelcome sensation, not least because it made me angrier, starting a downward spiral.

Athos and Dad stood by, looking lost. Mom ignored me. "I'll set up an appointment and you can come home with us."

"I'm not going home with you." I said it more loudly.

"I'm sure he'll see you. He said anytime you needed him—"

"I don't need him and I'm not going home with you." And then, because Mom had gotten her phone out, "Mom, don't call him. I'm serious."

She dialed and put the phone to her ear. I didn't know what else to do, so I grabbed the phone away from her and hung it up with a quick motion.

Now Athos and Dad were staring at me, and Mom was, too. "Meg," Dad said, "If you need Dr. Wallace—"

"I don't. I don't need him and I don't need you." I was responding to Dad but staring at Mom.

She looked more hurt than anything else, and god I hated that routine, that acting hurt when I wouldn't let her do whatever the fuck she wanted to me. "Give me my phone back," she said quietly.

"What are you going to do, kidnap me? I'm not going with you and I'm not going to see Wallace." I tossed the phone at her, and she swiped at it but missed. It fell to the blanket with a thud. "You can call him as much as you want, set up appointments every day from tomorrow til fuckin' eternity, but I'm not going to see him."

I knew Mom would be the one to break the silence, and she was. "Then we'll find another doctor, someone you can trust."

"Knock yourself out." I pulled my shirt over my swimsuit, wishing I had Hannah's quick-drying clothes. No, she was a dream, she wasn't—fuck. Fuck. "I'm not going to a doctor. I'm fine."

"Meg, honey," Dad said. "We brought some of your pills. Just in case, you know? Mom said you might need 'em."

I struggled into my pants. It was easy to shut out the thought of the pills just as I was shutting out all the other thoughts. "No pills. No doctor. Can I be more clear?"

They all looked at each other while I ignored them, and then Athos came over to me. "No pills, no doctor," he said. "Got it."

"All Dr. Wallace was doing was trying to make you happy. Don't you want to be happy?" Mom asked, and it was probably meant to sound plaintive and caring, but honestly it came across whiny to me. "Don't you want to get better?"

I folded my arms and stared at her. "Get better? Yes, I want to get better, which is why I'm not going to any doctor and I'm not going home with you." She tried to say something, and I held up a paw. "I know, I know. You guys care about me. You care so fucking much that you kept me on those pills for four years. You care so much that you made me keep going to Wallace even when I didn't want to. You know what he told me?"

Maybe I wasn't doing as good a job blocking out thoughts as I'd hoped. Mom had frozen, staring at me. Athos and Dad were off to my left, but only in my peripheral vision.

"He told me that when a kid suffers a triggered depression, which is what he thought mine was, he said that a lot of times that trigger comes from the family. From pressure and a difficult home life. You hear that? Your 'house of love' is what put me on the pills in the first place. So I'm not going back with you."

In the silence that followed, the cries of one of the armadillo kits echoed across the lake, a high sobbing noise that cut through the birdsong and wind. "You're making that up," Mom said.

"Nope." I stared her down.

"You said on the phone that you were making up…"

"About him hitting on me. I dunno, I still think he might've been doing that. He was a creep. But he told me that the likely cause of my depression was family."

"We talked…" Mom swallowed. "We talked about school, about peer pressure…"

"But he didn't recommend you take me out of the school, even after…" I shoved that memory aside. "Even when nobody liked me there, when I had no friends to lose. Didn't you ever wonder why?"

"Nobody likes change," Dad chimed in. "Sweetie, don't be angry at your mom because she's trying to help."

"You're always trying to help. And you don't know how because you never listen to me. I said: no doctor, no pills, and you can't let it fucking go. You think I'm just saying that because I don't like Wallace, because I don't like the pills, because I'm scared of them or something? I'm nineteen fucking years old, I'm an adult, and I can make my own decisions."

"What did we do that was so terrible?" Mom was still trying to sound hurt, but she was too angry. "We loved you and gave you whatever you wanted."

"Yeah, that's right." I was aware of Athos standing there, so I kept back some of what I wanted to say. "Anything you thought I wanted. Or you wanted me to have."

"You never…" Mom frowned, her whiskers all angling downward. "Never brought this up. Dr. Wallace never brought it up. Are you sure that's exactly what he said?"

"You don't believe me."

"Well." Mom chose her words carefully. "You have had problems with the truth in the past."

"You think I'm making it up to hurt you." I reached into the back pocket of my pants. "You know what this is? This is my application to that art school. This is something I made up." I ripped the paper in half and then in half again, and let the pieces fall to the blanket. "There's your truth."

Now both parents looked bewildered. Dad stooped to pick up the pieces, his tail swinging out behind him for balance. "Didn't you already turn it in?"

"Nope."

"Well, what are you going to do?" Mom had both paws on her hips over her bikini bottom. "Just going to beg in the street for rent money?"

"I'm making rent," I said.

"That art school would let you follow your dream."

"That art school would crush my soul. I know you don't give a shit about that, but I do."

"Meg!"

"Hey." Dad waded in between us, paws out. "I hate to see my two best gals like this. Meg, your mother and I love you and we just want to be sure you'll be all right." He gestured to Athos. "You've got a nice apartment, a nice boyfriend, and it seems like a pretty good life. We just don't want you to float through these years when you have so much potential."

"I'm following my own current," I said, "and he's—" I looked at Athos, who was definitely standing near me, ready to back me up. It didn't seem worth it to protest that he wasn't my boyfriend, so I just said, "He's helping."

"As much as I can." The fox smiled. "You're very independent."

"You don't shove me in directions I don't want." I took a breath. "You guys can stay a while longer. I'm going to go walk back that way."

I gestured to the car, and Mom nodded. Athos checked his phone and said, "We'll be back at the car by two."

"We?" I looked at him and he raised his ears and whiskers in a smile. "Yeah, we'll be back by two. Come on."

So he and I went walking and I guess Mom and Dad went for a swim or just talked about what a shitty daughter they had and what went wrong with my karma in the universe. Athos was kind enough to be quiet until we got to the parking area, and then, when I slowed, he pointed. "I think there was a trail back that way."

"Sounds fine." We headed toward a stand of tall birch, and the sounds of shrieking armadillos faded away into trills and rustling leaves and insect wings. I thought that it was nice to have him walking with me, just being with me and not asking or judging. More words surfaced from my memory: *You bring nothing but hurt.*

Those words hadn't been real. They'd been nothing but a chemical imbalance in my brain. That's what Dr. Wallace had said. But what if he'd been wrong? What if William were as real as Athos and Hannah? Certainly my parents were hurting. I'd already hurt Bellie and Athos, and just because Athos kept coming back didn't mean he wasn't going to end up hurt beyond repair eventually.

"You're probably wondering what the hell that was all about," I said when we'd left the road behind too, our paws kicking up dirt on a narrow trail.

His tail swished back and forth, brushing mine on each swing. "Seemed pretty clear," he said. "You've always told me there was a fundamental disconnect between you and them."

"You never wondered what it was?"

"Course I wondered." His smile stretched his lips but showed no teeth other than his canines. "But we never really got to the point of talking about it. Maybe now I'm your boyfriend…"

"Ugh, yeah, about that."

He patted my arm. "I don't intend to hold you to any promises made in heated discussions with parents. I will point out that your mother might have a point when she says you have issues telling them the truth."

I shook my head. "I don't start out intending to lie. Well, except sometimes, I guess. It's just easier to lie than to get into a whole thing with them. They worry about me and I can't convince them that I'm fine, that I know what I'm doing."

"Did your doctor really say your depression might be their fault?" He caught himself. "You don't have to answer that. I know you don't like to talk about it."

"Maybe later. He did say that, though. Or something to that effect. It's been a while." I brushed my fingers across a tree trunk.

"Careful of poison oak," Athos said.

"That's not poison oak. Poison oak looks like…" I scanned the vegetation. "Well, it's not here. But it's reddish and the leaves are different."

We had a pleasant conversation about plants and wildlife that in no way involved parents, shadows, depression, or unexpected things perceived on a lake one saw in a dream. By the time Athos checked his phone and saw that it was five to two, I'd almost managed to forget about the lake altogether.

Mom and Dad were at the car, and all four of us got in silently. Mom pulled out and drove back along the dirt road. "It's really a lovely lake," she said. "Thank you again for suggesting it, Meg."

"Welcome." I decided to imitate Dad on the way back, staring out the window at the scenery.

"Do you feel like talking about what you saw out there?"

"Nope."

So she asked Athos about Port City, and that's what occupied the drive back to Vidalia. I watched trees and cars go by and thought about art. I'd drawn the lake, so maybe I could work again. Maybe I wouldn't need my parents to loan me rent money.

When the dirty concrete buildings made their first appearance on the side of the highway, there was a small brush against my tail. I looked over and Athos had let his tail flop onto the seat between us, and now the tip rested against mine. I flicked my tail so that its tip rested atop his.

He turned and gave me a smile, and I smiled back before turning to watch Vidalia grow into being around us. I was pretty sure he understood that I was still getting used to being touched, and that it didn't mean anything more than that I was stressed. If he didn't, I could clarify it.

My parents didn't want to come in to the apartment, and I didn't really want them to. Asking for rent was out the window, and we were all still stiff and tense. So they hugged me and thanked me for the visit, and Dad said to Athos, "Take care of her."

"I will, sir," the grey fox said.

"I'll take care of him, too," I joked, but only Athos laughed.

Chapter 24

Alexei came back while we were eating dinner and pulled a chair up to the dining room table. He and Mike had gone out to a flea market or antique market, which he'd never been to and had loved. "All the old things that once belonged to someone, and the care that was used to make them," he said, his eyes bright.

"That's super-stereotypical," I told him. "Gay guys shopping for antiques? Next he'll have you wearing rainbow flag pins."

"Kendall wears pins like that." Alexei's smile vanished. "I will not."

"Okay. I think you're still allowed to be gay without one." I pushed my plate away.

Alexei flicked his ears in my direction. "How was your day?"

"Oh, you know," I said. "The usual. I freaked out, Mom freaked out, I yelled at her."

He frowned. "This is usual?" I shrugged. "What did you 'freak out' about?"

I glared at Athos, who put his ears down even though he hadn't done anything. "Why does everyone want to know that? It was nothing—I thought I saw something."

The two foxes looked at each other, and neither spoke. "Oh, fine, tell him," I said to Athos. "You'll do it when I'm not around anyway. Might as well get it over with."

So Athos told Alexei hesitantly what he'd seen, and I sat there and tried to pull the warmth of my kitchen, my cupboards, my chair, my table, into a protective shell around me. I tried to stop thinking about Hannah and Marie-Belle, but as Athos recounted the story, I smelled again the light floral scent from my dream, felt the chill in my blood and the presence under me in the lake.

No, there'd been no presence. I'd been afraid that there was, down there in the deep dark water where perhaps they hadn't cleaned enough, where little pockets of evil still lurked.

"So what was it?" Alexei turned to me.

"What?"

"The thing you saw." When I didn't reply, he said, "I have told you about my dreams, about things that you think may be crazy. Can you not tell me?"

"I didn't *see* it." I stared at the table. "It wasn't like that, and…" I looked up. "I know you both want me to believe in ghosts, but this wasn't ghosts. It had nothing to do with your Siberian bum, or Sol's fox, or anything."

"Then what?" Alexei said gently.

Half-truths were easier than either a full lie or a full truth. "Look," I said, "something bad happened in my pool at home a while ago. And my parents never…they never really got why it was so bad. That's why I was on the meds."

I expected a pause to explain "meds" to Alexei, but he frowned, ears lowering in concern. "You are on medication?"

"Was." I sighed. "All that happened was that I…I got a flashback to it. I think it happened because I went off the pills. It's…I'm dealing with it."

"You should talk to your parents," Alexei said. "They are nice people. If they do not understand, it is not because they do not try."

"*You* should talk to my parents. They'd love you."

"Fine." His ears went back and he looked away from me. "And you may talk to my parents and hear what the absence of love sounds like."

"No, thanks." I grabbed my plate and Athos's, since he was done, and took them to the sink. "Maybe we're all better off without parents."

"I like my parents," Athos objected.

"What could they have done that was so terrible?" Alexei came over to the sink. "They did not understand, so what? They loved you the wrong way? That is better than no love at all, no?"

"Maybe. Maybe not. Maybe in the end there isn't a lot of difference." I scrubbed at the plates. "They loved me just fine, but I feel like I'm not what they wanted and they keep trying to change me."

Alexei nodded. "I am sorry," he said, and patted me on the shoulder.

Even though he was sympathizing, I had the impression that I was letting him down. Mom and Dad had been hurt, yeah, because of me. "I'm sorry too. You know, things just got bad for me, and I couldn't figure out how to talk to them, and they never figured out how to talk to me, and things kept getting worse."

"You will call them?" He met my eyes.

Calling them would be nice. It would be the sort of thing a good daughter would do. I probably wouldn't. "Yeah, I'll call them."

"Okay." His grin came back. "You say to them what you need to say, and you tell us what you need to. We are your friends."

"Yeah. Thanks." I wanted to tell him to run away for his own good, but I couldn't bring myself to do it. "I'm going to call Sol tonight, too. Want to talk to him?"

"Yes." Alexei's tail wagged, and so I put the dishes away and we all sat around the table and put Sol on speaker.

He was doing okay, getting used to classes and overwhelmed with work. He'd already moved on from being interested in whatever guy he'd had a crush on last week, the dingo with the accent, to a snow leopard senior, and he asked about Niki.

"Niki is fine," Alexei said before I could say anything. "He sends his love."

"Say hi for me," Sol said, and I kept quiet.

Until we hung up, at least. "Does it worry anyone else that he's chasing every guy he meets at that school?"

"It's harmless," Athos said. "College is exciting and scary. He's only been there a couple weeks."

"Do you want him to change?" Alexei said with a twinkle of mischief. "Perhaps you should love him differently."

"Touché," I said, and got up. "I've had a long day and I'm going to bed. You two can stay up and talk about ghosts or me or whatever you talk about when I'm not around."

Athos stood to hug me goodnight, and again I let him. "We talk about things friends talk about," he said, and smiled into my eyes. "Don't let today get you down. You got through it, and you have me and Alexei here."

"And Sol not far away," Alexei added.

"Thanks." I wasn't quite sure how much that would help, but I appreciated the sentiment.

"Oh," Alexei said. "Speaking of Sol, he has told me where to send the rent. You have a check for me? It is next week."

"Yeah." I didn't look at him or Athos as I headed back to my room. "I will."

It took a long time for me to get to sleep. Once I was alone in the darkness, I kept wondering, what if it is all real? When it had been all in my head, that I could deal with. That I could take pills for and smoke pot for and understand. This was strange, and while I didn't really give a shit about Hannah one way or another, I thought I would like Marie-Belle to be real, and I really really did not want William to be. But I wasn't allowed to pick and choose, was I?

Focus on what I know is real, I told myself. Athos was real. He had helped calm me and had stood up to my parents for me, which had earned him lots of points in my book. I wanted to think his actions were the actions of a friend, but he'd taken the "boyfriend" label and I couldn't help wondering if he was being this caring and polite because he wanted a chance to sleep with me. Whether or not that was true, I'd appreciated his friendship and company today like I hadn't since some of the pre-Sol days in high school. Having someone stick up for you was a pretty good feeling.

Chapter 25

"Where is she?" Hannah faced down Angeline, even though the companion was taller. Hannah held her balled fists at her sides, her fingers aching from the tension.

"You should be thinking about your wedding," Angeline said, pushing the display forward at her.

"I know you know." Hannah glared up at her companion. "And if you don't know, I know you can find out. So tell me."

"I am not obliged to take orders from you."

"Fine." Hannah's mind turned around. What would Vanessa do in this situation? Threats? No; Vanessa would find a way of getting what she wanted without her companion. "Fine," she said again. "Then I will go ask the Holywaters."

"An excellent idea." Angeline tapped the display. "Now, pay attention. After you are introduced, you will walk along to here—"

"I'm going now." Hannah took off the light jacket and smoothed down her swimming dress.

Angeline stood, and Hannah felt a flicker of annoyance that her companion was still taller than she was. Designed that way, she reminded herself with Vanessa's sharp voice, designed to look down on me all my life. "You will attend to your wedding preparation, and after that there is Bible study, and then supper."

"*I* am not obliged to take orders from *you*." Hannah's heart beat fast, but she turned and strode out of the small room into the larger living area of her house, onto the balcony that overlooked the pool.

Angeline's shocked voice followed her out: "Hannah!" But the companion herself did not appear before Hannah bent and dove easily into the water.

Hannah! Come back this instant. Hannah pressed the privacy button, and Angeline's voice cut out, leaving her in the muffled, insulated underwater world. Her house's underwater hallways flashed by: paintings of the Otter Christ, a family portrait in which they were all limned in gold, a capture of her father receiving the stewardship of the Porterville Church from the previous pastor.

And then she was out in the open water, and sound assaulted her ears: swimming otters on their way to the town center, the hum of skimmers on the surface, the burble of the water purification machinery, a pet frog making a cheep-cheep noise somewhere to her right. She cut off an older couple swimming to town, but she only registered their annoyed expressions for a moment before they were behind her and forgotten.

The Holywaters' house had two entrances, and Hannah chose the rear, pausing to surface by the tree where she and Vanessa had kissed. Then she swam back to the oak, to the large wooden door.

The privacy screen clicked off; her five minutes were up—*this instant! Hannah! Do you hear me?*

She rubbed her paw down the grain of the wood. The section that should have held the speaker for guests to announce themselves was dark and lifeless. She bit her lip and then broadcast to the Holywaters: *It's Hannah. May I come in?*

Angeline's orders continued to batter her as she waited for a response. Finally Vanessa's mother spoke on her channel. *Vanessa's not here.*

Her tired resignation gripped Hannah more than Angeline's increasingly sharp tones. *I know*, she replied. *Where is she?*

Please go, Vanessa's mother said.

Where is she? Hannah repeated.

There was no answer. She pounded the door with a fist, but the echoes resounded dully, impotently. *I'm not going away!* she yelled, but still the only reply she received was Angeline's repeated order to come back. And then even that stopped.

Hannah touched the wood one last time, then swam around to Vanessa's room and put her ear to the wall. She closed her eyes and strained to hear anything in the silence.

Hannah!

She jerked herself away from the wall at her father's stentorian voice. *You will return home immediately.*

She rested her paw against Vanessa's house, then pushed off and swam slowly away.

∞

"When Angeline tells you to attend to the wedding preparations," her father said, "You will attend to the wedding preparations."

"She wouldn't tell me where Vanessa is." Hannah's blood raced with a mix of fear and desperate rebellion. "Nobody will tell me."

"And so you took it on yourself to burden the Holywaters, who are quite busy with their own affairs. 'Who may dwell in Your Holy Pool?'"

"They wouldn't tell me either." Hannah slapped her tail against the chair behind her and refused her father's pressure to recite the rest of the Psalm.

Mind your tail, Angeline said icily.

"If I tell you where she is, will you stop this foolishness?" Her father sat behind his desk, looking down at his display as he talked.

Hannah stilled her tail. "Yes, sir," she said. Her paws closed into tense fists.

"Very well." Her father exhaled. "She's been sent to a special short program for girls who are unhappy. It takes two weeks, and she'll come back much happier."

The bland words might have reassured Hannah but for the memory of her dream-self being filled with horror at the prospect of artificial happiness. "Are they giving her the blue pills?" she demanded.

Hannah! Mind your tone.

This time she ignored Angeline. Her father had snapped his head up to stare at her. "Are they?" she asked. "The pills that take away your heart?" She didn't know how else to describe the confused feelings from her dream.

"Blue pills? Where did you get that idea?" Her father narrowed his eyes. "Do you have another illegal book?"

"Nothing." Hannah's mind spun; the comment about the pills had made the conversation turbulent and dangerous. Her father didn't know about the pills; that was clear. Her dreams were from another place, but maybe they had things Hannah's world didn't. "Why didn't Vanessa tell me she was going away?"

"It happened very quickly. Often children don't realize they're unhappy and their parents have to step in." Her father didn't stand up, but his stare stayed locked on Hannah. "Tell me more about these blue pills."

"It's—I had—I thought that—it's something Mother Light talked about once." Hannah shocked herself with the ease of the lie.

"I don't remember hearing anything of the sort," Angeline said.

Hannah's father flicked his eyes to Angeline, then reached up to smooth back his whiskers before staring back at Hannah.

"You weren't there." Under her father's penetrating gaze, Hannah had to either confess the lie or compound it. "Mother Light didn't want you to hear about it because...because she was threatening Vanessa. She said that if Vanessa didn't behave properly, there were pills that could make her."

"And did she tell you they were blue?" Hannah's father asked.

Hannah swallowed. "I made that up. Because my headache pills are white and my devotionals are yellow, and I thought they would be blue because they cure sadness."

She hung suspended for a moment, and then the current of the room resumed its steady flow. "Well," her father said, and his gaze relaxed, "there are no blue pills. Vanessa is learning to be happier, and that means she will stop making you unhappy as well."

By this point, Hannah was conscious enough to keep from blurting out that Vanessa had only made her happy. She still felt the wrongness in what her father was telling her, but at least Vanessa would be back in two weeks and would tell her all about it then.

In the meantime, she thought, there was one more thing she might be able to do. "Are the traders here today?"

Her father had bent back to his display, but his small ears flicked at her question and he glanced up. "Why?"

"Mrs. Everett said the traders would be bringing daffodils for the wedding."

"It's the wrong season for daffodils," Angeline said.

"Yes, but the seeds." Hannah gestured with a paw. "We must plant them this fall so they will bloom in the spring."

"Daffodils grow from bulbs."

Hannah's father waved at them with a paw. "Take your flower talk outside, please. Angeline, take Hannah to the traders if she wishes it."

∞

Angeline tried to talk to Hannah all the way to the traders, but Hannah swam along in silence, listening to the sound of Angeline talking without taking in the words. Finally, her companion asked, *Are you angry with me?*

Again, Hannah didn't answer, but her thoughts had been interrupted. Angeline followed up that question with, *I had nothing to do with Vanessa being sent away.*

It was harder to subvocalize while swimming, so Hannah waited until they were at the big stand of cypress near the trading market before surfacing. "You broke your promise to me."

"I made no promise," her companion said. "I agreed not to tell your father about the incident that resulted in the damage to my paw, and I have not broken that agreement."

"Then you told the Holywaters!"

"You were the one who insisted I charge the repairs to them. Did you think they would not inquire as to the reason?"

Hannah gulped back her retort as the words penetrated her brain. She had caused this? "What—what did you tell them?"

"They demanded my recording of the incident and I complied."

She fell back against the cypress tree and slid down into the water. So Vanessa's parents had seen everything. "It is your fault," she moaned into the water.

I hope you are talking to yourself.

Hannah surfaced, sputtering, splashing Angeline. "I am talking about you! You betrayed us."

"Us?" Angeline came closer and gripped Hannah's shoulder, her voice ringing in Hannah's skull. *Listen to me. I have done everything I could to protect you. Your father reported to Mr. Holywater that their daughter had given you illegal books, and together they decided that both of you should be sent away. I pleaded on your behalf. I told your parents that you had been corrupted by unhappy thoughts but that you were a very happy girl, that you would not want anything to interfere with the wedding you were so looking forward to. It is only my fault that you are* not *with Vanessa Holywater right now, and I will proudly admit to that.*

"I would rather be with Vanessa!" Hannah cried.

Angeline's fingers dug into her muscle. *No, you would not. You are not listening. My job is to ensure you grow into a happy, healthy wife.*

"This treatment makes people happy. That's what Father said." Hannah knew there was something more sinister behind her father's words, but she also knew she could not ask Angeline directly about it.

Angeline looked from side to side and then back at Hannah. *It makes people behave as though they were happy.*

"Isn't that the same thing?"

Her companion's speckled brown eyes stayed steady on hers, the whiskered muzzle so real that Hannah could not remember when she had first understood that Angeline wasn't flesh and blood. *You are not so stupid that you do not understand the difference.*

Wh—what will they do to her?

Angeline let go of her and floated in the water, her whiskers drooping. *I do not know. Come along now. Let us look at daffodils.*

She followed, but Hannah was sure that that last denial had been a lie.

She brooded over it all the way to the raucous trading post, where they climbed out of the water into a chorus of conversation too loud to ignore. Female otters and the occasional muskrat wandered dirt paths between canopied stalls, fifty of them in all. Hannah tried to lose herself in the curiosity of the different species selling their wares and the wonders they had brought from all over the SCS and the Federated States and even farther, from the islands just south and the jungle lands beyond them.

Even that pleasure was tainted, though; at the pretty beads, the exotic flowers, the fruits and jams, everywhere she looked, she thought of Vanessa and how her friend would have loved the fruit, would have mocked the beads or wondered over the shells, would have disdained the flowers, though she would never have spoken less of Hannah for liking them.

Thoughts of Vanessa drove Hannah to pass by the raccoon selling daffodil bulbs, so that Angeline had to call sharply to her. She bought a hundred of them, which seemed right for her wedding, all the while looking beyond the raccoon and around.

"Whatever are you looking for?" Angeline spoke with good humor, as though their conversation at the cypress had never happened.

Hannah spotted him just then. "The necessary," she said.

"You know well where it is." Angeline pointed.

"Yes," Hannah said. "Why don't you go look at the beads and see if there are any that would match what Mother thought would look good in my fur? I will be back in five minutes."

"All right. Roman the hutia is two rows down. Meet me there."

So Hannah hurried in the direction of the necessary, only to turn away at the last minute toward a booth on the edge of the trading post where a lanky red wolf in a faded blue jacket and white undershirt leaned against a tree watching the customers that crowded the other tables.

His ears perked up as Hannah hurried toward his table, and he reached down to arrange the small bottles of perfume on it. "Finest scents from the barbarians to the north," he said in a pleasant light voice. "Smell like Darlene DiComo or Henrietta White."

Hannah reached up to turn on her privacy. "I'm not interested in perfumes," she said. "You're Vilan, right?"

His ears flattened. "Well, I can only think of one other reason a young lady would come to my table, and I'm flattered, but I've heard what happens to Northerners who try to make time with you Ladies of God. I like my bits all where they are, thank you."

"It's not that," she hissed. "I don't have much time. I'm a friend of Vanessa Holywater."

His eyes widened, and the ears perked back up. "Oh. Wait. A friend, or a 'friend'?"

"What?" Her brow creased.

"Never mind. Go on. What's your name, and how is Vanessa?"

"I'm Hannah. Vanessa has been—" She twisted her paws together. "They took her away to make her happy."

"Oh dear." Vilan's expressive ears flipped back down. "I'm so sorry for her."

"Then you know about it." Hannah leaned over the table. "Do you have anything in the North that can fix it? Undo it?"

Slowly, he shook his head. "If she could come with me, perhaps, but nothing I can bring down. I'm sorry."

Hannah's hopes imploded. She sagged against the table. "Nothing," she echoed.

"I can sell you a perfume. Those have been known to perk up the spirits." The red wolf grinned.

"No, thank you."

"Come on. I'll give you a discount on this one. I think it suits you."

His paw brought from under the table a small bottle full of a pale green liquid, while his eyes rested on Hannah. She hesitated, and he leaned forward, his voice dropping to a whisper. "And don't get any on your companion. Unless you're very angry with her."

"Oh," she said. "Yes, very well."

While he was wrapping the bottle, she said, "Will you be here in two weeks?"

"Either here or at the other trading post—well, but you don't come to that one."

"What other one?"

He held out the wrapped package to her. "The one the males use. I don't have much I can sell here, so I spend a lot of time there."

Hannah had gotten very good at estimating how long her privacy button would remain on and thought she had about fifteen seconds left. "Oh," she said quickly, bringing the small device Vanessa had given her out into her paw, "do you know how to install these? I can't make it work."

"Ah." He reached for it, then looked around.

"Not now." She dropped it back in her pocket.

He nodded quickly and raised a paw. "Give my best to Miss Holywater. I hope she is all right."

Hannah wanted to reply, but her earpiece clicked on and she hurried away from the booth, pushing the package into her pocket beside the small earpiece.

Chapter 26

Tap tap tap tap tap.

I struggled to sit up, groggy. My first thought was, *Vanessa's back!* I called, "Just a minute," and then as I toppled out of bed onto the floor and smelled construction dust and the faint haze of weed from the last cookie near my bed, I pieced back together the world I was in.

Hannah was standing up for herself and her friend, finally. Good to know that if she was real, she was taking lessons from my experiences somehow. It felt like she was having dreams about me the same way I was having dreams about her. In which case, poor kid. At least her life was interesting in a "weird future" kind of way. I couldn't imagine being forced to live my bland life through dreams.

If she was real, of course; that was the key question. My panic from Saturday was a memory (had Hannah seen that part of my life?), but a vivid one, and I still couldn't explain how I knew that lake so well from a dream. On the flip side, it was a lot easier to imagine a trick of mind or memory than to imagine that I was dreaming about a girl who wouldn't be born for decades. For years, Dr. Wallace had drilled into me how wonderful and powerful the mind was, how inventive and gullible both.

If it wasn't real, though, I would have to go back on the pills. That was looking more and more likely. And what did that mean for the rest of my life?

Sol's and Alexei's adventures had both left them with relatively undisturbed lives. So maybe I could get through this patch and forget about whether or not it was real until it ended. Whatever it was, I couldn't deny that something was happening.

To put off going outside, I checked my e-mail for any more commissions, but of course no new ones had come in; why would they? The universe loves you, Mom said, but it won't just drop the fish in your lap. My last existing commissioners had e-mailed, probably wanting to know when their pics would be done. Then amid the spam was an e-mail from someone named E. March that didn't quite look like junk. The subject was, "Hi, its Eve."

Eve…oh, Eve from the Café. I sat and stared at the e-mail. If it was scolding me for what I did with Bellie, then I really didn't want to read it now. And if it wasn't, then I could read it later. Either way, it was likely going to take up a fair amount of my time, and someone had knocked on my door to get me up.

Two foxy muzzles turned my way from the dining room table when I opened my bedroom door. "Great," I said. "This looks fucking ominous as hell."

"We were hoping you'd talk to us about what happened yesterday," Athos said.

"What has been happening," Alexei added.

"What is that supposed to mean?" I leaned back against my door frame and folded my arms.

"The comic." Athos turned to Alexei and the red fox nodded back at him. "I hear you've been doing more of it."

"So what?" I slapped my tail against the door to hide my nervousness, the flush under my fur. "I can draw the comic, can't I?"

"Instead of drawing for your customers?" Alexei said quietly. "Like that Chet the boar?"

"You've done a lot of comic pages in the time it would have taken you to do the couple commissions," Athos said.

"Thanks for the reminder. Are you offering to be my manager? I mean, I could use that, but I can't afford to pay you."

Alexei flicked his ears. "Are you drawing the comic to escape from something?"

I laughed, because the comic was what I was trying to escape from, and then I realized that the question meant that they didn't understand what was happening with the comic, and they didn't know about the dream. They thought something else was going on.

"No," I said. "The comic is just this story that I…I need to get out."

"It seemed to startle you, that day in the coffee shop," Athos said.

God, that seemed like forever ago. "I guess. I don't know. I'm surprised I have this story in me, you know?"

"Are you going to be able to pay rent?" Alexei asked.

Before I could answer, Athos raised his paw. "Yes. She'll be fine."

"I don't need—"

"If you don't need it," Athos cut me off, "then that's fine. But the alternative is you getting kicked out of your place, and I don't want that. So consider it a loan or whatever you like, but I'll take care of it."

Great. Fucking great. I pointed at him. "This doesn't buy you anything."

He grinned, lips curving up into his orange-and-grey cheek ruff. "You're welcome."

I had to smile at that. Fucker knew me too well. "So that's what you woke me up to tell me?"

"Oh!" Alexei laughed, and his tail swished along the chair. "No, we woke you up because we want to go get pancakes."

"While we were waiting for you to get up, we started talking about the comic," Athos said. "So...pancakes?"

I was hungry, so I said sure, but then they wanted to go down to Riverwalk and I couldn't think of a good reason to tell them not to; the nearest breakfast place that wasn't there was three times farther away. At least I picked a route that didn't take us by the La Croix, and Alexei promised to keep an eye out for Chet.

The pancakes were good and reassuringly normal. We talked about Alexei's visa application and his Saturday with Mike, and about Athos's job, and about movies, and nobody asked me about the comic or the lake.

But of course that couldn't last, and on the walk back, full of syrup and greasy sausage, they started asking again whether I was okay, trying to get at what had really happened at the lake. I put them off with the same story about a childhood trauma that I didn't want to talk about, and then they shifted to talking about the comic. Athos hadn't known there were spirits in it, so they pretty much demanded that I show them the whole thing when we got back to the apartment.

At that point I couldn't think of a good reason not to. So when we got back I grabbed the stacks of paper and threw them down on the table. "You guys look at that," I said. "I want to draw some more."

"Commissions?" Athos asked.

I already knew I wouldn't be able to draw commissions. I had an inkling of what Marie-Belle was going to do next, and I dreaded it and wanted to see it. "No."

"All right. We can take this down to the café, right?"

He started to gather up the pages, but I shook my head. "I'm not going to the café. Long story. Don't ask."

His ears went down, and Alexei looked puzzled, but the two of them let me be. I took a paper pad and my pencils into my room, but there I remembered Eve's e-mail. So I opened it up to look at it.

Hi, Meg,

Hope you don't mind. I got your e-mail information from Yolene. Well I guess you probably figured Bellie came in and told us all how your date with her went. Sherine called you a poser, whatever that means—some people want to be political and if you're not with 'em, you're against 'em. But I wanted to tell you I know when you're confused and trying to figure things out, sometimes things don't come out right and you can hurt people without meaning to. I told Sherine you might be coming out of season and that's why you were more on edge than usual, and she admitted she hadn't thought of that. If you want to come back and apologize to Bellie, I think that would be okay and we'd be behind you. Alain and I, I mean, and Sherine would be if you'd sit down and explain it. So think about it. Geoffrey says he wants our resident "otterist" back.

> Best,
> Eve

I was going along through the letter okay until I got to the "hurt people without meaning to," and then I got annoyed and ashamed all at once. I knew I'd hurt Bellie; I wasn't stupid. It was more the revelation that everyone knew I'd hurt her, and they were chalking it up to my youth and inexperience and coming out of season, but I wasn't sure I'd ever been *in* season. Anyway, it was at least partly Bellie's fault, trying to push me into something I wasn't ready for.

Just like Vanessa kissing Hannah behind her house, only Hannah had been ready and even eager for it.

Fuck, now I was comparing my behavior to dreams. I closed the e-mail and scooted back on my futon so I was leaning against the wall. It would be nice to go back to the café, but honestly it was a hassle now what with half of the people who knew me hating me because I'd fucked up commissions or told them I didn't want to fuck them. I might just as well leave it be.

I knew I should write back to Eve, but I couldn't think of what to say. I could write something like "sorry I fucked things up with Bellie," only I wasn't that sorry about it. I mean, I didn't like that I made her feel bad, but she was the one who forced me into that spot. Jesus, just thinking about it brought me back to that stuffy room with her paws rubbing at her naked body, and ugh. I couldn't write out a letter explaining all that, though. Even to myself, my justification sounded whiny. What I really wanted was for the whole thing to go away, and the only way to make that happen was for me to ignore it.

So I went back out to the dining room table to draw. And as I sat with the two foxes, a voice in the back of my head said, *how long before you end up ignoring them, too?*

Chapter 27

"Stop! What are you doing?"

Marie-Belle hurries down the back stairs of the Guignac house, not in time to prevent the lash descending once more across Toquine's back. Pierre raises his arm again, sees his fiancée, and hesitates.

"Don't worry," he says. "It's only ten lashes. She admitted to trafficking with the voodoo witch, you see."

Silence hangs like the porch roof over Marie-Belle's head, weighty and dark, broken only by a half-choked sob from the mouse pressed against the porch rail. The air is still and no breeze rustles the trees or the sugarcane. She stands in the dust, her thin tail curled below her dress. "For that you whip her?"

Pierre lowers the whip, puzzlement on his face. Toquine continues to crouch in the dirt, her shirt pulled up over her head, her body trembling. On her bare back, glimmers of red blood seep through the fur.

None of them speak for a moment, and then Pierre says, "Well...yes. It is forbidden, and she knew it was forbidden. Ten lashes is lenient."

"Lenient!" Marie-Belle hurries forward, crouches beside Toquine. "How many has she had so far?" When Pierre doesn't respond, she looks up. "How many?"

"Four." He scratches behind his ear and raises the arm that holds the whip. "Marie-Belle, please move. I would not want you to be struck."

Movement at the screen door catches her eye. Pierre's mother moves back into the shadows, but Marie-Belle knows who has arranged this tableau for her benefit. "I will not move." She puts a paw on Toquine's shoulder, tries to soothe the trembling mouse. "If you wish to dispense the last six lashes, you may dispense them upon me."

Now Pierre lowers the lash again. It twists in his paw as though impatient to bite. "Come now," he says. "What purpose would only four lashes serve?"

"Toquine," Marie-Belle says gently, "have you learned your lesson?"

"Yes, yes," the mouse sobs.

"There." Marie-Belle stands and holds out a paw. "She has learned her lesson. Give me the lash."

Pierre looks even more confused. "To what purpose?"

"So I may be sure you will not strike her again. And so she may be sure of the same thing."

Her fiancé shakes his head and does not release the lash. "This is ridiculous. To interfere in the discipline of a servant…"

"Who will soon be my servant as well." She matches his gaze.

"You have no servants. You don't understand discipline."

Marie-Belle looks from him out past the yard and the fields. There at the cottages, the servants who work the fields have gathered to watch them. They stand straight and still on their roofless porches, staring. Pierre goes on. "If this is not corrected, then she may bring the voodoo orgies back to the plantation. Dancing and shrieking and…and fornicating at all hours. Or, worse, you and me and our children may become victims like the DeLacs."

"The DeLacs?"

"I would never!" Toquine cries.

"Quiet." Pierre shakes the lash so that it makes a hissing sound.

"What happened to the DeLacs?" Marie-Belle asks.

Pierre looks at her and shakes his head. "Go inside and talk to Mother," he says. "I will tell you later. When I am finished here."

This is a test, a natural one, as surely as the whipping was a test arranged by Mrs. Guignac. Marie-Belle feels she has failed the first one already by interfering, and so what has she to lose? She bends and extends a paw to Toquine, but before she can speak, Pierre continues. "A wife must be obedient to her husband."

I am not yet your wife, Marie-Belle thinks, and then realizes the threat implicit in his statement. Will she throw away her family's best chance at rising to a better station? The alternative seems to be to throw away her pride in herself, her decency as a person.

"A husband does not ask of his wife that which he knows to be wrong," she says.

"Wrong? When you have lived here with servants for years, then perhaps you may judge what is right and what is wrong." Pierre rattles the lash again. "But today, now, you must go inside."

She is about to protest, but Toquine says, "Please, madam. Go. I can bear it."

Consorting with a voodoo witch is no crime, Marie-Belle wants to cry, and then she thinks, there may be another way. So she gathers her skirt around her and turns without a word, making her way up the porch stairs to the screen door and the room beyond that still smells of Mrs. Guignac's perfume.

∞

The only time she can escape her aunt's watchful eye now is after the sun has set. The swamp is familiar by smell and feel, but in the darkness shadows lurk, alligators and perhaps other dangers. The darkness in her future is more threatening still, so Marie-Belle kicks her way through the water. It streams cold through her fur, and the smells feel thicker in the night air. The plants that caress her fur are chilly and slimy, their messages murky and slow.

But she arrives at the dock without encountering an alligator or worse, brushes water impatiently from her fur, and does not dress before hurrying to the door of the cottage.

The windows show no light, but within moments of her knocking, footsteps come from inside, and then Toutou's voice filters through the door. "Who is it, at this hour?"

"Toutou, it is me, Marie-Belle, please let me in!"

"Marie-Belle?" The door creaks open, revealing Toutou's whiskers glowing in the light of a candle. "Child, what are you doing in the swamp this late?"

"Oh, Toutou, I need your help. The spirits spoke to me, but then Toquine was beaten for conferring with them and I must do something to prevent this engagement but I don't know how to ask them for it."

Her grandmother stares at her. "Oh, child, come in." She ushers Marie-Belle into the room and closes the door behind her.

The candle flickers, but even the jumping shadows in Toutou's cabin cannot unsettle Marie-Belle any further. Her grandmother pulls out a chair at the table, but the young muskrat paces back and forth, her tail flicking. "I cannot marry him," she cries. "He beat Toquine for asking your help! He talks about the DeLacs and Pelican Harbor as though they are reasons for cruelty. I don't even know what they are! Toutou, he is a monster, and Aunt Eloise wants to bind me to him…"

Her words run out and she stops to stare at her grandmother, who has folded her paws together on the table. After a small silence, the elder muskrat smiles and says, "First, you will sit down and calm yourself, and second, you will arrange your thoughts, and third, we will discuss your marriage and the spirits."

"Oh, Toutou." Marie-Belle feels pressure behind her eyes. "Aunt Eloise would not allow me to visit and I have been listening for the spirits and I spoke to one, but I have missed you so."

Toutou looks sharply at her. "You have spoken to a spirit?"

And so Marie-Belle tells her about the weasel in the top hat and his glib assurances and his question, and the way he disappeared into the late summer breeze with a laugh when she could not answer.

When her story is finished, she watches Toutou, but the old muskrat only taps the table. Outside, frogs croak and the slow lapping of water surrounds them. A slow, soft rustle comes from the back wall, and Marie-Belle sees that Sébastien has raised his head, the mirror making it seem as though another snake is looking back, away from the cottage. All around him, the voodoo altar flickers and jumps, grotesque shapes magnified by shadows like leering visages laughing at her story.

Finally, Toutou shakes her head. "You talked to one of the Guédé."

"The Baron of the Cross."

"Oh, child. Oh, my Marie-Belle." Toutou sighs. "The Guédé are seductive and charming, but are the most dangerous of the loa. They will tempt you and trick you."

"But they are also the most powerful, are they not?"

Toutou breathes in and then out. "They are powerful, yes. But it is because they traffic in lives. For a love potion, you may ask Ezili and the cost will be no more than you may bear. But the Barons care not for what you can bear."

"You would not let that happen." Marie-Belle thinks back to the weasel. He was so pleasant, so full of the joy of life. How could he take it away?

The croak of frogs grows louder, then fades. "Would I not?" Toutou asks quietly. "You asked about the DeLacs. I knew their servant Lara, the one who did it."

"Did what?"

Toutou sags, shoulders bowing inwards. "She was expecting a child. She did not want it born into poverty and servitude. You understand, child?" Marie-Belle nods. "So she asked me to help them escape. I cannot do that. I cannot ask the loa to break men's laws."

"So they tried to escape?" Marie-Belle holds her breath.

"They summoned Baron Samedi. This is what Lara told me, after. But they misunderstood him. The Baron told them 'life is worth life.' So they slaughtered their masters. And in the end, they were captured and killed."

Marie-Belle squeezes her paws together. "I am sorry. It sounds horrible." A thought occurs to her. "What happened to her child?"

"Her child was born and then given to the state."

So, Marie-Belle thinks, he might have been adopted. He might not have lived in servitude. And the Baron had kept his promise.

Toutou reaches across the table. "You see, my dear, it is best not to speak to the Guédé, nor to believe their promises."

"But Toutou," Marie-Belle says, reaching out to take the offered paw, "this proves I can talk to the spirits, does it not?"

"It does." Her grandmother's fingers are warm, the pads old and callused. "It does. And perhaps we may yet make a vodou priestess of you. But will you defy your aunt?"

"Yes," Marie-Belle says quickly, but it is easy to make promises here in the safety of the cabin. "I want nothing to do with Pierre. My family may—there will be other ways."

"Your cousins are already married, and your other aunt is childless and likely to remain so. If you do not marry into town, it will fall to your cousin's children, another generation, and who can say whether the chance will come again? Perhaps your grandchildren will still be living in the swamps."

"It is better for them." Marie-Belle thrusts out her lower lip. "The swamps are closer to nature, to our roots."

Toutou waves to a corner of the cabin, where a thick oak root comes through the wall. "And some roots that are not ours. But are you willing to make this decision for your family?"

"Should I let them make this decision for me?"

"My dear, such is the way of the world."

"You told me," Marie-Belle says, feeling betrayed, "that we may change the world if we are strong enough to do it."

"Yes, we may. That does not mean we should."

"Will you not help me? I want to work at your side."

Toutou sighs. "Not with the Guédé. I am sorry, dear child, but if you may talk to Ezili, or Ayida Wèyo…"

"I have no time! The betrothal will be announced next week, and then…"

"And then?"

"And then people will know."

Toutou shakes her head. "If you care so little now, why do you care what people think?"

It is true, but it would be easier, that is all. Marie-Belle knows what Toutou would say to that, so she keeps her mouth shut. "Give it time, child," Toutou says, and then perks her little ear to the corner where the snake's head bobs. "Oh, now you've woken Sébastien."

She gets up from the table and walks slowly to the shrine. The long, narrow shadow rises on a sinuous neck to meet her. Marie-Belle is about to

"His head is level with her paw"

say that she saw the snake move earlier, that he has been listening this whole time, but then she has an idea.

"May I ask Sébastien?" she asks timidly.

Toutou gives her a sharp look. Her paws stroke the snake's scaly neck, and she whispers to it softly. The snake's head bobs in reply. "As you have woken him," she says finally, "he is agreeable. But one question, and quickly."

Marie-Belle gets up and pads to the corner, where she sits cross-legged on the floor. The air here is warmer, and the smell of the long reptile rises thick, dry and pleasant.

Sébastien's scales rustle over one another with a sound like leaves blowing in autumn. The great black snake slides from Toutou's paws to Marie-Belle. "Lift your arm," Toutou orders her, and when Marie-Belle does, Sébastien slithers around her forearm and up. His tongue flicks through her fur, but she does not shiver at all. She has always liked the elegance of his glossy black scales, the shine of his round yellow eyes, and his slow, deliberate movements. Sébastien is like her old Uncle Laurent, and she imagines him speaking in Laurent's crackling voice, with a witty barb attached to each line.

When he has circled her arm and his head is level with her paw and his eyes stare into hers, she clears her throat. "Sébastien," she says, and the long, flat head bobs slightly. She doesn't know what to say, and then all the words come out in a rush. "Is my first duty to my family or to myself?"

She meant to ask whether she should trust the Guédé, but the snake's eyes drew a different question out of her.

"It is easier if you ask a yes or no question," Toutou says, but she is smiling, across the tree root from Marie-Belle, her paws still holding Sébastien's tail.

Marie-Belle tries again. "Is my first duty to..." But she stammers, because Sébastien is moving around her arm and sliding his head closer to her nose. Her world shrinks to the small nostrils, the bright unblinking eyes, the flickers of candlelight over the scales, the black and pink forked tongue shooting out at her and withdrawing. It touches her nose so lightly that it might be nothing more than a thought, and then Sébastien withdraws his head.

Slowly, he unwinds himself from her arm, though his head stays level with hers. And then he lowers himself and returns to his nest before the mirror of the shrine.

"He didn't answer my question," Marie-Belle says softly.

Toutou gets to her feet and reaches down to help Marie-Belle up. "I think he did," she says.

"How? What did he say?"

"You will have to figure that out for yourself. Especially if you want to be a vodou priestess." Toutou's paw tightens around Marie-Belle's. "But remember all that I have taught you, and above all, beware of the Guédé. If they are showing an interest in you, it is because you are approaching a decision and they see possibilities. And the possibilities of the Guédé are not always to our benefit."

"But sometimes they may be?"

The frogs go silent. Toutou turns to Marie-Belle and her eyes are dark, though reflections flicker across them. "Sometimes," she says. "But when the Guédé benefit people, someone gets hurt."

Marie-Belle turns away, seeing the red seeping through Toquine's fur. "Yes, Toutou," she says. "Shall I do nothing, then?"

"Until you are certain of the right thing, do nothing."

Chapter 28

"Meg?"

I stared down at the old muskrat's picture. *Until you are certain of the right thing.*

"Meg!"

Athos was shaking me by the shoulder. *Do nothing.*

"Yeah, I'm okay," I said. "What's wrong?"

Athos's grey and orange muzzle hovered near mine, bobbing much as I imagined Sébastien the snake's had. "It's been three and a half hours," he said. "You were...well, in a trance, kind of. Alexei went and got lunch for us."

A wrapped fast food sandwich and a paper soda cup dripping with condensation sat by my right paw. I reached out, realizing my throat was parched, and sucked slightly cool Coke through the straw. "How long ago was that?"

"Like an hour and a half."

"Wow. I don't remember it at all." The Coke reinvigorated me even though it wasn't cold. I was hungry, too, so I reached for the sandwich. "Where's fox-boy? Sorry, red fox-boy, I guess."

"Went out with his boyfriend. He said they were going to have dinner later and we're invited."

"Oh." The paper fell back and I smelled fish. My stomach rumbled eagerly and I took a bite of sharpish tartar sauce and lukewarm fish. It was great. Slowly, Marie-Belle's world fell away and I was left in my own complicated life. "Why'd you shake me? Was I doing something?"

"Oh, well. Mostly you were drawing, but then you stopped and stared at the paper. I mean, the trance thing was a little scary. I've never seen anything like it."

I talked while chewing. "Was I making noises?"

He shook his head. "Just...just really focused on the paper. You barely stopped drawing."

"Great, considering I can't draw any other time." I snorted.

"Have you tried right after drawing your comic? Maybe if it's out of you..."

"Yeah, thought of that. It's hard to get the momentum going." As I said it, I wondered if I really had tried it. The first few times, the comic had unnerved me so much I'd stopped, and the last time I'd emerged from the trance starving. So I finished off the sandwich and then pulled out the piece of paper on which I'd started a pirate commission. The lines that wouldn't work right for me looked obvious now; I erased them and started over again.

They came easier this time, and Athos watched quietly as I sketched outlines. "Looks better," he observed when I paused.

I think he was testing whether I was in a trance again. "Yeah," I said. "It's coming easier."

His smile told me I was right. "Good. Have I told you how impressive your art is? I mean, the story of the comic is really interesting, but you've got obvious skill even with those rough lines. It's something I never really saw until this summer, and watching you draw is even more amazing than seeing the finished product."

"Before this summer I was on anti-depressants and it fucked up my art." I breathed in and out and the pencil moved across the paper. "Getting off them was like being let out of jail."

"I imagine." He watched me, and his tail swished back and forth. I could feel the air even though it didn't quite touch mine. "And you haven't—I mean, you seem fine without the drugs."

"Fine" clearly didn't include having art trances or crazy dreams, but that wasn't worth getting into now. I kept drawing because it felt good, and Athos picked up the comic I'd drawn. He seemed able enough to read even my hasty sketches and scribbled words.

By the time he put it down, I was a little farther along my commission and optimistic about being able to work on art again. I felt good enough that I agreed to go meet Alexei and Mike for dinner.

On the way there, on the bus, Athos asked, "So do you know what happens next in the comic? Does she deal with the Guédé or go ahead with the marriage and exert her influence with the family?"

It would be weird for me not to know. I hesitated anyway. "Well, she—I think she does the deal with the Guédé, but it might not be as bad as…" I trailed off, because I didn't know. In the original story, the vodou spirit (I hadn't known about the Guédé then, or the Barons) freed her from the promised marriage. The way the comic was going, I didn't know if that was a possible ending.

"It looked like that might be pretty bad," Athos said. "But maybe that's what you should write. You know, having the worst thing happen is good for the story."

"What if I don't want the worst thing to happen to her?" Which sounded better than saying that I wasn't sure that I was writing this story; I felt more like I was drawing it as it was being told to me.

He smiled. "It's your story, I suppose."

I distracted him by pointing out a weird-looking red panda guy at the front of the bus who was singing some hardcore rap. We speculated on whether he was mentally unstable or just clueless, and the "unstable" theory gained weight when the driver told him to stop, and he was quiet for thirty seconds before starting up again. I wondered if the rap was coming to him like my comic was coming to me, if he couldn't *not* sing it.

Alexei and Mike were at Butter Betty's, one of those places with pictures of Little League ball teams up in the entryway and pennants of local sports teams around the big bar in the center of the restaurant. Most of the things on the menu mentioned butter; the featured dish was the "butter-grilled burger." Athos texted me while we were looking at the menu that he was going to gain ten pounds just from tonight, and I told him I would match him so we could waddle home together.

The whole night felt strangely, wonderfully normal. As much as I wanted to make cracks at them, Alexei and Mike were sickeningly adorable together, joking with a friendship and intimacy that slightly surpassed what Alexei and Sol had and reminded me of myself and Sol—or myself and Athos, any time before last month. I leaned an elbow on the table, very aware of the grey fox next to me. We were making strides in getting that intimacy back, but Alexei and Mike's rapport put me to shame. Athos had been patient with me through my weird troubles, supportive with my parents, basically more than made up for whatever he might have done wrong a month ago. I stared down at the menu, and when the waiter came, I picked something more or less at random.

For an hour and a half, I left Marie-Belle and Hannah behind and enjoyed dinner. Nobody asked me about my art or my jobs, apart from one question from Mike about what I was going to do now that Sol was off to college. "Pretty much just what I been doing," I said, and Alexei caught my look and changed the subject.

At the end of the dinner, we walked out together, and I said, "Coming back on the bus, fox-boy?"

Alexei grinned and took Mike's white hand in his black paw. "Mike has asked me to stay with him tonight."

"Great," Athos said. "Thanks for inviting us to dinner. It was a lot of fun."

"When are you going back north?" Alexei asked him.

"Oh, my ticket was for tomorrow night, but it's a full fare, so I can change it if I need to."

I turned to him. "Why would you need to change it?"

"Well," he said, meeting my eyes, "I guess if there were a reason for me to stick around."

"Hey, you can make up reasons if you want to. Sol ain't comin' back anytime soon, so his bed's free, and as long as Alexei doesn't mind you using it—"

"Of course not," the red fox put in.

"Stay as long as you want," I finished.

He laughed. "I do have to go back to the office eventually."

"I will hope to see you tomorrow, then, but in case." Alexei hugged Athos and then Mike shook his paw and mine and we parted ways.

Athos was quiet all the way back, as I was too. I knew I should open up to him both about my failed lesbian experiment and about Drowned William. I used to tell him everything about high school, and having him share the experience of the comic made me less apprehensive about it. But I was still ashamed about the date with Bellie and a little afraid of Drowned William.

I shifted to thinking that maybe I should call Sol now that I had a better handle on what was going on. It was one thing when I was just having weird dreams, but now that things had escalated, maybe it was worth having Sol laugh at me for not believing him this past spring.

Maybe. If I could keep his questions limited to what was happening now.

When we got home, Athos checked his work e-mail to see whether he could stay an extra day even though I hadn't asked him to. That was fine. I logged back into mine and saw Eve's message again. Still couldn't think of what to say to her, so I dashed off a quick response saying, "Thanks, still sorting through things." Then I went to open up the two commission e-mails, feeling up to the task of reassuring them that their pictures would in fact be done.

"Fuck," I said, not even aware that I'd said it aloud until Athos appeared at the bedroom door.

"What's wrong?" he asked.

I turned the computer off and scooted back on the futon, leaning back against the wall and closing my eyes. "Both the commissions I had left wrote to cancel."

"Can you talk them out of it?"

"Maybe." I didn't move. Neither of them had said they'd heard from Corra or Chet, but the abrupt nature of the requests—one of them wasn't even late yet—left me no doubt.

After a moment, he said, "May I come in?"

I raised a paw and waved. My whiskers registered the movement of air as he walked into my room, and I heard him settle on the floor near the futon. "So now," I said, "in addition to not having enough money for rent, I have to give back money to two people."

"We can work on getting you more commissions," he said.

"Where? My reputation is pretty much shit everywhere now. Even if I can draw again, who'll pay me up front?"

"You don't have to get payment up front. Do something like, say, they pay half when you make a sketch, and then the rest when it's finished."

"Sounds great." I didn't move or open my eyes. "All I need is ten of these imaginary customers in the next week and I'll be fine."

"I can loan you the money." When I didn't respond, he said, "Or I could give it to you."

"No. I'll pay it back. I just…" I sighed and drew my knees up to my chest. "I fucked everything up."

"You didn't." He leaned closer; I could feel it even if I couldn't see it. "I think there is something going on with you. There's a spirit or something haunting you."

He had his elbows on the edge of the futon, paws crossed over each other, and he was looking up at me with an optimistic smile. "So if you figure out what it wants…"

"You've done a one-eighty on this in the last month. Not everything is about spirits."

"Then what is it?"

"I don't know. I'm confused, I'm stressed about a lot of shit, art school and sex and whatever."

His smile dimmed and his ears lowered. "I don't mean to stress you or put any pressure on you."

"No, you're not," I lied. Well, sort of lied. He was part of why I was pressuring myself. "It's just a lot of shit going on, and then Alexei and I on our own."

"And him with Mike."

"Yeah, that too."

The fox was quiet a moment, and then his tail swished across the floor. "You have any cookies left?"

"Hell, yes," I said, and reached for the baggie under the bed. "I also have that weed Dad gave me, but you probably don't want to smoke."

"The cookie's fine. I'll get some water." Athos got up and walked out to the kitchen.

A minute later, the sweet herbal taste of the cookie in my mouth, I took a drink from the glass he'd brought. He sat on the futon and I didn't object. His tail dropped between us as I gave him the other half of the cookie.

"Thanks." He leaned against the wall and chewed, sitting cross-legged, paws folded in his lap. When he swallowed, I held out the glass of water, and he took a drink, tipping the wide cup to the end of his muzzle. "So… can I ask you what happens when you draw the comic?"

"Fuck, I dunno. I'm not high enough yet to answer that."

He laughed. "I mean, is it a spirit guiding you?"

"There's no spirit," I snapped. "There's nothing. It's just…" I shifted and put my paw down between us, and it landed on his tail. "Oh. Sorry."

"It's okay," he said, and though I'd already lifted my paw, I put it back down again. His tail was fluffy, and the contact was nice. I ran my fingers through the long fur.

"I had the story in my head a long time," I said. "Years. I tried to draw it before, but it wasn't 'til I was off the pills that I really felt like I could do it. And a week or two ago, I just sat down and thought I'd give it a shot." And Marie-Belle was looking at me in the last panel. "And it kinda took over my brain, I guess. It wanted to get out. And when I tried not to draw it, it got into the other things I was drawing."

"But you don't feel like there's a spirit guiding you? I mean, the trance you were in resembles trances experienced by mediums—"

"Faked by mediums, you mean."

"Well, yeah. But remember when Alexei was in shock. That was a deep trance of a similar sort, I think."

"I still say he was just in shock."

Athos didn't say anything, but he dropped his paw to cover mine, on his tail. "I'm here to help you with this." I stayed quiet and he went on. "But I don't want to intrude on your privacy or anything. If I'm persistent, it's because it feels like you could really use…"

"What? Help?"

His paw lifted slightly. "A friend."

What a loaded word that was between us. We knew that's what we were, and the tension was about where we would go from there. But he'd helped me out with my parents, really stood by and helped stabilize me, and though he'd pushed me about the comic, it really did seem to be about helping me get through it.

So I said, "Yeah, I do." And his paw settled back over mine.

The companionship warmed me even though the pot hadn't kicked in yet. That was probably the first moment where the thought of sex entered my mind. That night, I mean. I'd had sex now—okay, maybe not me personally, but after the night with Bellie I didn't feel like a virgin anymore. I'd been through it and survived, and I knew I could survive it again if I had to. The trick would be to avoid the kind of debacle that had happened with Bellie. I couldn't afford to lose Athos.

On the other side of the pool, I really did like him, where I didn't have that bond with Bellie. And I'd established that I wasn't attracted to mostly-naked girls, but I hadn't tried that with a guy yet. Maybe I was straight. Hell, maybe the fact that I was thinking about sex meant that I really was entering my season now—a bit late, but my body chemistry was fucked all to hell anyway.

Besides, even though I didn't really want to have sex, I could tell he did. Now that I was thinking about it, I noticed him fidgeting and shifting his weight around. Shit. Maybe rubbing his tail was getting him worked up? I didn't know if guys worked that way. Bellie didn't seem to care much about my tail, but then, mine wasn't long and fluffy like hers, and I hadn't had much inclination to explore hers.

The tip of Athos's tail, as black as Alexei's was white, curled up and then lay back on the bed. How would I initiate sex? With Bellie, it had all just progressed. The night was blurry enough that I couldn't put myself in her place, and I didn't want to look like the clumsy idiot I felt like. All I had to guide me was, well, an entire childhood filled with my parents' stupid romantic comedies.

Then Athos said, "I was only thinking it was a spirit because of Alexei's visitation," and I decided I didn't want to talk about that anymore. Romantic comedies, take me away.

"Hey," I said, and he turned to look at me. "I really appreciate everything you've done, and I'm really glad to have you here."

"Oh." He smiled, and his tail curled again, trying to wag, I guess. "It's my pleasure, really."

"What I mean is…uh…you don't have to stay in Sol's bed tonight."

His smile froze and his ears stayed up. Only his whiskers twitched. "Are you sure?" he said softly.

"Yeah." The moment was getting a little too serious, so I said, "Alexei's gone. You can stay in his."

He laughed, and then stopped laughing and searched my eyes. "You don't have to do this just to pay me back, or something."

"No, I know." I curled my fingers around his tail. "I like you a lot and I want to."

The smile returned, a little goofy like on his last visit, and then he reached around with his other paw and pulled me into a hug.

We hugged for a while, and then the pot kicked in all the way and a while became a longer while, or maybe it just seemed that way. I used some of Bellie's moves on him, reaching under his shirt and all, and he was a lot more hesitant with me, but finally we were both down to underwear and our paws were all over each other. He was grinning a lot and panting a little, and while he wasn't doing anything for me in that way, at least I didn't feel completely out of my skin like I did with Bellie. It was cute the way he tensed and twisted sometimes, and he had a nice enough body to look at, too.

"You, ah, you sure you want to…" He stopped with his paws around one of mine, though he was looking at my bare chest with a hunger that would've unsettled me if I hadn't seen it on Bellie's muzzle as well.

We weren't going to get pregnant this way, not a fox and otter, so my only non-emotional hesitation was whether he had one of the horrible diseases we'd had drilled into us in high school. But I figured moral, upright Athos would tell me if he suspected that. So I took his paws and put them on my breasts, and said, "Yeah."

"You like this?" He tried playing with them.

It felt okay, a little weird, but he was a guy I trusted, so the violation of my personal space was bearable. "Yeah."

We were in uncharted territory after that, but I was pretty sure it involved getting his underwear off, and after that the only really weird part was the actual, you know, sex. I kept having these thoughts running through my head about how weird it was that someone was putting part of their body *inside* me (clinically I know how sex works, of course, but still, I mean, if someone shoved their fingers into your mouth, you'd be weirded out).

Fortunately, as I had read, boys are pretty easy, and I barely had time to get freaked out before he went all stiff and then collapsed like a pricked balloon. I held him and waited for him to get out, but he just looked at me with—Christ, if the previous smile was goofy, this one was flat-out ridiculously ecstatic—and said, "Did you, ah, you know…enjoy it?"

"Oh, uh." I couldn't lie fast enough.

"I'll keep at it," he offered, moving his hips around. That just reminded me of what was happening, and I jerked my hips back.

"No, no. It's fine," I said, and touched my nose to his. "Look, I'll—it's fine, it was really nice." He could tell I hadn't enjoyed it. He was going to get up and leave. My heart pounded faster.

His ears flopped to the side. "I can, you know, do other stuff. I will. I can make it better."

"No." I pressed a paw to his stomach and got up. Why was I so nervous? Oh, right. I was still high. And so was he.

His nose twitched. "This was your first time, right?"

"Yeah."

"Oh." He looked relieved. "I read that a lot of times the first time is hardest and after that it gets easier."

"Right," I said. Looking down at him, there was no question that he'd enjoyed it, and that at least gave me a little comfort, quieted the worries. His eyelids were drooping and the tip of his tongue poked out through his smile. "I'm just going to go clean up."

His tail flopped in a lazy wag from side to side. "Can I...may I stay here?"

"Yeah, sure." I turned as his eyes drifted even farther down.

"Mmkay." The word followed me out the door.

I cleaned up in the bathroom, a process during which I successfully did not think about what I was doing, and threw the messy towel in the hamper without looking at it or smelling it too much. The smell on it was all him; little or none of mine and certainly nothing near the volume of what had come off Bellie. There was no question that any enjoyment I'd gotten out of sex had been only because I'd been doing something nice for a friend. So I wasn't gay, and I wasn't straight, and that seemed to rule out bi, too. Maybe I really was asexual.

I sat naked on the toilet, my tail hanging behind me, and tried to think not about what I was, but what I'd just done. It was such an insignificant, quick thing, and now I was no longer a virgin by any definition, gay or straight. Funny. I didn't feel any different, except maybe a little dirtier. Mostly I was just relieved that it was over and I hadn't done anything to fuck it up.

Fucking up the fucking. Oh, god. I put my paws over my muzzle and breathed in and out, alone. I'd done a nice thing for Athos. He was happy. I was going to go back in there and lie down next to him and fall asleep, and in the morning we would find some more people for me to draw and he would give me money for rent...

Shit.

Shit shit shit. Had I just had sex for money?

No. I mean, I was pretty sure. But what if he thought I had?

Okay, shut up. You're still high, you're overthinking everything. Christ, how long had I been in the bathroom? Like half an hour? He was going to freak out or think I was freaking out. I should get back.

I stood and caught sight of myself in the mirror. For some reason, my wide eyes made me think of Hannah, even though I had no idea what she looked like—I mean, in my dreams I was her, and I rarely looked in a mirror. She'd never had sex, probably wouldn't until she got married. I reached up to my whiskers and brushed my fingers along them, staring in the mirror. I didn't think I looked any different.

Athos was sprawled out in my futon, one arm splayed out across the empty side. "Athos," I whispered, but he didn't stir.

At the edge of the futon, my phone sat on the plastic crate beside the computer. I reached for it and tapped it on. I could call Sol now. He was a college student, he stayed up until like three a.m., right?

So I took the phone and padded back to the bathroom. Athos was asleep. He wouldn't know or care.

The wolf answered on the fifth ring. "Unh," he mumbled. "What's wrong?"

"What?"

There was some scuffling around and his voice hissed, "It's twelve thirty in the morning!"

"I know. I just wanted to say hi. I haven't talked to you in forever."

More scuffling, more movement, and then the clicks of a door closing. His voice sounded more normal when he talked again. "I have an orientation seminar at nine a.m.!"

"Really?"

"And my roommate likes to get up early."

"You haven't told me anything about your roommate. Is he one of the guys you have a crush on?"

"What? No!"

"So he's one of the, what, two guys on campus?"

Sol made an exasperated noise. "Did you call just to annoy me about having a crush?"

"If you'd only had one, maybe I wouldn't have to."

"I'm hanging up. Go to sleep."

"No, no, Sol, wait!" I said it louder than I intended to and then held my breath, listening. No movement from Athos.

Sol waited, and then said. "Well?" When I didn't respond right away, he said, "Are you high? Is Alexei there?"

"No," I said, and didn't clarify which question I was responding to. "No, look, Athos is here, Alexei's over at Mike's, but that's not why I called."

He waited some more. "Meg? Why did you call?"

He didn't know. If I told him, would he judge me? Call me a slut? No, he'd know I'd only slept with Athos to keep him from leaving and he'd call me a liar, a fake. I had to think of something else to ask him. "Oh. Hey, listen. When you were having those dreams…"

"Yeah?" His voice got sharper, more attentive.

The barrier to telling him anything had been lowered by the pot. All my paranoia was taken up by worrying about Athos and sex, and as long as I didn't say anything to Sol about that, I was okay. "It ended with your fox getting killed, right?"

"You know that."

"Yeah, but…why did it end there? Did you know it was going to end?"

"It was the end of the book," he said, confused. "What's going on? Are you seeing Niki?"

"Jesus, Sol, no. Your fucking dream fox is in your bedroom where he has been."

"But something's happening, isn't it?"

I took a breath and focused on the mellow. "Yeah, kind of. I'm writing this comic and the story is sort of…it's getting away from me."

"What's that mean? 'Getting away from you'?"

"I go into a sort of trance and draw the comic, but the story seems to be going…going through me, you know. Not like I'm making it up."

"And then you're dreaming about the story?"

"No." I hesitated, wondering whether to tell him about the Hannah dreams. They were sort of related in that they'd started around the same time. "I'm having weird dreams, but they're not part of the comic."

"So there is a spirit guiding you. But it's not Niki?"

"There's no spirit, Sol. Dammit. The dreams are in the future, and they're real. That's what's freaking me out. They're fucking real."

It all came spilling out as I sat there on the closed toilet: the future with androids, the lake, and so on. "I feel like I'm going crazy, but Sol, I'm not going back on the pills."

"Whoa, slow down. Pills?"

"Did I not tell you about the pills?"

He paused. "Who is this?"

"Jesus fuck, Sol, okay, I was on antidepressants for a while."

"How long is a while?"

"Athos lay under the covers"

I stood and stared at myself in the mirror. "Like…four years."

He made a noise. "When did you stop taking them?"

"A few months ago. Right around when you were having your dreams. When I turned nineteen."

"Your nineteenth birthday was like a week or two before we got assigned that report."

"Okay, you get a gold star for memorization of stupid dates. No wonder you got an A in history. The point is, I stopped taking them months ago so that can't be what's happening now. I just want to know when it's going to end."

"Well, why *is* it happening now?"

"Fucked if I know." Then I giggled and then covered up the giggle, and cleared my throat. "I don't care anymore. I was trying to figure that out, you know, but I just want to know when it's going to end. You and Alexei had your episodes and then they were over and done and you went on with your lives. Well, you not so much."

"Thanks," he said. "Hey, could you call back to mock me some other time?"

"Sure. What's good for you? Tuesday?"

"Good-bye, Meg."

"Wait!"

He exhaled again, loudly, deliberately. "I don't know what to say. I'm trying not to say 'I told you so,' so hard like you would not believe. Does your comic have an ending? Maybe when it's over, your dreams and shit will go away. In the meantime, I need to get up in seven hours—no, six and a half—and I am going to sleep."

"All right. Hey, Sol?"

"Yeah?"

"The not having a crush on your roommate thing? That's good. Keep that up."

"Good-bye, Meg."

I sat there in the bathroom with the dead phone, weighing it in a paw. Sol was about as much help as talking to my own thoughts, but it was reassuring to talk to him again.

Now I had to walk back in there and lie down next to Athos. That wasn't so bad, really. I could sleep on the couch if I really wanted to, but then Athos would get up in the morning and he'd be sad, and he'd come out and ask me what was wrong, and that was a whole conversation I wouldn't want to have. So it was better and easier to just go back into the room, resist the temptation to put on clothes, and lie next to him. And hopefully he wouldn't want to have sex again in the morning.

The bedroom remained partly lit by lights from the construction site. Athos lay under the covers of my futon, which was weird enough, along with the smell of him and the sound of his breathing, which I could somehow hear over the noise of the construction. I don't walk around the apartment naked a lot, so that was weird too.

I ended up not resisting the temptation to put on clothes. It was a little too much otherwise, and even though he was naked—maybe because he was naked—I didn't want to be.

So I pulled on a long t-shirt thing I liked to sleep in and stood there staring down at him for another half minute, or maybe ten minutes or whatever, and then I crawled into bed.

Lying beside him, I felt his warmth and his breath, and his scent was even stronger. I'd always slept alone, and having someone else in the bed made me self-conscious about falling asleep. What if I rolled over? What if I kicked him? What if he kicked me? What if he wanted to cuddle? Could we, like, start having sex in our sleep if we rolled together the right way?

Ha ha. That was ridiculous, the kind of stupid story Sol found on the Internet and we laughed about. Still, I rolled onto my side to face away from him, keeping my thick tail between the two of us. That he was lying beside me in bed, naked, that was a little strange, but if not for the sex itself, I thought I could get used to it. It was Athos, after all. So to keep myself from thinking about the sex, I focused on Marie-Belle's story.

Even that, though, led me to thinking about her marriage to Pierre. She wasn't attracted to him, but I thought she was straight; sex just hadn't been part of her story so far. Whereas if I were straight, Athos would be a fine boyfriend. I mean, there were other issues, like him living in Port City, but if I had to have a boyfriend, I mean, he was the only guy I'd met who I didn't want to strangle. Usually. And we were rebuilding our close friendship, truly intimate now, except that I was hiding how I truly felt about sex from him.

I could still be straight. First times were difficult and not always enjoyable, I knew that. Everything would be so much easier if I were straight. We could go on and have sex, and me not telling him that I hadn't enjoyed the first time at all would become insignificant.

I waited for the voice in my head to say, *You're broken*, but for once I didn't hear those words.

Maybe the voice knew that I already knew.

Chapter 29

I woke to an empty bed and an open bedroom door. Athos's scent lingered on the sheets near me, as did the feeling and the memory of sex. It hadn't been as bad as with Bellie, where I'd felt completely out of place. The main problem would be Athos's over-considerate worry that I enjoy it.

When I finally got out of bed, I saw that concern on full display in the kitchen. He'd gone out to get eggs and had somehow made toast.

"Morning!" His tail wagged as he indicated a plate on the table. "Sit down, I'll make you some eggs if you want."

"Sure." I sat and stared at the plate.

Athos slid a piece of toast onto it. "There's butter and strawberry jam, too." Those appeared on the table with a clunk a moment later.

"Where did you go for all this?" I didn't touch any of it.

"Found a little market about a mile that way." He gestured. "Or... or that way, maybe. Anyway, you didn't have any breakfast stuff around."

"We have cereal and milk."

He cracked two eggs into my saucepan. "I mean a real breakfast."

"I haven't had eggs for breakfast since..." I scratched my ears. "I guess Christmas? When we went to Aunt Charity's place. Mom wasn't big on eggs."

"You're okay with eggs, though?" He turned, worried, the paw holding the spatula hovering over the pan as though he would chuck the whole mess if I said no.

I smiled. "I'm fine. Just put soy sauce on 'em." It was nice to have someone care that much about whether I liked eggs. But at the same time, I didn't really want anyone taking care of me.

Shut up, brain, I ordered. He's making breakfast, that's all. It's not a marriage contract.

"Soy sauce?" He wrinkled his nose.

"In the fridge. And how did you make toast?"

"On the burner." He indicated the stove.

"Huh." I bit down on the toast. It was surprisingly good. I reached for the butter.

Athos sat down with me when the eggs were done and dripped a bit of soy sauce onto his. "Not bad," he said. "If you like soy sauce."

"I pretty much season everything with it." I scooped eggs onto the toast.

We ate in silence, and then he took the dishes to clean them. I stopped him. "Come on," I said. "You cooked."

"All right." He stepped back and let me handle the sink, but stayed beside me while I washed. "So, ah. Uh, last night was…was okay?"

At least I didn't have to look at him. I scrubbed the plate. "Yeah, it was fine."

"Just fine?"

I took a breath. "It was really nice. Did you enjoy it?"

That was an easy one; I already knew the answer. "Well, yeah," he said, and though I wasn't looking at him, I could tell he was relaxing from the easy chuckle behind his words. "It was great. And I'm glad you changed your mind about it." I kept scrubbing, and he kept talking. "I mean, I would totally just be friends, but it felt right, you know?"

I nodded, and put one of the plates in the drying rack. His paw touched my hip as I moved back to the sink, and his muzzle moved a bit closer. "Hey. Say something. Like, 'it's just sex, get the fuck over it.'"

So I said, "It's just sex, get the fuck over it."

He laughed. "Seriously, I mean, are you okay?"

"I told you, I'm fine."

He cleared his throat. "Look, I know I wasn't that good, but…"

I put the second plate in the drying rack even though there were still soap bubbles clinging to it and turned to face him. "Hey. You were f—you were good. I had a really good time. And it wasn't just sex, it was a change in our—our relationship, and you know, we should figure out what we want. Do we want to be friends who have sex, or—" I didn't really have to finish the sentence; his answer was naked on his face in his eyes and the lowering of his ears. "—or do we want to start being more?"

"I want to start being more." It came out in such a rush that he had to take a breath after it. "I don't know what that means, but you could do your art up in Port City, right?"

"Whoa there." I dried my paws, leaning against the counter. "It's gonna take more than a night in bed to get me to move to Port City. I mean, my friends are here, my family…" There I faltered. "Well, I might want to talk to them again someday."

"I'm sure you'll patch things up. You just yelled a bit."

"You ever yell at your parents?"

"Uh." He shook his head. "But I'm a northern middle-class liberal, and also a fox. We don't yell, we go and sulk in corners and then smile when we get together."

"Alexei yelled at his parents."

His eyes looked past me to the fox's room. "He's Siberian," he said. "Also, you…you heard about his parents."

"We never yelled much at family gatherings," I said. "Mom kept trying to get everyone to play nice and get along. I sat in the corner with my black fur and glared at anyone who tried to talk to me. It was fun."

He tilted his muzzle. "Sounds like it."

"I made my little cousin Jerome cry once."

"Only once?"

I grinned at him, because that was a pretty good one. "Okay, so what are we doing today and when are you heading back?"

"I think maybe talking about things? And I've got a ticket for tonight, but I could call in to work."

"Don't miss work on my account. We don't have to spend every minute together from now on."

He sighed and reached out to take my paw. "I know. I kind of want to anyway."

I didn't really want to spend all that time with him, not yet, but on the other side, I felt more stable with him around than without. Certainly he was helping me deal with the comic thing and by association the dreams. "You think there are people in Port City who would want commissions drawn?"

"Sure. But you could also do the work over the Internet." His ears perked up. "Plus then people wouldn't know where to find you."

"That's a plus." I turned to the door of my bedroom. "But…I know it's stuffy here, and the neighborhood is crappy…"

"Think about it," he said. "My apartment is small, but there's room for you to draw and there's a coffee shop two blocks away. You don't have to make a decision now."

Then he got a goofy smile and leaned forward and kissed me. I wasn't quite ready for it, but I recovered in time to kiss him back. "So is this kissing going to become a regular thing?" I asked when we were done.

"Maybe." His tail wagged. "Like it?"

There it was again. If it was a thing people did, why the fuck did it matter if I liked it. "It was fine," I said.

He shook his head and smiled. "I guess I'm going to have to recalibrate the way I view 'fine.' So that kiss was as good as sex?"

Probably wouldn't be good to say, "Better, actually, because it was shorter and there were fewer things going into me." I was going to have to watch what I said around Athos, which was annoying because of all my friends, he was the one for whom I'd had to do that the least. So I grinned back and said, "Well, you said you'd get better."

"Ouch." But he kept smiling, and he reached out to rub my arm. "Yeah, about that…"

"Can we hold the sex talk?" I clasped his paw back, keeping it on my arm but also keeping it still. "I mean, that's something that will work itself out, right?"

"Oh, no." He was cute when he got serious. "It's important to talk about it. Otherwise we might not know what the other wants."

"Okay, fine, but…not now. I mean, you're already talking about Port City and all and I don't know, let me think about stuff."

He nodded slowly. "It's a lot, but I feel like it's right. I hope you will, too."

While he was showering, I went back to my bedroom and sat on my futon. He very definitely had said "hope you will" and not "hope you do," asking the same question I was asking myself: would my feelings change? Or, as he'd joked about with "fine," would I change what I felt was "right"? Could I change it to include keeping Athos around in exchange for sex I didn't enjoy? Moving to a strange city and leaving my friends behind?

How often did couples have sex? I checked the Internet and got back everything from five times a week to once a month. While I was there, I looked up info on "didn't enjoy sex first time," and found a lot of links from females who'd had inexperienced partners, who said that eventually it got more enjoyable. A few said that once they got a handle on when their seasons came around, sex was more enjoyable. Maybe it really was as simple as that for me, too.

There were a fair number of stories that also went along the lines of "I never learned to enjoy sex," and under one of them in the comments there was a long discussion from someone suggesting that the writer might be asexual.

I'd read about asexuality, of course; someone who had no sexual thoughts or interest who wasn't scared to search the Internet could hardly avoid it. But it was so rare, it seemed, and the drugs were a much simpler explanation. Now, off the drugs, there weren't many other possibilities.

But still, it had been my first time. Athos had seemed about as unsure and fumbling as I was, if much more into the whole experience. Maybe it would get better, maybe we'd be a good couple, and I could sit down with Sol and Alexei and compare boyfriends and techniques.

Still…as I followed the commenter to more stories of asexual people, the more they resonated with my own life: *never wanted to talk about sex in high school like my friends did, never got aroused looking at porn, never got aroused or thought about sex, didn't feel my season come on at all, got uncomfortable with how into sex everyone else was, don't masturbate at all...*

The missing seasons and the lack of masturbation, those were the big ones. Us ladies don't pleasure ourselves as often or as reliably as guys do, I guess, but that was the comment that got every female on the board to say "oh, I felt the same until I read Cosmo," or "maybe you need a vibrator," or even, "you're lying, everyone masturbates."

But me, I felt a huge wave of relief reading that. I'd read *about* asexuality, but I hadn't read first-person accounts of it. There was someone else somewhere who didn't feel her seasons, who didn't get aroused or enjoy sex, who didn't even feel the need to pleasure herself? There was someone else like me?

And then the relief was swamped by fear and anger: I was asexual? That was great, that was perfect; I really *was* broken. Now how could I move in with Athos? Knowing there was someone else out there like me didn't help me deal with a would-be boyfriend who definitely liked sex and would want to keep doing it. Maybe I wasn't asexual after all. Maybe I was just confused, recovering from the drugs and a fairly typical first time.

But as hard as I tried to get back that hope, it wouldn't come. There was a difference between what I wanted to be true and what I felt to be true, and as much as I didn't want to be asexual, these were the facts: I didn't have seasons, I didn't want to masturbate, and hadn't since before taking the drugs. I'd now had sex with both a boy and a girl and neither one did anything for me. I might not know whether Marie-Belle or Hannah were truly real, but this one I felt down in my bones.

I would have to tell Athos about this, but I didn't know if I could handle that conversation on top of all the weird stuff going on. What I could do was put off a decision until Athos went home, and we'd talk about it over the phone or Internet, and I'd talk to Alexei and Sol about the move, maybe about the sex stuff. So I didn't have to deal with it right now, but I felt its inevitability like water soaking into my fur.

Chapter 30

Marie-Belle's paws shake slightly as she sets down the snake vertebrae. The bones are only three years old, not forty like Toutou's, but she has kept them because she thought they might be useful one day when she becomes a priestess. The small pig beside her roots in the ground, unconcerned, its skin fresh from the bath and smelling of the lavender oil she stole from her aunt.

She looks up, but her aunt is in town and Pierre would have no reason to come by this house in the early evening. She would prefer to do the ritual at night, but her aunt will be back by then. So she places the herbs in the middle of the circle of vertebrae, next to the stoppered bottle of whisky, and looks up toward the evening star. Clasping her paws together to steady them, she inhales the scent of the herbs. She remembers the dances that Toutou has led, the giddy ecstasy in them, and she wishes there were more than her to join in. But she gets up and takes a few steps, forces herself to dance, and then she has to stop in order to speak.

"Baron La Croix," she says, kneeling again. "I ask for your assistance. You have come to my side once before; you know me. You know my grandmother as well. We have worked together for many years and I ask you to come in recognition of that bond, to come for the call of the great serpent god Damballa, to come for the sacrifices of meat and whisky I make to you."

The birds that had been singing fall silent. Leaves around and above her rustle. She reaches to her side for the butcher knife and then looks beside her for the pig.

Chapter 31

No! Shit, no. Don't do that, I tried to scream down at the comic page.

I'd started drawing to escape from thinking about Athos and sex and moving, only to get sucked into Marie-Belle's ritual, and now she was going to slaughter a pig? I had a really bad feeling about how that was going to go, and I didn't want to draw it. Whether or not the worst thing was the best for the story, Marie-Belle was real to me and I didn't want her making mistakes like that. The sooner this story was over, the better. But I was for damned sure not going to draw a pig being slaughtered.

Okay. She was going to put down the knife. She was going to reconsider and figure out how to solve her problem without calling that shady Baron.

I stared down at the paper.

"Everything okay?" Athos asked. He looked up from his laptop. I hadn't even registered the sound of typing.

"Yeah." I had sketched in the knife in her paw. I could just erase it, right?

"Sol called."

"What?" I looked up at Athos's narrow muzzle and got briefly distracted by the memory of him kissing me. Would he want to do that again right now?

He didn't, but his ears did swivel back a little bit. "Uh, your phone rang, and I saw it was Sol, so I picked it up. He said he had more time to talk now."

"Okay. I'll call him in a minute. I'm sort of in the middle of something here."

I picked up the eraser and rubbed out the lines of the knife on the page. But the picture didn't look right. I redrew her paw and still it didn't look right. I drew it again, again, and again, and I couldn't make it look right.

Frustrated, I drew a stick in her paw. Still didn't work. I drew a fan, a parasol, a pencil, even a rubber chicken. None of it looked right. I erased so often that the paper started to wear, and I stared at the blank space at the end of her wrist. Maybe I could leave the panel unfinished and move on to the next one.

But when I tried to draw the next panel, my eyes kept sliding back to the empty spot where the knife should be. And my fingers drew Marie-Belle's arm raised.

She was going to slaughter the pig and complete the ritual. She was going to call that spirit and terrible things were going to happen. I was supposed to be the creator of this story, but I'd never felt less in control.

I sighed and touched my pencil to the paper again.

Chapter 32

The pig only struggles when she holds it down. Blood sprays from the throat as the knife plunges into it, and Marie-Belle's stomach turns. She has slaughtered animals before, but this is more intimate and more dangerous.

Blood pools in the center of the snake vertebrae, black in the evening light. Marie-Belle ignores the smell as best she can and closes her eyes. "Baron La Croix. Hear me—"

"Now that is a poke in a pig." The pleasant voice cuts across her invocation.

She looks up into the eyes of Pierre Guignac. He smiles down over his flat nose and straightens his collar.

"Pierre," she gasps, struggling to her feet, ice clenching her heart. "What are you doing here?"

His smile remains broad and easy as he extends a paw to her. "Why, I just felt propelled to walk over here to see my fiancée."

Her fingers drip blood, but that doesn't seem to deter him. Still, she is reluctant to take his paw. "I—I can explain this."

"I'm certain you can. But perhaps you'll favor me with a dance, first?"

His voice is not Pierre's; it is higher, more playful. And now jazz music swells around her, from all sides. Pierre's smile, now that she looks closer, is too broad, too easy for the tight Mr. Guignac. "Baron?" she whispers.

"You summoned me, did you not?" His paw remains extended.

"You have brought Mr. Guignac here?"

"I needed a host, clumsy as this body is." His fingers gesture impatiently. "I believe this has relations to the favor you were going to ask of me."

She swallows. "You will not harm him?"

"Oh," he says, "harm, do not harm, it all comes to the same in the end, *se pa li*? Dance."

It is no longer a question, but an order, and now his fingers grip Marie-Belle's paw with more force than mild Pierre Guignac ever used save on his whip. Pig's blood seals the space between their fur as the loa in her fiancé's body whirls her about and around, lifting his feet and dancing until she matches his movements. The music echoes from the back wall of her house and lifts the leaves of the scrub all around, lifts Marie-Belle's feet so that her worry and fear melt away. The Baron twirls her, both of them kicking up clods of dirt and grass in a larger circle around Marie-Belle's ritual circle.

"Do you like the music?" he shouts to her. How could she ever have thought this was Pierre's voice?

"It's wonderful!" she cries back, though she does not like jazz. She is swept up in the rhythm, the free melodies skipping with the blare of trombone and the sweet caress of saxophone, following the deep bass rhythm with her feet and shaking her free paw with the jingle of a tambourine, and now laughter and cheers rise behind the music. She is on a stage, dancing with Baron/Pierre, and all around them, spiritual hands rise and applaud her.

He pulls her close, and he is as warm as a summer day, his breath redolent of sweetmeats and rum. His fingers work behind her, but she only realizes what he is doing when her old work dress sags against her shoulders.

"Wait," she says, though her blood sings and now that the dress has partly fallen away, she wants nothing more than to be rid of it. "Wait, wait…"

"Wait?" He smiles. His chest is bare. "Is this not what you wanted?"

She does, now; she longs for it, burning with the need to hold him close, to feel him against her and welcome him into her. "Is this part of the price?" she whispers, struggling for control.

"It is part of the price and part of the favor." Pierre's lazy smile remains even as his fingers slide through her fur, pushing her dress off of her left shoulder. "And a little extra for you besides."

Chapter 33

Seriously? *Seriously?*

"His weight settles atop her"

Chapter 34

She allows the dress to slide free, and allows him to take her to the ground. He kisses her with a passion she would not have imagined in Pierre (of course, it is not Pierre's passion), and looks down with amusement. "These front teeth are a challenge," he says, curling his tongue around them, "but we will make it work, *pa enkyete.*"

"I'm not worried," she murmurs, placing her paws on her fiancé's back as his weight settles atop her.

He makes love to her whole body, caressing the fur, kissing her ears, her cheeks, her neck. The jazz swells around her and the invisible crowd cheers and dances, and Marie-Belle gasps and succumbs to it.

When it is over, Baron/Pierre rolls over and stretches out on the ground. Marie-Belle's paws still bear the dried blood of the pig, but she rubs them down her stomach and hips anyway and is glad to see an answering smile on Baron/Pierre's blunt muzzle. "I don't mind paying that price," she says.

"If he could make love like that every time, you might think again about being released from him, eh?"

She looks down Pierre's body, the carefully groomed fur all in disarray, the tail lying carelessly behind him. "Perhaps not. But it is too late for that now."

"Nearly." He reaches out and takes the bottle of whisky, unstoppers it, and gulps from it. "Next time, bring rum."

"Yes, sir." She is not sure if "sir" is correct for a recently intimate partner. "So...how will you do it?"

"How?" He lowers the bottle and grins. "I have done it, nearly. All that remains is for me to release this body."

Marie-Belle struggles to sit up. "But—but then Pierre will wake here!"

"Yes." He trails fingers down his naked form, grips himself between the legs and leers. "I presume he will be rather startled. At first. And after, I am sure there will be no trouble in releasing you from your engagement."

All the warmth in her turns ice cold. "No," she says. "No, you cannot. I will be—" She sees again his arm rising and falling, the lash biting Toquine in the back. What would he do to her if he saw this? "We will be ruined."

"Ruined?" He laughs. "You will be known for what you are, and able to live freely, and what is more desirable than that?"

The house they are lying behind, the house her aunt owns where she has lived her whole life, she would no longer be allowed to live there. She imagines the angry mob from town, torches held high, and then planks burning, the warped window glass of her bedroom cracking and melting, her aunt's screams and curses as they flee into the swamp. "Please," she says. "Pierre cannot know about this. There must be another way."

"There is always another way." Pierre's eyes glitter.

Chapter 35

No. No no no. I will not draw this. I will not.

My fingers pressed the pencil to the paper, drew a square outlining the last panel on the page.

Stop!

Marie-Belle would not be in this panel, but I could see her expression: scared, worried, unsure of her future.

The outline of a paw took shape.

I made a noise in my throat. Athos wasn't there. He was in the bathroom maybe, or in my bedroom. Maybe he'd gone out or maybe he was working. I tried to make a louder noise, even though my throat was dry. Through all that, my fingers kept working.

Claws scratched on the carpet back near my room. "You okay?"

I dragged my attention away from the paper. "I. Don't. Want. To."

"To what?" My whiskers felt his presence a moment before his arm draped across my shoulders.

"Draw this." I fought with the pencil. "I don't want to draw this."

"Then don't." He reached out and took the pencil from my paw.

Is it that easy? Of course not. I breathed and leaned against him. "So what, just leave the story unfinished?"

He peered down at the page. "Wow, it got a bit racy there." He nuzzled my ear. "Nice to know I could be inspiring."

I tried to clear my throat. "Could you get me a glass of water?"

"Sure." He moved around me to the sink. "What don't you want to draw?"

I stared down at the page. The last panel, the one I stopped at, was as clear in my mind as if the pencil were still tracing its lines on the page. "It gets bad here."

"That's good for the story, right?" He filled a glass and brought it over. "I mean, you want Marie to learn a lesson."

Her name was Marie-Belle. I didn't correct him. "What if it's real, though?"

"If it's real…" He sat in the chair beside me. "Then it's already happened and nothing you do will change it, right?"

"I guess." I stared down. "But…if I don't draw it…"

"Do you want to stop drawing the comic?"

I shook my head slowly. "I don't think I can."

"Well then." He patted my paw. "Sometimes bad things happen. Won't it be better for you to get it out?" He glanced at the glass. "You want something stronger than water?"

Next time, bring rum. "No."

"Okay." His paw rested on mine and he waited.

I stared down at the paper. Even if Marie-Belle's story was as real as Hannah's, it sure felt to me like it wouldn't be completely real until I finished drawing it. But if my part was so critical to it, why couldn't I change anything about it?

I reached over and picked up the pencil.

Chapter 36

Even when Pierre picks up the knife, Marie-Belle does not realize at first what he means to do. His smile is so easy, so relaxed, and his motion so casual that even when he drives the knife point-first into his chest, it takes her a moment to process what has happened.

"No!" she yells. Her arm snaps forward as though by pulling the knife out, she might undo what has just happened.

He is faster still. His paw seizes her wrist inches from the knife's bloody wood handle and his smile does not waver. "He will never know. It is just as you asked."

"But he's dead!"

"*Wi*." The Baron laughs, showing Pierre's fine teeth. "Well, not *quite* yet."

She struggles to free herself from the grip of the loa. As he speaks, a shadowy top hat glimmers into existence atop Pierre's head and the white lines of a skull drip down his face's fur. "He is too young!" Marie-Belle cries. "It is not his time!"

How could she have thought this smile casual and easy? It is uncaring and cruel. "Bah, death comes to all of you in the end. Now or in four years or in forty, what difference does it make? It is a great joke, that you are here in this world only long enough to sample its pleasures and then you are taken away from it."

She does not know how to answer that. "But you cannot—he does not deserve to die." She thought she cared so little for Pierre and yet the knife might as well have pierced her own skin and drawn her blood for the pain it causes her. She remembers only the kindnesses Pierre showed her, his easy amiability, his concern for her even in the midst of his cruelty to Toquine.

The paw that is not holding her wrist touches her cheek. "Oh, my dear. Of course he deserves to die."

"Why?" The word wrenches free of her.

He releases her wrist and rolls back, sitting up with the knife still sticking from his chest and remarkably little blood dripping from it. "Why?" He laughs. "Because he was born."

She gets to her feet as he does, and he warns her away with an outstretched paw. "Don't worry. I shan't leave him here. That would be embarrassing. I will walk him down one of the back roads to town and leave him there." He reaches for his pants and pulls them on.

"Please," Marie-Belle whimpers.

His eyes meet hers, and there is more than moonlight shining out of them. "My dear, you have struck a bargain with the Guédé and gotten what you wished for, besides which you have been left alive to tell the tale. Some would call that charmed." He picks up his white shirt and slides one arm through a sleeve, then another. As he buttons it around the knife, he looks down at the red stains soaking through the cloth. "Pity about the shirt."

—*Marie-Belle.* The voice sounds in her head.

Toutou?

—*Let me in. I will not possess you as the loa do, but if you let me in, I may help.*

Yes, please!

There is a rush and then she stands straighter. When she looks at Pierre now, she sees the weasel in his top hat and evening coat overlaid atop the muskrat as though his features are painted onto Pierre's, or perhaps projected onto him with a magic lantern. Pierre continues to grin placidly, but the weasel's eyes narrow. "Madame Lefour."

Marie-Belle's mouth speaks. "Baron La Croix."

"Such a joy to see you again. Your granddaughter is quite delectable, you know."

"Baron, you must release this young fellow alive."

"Must I?" His eyes dance. "You have not brought me a pig, nor rum."

Marie-Belle's arm lifts, extending a dark bloody paw. "I have brought you a spirit in exchange."

No! She wants to pull her arm back, to take the words back. She would sooner lose Pierre than Toutou. But she has lost control of her body and can only watch as the weasel's smile grows to match Pierre's.

"Well," he says, "it is a tempting offer. I could simply take both, could I not?"

"You will walk the young M. Guignac back to his house, and I will accompany you. When you have released him, then I will go with you."

Toutou! No!

—*Quiet,* her grandmother says. *It is my time and my life and I may choose what to do with it.*

The weasel doffs his top hat and bows. "I accept your bargain." He offers his arm, and though Marie-Belle screams inside, her paw takes it.

They walk back to the Guignac house in silence, the most excruciating half hour of Marie-Belle's life. She tries to talk Toutou out of this bargain, but every time she does, her grandmother turns her head to make her look at the knife still protruding from Pierre's chest. The Baron has left it there out of laziness or warning, but she takes it as the latter.

When the house is in sight, he reaches up and slides the knife out with no more than a slight wince. The flesh knits up under Marie-Belle's startled eyes as he extends the knife to her with a smirk.

She throws it into the bushes by the side of the plantation. Baron/ Pierre buttons up his shirt, shaking his head. "No wish to remember our evening together?"

"Go up to his room and come back," she says, clearly.

He bows again. "But of course. Just a moment." As he straightens, he takes Marie-Belle's paw and kisses it, blood and all, and looks up at her. She is certain he is looking at her and not at Toutou, and when he says, "It has been a distinct pleasure," she knows the words are meant for her.

—*Now*, Toutou says as Pierre's body walks up the porch stairs. *Three things.*

Oh, Toutou, I am so sorry. Marie-Belle's eyes remain dry, but inside, she sobs.

—*Hush, kitling. We have not much time. The first thing: you must find a pump and wash your paws, then clean up your aunt's back yard.*

Yes, Toutou.

—*The second thing: you must swim to my cabin in the morning and tell Sébastien to leave. There is nobody now to live in my cabin and I would not have him starve.*

I could live in your cabin.

—*You will live in this house.* Marie-Belle's head turns and stares up at the second and third stories of the house, the windows and railings and small decks that retain their elegant style even in disrepair. *You will care for Toquine and the others and you will bring many children into the world.*

Yes, Toutou. She looks at the house with both her grandmother's eyes and her own. *Is that the third thing?*

—*No. The third thing is this: you must fulfill one last obligation for me. There is a rat in town, Desiree Trounoir, who fears her brother is dead and wishes to contact him. You must simply be in my cabin the day after tomorrow at sunset. Can you do that?*

Hope flares in her heart. *So I am to be a vodou priestess after all?*

—*No. It is not enough merely to speak to the loa. A priestess must always keep the needs of others in her mind, not merely of herself.*

The hope dies as easily as the pig did. She rubs her paws together, sticky with blood. *How am I to help this rat, then?*

—You already know Baron La Croix. He will help you.

I don't want to see him ever again!

—Ah, kitling. Once the loa know you, you are not easily rid of them. But it is not an entirely bad thing. He is not good nor evil.

How can you say he is not evil?

The weasel is there in front of them in his top hat, coat, and cravat, the house visible through his outlines. "Because I do not seek to harm. I told you, I bring only joy."

Joy! Marie-Belle cannot use her mouth yet, but he can hear her anyway. *You were going to kill Pierre!*

"Ah." He waves a paw dismissively. "He took little enough joy from the world. And for all the joy lost by his passing, you would have had twice that from your freedom. But your grandmother has chosen to sacrifice herself for you, so there is no need."

"Baron, you will help Marie-Belle the day after tomorrow with one last séance, please? She will provide rum."

The weasel smiles. "I will be delighted to see her again. Shall I leave my clothing behind?"

Marie-Belle shudders. "No," she says, and realizes she controls her mouth again.

Beside her, as ghostly as the loa, is the shape of her grandmother. "I am ready to go, then," the spirit says.

Baron La Croix smiles and extends his paws to her. "Then come, sweet morsel, and dance the last dance with me."

She takes his paws and turns to Marie-Belle with a bright smile. "Remember what I have told you," she says.

"Goodbye!" Marie-Belle cries. She tries to hug Toutou but passes through the spirit without touching. "I'm so sorry! I never meant for you to die!"

The last thing she sees before they disappear is the weasel's crafty, wide smile, and he says, "What difference does it make?"

Chapter 37

I pushed my chair back from the table, hard. I didn't want to look at the comic anymore, didn't want to think about it. My breath came in hard gasps as I focused on the soy sauce smell and bright sunlight of the apartment, the cracks in the table I knew well enough to draw them without reference, the feel of my fur as I rubbed my paws against each other. Those were real, those were here with me in the kitchen at the table. The sound of my breathing was real, the sound of Athos typing in the other room was real.

My phone sat next to the papers on the table where Athos had left it. I picked it up and dialed "last called" to get Sol again. The phone rang and rang, and finally he picked up.

"Hey," he said. "What happened now? Another dream?"

"No. I was drawing today, the comic, and I tried to make it stop. I tried not to draw the knife. I couldn't do it, wolfy, I had to draw the guy with the knife sticking out of his chest and Jesus, you can't—"

"Whoa. Back up. What guy got killed?"

"He didn't get killed."

"Just stabbed in the chest?"

I pressed my fingers to my muzzle. "You want me to tell you the whole story?"

"No, I'm going to lunch."

"Oh, well, wouldn't want you to miss your three squares a day. I'll sit here and go crazy, don't mind me."

He sighed noisily. "Don't be so dramatic."

"Do you *know* me?"

"Yeah. You paint your face black and dare people to make fun of you."

"Ha ha. Thanks for reducing my life to that."

He got a little bit of a growl in his voice. "If you want, I'll—I'll put off lunch. It's just, I'm supposed to meet this guy..."

"Who, the dingo? No, wait, the snow leopard?"

"Uh."

"Another new guy? Jesus, Sol, I thought you were only going to play the field in baseball."

"I knew you'd give me shit about this. Bret was cool, and Lars, too, but Ken is a wolf and he plays lacrosse, so we have athletics in common."

I leaned back in the chair. "It's cool. Go meet your wolf. Athos is here, I can talk to him."

"Sorry. If you really want to talk to me, I'll stick around."

"I'll call you tonight." I wanted to ask him about moving to Port City, but that was going to be a longer conversation. And Alexei should be part of it, too.

I set the phone down on the table, thinking about that. Sol was already gone. I could call the guys, talk to them online. If William was right…if William was real…they'd be better off without me.

"Everything okay?" Athos came up behind me.

"Sol's getting all sucked into college life and is on his third boyfriend in like two weeks and my story isn't mine and it's fucked up like you wouldn't believe, but other than that, sure."

He rested a paw on my shoulder and looked at the comic. "Mind if I read it?"

I waved him over to it. "Go ahead."

While he was reading, I went to the cupboard for some crackers, then saw the loaf of bread Athos had bought. I spread some butter and jam on it and folded it over.

I'd eaten two of the slices by the time he looked up. "It gets really rough toward the last few pages, but I get it." He wasn't smiling, though he was looking at me attentively with ears perked and his whiskers all up. "You think this is real?"

"Was real. It was like a hundred years ago." I refilled my water glass and drank. "But how the hell is it getting into my head if it's real?"

He rested his elbows on the table and pressed his paws together, looking at me over steepled fingers. "May I assume that you are somewhat more open to the idea of spirits?"

I looked away from him. "Fuck. Maybe? I don't know. It's either spirits or I'm insane, and…"

"I don't think you're insane."

"Thanks," I said, "but that's actually the easier explanation to cope with. I'm used to thinking there's something wrong with my head."

"You're not reacting to this in an insane way."

I looked levelly back at him and put the water glass down. "Some people might say that allowing for the possibility that a hundred-year-old story is being channeled through my head is fairly insane."

"Fortunately for you, I am no longer one of those people." Now he smiled, pulled those black lips back up so they lifted his cheek ruffs, and his eyes brightened. "I hope it's a real story, actually."

"Why?" I still couldn't make myself look at the pages I'd drawn. I'd felt Marie-Belle's sick horror at what she'd done, at the grotesque body of her fiancé with the knife hilt-deep in his chest, at the shade of her grandmother, at the thought of finding the cabin empty. "Because now you want ghosts to be real?"

"No. Because otherwise I'd be worried about you following up a sex scene with the guy getting stabbed. Very 80's-horror-movie sensibility."

That got me to look up and meet his eyes and smile with him. "I don't think I want to stab you, but you can lock up the knives if you're really worried."

"I'm not," he said, and got up. "Come on, let's go for a walk."

"All right," I said.

He went to the bathroom before we left, and I took the opportunity to hurry into Alexei's room. I felt like an idiot standing in front of the portrait of Niki on the wall, but I only had a minute before Athos came out. "Hey, fox," I said. "So look, if I am being haunted, is it you? Can you help me? Or at least tell me what's going on?"

The painting hung there. I waited another moment, then heard Athos finishing up. "That's what I thought," I said, and walked back out.

⤫

By the time we got back, hungry for dinner, Alexei was home, so the three of us ordered pizza and sat around talking. Athos told Alexei that he was staying an extra day, and Alexei offered to make up Sol's bed again, and Athos looked at me and said, "Ah, I don't think that will be necessary."

The red fox looked at me with wide eyes. "You are making him sleep on the couch again?"

"No, no," Athos hurried to say, but I cut him off.

"He's making a joke. He understands."

Alexei's eyes sparkled, and he grinned. "I am very happy for both of you."

"Uh, yes." Athos cleared his throat. "In fact, er, Meg might be moving up to Port City."

At that, Alexei's ears drooped and he lost the smile. "I am still happy, but I will miss you when you go. When? After a few months?"

"Maybe." I was holding a slice of pizza and started to take a bite so I wouldn't have to answer, then thought that was kind of a jerky thing to do, so I put the slice down. "Maybe, like, end of this month."

"One *week*?"

I couldn't say anything back to his shocked expression. Athos stepped in again. "Maybe not quite that fast, and we'll settle the rent here, of course. But there's nothing really to keep her here."

Alexei looked at the other fox and then back at me. "I am sorry," he said to Athos, "I do not know a polite way to do this, but I wish to talk to Meg alone."

"I know it's sudden—"

I cut Athos off. "Let's go into your room," I said to Alexei, and then pointed at Athos. "No listening at the door, mister ears."

He made a cross over his heart, then folded his arms and watched us go in.

Alexei closed the door behind us. "Listen," I said, but he held up a paw, hurrying to his computer. He fiddled with it and turned on music.

"There." He turned to me. "He cannot hear what we say with that music on."

"Takes a fox to fool a fox," I said, moving closer so I could talk to him without shouting. "Listen, I'm sorry about this. I didn't mean it to happen so fast, but he's excited, and…"

He took one of my paws. "Is it best thing for you?"

"Ah, shit." I sat down on Sol's bed and he sat beside me. "I think so. I dunno, fox-boy, I mean, you've got Mike and Sol's got college and what do I have?"

"You have us." He curled his tail around his hip.

"You have your own lives. I can't impose on you to be my social network all the time."

His fingers curled against my paw. "It is not imposing. We are your friends."

"I know." I leaned back, resting my weight against my tail. "I just thought—why put this off? Why not go for it?"

"Mmm. Do you now believe in…"

"What, ghosts?"

His eyebrows rose and his tail curled, the white tip resting on his blue jeans. "I was going to say, 'love.' "

"Oh. Well—maybe a little more than I used to."

"Which one?"

His paw was warm against mine. It frightened me to have that contact, but I didn't want to let him go. "Both?"

He laughed. "I would not have believed it one week ago."

"I'm not sure I believe it."

"You don't believe that you believe?" He tilted his muzzle. "Is this an expression?"

"No, just confusion." I shook my head.

He nodded. "Sol and I had dreams, but you have this comic and you are awake while it is happening. I know that must be confusing. You have not had dreams?"

"Uh…not really. Not about the comic."

"But other dreams?"

I pulled my paw back from his. "Did Sol call you?"

He frowned and his ears folded back. "No. Why? What is going on?"

"Fuck. Okay, don't tell Athos. I'm having dreams that aren't related to the comic. I don't know why, but they feel real too."

He turned to look up at the picture on the wall. "Are they about Niki?"

"Oh, god, can you imagine? Sol would shit a brick." He wrinkled his forehead. "He'd be really upset," I clarified.

"What are the dreams about?"

"They're—I think they're in the future or something? It's weird. A lot of it doesn't make sense, and it's about—" There I stopped. I didn't want to tell him about all the lesbian shit I'd been going through. "About, uh, like, freedom and slavery and stuff."

"Is there a spirit you are talking to?"

"No. In the dreams, I'm an otter…a sixteen-year-old, I think? She's supposed to get married and she doesn't want to."

"Ah." He looked at me again, and then turned slightly in Athos's direction. "And you are going to move in with Athos."

I nodded. "I haven't decided yet, but probably."

"Is it what you want?"

I considered that question for a while, and gave Alexei an answer that he couldn't understand the significance of. "What difference does it make?"

The truth was that what I wanted, the only thing I knew for sure that I wanted, was for the comic and the dreams to go away. I wanted to draw for a living, and I could do that anywhere. And yeah, I wanted to live down here with my friends. I wanted Sol to come back over the summer and Alexei to get his visa and stay in the country and fuck, even marry Mike if that would make him happy. I wanted to be friends with Athos, maybe really close friends who could talk about anything without touching each other, but life was full of compromises and I probably wasn't going to get all of that even in the best of cases.

"I think it is important, knowing what you want," Alexei said, breaking my mournful reverie.

"Yeah, well. I want to be able to draw in peace, and maybe when I finish doing this goddamn comic, I'll be able to do that again, but all the people around here already think I'm a fucking flake, so I might as well move somewhere new. And if Athos is paying the rent, I won't have to worry about leaving you in the lurch."

Then I had to explain "flake" to him, and he got "lurch" from context but we talked language for a while, and finally he said, "As long as you are sure."

"Is this about Athos? Do you not trust him?" I kept my voice low.

"I trust him." He smiled. "I do not know that I trust you."

"You think I would do this just to make him feel better?"

"Hah. Perhaps not." He laughed. "But you are not selfish, though you want people to think you are."

I snorted. "Everyone's selfish."

"You care about your friends," Alexei said.

That made me think guiltily about the e-mail from Eve, perversely enough. I should go down there and talk to her. Maybe tonight, even. Bellie would be working, so I could go down without worrying I'd run into her. I could take Alexei and Athos, maybe. "I care about them when they're going to fuck up their lives. But I think you and Sol are past that. Well, you are." I looked up at the picture.

"Sol still wants to meet Niki."

"Yeah. I think he's going through a million boyfriends just to try to find someone like him."

Alexei smoothed his whiskers back. "I think perhaps he is simply excited to be in a place where there are many people he can date."

"Maybe. I hope you're right. He keeps asking about Niki, though."

"He will always love Niki."

"That's what I'm afraid of." I sighed. "Come on, we'd better go out or Athos will be even more worried than he already is."

When we came out, Athos looked up from his phone. "Did he talk you into staying?" he asked.

"I was not trying that." Alexei bristled.

"Can't think why you would need to talk to her alone otherwise."

"Hey," I said, "not everything I share with each of you can be discussed in front of the other, so just chill out. You guys want to walk down to the café and get dessert?"

Chapter 38

So we walked down to the café at nine at night, which was a very normal thing to do and got my mind off the pages sitting in a box in my closet. When I saw the "Café La Croix" sign, for a moment I had a vision of a weasel in a top hat, but it passed quickly. Coincidence of names, I told myself. After all, in the ultra-religious South, how common was the word "Cross," in any language?

Eve didn't see me until we were all right at the counter, and then she came around the end to put her arms around me. "Oh, honey," she said, and then when she stepped away, she took my paw in hers.

"I'm glad to see you too," I said.

She nodded, and then brought her paw down hard on the back of my wrist, and for a raccoon, she's got some strength. "Ow!"

"That's for disappearing for days and not answering my e-mail," she said.

"Sorry!" I glanced at the two foxes with me; Athos looked startled while Alexei was smiling, the idiot. "It's been a rough few days."

"You made a mistake, you own up to it and move on. I know you're only a child—"

"I'm nineteen," I muttered.

"—but you have to learn that or you'll never escape your mistakes. What, were you going to avoid the café forever?"

"I came back," I said, louder.

"That's why you only got a slap." She grinned at me. "What're you drinking? It's on me."

Alain leaned over to say hi as well, his ears perked toward Alexei. "Another boy? Please tell me he's not straight."

"I have a boyfriend." When I turned, Alexei was grinning even wider and his tail wagged from side to side.

"Lucky guy," Alain said.

"Thank you."

"I meant your boyfriend." He winked at Alexei, whose ears flattened.

Before he could say anything more, I said, "Decaf for me, and something nice for dessert." I would explain Alain's flirting to Alexei later—if I had to; Alexei already looked pleased, his ears coming back up.

We sat at a table in the corner where I could look out at the rest of the café. I had noticed that Eve hadn't mentioned Sherine, so I was still a little stressed about her, but it was nice to be here again and feel comfortable, especially with Alexei and Athos.

Sitting next to the grey fox reminded me that he would want to sleep in my bed again tonight, and maybe more, but as long as we were sipping coffee and eating messy chunks of chocolate cupcake, I didn't have to think about that. "I like this coffee shop," Alexei said. "We should come here more. And they know you."

I shifted and licked chocolate icing off my fingers. "I come here a lot, but mostly during the day. I used to draw here. It's a nice environment for that."

"Nice people, too," Athos said.

"Oh, you know this place?" Alexei's ears flicked toward me. "Why have we not come here for coffee?"

"Uh…" They were both looking at me. "I didn't want to get into a whole thing with the people here. We needed to grab coffee and get you to work."

"So that wasn't related to you not coming here? What Eve was talking about?" Athos talked gently, but the quiet in his voice felt intense.

"Sort of." I avoided his eyes. "You know, after my panic attacks here, I didn't want to come back. It was embarrassing."

"So that was the 'mistake' she was talking about?"

I stuffed the rest of the cupcake into my mouth and shrugged, mumbling, "I had an argument with one of the regulars here."

They were both quiet. I washed the cupcake down with my coffee and Athos rescued me, looking over my shoulder. "That's the owner, isn't it? The one who sold us the banana bread?"

I turned. The elegant Geoffrey's cat, sporting a long evening coat and a bowtie, raised a paw as he glided between the tables. "Yeah." I waved, relieved at the distraction. "I've only met him a few times, but he's really interesting. Loves the arts and food and stuff—well, you heard him."

Something tickled at my mind as I said those words, but I didn't have time to follow it up. Geoffrey stopped over our table and smiled down. "Every time I see you lately, you've an extra fellow in your company," he said in his deep, hearty voice. "You have been enjoying my cupcakes, I see."

"Chocolate," Alexei said. "It was delicious."

"You should try the red velvet," Geoffrey said. "Although they are all delectable enough that it doesn't make a bit of difference."

I introduced Alexei, and they talked about his job for a short time. Geoffrey had turned to Athos when Eve called from behind the counter, "Mr. Baron!"

Geoffrey turned and she said something about the register and he said something to us and then walked over to her. I didn't hear any of it. Athos leaned over to me, but his words, too, fell unheard against the furious workings of my mind.

Alexei reached out a paw and touched mine, breaking my train of thought. "You look strange."

"I'll be right back," I said, and pushed my chair back. My mind was humming like a warm night full of insects, a million thoughts beating their wings against the inside of my skull. Pierre and his knife, Bellie and Geoffrey and Marie-Belle. *What do you want? What difference does it make?*

The cat turned as I approached the counter. I saw or imagined a top hat on him over the formal evening coat. "My resident otterist," he said. "Are you in need of a refill?"

The rest of the café faded from my perception as though it were sunk in twilight. "I want answers," I said, and then added, "Mister Baron of the Cross."

He raised his eyebrows. "You invoke powerful spirits, my dear. What answers about them can I provide?"

"You can tell me why you're doing this."

"Meg!" Eve reached over the counter, brown fingers splayed toward me.

Geoffrey laughed easily. "It is my café. I think I am entitled to look at the receipts."

"Not that." I was keeping my voice even, but the people around us had quieted and so everything felt loud, sharp, and crisp. Eve hissed at me, but I ignored it. "What you're doing to me. Making me tell Marie-Belle's story. Is there a point to it? Is there an ending?"

He inclined his head. "My dear, I am perfectly willing to accommodate the tempestuous nature of an artist, but I cannot take responsibility for the muse that guides her paw."

"You killed Pierre!" I stabbed a finger toward his chest. "Or you would have."

"Mr. Baron?" Eve said. "Meg?"

We both turned. The raccoon's fingers held a cell phone, poised to dial. Alain's muzzle hung open, his eyes wide and staring. Geoffrey raised a paw to Eve and shook his head. "I fear Meg is suffering from stress, possibly due to overwork and deadlines. I prescribe a good night's sleep."

"Why?" I snapped. "Did you send me those dreams too?"

"Meg, are you okay?" Athos stepped up on my left side, and I felt Alexei behind him.

"I'm fine," I snapped, though truthfully I felt tenuous and yet sharp, like a shadow on a sunny day who finally glimpses the person casting her. "When does this end?"

He kept his pleasant smile as Athos laid a paw on my arm. "It ends," Geoffrey Baron said, "with your friends taking you home, I suspect. Indulgence is all well and good, but it should not cause trouble to those around us."

"Is that what this is about? Is that the point of the lesson?"

"Come on." Athos pulled, and now Alexei helped him from the other side.

"You are welcome back when your mind is more clear," Geoffrey said, stepping back.

The top hat wasn't really there, but I felt its presence. "I know you now," I said. "I know you."

"Meg," Alexei hissed. "Please stop. What are you doing?"

I stopped and looked around the café. A hundred eyes all faced me, and whispers around tables reached me as sibilant background. The insects buzzing in my head fell quiet. "It's him," I said weakly, but my skin felt warm as the conversation played back in my head. For a few moments I had been so sure—

Yes, Meg, and when else have you been so sure about something?

I turned to Alexei and saw his ears back, his eyes locked on mine with his usual kindness and something else there, too: curiosity and sympathy.

"Get me out of here," I whispered.

⌒

Back at the apartment, I sank into the couch. Athos sat beside me while Alexei crouched in front of me. "Now will you tell us what is the matter?" the red fox asked.

Athos reached for my paw, which he'd held all the way home, and I let him take it again because that helped it not shake. "I got confused," I muttered. "That's all."

"Was the cat someone from your dreams?" Alexei looked up earnestly. "No."

"From the comic?" Athos asked.

I hunched in on myself. "He's a guy who owns a coffee shop. I'm an idiot."

"But you thought he might be someone from your dream," Alexei persisted. "It is okay, Meg. He might be."

"He's not." There was no life in my voice and I couldn't put any in. "He's a regular cat and I'm an idiot."

"I know how it is to be scared, to think perhaps you are going crazy—"

"Yeah, I remember," I said. "Only you never admitted you were crazy, did you? So you don't actually know what it's like to know you're crazy."

Alexei's ears went back. "I do not understand."

"Thank you for making my point for me."

God, I hated how hurt he looked, and I wanted to reach out and tell him, *Please don't worry, you can't help me, there's only one person who can now*, but I knew that that would only make him want to help more. It occurred to me that it would be better for him to be hurt now, that it would cushion the blow if I moved. And it was easier not to say anything, as numb as I felt.

He tried one more time. "I only wish to help."

"You can't." Two words, but they were hard as nails to force out.

I couldn't look at him. After a few seconds he said, "Very well," then turned and walked slowly to his room, and I felt guilty and angry with each step. As the door closed, Athos said, "You shouldn't be so mean to him. He wants you to trust him."

"I do trust him. I just don't want to talk about these dreams with him." Athos looked pained. "Or you. I didn't want to talk about the comic either, but then you guys wouldn't leave it the fuck alone and then look what happened? I ended up yelling at Geoffrey." I put my paws over my muzzle and lowered my head.

"Who did you think he was?" Athos asked quietly.

"It doesn't matter."

"You mentioned Pierre—was that the Pierre from the comic? You thought...you thought he was Baron La Croix?"

"Maybe. For a minute. But he wasn't, of course he wasn't."

Athos put a paw on my shoulder. "Meg...I wouldn't discount that."

He wasn't going to be as easy to get rid of. So I said, as mildly as I could, "No, I guess not. Hey, I've still got some weed and I'd really like to calm down. Wanna smoke?"

"Ah." He inspected my muzzle. "Sure."

"I'll roll up a joint." I got up, and then said, as though it were an after-thought, "Hey, could you do me a favor? Could you talk to Alexei, tell him I'm stressed and I'm sorry?"

"I think that would be best coming from you," he said gently.

"I know. But you and he are friends and he probably doesn't want to talk to me just yet."

"I suppose...maybe that would be best." He stood with me and grasped my paws in his. "It's going to be okay. If it is the Baron, we can work out some way to get you free of him."

I said, "Right," because if I'd said, "Oh, of course, a few kids will easily be able to outsmart a voodoo god who's been around for hundreds of years," or, "And next we can work on getting me free of Santa Claus," which were my two best options, Athos wouldn't have left me at that point.

But leave me he did, and I went to my room while he went to Alexei's. I left my door open until I heard them talking, and then I picked up my phone.

The number was still there. Maybe I'd always known I would need it someday and that's why I hadn't deleted it. I dialed, and a chirpy female voice answered.

"Hi," I said. "I'm Meg Kinnick. I was a patient of Dr. Wallace's. Can you have him call me tomorrow morning?" I gave her my number.

"Do you need care now?" she asked.

"No, thanks. Tomorrow morning will be fine."

"I'll pass the message along."

I hung up feeling cold and empty inside. I'd lost, finally. But what other choice did I have? I was on the edge of hallucinating again, not in a dream, not in a comic, but in actual real life. I was endangering myself, and who the fuck knew what would happen next. If Geoffrey had told me to do something, what would I have done? Could I have resisted? What if he took possession of Athos and decided to free me by jumping the fox into the river or something? This wasn't something I could just ask a passing pronghorn to walk me out of.

I could no longer summon the fear I'd felt at the lake when everything seemed real; I had only the memory of the certainty and the feeling of being trapped. When I focused on that, glimmers of hope came to me. Maybe Geoffrey had really been Baron La Croix, or at least possessed by him in certain moments. Maybe the spirits were real.

In which case, Dr. Wallace would help me stop seeing them again, as he had for four years. And if they weren't real, then he would help me build the bulwark against crazy back up in my mind, because that shit was eroding something fierce. And the dread of talking to Dr. Wallace again was at least better than the terror of staring down into the blackness waiting for it to talk to me.

I rolled up a joint and was sitting on my futon staring out the window when Athos came back in. "Can I turn on the light?" he asked.

The construction workers were just arriving. They hadn't turned the big Kliegs on yet. "Sure."

I shielded my eyes as the light came on. There was the thump of Athos's bag hitting the floor, and then I felt the fox moving toward me before he plopped down beside me on the futon. I held out the joint to him. "You don't mind the smoke?"

He shrugged and lit the end. "I can live with it. You first."

I brought it to my lips and inhaled. "Thanks," I said, exhaling as I passed it back to him.

He took a drag as well. We sat together waiting for it to kick in.

"It doesn't seem like you need this that much," he said, staring down at the lightly glowing end of the joint between his fingers.

"Habit," I said. "It feels good."

"What I mean is…" He offered it to me, but I could still taste it and I refused, so he brought it to his lips again. The tip glowed brightly for a moment. "When you called me all panicked because you were out of it…" The words came in a cloud of smoke. "It was because you were freaking out about the comic, right? Or the dreams, maybe, whatever the dreams are?"

It seemed so long ago now. "I guess so, yeah."

"Well." He shaped his words carefully. "Thinking you saw a voodoo spirit in a coffee shop seems a lot weirder."

Now I took the joint back and inhaled before I answered. "I guess so," I said again.

"You guess…" He laughed shortly. "So are you getting used to the idea? Or—I mean…does it help that I'm here?"

Smoke plumed out from my mouth and I watched it swirl and disappear into the air. Athos turned away, covering his nose. "It helps," I said.

I extinguished the joint with two fingers and rested it on my milk crate, so the ends weren't touching plastic. When I turned back, he was looking at me, and so I said, "It helps a lot," and I leaned forward to kiss him.

Our mouths tasted of weed and smoke. He put an arm around my shoulders and made a contented noise. I put my arms around him too, but I was thinking of Dr. Wallace, and the coldness in me didn't go away.

The sex was easier that time because I knew what to expect. It was harder because I still didn't enjoy it, not even when Athos did a few things he had apparently been looking up on the Internet that day. The hardest part was looking at his smile afterwards and forcing an expression that felt like a ghastly jack-o-lantern but which I guess was good enough for him. He put his arms around me and we lay there in the dark together.

Chapter 39

In the week since she'd met the red wolf trader, Hannah had concocted a plan that was based partly in reality, but much more in some of the movies she'd watched. If she substituted herself for the dashing male otter who rescued the girl in nearly all of them, then things became more clear. When Vanessa came back, she would find a pretext to go to the market with her and they would meet Vilan there. He would help them get to a (nebulous) place from which he could take them back north while (somehow) preventing Angeline and Nephaline from finding and following them. Hannah had great faith in the northern trader largely because he was an outsider, and male.

Her lessons and companion did not hinder her planning; what did was the dreams. The otter in her dreams, whose independence had previously been an inspiration, had in the last dream been overwhelmed by the spirits haunting her. Hannah didn't know what the blue pills were exactly, but she knew that they felt like the opposite of independence. She was not going to be beaten down by life in that way, she determined, but the mornings after the last two dreams, it had taken her until lunchtime to recover her spirit. This last dream had left her feeling floaty and relaxed as if her mind were in a hot bath, and she spent the morning (which seemed to take forever) terrified that someone would notice. But nobody did.

Plans for the wedding had taken over more of her days as well: her mother had told her who would be in her wedding party, a list of Hannah's friends that did not include Vanessa. When Hannah insisted that her best friend be included, expecting a fight, her mother simply said, "Yes, I think that will work," and had added Vanessa's name to the list.

Inquiries about Vanessa's whereabouts or return still got no response, but at least Hannah knew she would be back by the wedding. If her plan had to wait until after that, so be it.

There was one afternoon when Hannah and her mother sat talking about the guests and her mother mentioned a distant cousin who lived far to the west in the arid plains north of Sonora. "I used to visit them quite often," she said. "I thought I might like to live there once."

Hannah did not recall her mother ever expressing any love of adventure. "Really? Away from the water?"

"There's water; artificial lakes and canals." Her mother sighed. "You can see forever, and the church there stretched nearly a mile wide under a huge white dome. The fox who preached there had a—"

"A fox, preaching?" Hannah frowned. "I thought only otters were permitted."

"In our church, yes. But in other churches, any species may preach." She sat and digested that. "Do you still want to go back?"

Her mother smiled. "No, it was a young girl's foolishness. This is God's country for otters and once I had you, I knew I could never leave." Her paw caressed Hannah's ear. "You'll know what I mean once you have your own kit."

The words stayed with Hannah. She knew she was expected to have a kit within a year of her wedding, but that had not figured into her vague plans. She'd thought she would be gone well before then, but here she was thinking that it might wait until after her wedding. What if she were married and then kept putting it off? What would the otter in her dreams—in the earlier dreams—have done?

Thinking about her dreams had come to dull her drive these days, so she pushed the thoughts away. Angeline noticed the change, though, and two days after the conversation with her mother, though Hannah had not dreamed since then, Angeline took advantage of a quiet moment to ask her about them.

"Your sleep has been more troubled of late," the companion otter said.

"I slept well last night," Hannah said truthfully.

"Four nights ago," Angeline said. "You woke in the night and were crying."

Hannah touched her cheek. "I don't remember."

"Your dreams have been more restless. In the last six weeks you have experienced immersive dreams five times, waking three times from them in a state of excitement, including last night."

"I don't think I usually cry when I'm excited." Hannah tried to keep herself calm.

" 'Excitement' can refer to any heightened emotional state," Angeline said. "What have you been dreaming about?"

Hannah stayed quiet. The connection with her dream otter was private and she'd grown to cherish this one thing that was only hers. She hadn't even shared the dreams with Vanessa. "I don't remember," she said again.

"Physiologically it is likely that you remember at least the most recent, given when you woke." When Hannah still didn't say anything, Angeline lowered her voice. "If you have been dreaming about Vanessa, there is no shame in it. Our minds often show us temptations, and if we leave them in our minds they may grow there, as mushrooms grow in the hidden darkness beneath logs. But if we expose them to the light, then others may help us to resist them."

Hannah swallowed. "Yes," she said. "I was dreaming about Vanessa. I dreamed she came back and she said we couldn't be friends anymore. So I was very sad when I woke up."

"You said you didn't remember." Angeline raised a finger. "Was that a lie?"

"Er." Hannah nodded, ducking her head. "I am sorry."

"Do not be afraid of the truth." Angeline lowered her paw. "You may spend an extra ten minutes in prayer this Sunday. Were you hiding the dream from me because you feared I would worry about you, or because you feared I would warn you about it?"

Hannah weighed a third lie, harder to disprove, against the truth. "I was ashamed of it," she said, which was at least partly true, even if the subject of the dream wasn't.

Angeline studied her and then nodded. "At least you understand. But you know, it is all right that you dream of seeing your friend. And in your *dreams*, it may become more than friendship." She met Hannah's startled gaze. "Yes, I know what has been discussed between you and Vanessa. I know what your father took from you and I saw what she was doing to you behind her house. This sort of thing is a known temptation that we must pray to God for the strength to resist."

"Yes, I know." Hannah kept her head down as if in prayer.

"I can help you," Angeline said quietly. "I know it is not easy when God throws obstacles into our path, but believe me, they do not remain there forever. I have attended your mother and your grandmother, and I have seen the demons they wrestled with. They defeated them and grew into wonderful mothers and important members of the community."

"Did they…" Hannah's heart quickened. "Did they have friends like Vanessa?"

"No," Angeline said. "Their demons were their own."

"Mama said she once wanted to go live on the plains where Cousin Betty lives."

"Yes, I recall." Angeline smiled. "The sun dried out her fur, but she loved the sky and the way the clouds moved across it. She loved the way people spoke and the spice of the foods. We still get spices from Elizabeth. You remember the catfish from last month, the one that made your eyes water?"

Hannah nodded. "But mother said that when I was born, she gave all that up. Was that when you knew she didn't need you?"

"Of course. A child is God's greatest gift and shows us our true path." Angeline beamed. "But until you have a child, I will be here to help you."

It was the next day that Vanessa returned.

Hannah came out of her etiquette lesson to find Angeline waiting, which was expected, but her companion was beaming, which was not. "Oh, Hannah, come along," she said. "We have a guest for lunch."

"A guest?"

Angeline led the way through the water to the back of Hannah's house, where a small deck held a tray with sandwiches and glasses of lemonade. Sitting cross-legged on the deck was Nephaline, and floating in the water in a light blue dress and large flowery hat...

"Vanessa!"

Hannah ducked under the wooden barrier and surfaced in the pool in the middle of the deck. She arrowed to her friend and wrapped her arms around her, grinning from ear to ear. "Oh, how have you been? I've missed you! You know what that little Georgette said in etiquette yesterday?"

Arms circled her stiffly and then let her go. Vanessa said, "It is very good to see you again, Hannah."

It was Vanessa's voice and Vanessa's words, but restrained and confined. Hannah released her friend and swam back, studying the familiar whiskers, eyes, and smile. "That's a nice hat," she said.

"My mother gave it to me as a welcome-back present." Vanessa reached up to touch the brim. "I chose the cornflowers." There was a short hesitation. "They go well with this dress, don't they? It was made by Genevieve Perron."

"Yes," Hannah said. "But Vanessa..." She stopped, feeling Angeline behind her and Nephaline up on the deck. "You know you can't wear a hat to etiquette class."

"Oh, I won't be attending etiquette class any longer," Vanessa said. "Mother has scheduled an appointment with Mother Light for me to demonstrate my etiquette. They taught me while I was away, you see."

"I see," Hannah said. She groped for something to say. She wanted to tell Vanessa that she'd seen Vilan, but of course, not in front of the companions.

Angeline coughed delicately behind her. "Perhaps you two would like some time alone?"

Hannah gaped. Vanessa opened her mouth and then closed it again, remaining primly silent. Behind Vanessa, Nephaline stood and brushed down her white robe. "I think that is an excellent idea," Vanessa's companion said.

Nephaline waited while Angeline climbed out onto the deck and then walked toward Hannah's house as Angeline's robe whirred itself dry. They stepped through the air door and were gone.

Hannah stared after them. "Well," she said. "I wish they'd have done that more often. Don't you?"

"Yes, I—I mean, I think that we can always benefit from our companions. But we also need time to grow as individuals."

Hannah lowered her voice to a whisper. "What did they do?"

Vanessa grimaced and put a paw to her head, just under the hat. At first Hannah thought Vanessa was turning on her privacy, and her paw shot to her own ear to do the same. But when her friend spoke, the words still held nothing of the Vanessa Hannah had known. "I am sorry," she said, "if I led you astray in the past. I had only the best intentions."

"You didn't—"

"I have been reminded of the good word of the Lord." Vanessa interrupted her. "You are already—" Again her paw went to her head and she closed her eyes. "You are already virtuous. Without me you have no doubt returned to the fold. I hope you will always feel love. God's love."

"What's the matter?"

"Nothing." Vanessa lowered her paw and smiled serenely. "Nothing is the matter."

It was the hat, something under the hat. Vanessa had never liked hats. Probably the companions would be back soon, so Hannah didn't have much time if she wanted to do anything. "Would you like some sandwiches?"

"That would be lovely, thank you."

As she climbed up onto the deck to prepare a small plate for her friend, Hannah watched the other otter's placid demeanor. Perhaps they had given Vanessa the blue pills she'd dreamed of, or done something to her head that the hat was hiding. In any case, it was easy enough to come around the deck behind Vanessa and hold the plate down.

For a moment, she hesitated, but movement caught her eye: the two companions approaching from the inside of the house. Hannah let go of the plate as Vanessa gripped it in both paws, and as the otter who had been her friend began to say "Thank you," Hannah grabbed at the hat and pulled.

It resisted, attached to the fur somehow, and Vanessa cried out and dropped her plate into the water. She reached up to clutch the brim of her hat, but Hannah wrenched it partly free, enough to see the gleam of metal and the sharp corner of a small plate underneath, enough to see the ugly skin around it, shaved and scabbed.

She stumbled back and fell on her tail on the deck, staring in horror. Vanessa calmly adjusted her hat and turned to Hannah. "You must never do that," she said severely.

"Are you...are you going to become a companion now?" Hannah whispered.

Vanessa laughed, an artificial proper sound that made Hannah's ears fold down. "I'm not a machine, Hannah. I'm Vanessa, your friend."

Hannah couldn't force any words past her throat. A shadow fell over her and she looked up to see Angeline standing over her, with Nephaline behind. "What have I warned you about overstepping your bounds?" her companion asked, while Nephaline walked to Vanessa.

"They put a *box* in her head." Hannah pointed. "Why—why would they—"

The three of them stared at Vanessa, and then Nephaline said gently, "Vanessa, you may tell Hannah about your Voice."

Angeline interrupted as Vanessa opened her mouth. "Do you think that is wise?"

"She has already seen it. An explanation is preferable to allowing her imagination to run wild."

Hannah continued to stare at Vanessa, who slowly picked pieces of sandwich out of the water and placed them on the plate on the deck behind her, just as though they were leaves in the water and it was a lazy Sunday afternoon, just as though she'd put the hat on her head as a prank. Any moment now she would look up and laugh, throw it across the water, and reach for Hannah with the warm glow in her eyes that Hannah wanted to see again more than anything else in the world.

The companions had moved to non-verbal or else were just staring at each other over Hannah's head, until eventually Angeline said, "Very well."

Into Hannah's head, Angeline said, *If you have any questions, we may talk about it after lunch.*

Hannah didn't respond to Angeline, keeping her eyes fixed on Vanessa as her friend raised her head. "The device you saw allows an angel to speak to me even more directly than Nephaline was able. He can see our thoughts and now he can tell me when one of them is wrong. He can tell me what to say. So you see, I'm still your friend. I just won't say so many terrible things anymore."

"You never said terrible things," Hannah said softly.

"Oh, I did." Vanessa leaned toward her. "I tried to lead you astray. If not for my companion and my family, who knows what might have happened?"

Freedom. Love. Hannah thought the words so loudly she was sure Angeline could hear them. But her companion said nothing. "I wanted to—"

Vanessa reached out and took her paw. "The fault was mine, Hannah. I know it. You are good."

Her eyes beseeched Hannah's, and for a moment there was a flash of the old Vanessa, the one who cared for Hannah and wanted to run away with her. At least, Hannah was sure she saw it, a pinch of the eyebrows and a tremble of the lower lip, and even the way she said, "You are good."

"I am glad you've found the word of our Lord," Hannah said. "I have high hopes that He may save both of us."

She hoped that Vanessa would understand her double meaning, but her friend showed no indication whether she had or not. She eased herself back against the deck and said, "Now, shall we continue our lunch?"

Chapter 40

"Meg! Hey, Meg!"

I surfaced from the dream still feeling water on my fur and the sick taste of dread in my throat. After Marie-Belle, this is what I dream about?

"Meg!"

A paw shook my shoulder. I focused on the face above me: slender muzzle, little black nose, grey and orange and white fur muted in the glow of the construction lights. "Mmwha?" I mumbled.

"You were moaning in your sleep. You kicked me."

"Sorry." I struggled awake as the reality of the room reasserted itself, as I felt Athos's warm body next to mine, the pressure of his fingers on my shoulder. My eyes flew to the spot behind his ear, but there was no hat there, no silver plate, nothing but soft grey fur.

"Bad dream, huh?" His fingers stayed on my shoulder and his eyes searched mine.

"Hole in one." I squeezed my eyes shut, but then I saw Vanessa's placid expression and shuddered. "But really, you didn't even need to ask. These days I don't have any other fuckin' kind."

He kept rubbing my shoulder, which I let him do even though I felt like he was pinning me to the mattress. "Sorry."

"Yeah, you and me both." I exhaled.

We were both quiet without moving, and then he said, "But I'm here."

He tried to hug me, and I sort of let him, and I said, "Thanks," because what the hell else was I going to say? *What difference does it make?* would be rude, and sort of misleading, because it was nice to have him there even if he couldn't help at all with the dreams. Also I was aware that even though he wasn't saying anything about it, he was kind of, shall we say, excited. I hoped it was just an effect of being naked in bed with a girl and also of being young and male, and not that he was turned on by me having spooky dreams, because that would definitely put a pall on our relationship. Though it would explain a lot.

No, no, he was just a guy, and after the hug, I think he was embarrassed by his state, because he lay back on his back. I lay there wondering if I should ask if he wanted to have sex again, and then I decided that it was one thing to have it when we were both generally expecting it and another for me to initiate it out of nowhere as if I wanted it. That would definitely send the wrong message. Then I wondered if he was thinking that him pressing

279

against me had been a signal and I was supposed to pick up on it, and not responding was the same as responding in the negative. I'd seen all the sappy romantic idiotic movies where the newly-together couple can't keep their paws off each other and they end up screwing under tables and in dressing rooms and whatever.

Well, we weren't in a sappy romantic movie. If he wanted more sex, he could ask for it.

The side effect of worrying about what he wanted was that the ache of the dream faded while I was working through all of that. So when he asked if I wanted to talk about it, I said, "No, I'm already feeling better," which was true, and it was also true that it was because of him, so I left it there.

But I kept seeing that desperate trapped flash in Vanessa's eyes.

In the morning, lying in bed, Athos asked me seriously to tell him about the dreams. I tried to resist, but he said that if he knew about them, he might be able to help me figure some shit out. So I said fine, and I told him in very vague terms that they were about a lesbian otter trapped in a theological misogynistic cult and her best friend who had just been implanted with a device that corrected her behavior with "the Voice of an angel." I didn't tell him that Hannah had been dreaming about me, nor that she'd been getting spunkier since I'd started dreaming about *her*. I didn't hate her for being a sap anymore; now I kind of hated her for having the strength to plan a way out of her life.

"That's a pretty bad dream," he said, propping himself up on one elbow so he could look at me. "I'm sure you see the relevance to your situation."

For a minute, I thought he meant Bellie, and I was going to snap something about not being a lesbian, but then I caught myself because I hadn't told him about that. "Sure," I said. "I'm really sick and fucking tired of my parents taking me to church and making me marry a good Christian otter."

"The underlying story," he said patiently, "is of a girl trying to escape the rules of society, like you're doing."

"So which friend of mine just got ass-whupped back into obedience?"

"That's also you."

I squinted at him. "Dream theory, right? Everyone in my dreams is me?"

He nodded. "It's the you that you're afraid of becoming. It's interesting that the correction is made through a Voice, though, and not pills of some kind."

"Hannah doesn't know about the pills," I said without thinking.

"Uh-huh."

"But the voice totally makes sense." I hurried away from the topic of what Hannah knew and talking about her as though she was real, and fortunately had a good reason why I would know about voices in people's heads. "There's studies about how if we get voices inside our heads, they bypass our logic filters and we take them as fact."

"How do we get voices inside our heads?"

"Hallucinations, I guess? Malfunctioning speech centers, or parts of the brain that used to evolve into speech centers. There's this book by this one guy who thinks that when people talked about ancestor worship, they were actually hearing internal voices and attributing them to their ancestors."

"Huh." He tilted his muzzle. "And we evolved beyond that?"

"I dunno." I shrugged. "I only read the free preview."

He chuckled. "So you incorporated that into your dream as well. Interesting. Why did you read that book?"

I'd had time to prepare a reasonable answer that didn't reveal the real reason. Also time to feel guilty about not revealing the real reason, and to reassure myself that this wasn't the time or place. "When Sol and Alexei started having weird experiences, I read a lot of shit."

He reached over and rested a paw on my stomach. "Don't worry about this. You'll get past it. Alexei feels a lot better having gone through his, and it's helping him deal with…you know."

I nodded. "Mike's good for him too."

"You should go apologize to him for last night." Athos's fingers rubbed through my fur. I relaxed enough to not mind it.

I didn't really want to apologize. I wanted everyone to forget about it. But Athos was probably right, and since obviously everyone was not going to forget about it, I really should make sure Alexei was doing okay.

We went out to the dining room after throwing on some clothes and found a note on the table. *Gone to Mike's. See you Monday night. —Alexei.*

I sighed. "Drama queen."

"You should call him," Athos said. "Or at least text."

"You know, the otter in my dream had an annoying companion who always told her to do the right thing."

"Oh?" He raised his eyebrows. "Did she sleep with her?"

"No." The memory of Hannah shuddered at that, as though he'd suggested she sleep with her mother. I went back to my room for my phone and found a voicemail already on it. It wasn't from Alexei, though.

"Hi, Meg. This is Dr. Wallace. I'm sorry to hear you're having trouble again. Let's set up an appointment. I can make time for you this afternoon, Tuesday or Thursday afternoon, or Thursday or Friday morning."

He left the number for me to call, and I set the phone down numbly. Last night I'd been so sure there was nothing left for me to do, and I still thought that, but I kept seeing Vanessa's eyes. Is that how I would look?

No, the pills *stopped* the voices. They didn't enable them.

Athos came in holding his own phone. "Something wrong? Did Alexei call?"

"No." I held the phone in my paw and stared at it. "No. I'll text him."

So I texted, *Hey fox, sorry about being a bitch last night. I was scared.* Athos asked me what I was thinking about with the phone, and I told him it was nothing. Alexei texted back while we were talking that he would be back tonight; I showed Athos that and he went off to text Alexei that he was sorry he'd miss him, and that ended that conversation.

We went out to the other little coffee shop for breakfast, and Athos talked about the coffee shops in Port City, the art scene there, and how he was looking forward to showing me places. He thought I'd fit in with a lot of the artist crowd and that I would like his bookish friends, too. I listened with one ear and nodded, saying how interesting it sounded, but it made me think of bringing him to my coffee shop and that led me to last night, which I didn't want to think about at all.

I imagined myself walking into one of the artsy hangouts in Port City and seeing Angeline in the face of one of the people there, yelling at her about keeping Hannah down. Or maybe running into another lesbian like Bellie who was convinced I was gay. I guess having Athos around would help with that, maybe, but the whole thing made me feel tired and a little ill.

His flight was for mid-afternoon, and I was going to wait to call Dr. Wallace back until after he left. I suggested we watch some shows on the computer through the morning, but Athos said, "You sure you don't want to draw something?"

"I don't think so," I said.

"Maybe your comic story is almost over." He smiled. "Getting it finished might help you get some closure."

I thought about that. He wasn't completely off. And I wasn't dreading drawing the rest of Marie-Belle's story anymore. My life was pretty completely fucked up, so what could get worse? But I almost wished I did dread it. At least then I'd feel something, at least then I wouldn't be killing time waiting to descend back into Dr. Wallace's office, back to the scared fifteen-year-old I'd thought I'd left behind.

So I took out the paper and sat at the dining room table while Athos watched. I remembered where I'd left the story, with Toutou's death, and I did not want to draw Marie-Belle grieving. Fortunately, I didn't.

Chapter 41

The Guignacs insisted that the ceremony be held indoors, so Marie-Belle dresses in the hot, stuffy back room of the large town hall. Aunt Eloise helps with the dress, a gift from Mme. Guignac that does not quite fit, but discreet pins make it look quite presentable. "How lucky you will be to go live in that lovely estate," Eloise says. "You must have us over for tea."

"Of course," Marie-Belle replies automatically. She had asked that Toquine be allowed to attend her, but the Guignacs could not spare her from the kitchen. There will be nearly a hundred guests to be fed, after all, and there are catfish to fry and crawfish to boil, there is dough to shape and fry and beer to pour.

She looks longingly out the window at the buildings, the fields beyond, the cypress trees beyond that. To live in the open air, under the trees and above the water: why is it so reviled? That is where she belongs, that is where she has been happy. But the Guignacs and her family wish to appear civilized, to live on dry land and behave like land-dwellers.

"And if you come into a bit of property somewhere, we could always sell the little cabin."

Toutou's cabin has been sold; Sébastien slithered away free into the swamp and the spirits bound to the shrine have been released. Marie-Belle arranged the sale, as the heir to her grandmother's estate, but she has not visited the cabin after the one time to meet Desirée Trounoir, who had spoken to her dead brother briefly and unsatisfyingly. Baron La Croix's presence had been brief, limited to what was necessary. Perhaps he had extracted some price from Desirée; the idea nagged at Marie-Belle if she let it, but what was she to do about it now?

One of the things Toutou had always lamented was that people wanted to speak to the dead so often (not counting the spirits who had remained in her cabin to help her). Either the dead wished to be left in peace and did not come, which was the usual way, or they did come and spoke longingly of life or angrily of death. They could not rejoin the world, and the living who attempted to talk to them could not comfort them, and so on the whole, she disliked those requests the most. But she never turned one away.

"Come along," Aunt Eloise says. "It is time."

Music begins from the other side of the door; or perhaps it has been going on for a few minutes and Marie-Belle has been unaware of it. She gathers the dress around her and rises.

"You are the most beautiful bride I have ever seen," Eloise says.

Marie-Belle supposes that that is because to Eloise, she looks like respect and an elegant two-story house painted eggshell blue and soft ivory, tea services every afternoon, visits from the mayor and judge, from traders and travellers, from family and friends. In the glass of the room, Marie-Belle sees a plain muskrat in someone else's dress, a future of other people's drawing-rooms and manners, of ceilings and lashes. She will live it because her Toutou told her to, because she does not deserve her freedom.

The ceremony itself takes nearly an hour and a half, and despite the airy look of the hall, wooden beams crossing thirty feet up beneath the gabled roof, the air here is warm and no less thick than in the small back room. Here it also smells of a hundred Guignacs and their relatives, of Pierre standing beaming oafishly at her.

Of all the parts of this wedding that chafe at her, Pierre surprisingly is the least of them. She cannot forget the knife in his chest, that she saved him from death and preferred him alive. In this sense he is her responsibility, and her feelings toward him have moderated to affection, if not love.

This newfound bond between them has not gone untested. Pierre contrived to get her alone two nights before, unwilling to wait for the wedding day. She had never lain with anyone, and her body barely quickened with arousal before Pierre rolled off, grinning and panting. It wasn't that no males interested her, but Pierre did not, and when she tried to imagine someone she might better like pressed to her body, the only face that came into her mind was the grinning weasel Baron La Croix. She could not help thinking in that moment that if he would possess Pierre's body again for a bottle of rum, Marie-Belle would lay in a bedroom closet full of bottles. That she is ashamed of herself for thinking this does not make it less true.

She does not want to look at Pierre's grinning face during the ceremony, but remembering his awkward lovemaking is better than looking at his chest and remembering the knife. So Marie-Belle fixes her gaze on her almost-husband's smile while the pastor drones like a hive of hornets and his foul breath washes over them in waves worse than anything the swamp could produce.

When they are declared married, a great cheer fills the hall, and Marie-Belle smiles. The joy of a hundred people warms her for a moment, long enough that she can step outside herself and dwell on their happiness for her rather than her own lifeless future.

There is an interminable reception line. Mme. Guignac stands next to Marie-Belle on her left; Pierre to her right is the end of the line. With every muskrat and otter that approaches, Marie-Belle's mother-in-law whispers in her ear their name and station, and Marie-Belle must hold out a paw to be kissed and repeat the name and title with a "Thank you," as they congratulate her.

Then there is a young otter, no more than fifteen, wearing a bright yellow dress and a bright wide smile, and Mme. Guignac pays her no mind. She is with the stout matronly otter in front of her ("Mrs. Robinson, the wife of the county clerk") or the slender female otter behind her ("Mme. Lowry, the wife of James Lowry the sugar trader"), perhaps. Marie-Belle smiles as the young otter looks gravely up at her.

They clasp paws, but the young otter does not move on. "I have a secret," she announces.

Mme. Lowry smiles tolerantly. "What secret is that, Adelaide?"

"It is for Mme. Guignac."

Marie-Belle's mother-in-law leans forward, but the otter shakes her head and points to Marie-Belle. "That Madame Guignac."

The older muskrat's ears flick in annoyance. "Very well. Hurry up about it. You are inconveniencing the whole line."

Marie-Belle bends over so the young otter can approach her ear. The little muzzle comes close, and she whispers, "*There is joy everywhere, sweet morsel. If you know how to look.*"

Marie-Belle straightens and stares down at the young child. "Who are you?" she whispers.

"I'm Adelaide Lowry," the young otter says, her smile wide and bright as the sun shining through the western windows of the hall, and she skips past Pierre without even offering her paw.

Marie-Belle stares after her as she takes her mother's paw, the two thick tails bobbing in unison. James Lowry comes next in the line and tells her how clever his daughter is, and Marie-Belle says how wonderful that is, watching the yellow sundress dance out the door into the bright afternoon.

It is a great trial not to burst into tears. The child's innocence behind the Baron's honeyed words, the promise he made that she will never, ever act on, all serve to remind her how her own selfish actions led her to this wedding.

And then, with the warmth of the sun coming through the clouds, she feels her grandmother's presence with her as well. The child skipping away becomes a portent of the children she may have eventually. The Guedé are not evil, she remembers, and the Baron has reminded her that her husband may be clumsy, but he loves her; the house may seem a prison now, but there are sweet vegetables and drinks.

"That's all the guests," Mme. Guignac says. "We may leave now."

Marie-Belle knows it is a lie, but she follows anyway. Presently, she thinks as she walks out onto the lawn, there will be music and dancing. And all around her are smiles, so many smiles that she cannot help but smile herself.

Chapter 42

Athos took the pages as I lifted my paw from them, blinking. The pencil slid from my fingers to the table.

Pages shuffled. "Does she talk to the Baron again?" Athos asked finally, setting the pages down.

The pencil lay next to a scar that had been on the table since we'd gotten it. "I don't think there is any more."

"So...she marries him and lives with him and has kits?"

I nodded slowly. "I guess. I don't really know. I just feel...empty. Like it's over."

His whiskers dipped and came back up. "Was the dream last night the last one, too? Maybe everything's over."

"No. I don't think everything's over." The story might be over, but there was still something Marie-Belle wanted from me.

"Adelaide Lowry," he said, pulling out the next to last page.

"What?" I leaned over.

He showed me. "The name comes up several times, so I thought it might be important."

"Maybe." I shook my head again. "It doesn't mean anything to me."

"All right." He set the pages down and rested both paws on the table, staring at the comic. "Is everything all right?"

"We'll see. If it's over, then...maybe."

"I mean..." He took a breath. "I haven't really dated a lot." His finger touched one of the panels where I'd sketched in Marie-Belle next to her husband. "But I feel really happy about us, and you seem..." He looked down again. "Not so happy."

"Maybe that has something to do with the freaky dreams, the panic attacks, the public drama, and," I gestured to the comic, "having *this* thing going on." When he didn't respond, I said, "I did say it was helpful you being here."

"I know. Sorry. I guess I'm just feeling like, I'm leaving in a couple hours and..." He lifted a sheaf of pages, going back to the one where Marie-Belle was remembering the awkward sex with Pierre.

"I don't want to marry you, if that's what you mean." My stomach skittered uneasily.

"Of course not." He dropped the pages and laughed shortly. "It's funny, that's all. I mean, we sleep together for the first time, and I know—I know there were problems." He ducked his head, his ears back.

"It was—"

"Fine, I know." He didn't let me finish. "Then I suggest you move in with me, and you draw this comic where a bride has unenjoyable sex and then is pushing herself to be happy at her wedding, where she clearly doesn't want to be."

"I think she really is happy." I didn't want to look at the pages. "Anyway, I made up this story like four years ago."

"But you told me you weren't sure how it was going to turn out."

When I'd made it up, I was sure that Marie-Belle had escaped her marriage and run off to be a voodoo priestess. I was pretty sure I hadn't told him that, but it wasn't relevant anyway. "Look, if you believe in all this spirit stuff, then…then you know that this isn't coming from inside me. It's coming through me. All I'm doing is drawing it."

His ears came back up and he lifted a paw from the comic to rub his whiskers. "True. But in that case, why are you being told this story?"

I rocked back in the chair. "Jesus, if you can figure that out, please for the love of god tell me."

"Right. Right. Sorry." He stared back down at the comic, then lifted his head. "So can we still talk about you moving…?"

I gathered up the papers and stood. "I need to talk to Alexei. We can talk about it later in the week."

He followed me into my bedroom, where I could smell him from behind me and from the futon in front of me. I threw the comic pages with the others on the floor of my closet. "I know you have to talk to Alexei," he said. "I will too. But do you want to?"

"I don't know," I said. Saying yes would avoid trouble, and what else was I going to do with my life? If I had to go back on the pills, my choices were either live with my parents or live with Athos, and when you put it that way it wasn't a choice at all. Marie-Belle was bound in a marriage she didn't want, and Hannah was about to be; why should I be any different?

Because they're stories, I told myself, and you're real. Right. Even in my head, that didn't sound convincing anymore. Thinking about Hannah, I had the creepy feeling that maybe she was dreaming about me having this conversation. She'd been getting better since I'd been dreaming about her, or at least I sympathized with her more because we were both trapped. So if I gave in to Athos, what would she do? Would she just go off and get married?

Fuck, I hadn't asked for this responsibility. If Hannah couldn't sort out her own life, I couldn't worry about her. I needed to sort out my own.

Athos's tail was curled between his legs, and after years of friendship with Sol, I knew canid body language well enough to know that he was more down than he was letting on in his tone or his still-upright ears. "I've got forty minutes before I should leave." He sat on the futon and patted the space next to him. "So let's talk about it."

I couldn't think of a good reason not to, so I flipped my tail back and sat next to him. "Do you love me?" he asked.

"Wow," I said. "I thought you were going to go right to the hard questions, like asking if I've noticed this weather we've been having."

"Sorry." He exhaled. "It took a lot of nerve to ask that. I know you don't believe in True Love with capital letters, but you've got to admit that there is a condition where two people have a great deal of affection for each other and want to share a lot of their lives, and it's quicker just to call that love."

"You know that backing me into a corner like that isn't helpful? Of course I'm going to say yes, because you obviously love me and if I say no, you'll walk out of here with everything drooping." I knew I was babbling, but I was rather desperate.

"Are you saying yes?" He tried a smile, but it barely lifted his whiskers.

"Christ." I slumped my shoulders. "I have a lot of affection for you and I like having you around and I will be sad when you're back home. I'm already sharing more of my life with you than anyone else. So you tell me: do I love you?"

He swung his tail over, but mine was lying to the other side, so they barely touched. "I suppose that's the best I could hope for."

That was a relief. The last thing I wanted was for him to go home broody and depressed. Well—okay, there were probably half a dozen things I wanted less: sex, another comic like Marie-Belle's, another Hannah nightmare—but few of them were anything I had control over. "Look," I said, "it'd make a lot of things easier if I move. It'd just also make a couple things harder, and Alexei and Sol are important to me, so I have to deal with that."

"I know." He folded his paws together in his lap. "I'm sorry for making a big deal about it, but it's a big deal for me, too."

"I know," I said.

We sat quietly, and honestly it was the most peaceful I'd felt in days. When he reached out and took my paw, I let him, and I even squeezed back. "Hey," I said, "if I move in with you, we won't have to have conversations like this every day, will we?"

He laughed again. "No, things will settle down." Then he cleared his throat and his ears folded partway back. "Uh, and the, uh, the sex will get better too."

My warmth faded. "What?"

"Well, uh, you know, it was both of our first times, and so it's going to get better. I was reading about it and, and, Kevin said that too."

"Wait." I kept hold of his paw. "It was your first time, too?"

"Well, yeah." His ears went farther down. "I told you I'd never...I mean, we talked about it last year."

Ah, shit. I vaguely remembered an online conversation when I was talking about what I could do when I turned eighteen, and on the topic of sex, he'd said something about not rushing into anything...for a twenty-something virgin, that was probably super-revealing, but I'd barely thought about it until now. "Oh, right," I said.

"I'm really glad my first time was with you." He leaned over and nuzzled me. "And that you chose to make yours with me." I didn't say anything, so he kept talking. "I know it didn't feel great, but I hope it was still special."

Goddammit. I was going to have to be honest with him about sex.

Right now? I pleaded with myself. *Maybe it'll get better. Maybe I'll figure out how to enjoy sex.*

There wouldn't be a better time. What, was I going to wait until we were making plans for me to move and then say, *Hey, by the way, don't really like sex at all?* Besides, he'd just come out with his "first time" confession. I owed him honesty.

But maybe I wouldn't move. Or maybe I didn't have to tell him. That was my original plan, after all.

Yeah. Great plan. Did I really think I could keep a secret from Athos all my fucking life? We'd already had two intense relationship talks since having sex two days ago. One of these days I would snap and tell him, and the longer I waited, the worse it would be.

In my head, I saw the panel of the comic in which Toutou asks Marie-Belle, "What do you want?" I felt Vanessa whisper the same thing to Hannah.

What did I want? Did I want safety and security, companionship built on little lies? Or did I want Athos to know who I was? This was the part of "love" he hadn't mentioned, this whole uncovering of all your dark places to someone and trusting that they would still want to be with you.

Did I trust Athos? I thought so. Sex was as important to him as to any other guy, but it wasn't what our friendship had been built on. He could handle it.

All right, I thought, you asked for it and here it is. "Actually," I said, "about that."

His ears perked to listen. I took a breath. "Do you know what 'asexual' means?"

He shook his head, then said, "Without sex? Like someone who's… not sexual?" I nodded, and his brow creased, ears folding back down. "But you are sexual. I mean, we had sex."

"That's not what it means. It's—well, like, when you look at me—or if you look at porn on the Internet…" He tried to protest, but I went on, "which you do, don't deny it, all guys do it, anyway, the point is, you get excited, right? You get…" I waved at his hips. "Like guys do."

"Ah, well, yes…" He forced a grin, which held for a moment. "You know how I get."

"Right. Well, I don't. I don't get that at all."

He tilted his head. "I know that female arousal is different—"

"No. I know. I've—" I forced away the image of Bellie. "I've talked to girls too. I don't get that either."

"I don't understand," he said. "You said you weren't—you aren't a lesbian."

"I'm not."

"So you must be straight."

"No." I pushed away the words, *I don't get that with you either.* "There might be another option. I'm—I might be nothing."

He pulled his paw back. He was thinking about it, but I could see his mind going around in circles. "You're not nothing."

"You know what I mean." He still didn't say anything. "Look, you already believe in ghosts. Asexuals aren't that big a stretch."

"It seems weird." His voice was a little distant. "But I guess I can understand an absence of sexual desire."

"It is weird." I started to correct myself, because the one thing the lady on the Internet insisted was that it wasn't wrong or broken and I was still struggling with that. Athos cut me off before I could.

"So when we…had sex, the other night…you didn't want to?"

I puzzled out how to answer that. "I wanted to because you wanted to."

"But you didn't enjoy it."

He still wasn't looking at me and I wasn't sure what he was getting at. "You knew I didn't enjoy it. It didn't matter to you when you thought it was because it was my first time. Why should it matter now?"

"Because—because not enjoying your first time is natural!" He spread his paws, then saw my expression. "Hey, I'm sorry." Now he tried to smile again, but again his whiskers barely lifted and the smile faltered before it even got started. "I didn't mean it that way."

"Yes, you did. It's fine, it's weird. I'm still not completely sure, but I feel like…" I shook my head. "There are people online who identify as ace."

"That's great." He still sounded distracted. "So why did you come on to me?"

"What? Because—because I like you. I knew you wanted to do it and I wasn't sure. I thought maybe I'd enjoy it."

"Heh." There was no humor in his laugh. He looked down at his lap and curled his paws against each other in little impotent fists. "So it was like an experiment. That's great."

I'd thought that this whole honesty thing was going to end with both of us feeling better. "Hey, it took me a lot to tell you. I wasn't sure until a couple days ago."

"When you tried it with me."

"Um." He didn't sound happy about it. "Well…yes."

"All the years we've known each other, you couldn't have talked to me about this before we…"

"I didn't *know!*"

"You could've told me you were worried about it. I could've—I could've done something different, been more careful, slower…"

He'd curled his tail back to his own side of the futon and his shoulders hunched over. I reached out to his paw, but it just hung limply in mine. "Look, I cared enough to try it with you."

"Yeah." His voice stayed flat. "I appreciate that. I appreciate you telling me now. I know it was hard for you."

I had no idea what to say to him or what was even bothering him. Was he upset that I had sex even though I didn't want to? Shouldn't I be the one upset about that? "Okay, well…should we go? I mean, are we done talking?"

He slipped his paw from mine. "Yes, we're done," he said. "We can go."

On the way to the airport, he seemed to perk up some, but I didn't bring up the move and neither did he. Nor did he ask when he could come visit again. He actually spent a lot of time texting his friends back home rather than talking to me at all. I would've texted some of my friends, but Alexei was still working and Sol was probably in class or something.

Dr. Wallace called me back again and as circumspectly as I could, I made an appointment for Thursday. He said he'd have his office send me an e-mail with details and I said I'd figure out how to get there somehow. He asked how I was doing and I said I'd talk to him Thursday. I'm sure Athos heard me, but he kept texting and didn't say anything about it.

When we said good-bye, we hugged, but he didn't try to kiss me, and dammit, that bothered me. All the way home it bothered me, and I knew it shouldn't. I mean, I didn't want him to kiss me, but I wanted him to want to.

Alexei was home when I got back, sitting at the computer in his room talking on the phone. He turned when I came in and raised a paw. "Sol," he said, and then flicked an ear at the phone. "It is Meg, she is home now."

I raised a paw back. "I'll talk to him if he wants."

While I was waiting for Alexei to finish his conversation and trying not to listen to it (he was talking softly, so I couldn't really hear anything), I checked our fridge for dinner. There were a few leftovers, enough stuff I could heat up. I stared at them, thinking about Athos.

When Alexei came out with the phone in his paw, the refrigerator was still open and I hadn't picked anything. I closed it and took the phone.

"What did you say to Alexei?" Sol demanded.

"Hello to you too." I looked up as Alexei sat back down at his computer. "Weren't you just talking to him?"

"He won't tell me. You know how he is. What did you say?"

"I didn't say anything! I told him that he wasn't crazy."

"Uh-huh. How did you say it?"

I sat on the floor in front of the fridge. "What the fuck is with the third degree?"

"He said he's thinking about moving in with Mike. I asked him what you would do and he said you might be moving out and that it was your idea. Then I asked if everything was okay and he said it was fine, but in that, you know, Siberian 'fine' way. So are you moving out?"

"Ugh. Thinking about it. I dunno." I raised my eyes to look at the bedroom. I could see Alexei's red tail swishing, but nothing of the rest of him.

"With Athos?"

"Yeah…"

"Alexei said you guys…did it?"

I leaned my head back against the wall. "Yeaaaah."

"How was it?"

"I dunno. It was fine. It was…you know, it was how it was."

He chuckled. "I guess the first time is a bigger deal for guys."

"I guess. You still looking forward to yours?"

He snorted and then was quiet. I sat up. "You had sex."

"Uh."

"Well, hey. Both of us the same week. Congratulations. Tell me about it."

"It wasn't..." He took a breath.

"What was his name?"

"Val."

"This was the...the dingo? No, wait, you were over him. Snow leopard?"

"No..."

"Come on, it's like pulling teeth. Why aren't you more excited about it?"

He made a low growling noise. "*Her* name was Val, and it was at a party with some of the baseball guys this weekend. She's a coyote on the lacrosse team."

"Whoa, wait. With a girl? What the fuck?"

"Shh! I didn't tell Alexei."

"What? Why not?" I craned my neck to see if Alexei had turned, but his tail kept swishing.

"It meant a lot to him to have another gay friend. I feel like I betrayed him sort of."

"Screw that. How do *you* feel about it?"

"I dunno. It's...it was good, I guess."

"You got off, then."

He chuckled, nervous. "Well, *yeah*."

"But you're not going to switch teams."

"Oh, heck, no. I mean, you know, you can just have sex with anyone, but you don't have to be attracted to them. I mean, I guess it's harder for girls—or maybe it's easier?"

I wedged myself into the corner between the wall and the fridge. "Easier to do it. Harder to enjoy it."

"Yeah. Hey." I could almost see his ears perk up. "Did you enjoy it?"

"Enh." I took a breath. "I'm...I'm sort of in your boat."

"What? You're not gay, though."

"No, I'm..." The prospect of explaining asexuality for the second time in a day fatigued me. "Look up 'asexual' on the Internet sometime. I think that's what I am."

"Should I call you back when I've looked it up?"

I sighed. "Short version: It means I'm not wired to enjoy sex."

"Oh. Can that happen?" Before I could answer, he went on. "Sorry. Obviously it can. That sucks."

That was one reason I liked Sol: he cut through all the bullshit about how hard it was and got right to why it would be hard for me. It *did* suck. "We all got shit to deal with, I guess. If you were straight, wouldn't your life be easier? You'd be a lot happier about having banged that coyote."

"I still like sex, though. I mean, I wasn't attracted to her, but it was still—I mean—you know, they say there's no such thing as bad sex."

"Maybe for you sexual people."

"See? Sucks. I'm sorry. Can you do anything about it?"

"I dunno. Maybe some ghost can fix it."

"All right, all right." We sat silently for a moment, during which I was thinking about whether I'd want a ghost—or a doctor, for that matter—to "fix" my sexuality. It'd be easier if I liked sex, but I'd kind of gotten used to the way I was, and it seemed like sex made lives more complicated, not less.

While I was thinking that, Sol was putting a couple things together. "So wait, you're not interested in sex but you slept with Athos anyway? You must really like him."

"You'd think that would be the reason, wouldn't you?" I shifted to let my tail curl around behind me. It was getting a bit grungy on the floor, but I didn't care.

"Well, why'd you do it then?"

"Seemed like the right thing to do at the time."

"Did he…" His voice got that growl again. "Did he force himself on you?"

"No. No, if anything, I started it. He was being so nice and doing all this shit for me and I knew he was expecting—well, hoping maybe—that we'd fuck, and so I figured if I didn't, I'd come off as a shitty friend, or maybe a bitch, tease, whatever you want to call it."

"Out of obligation, then?"

"Not only that. I mean, I didn't really know about myself. Everyone was telling me I needed to try it to be sure. So…I tried." I cracked open an eye to look at Alexei's tail, still swishing the white tip back and forth like a metronome. He must be listening to music. Polite as always. "What about you?"

"Me?"

"Why did you sleep with someone you weren't attracted to?"

Long sigh. "Couple of the guys from the team were pushing me, and Val liked me. She grabbed me and said, 'You're new,' and we were dancing and then she said she was parked outside—"

"Wait. You did it in a *car*?"

He got that ears-folded-back tone. "Yeah."

I couldn't help it; I laughed. "Aw, Sol. You didn't tell me she was from the eighties."

"Shut up," he said. "It wasn't bad."

"Apart from her being a girl."

He still sounded more amused than defensive. "It was a chance to have sex, Meg. I guess for you that'd be like someone offering you a free bottle of some alcohol you don't really like."

"Funny." I let that one go. "So how do you feel about that being your first time?"

"I'm still looking forward to my first time that *matters*."

"Ouch. Poor Val. Careful she doesn't come after you with a lacrosse stick. I know you like things stuck up there, but—"

"Har har." He growled again. "I'm going to see Limon tomorrow night for coffee."

"Which one is that?"

"He's a mouse. Contacted me through the message boards."

"All right, well. Good luck."

"Thanks. Hey, how are the comic and the dreams and all? Did they stop?"

I drew my legs up and checked Alexei's tail again. Still moving. "The comic's over, I think. The dreams…aren't."

"Don't worry," he said. "If you die in the dream, you don't die in real life."

"If mine are the same as yours."

"It'd be weird if they weren't," he said. "Hey, I have a long weekend over fall break in October. Maybe I can come back for a bit and we can talk about it. I really want to hear more."

"Yeah, maybe." I rested my chin on my knees. "We'll see how it goes. It's pretty fucked up."

"At least you believe now." Now he sounded tail-waggy. "Alexei and I really wanted to be able to talk to you about stuff. Oh—if you haven't moved, I mean."

"We'll see how that goes, too." I closed my eyes again. "But nah, I'm handling it. It's under control. Or it will be."

"All right. Take care of yourself. I'll talk to you soon."

When I hung up, I walked into Alexei's room to return his phone. He turned when I set it on the desk and took the earphones out of his ears. "You talked for a long time," he said.

"Yeah." I reached a paw back to Sol's bed, still made up from the last time Athos had been here. "Can I talk to you for a minute?"

"Of course." He turned his chair and rested his paws in his lap. His tail kept swishing.

I sat down on Sol's bed. "Sorry for what I said about you not being crazy."

He tilted his head. "You now think I am crazy?"

"I'm sorry I said it the way I did. The thing is, all this shit that's happening, I know what I need to do about it. I didn't want to do it because…" I took a breath. "It's kind of like numbing yourself. You don't feel the bad, but you don't feel the good either."

His ears went halfway back and he frowned. "Why must you numb yourself? It is so bad?"

"It can be."

He leaned forward as if sniffing at something. "This is not the first time this has happened to you."

I froze, my fur prickling. I couldn't come up with a good lie in time, so I settled back on sarcastic evasion. "Yeah, it's not like chicken pox, I guess. No immunity."

"What happened before?"

I rested my paws on the bed and leaned back. "You know, it doesn't matter. I dealt with it then, it's over, I don't want to relive it."

"It was worse than what is happening now?"

"Uh…" I swallowed and nodded.

For one tense moment I was afraid he would ask me for details. But his eyes drifted away for a moment and I think he was reliving his own nightmares. Finally he came back to me and gave one quick nod. "All right." He settled back into the chair. "But if you want to talk sometime, if that would help…" His ears came up.

"I know. Thanks." I cleared my throat. "Hey, so about the moving thing…Sol said you talked to Mike?"

"Yes. Mike thinks it is too soon for us to move in, but he has a friend with a spare room and I can live there cheaply. So we are talking about that."

"Okay. Good. I'm sorry to run out on you like this."

He smiled. "When there is love, I know you must follow your heart. But I will miss you."

"Oh, come off it. Mike's way better company than I am."

"Perhaps in some respects." He tilted his head. "If I did not know Athos, I might worry about you."

"Don't worry about me. I took care of myself for a while. I can do it again." It's easy to say things like that when you know you've got pills on your side.

"What do your parents think of your move?"

I looked away from him. "Who cares? I'll tell them when I get a chance." He opened his muzzle to protest and I kept talking. "They aren't really interested in me. All they want is for me to do whatever it takes to be normal. I'm not going to go to their stupid art school. One thing sucking the joy out of my life is enough."

"But they are your parents—" He stopped and tilted his head. "What one thing is that? You mean the dreams?"

"No, I—dammit." I bit my lip. "I meant, you know, that construction out back. Jesus, that's a pain. Can't open the windows at night, can't look out..."

Alexei didn't smile. "What is going on?"

I sighed. "Okay, don't tell—I haven't told anyone else about this yet. I'm going back on the antidepressants."

He widened his eyes. "You are depressed again?"

"No. But...last time I...I almost did something. I can't let it get to that point again and it's heading there, I know it is. You were there in the café. You saw it."

"Yes." He kept his eyes on me, ears straight up. "And you saw me when Konstantin visited us. Do you think I should also be on pills?"

"It's different!" I snapped.

"Why?"

"Because..." I swallowed. Alexei waited patiently. "Because that was your business, and you handled it the way you wanted to..."

"Yes...?"

"What do you want me to say? Yours was real?"

His eyebrows rose. "And yours was not?"

"No! I—listen, I know about these things."

"How?"

The construction machines started up outside. I ignored them, biting my lip again, and then slumped over on Sol's bed. "Okay. When I was fifteen..."

I paused, and Alexei stood. "Should I make myself be comfortable?"

"Probably." I slid over on Sol's bed. Alexei hopped up and sat cross-legged on it close to me. His tail tip flicked up and down, and I focused on that because it was easier than staring at his grey eyes, however friendly they were.

I told him about that night, with the slumber party and Margie and Amelia, and how uncomfortable I was with the sex talk. I told him about the alcohol and about waking up in the night and seeing the shadow in my pool. I told him what Drowned William had said about my life.

That's when it got hard to tell the story. I met Alexei's eyes and tried to crack a smile. "This was four years ago, okay? Just remember that." He nodded. "Okay. Anyway. He told me to go get Mom's sleeping pills. And… eat them all."

Alexei bit his lip. "And you did."

I nodded. "I woke up in the hospital. This Dr. Wallace guy was my psychiatrist and put me on the pills, and I didn't hear voices or anything. Until, you know, a few weeks ago."

He reached out a paw to me, though he wasn't close enough to touch my leg. I stretched my paw out to let him grasp it. "You told me you almost died," he said. "But I thought it was just…teenage things. I did not know there was more."

"Yeah, well, I don't make a big thing of it. For obvious reasons."

"Yes." He nodded. "You have not wanted to…since then?"

I shook my head. "Not really. I mean, no." I squeezed his paw to reassure him. "I'm not dumb enough to kill myself."

He grinned briefly. "I am glad to hear it. I know things have been difficult lately."

"Yeah, but not kill-myself difficult. I mean, I always have a place to go, right?"

"Yes." Alexei's ears folded down. "Now it is in Port City, yes?"

"I guess it is. I mean…we'll see, but I can't really see anything else to do."

He patted my paw. "You should be happy about this."

"Yeah. I am." I tried to see it as Marie-Belle had, to put the positive spin on it: it would make Athos happy. There would be new coffee shops and interesting people in Port City.

His slit-pupiled eyes narrowed. "You forget that I have actually seen you be happy. This…" His free paw waved at me. "This is not you happy."

"I'm sorry I can't be more chipper after telling you about the time I tried to kill myself."

His ears stayed flat. "Before then, too. When I had the chance to come to the States, I smiled every moment I was on the airplane. When Mike asked me to stay the night…" His tail wagged and he inclined his head back toward it. "But when you talk about moving in with Athos, it is like…it is like when you talk about the art school. It is something you know you must do but you do not want to do."

I hated it when he saw things like that, and at the same time it was what made him such a great guy. "What other choice do I have? If I go back on the pills, I can't do art, I can't pay rent here. You can't pay for both of us. So I can go home and live with my fucking parents who got me into this shit, or I can go live with Athos, who, y'know, at least cares about me."

"But do you love him?"

I tried to pull up my best smirk but I only got halfway there. "Hey, you know how I feel about love. I draw people in all kinds of imaginary situations."

He shook his head. "So what do you think about me and Mike?"

"I think you guys get along well, and you like each other, and maybe you'll get along well enough to support each other and live together for a while. Maybe the rest of your lives. And at least you've got—you enjoy the—uh."

His eyes lost the narrow squint. "We enjoy what?" When I didn't answer, he said, "Sex?"

I still didn't say anything. He leaned forward. "But you are not…gay?"

"No, I'm…" Ugh. Not again. Not again.

"Not attracted to him?"

Fuck. "No, listen." So I tried to explain asexuality to him, and he sort of got it, in that Alexei kind of way where he accepted it because I told him, but it didn't quite register, I thought. So I ended with, "I just told Sol, too, so you can talk to him about it. Everyone can talk about my fucked-up biology."

"Everyone has problems," Alexei said. He hadn't let go of my paw. "We do not make fun of you when we talk about you."

"Yeah, well."

His nostrils flared. "Do you make fun of me? Or Sol?"

"No more than I do to your noses." I raised my eyebrows with a weak grin. "Living in dreamworlds."

"It is a big world. There is room for you, too."

I lost the grin. "Yeah, I don't know about that. Hey…you never told me more about your first time with Mike. You said it went well, right?"

"Yes." He nodded and his ears came all the way up.

"Can I ask you something about it?"

He let go of my paw then and sat back. Tilting his head to the side, his lips curved into a smile. "I thought you did not care about love."

"Okay, first off, I said I didn't believe in it. I didn't say I don't care about it. Second of all, I'm not asking you about love, just sex."

"All right. I will not talk about private details…"

"I don't want details. I want to know…why was it so good? Was it physical? Like, the sensations were better?"

"Oh, God." He laughed. "The sensations were different, but…it was Mike. You said you are not asking me about love, but you are. Sex is physical, but with Mike it was better. He cares about me and he was—we were both so happy."

"Was there something about it being your first time?"

Again, he chuckled. "Mike was worried. He said first times are difficult and if it was not good, he worried it would make me like him less. I said that if it was difficult I would let him try again."

"What?"

He ducked his muzzle and grinned. "Sol taught me that one."

Should I have said something like that to Athos? Wait, he'd said something like that to me. "But it wasn't difficult?"

"No. Not very. Well…" He grinned at me. "I will not give you details. The second time was better, but the first time was still good because it was Mike."

"All right, I think that's about enough of the love." I leaned back. "I'll let you know how things go with Athos."

"We will have to have Sol back before we all move. He will want to see you again."

"Yeah. Thanks." I pushed myself off the bed.

"Meg." Alexei remained on the bed. His muzzle was turned up toward me and his eyes were serious, grey and bright. "If this thing with Athos is not what you want, then do not do it."

"I know in your world, you only get to do the things you really want to." I smiled a bit so he wouldn't think I'd forgotten his flight from Siberia and everything that had happened before. "But some of us get stuck in no-win situations. That's why that's a phrase, 'no win situation.' It means a situation where you have no winning move."

"Then you wait for a different situation." He flicked his ears. "You have friends."

"Thanks," I said.

"One more thing," he said as I was at the door.

"Christ, what now?" I turned.

"The blackberry liquor…"

"Yeah." I nodded. "That's why that bottle's in the cabinet. Dr. Wallace said I should keep it around so I wouldn't be afraid of it, but I haven't been able to make myself drink it. I never wanted to, you know?"

"I see." He smiled. "No more questions."

Back in my room, I sat on the futon and pulled up my e-mail. Three days until the appointment with Dr. Wallace. His office's e-mail sat there in my box, right under one from Athos that had come in a few minutes ago.

The subject line of that one was "Call me." I clicked, wondering what might have gone wrong, but the message only said he wanted to discuss something with me that he'd been thinking about all the way home. So I called him, hoping he'd figured out something about the comic or the dreams, or maybe a way to ease the move.

He started with small talk about his flight, and I let that go for a while until it became painful. Then I asked what he'd been thinking about.

He sighed. "I think we might be moving fast on this—you know, on the moving thing. I mean, we don't really know each other all that well. Maybe we should just keep visiting and talking."

"Whoa," I said. "Where's this coming from?"

"I dunno. I guess I got caught up in the excitement…you know, the first couple days this weekend were really nice."

The part where I was going crazy and also having sex with him. Yeah, I guess I could see where he'd be excited by that. I wanted to say something like, "Fine, whatever," like I didn't really care. Not having to move to Port City would be a lot less hassle, to be honest, even if I did then have a lot of shit to figure out.

I did care, was the problem. Athos had really made the last few days easier, not to mention the years of high school before that. I put a paw down on my futon and thought about waking up from the dream with him there, and him supporting me against my parents.

"Meg?"

And here he was pushing me away because of…I tried to remember when he'd gone all quiet. "Wait, is this because I'm asexual? Is that what this is?"

"It's not that." Lukewarm denial.

My fur got all hot and prickly. Sol and Alexei had been fine with it and I'd thought Athos was too. I'd told them *because* I'd thought he was. "Because fuck you if it is. You understand that I didn't want to, right?"

"Yeah," he said, more animated now. "And you didn't tell me that."

"I told you today."

"After we'd already had sex twice."

"So what difference does that make?" I heard myself say those words and I cringed, and then I remembered Sol saying, *the first time that matters*, and my fur got even more prickly. It had been Athos's first time, too.

"I don't know, it just does. Look, I'm not saying we can't work this out, but…I want to talk more."

"Jesus. You know I already talked to Alexei about moving out?"

"That's why I wanted to talk to you tonight. Nothing's firm, right? I mean, you can stay there a while longer? I'll still lend you the money for rent—"

"No. I'll be fine."

"You'll be—where are you going to get rent from, then?"

I drew my legs up onto the futon. "I'll figure it out."

Now he sighed. "Meg, I'm sorry, but don't be brick-headed about this just because I want to slow things down."

Letting him take care of me. That's what Hannah would have done—well, maybe at the start of my dreams. Marie-Belle wouldn't let a boyfriend take care of her. In fact, she'd had to look after hers. And then on top of it he had to call me names. "Brick-headed? Brick-headed? No, it's fine. I don't feel rejected for my asexuality at all."

"Meg—"

"Let's keep talking, like you said. When you figure out how to deal with the way I am, and I figure out how to deal with the way you are, then we can work something out."

"That's not fair—the way I am?"

Everything in my body felt tight. "Yeah, all like 'full speed ahead' and then slamming on the brakes. And so focused on sex."

"Wait a minute!" His voice rose sharply. "I'm not 'focused on sex.' I'm focused on, on honesty, and communication."

"Right," I said. "Which is why you got second thoughts when I was honest with you."

"That's not fair. It's because you weren't honest before."

"Oh, got it. Well, I won't make that mistake again."

Anger couldn't quite whitewash the sickness in me, the betrayal, and yet there was a little bit of relief, too. Maybe I hadn't really wanted to move to Port City, and this way I got to get out of it without being the bad guy. I really didn't want to lose my friendship with Athos, but that felt like it was happening anyway. Maybe the whole idea of love had been as imaginary as a ghost in a pool, something I'd tricked myself into seeing. When he'd wanted to sleep with me, he "loved" me. When I didn't want to sleep with him, poof, the ghost was gone.

"Look," he said, "I'm sorry for how this came out. I still want to keep seeing you. Maybe I can come down in a couple weeks and we can talk about it again."

"Sure." I was trying to balance all my emotions. I wanted to tell him not to bother, and part of me wanted to tell him to come down next weekend, and I wanted to yell and cry and hang up. Saying "Sure" put off the decision about what to do. Nothing I said was going to change his mind, and there was no point in continuing to fight over the phone, because what I wanted he wouldn't give me. Sometimes, I told Hannah silently in my head, you have to save the fight for another day. Listen. Know what you want. Know how to ask for it.

So we wound down the conversation with awkward, "Okay, see you then" exchanges, and he said something about calling again during the week. I made a noncommittal noise and hung up.

Alexei'd kept his earphones in, so he greeted me with a bright smile when I came in to ask about dinner. I told him everything was cool but that I might not be moving out yet, and asked him not to ask questions.

"May I ask one? You do not have to answer, but…" When I nodded, he went on. "Do you need money?"

I sighed. "I'll—I'll figure something out. Maybe I can still go to that art school, y'know?" And the doctor would cost money, although Dr. Wallace would probably let me slide for a bit. "But if you could cover dinner, I'd appreciate it."

He smiled and nodded. "I can do that."

Chapter 43

Hannah pulled Vanessa through the cypress roots. Walking for so long felt odd, but the streams and open water were watched, she knew. Vanessa seemed even less at ease, picking her way around and hiking her dress over snags. Hannah's already resembled a beggar's shawl around her knees, and the bundle over her shoulder kept catching on branches, but she didn't care. "Come on!"

"I know, I know." Vanessa said it low. Hannah wasn't sure whether her friend was talking to her or to the Voice. There was a short pause before she went on. "Your surprise isn't going to run away, is it?"

If we don't hurry, Hannah thought, it will. "I want to get there and back before dark, and the sun will be setting soon."

"How far are we going?" Vanessa clambered over a root as high as her waist. "And why can't we swim there?"

"It's on land." Hannah stopped to look around. The high cypress that was the church's steeple lay between them and the afternoon sun, as Vilan had told her, and so they should be coming to the cemetery soon. Surely it had been a mile already. They had taken half an hour to get to the church without swimming, and it had been at least another hour since then. Hannah's fur felt dry and itchy, and bugs kept flying into her eyes. She hadn't realized until this trek how much she hated walking, but the hardship would be worth it.

"Nothing is this far on land around here." Vanessa followed Hannah along the surface of a thick root onto a clump of sedge grass. "Look, there's water just through those bushes." She stopped to wave. "Hallo!"

"Shh!" Hannah's heart skipped a beat. She grabbed Vanessa's paw. "Come on!"

"But why don't we want them to see us? We're just on the way to your surprise." She paused again. "It isn't a surprise I will be unhappy with, is it?"

Those pauses always reminded Hannah of the box, and her fingers curled despite herself. "You'll be very happy," she promised.

Vanessa's muzzle relaxed into a smile. "Good."

Over the past week, Hannah had gotten used to watching for those flashes, those brief moments when she saw her friend struggling against the Voice of the angel. They were so brief that minutes afterwards, Hannah was no longer sure she'd seen them. "I can't wait for you to see it," she said.

They pushed through a large bush some fifteen minutes later, and aging wrought-iron fencing rose before them, each rail looking as though it had sprung from the thick growth of white-rimmed green ivy that clustered around the fencing. Vanessa stopped and stared, and only after a moment noticed the marble slabs and mausoleums beyond.

"Oh, no," she said. "We can't go in there."

Even the insects had grown silent and the wind dropped to a dead calm. Vanessa's words sank into the ivy and left the clearing and the small hill as silent as before. Hannah suppressed a shiver of her own. "We won't stay," she said. "And we'll be out before dark."

"It's wrong," Vanessa insisted.

"That's the angel talking," Hannah said, but she didn't move either. "Please, Vanessa. We have to go in. He's waiting for us."

"He?" Vanessa's eyes widened and then she paused, and the shock became suspicion. "Who?"

"It's—it's a surprise," Hannah said. She'd expected to see Vilan by this point, but the red wolf was nowhere in sight. The sun was almost to the tops of the trees; perhaps they were too late and he'd already gone. "Look, I'll be with you all the way."

"No. I'm not allowed to go in there. You're not—we're not allowed to go in there."

Hannah thought about her dream, how crushed her dream-self had been when the escape from her life was taken away from her, and how little she'd seemed to actually value it. Then again, she wasn't being forced to marry someone, and she hadn't had her best friend taken away from her. No, she remembered, that wasn't quite true. That last dream, when she'd been talking to her friend the fox who didn't want to be with her because she didn't like sex, that had stirred Hannah. Her dream-self had been fiery, standing up for herself, and Hannah felt she could do no less.

"We're not allowed," she said, "but we're going. We'll go around the fence for a while and only go in when we see the marker."

"I'm not." Vanessa folded her arms. "I can't do it. I won't go with you."

"But…" Hannah reached out to grab her friend's wrist. Vanessa's fur felt as dry as her own. "You *have* to. I won't leave you."

"Leave me!" Vanessa said it quickly. "Leave—" And then she winced. "Stay here. We both have to stay right here."

"Come *on!*" Hannah gritted her teeth and yanked Vanessa so hard her friend almost fell. She kept pulling, keeping Vanessa off balance so that the other otter had to run just to stay upright.

"Hannah!" Vanessa gasped. "No!"

Hannah gritted her teeth and kept going. They hurried through the short grass and got around one of the mausoleums before Vanessa dug in her heels. "We're staying here," she said. "They'll be here to pick us up soon."

"No!" They were so close. Hannah looked up the hill and saw there the stone wings that Vilan had told her to look for. "Vilan!" she cried. "Vilan, we're here!"

"Vilan?" By the time Hannah turned to look at her, Vanessa's face had twisted in horror, whiskers splayed and lips pulled back to show her teeth. "The northern trader?"

"He can help you! He can turn off the voice!"

"I…" Vanessa squeezed her eyes shut and put her paws up to her ears, hunching over. "No. It's too late."

"Hannah?"

She looked up to see a shape emerging from behind the wings of the stone angel, silhouetted against the sun. The lanky canid figure approached with his familiar swaggering gait, ears up, muzzle turning this way and that. "We're here," she called. "I can't get her to move."

"I can't help you with that. It's kidnapping."

"You have to."

Vanessa's paws remained pressed to the side of her head as she emitted a keening moan. "Stop!" she panted. "Please stop!"

"They're hurting her!" Hannah tugged on Vilan's arm.

"If you want to come with me," the tall red wolf said, "we have to go now, and we have to leave her behind. They mightn't pursue me if you came willingly, but if I kidnap someone, that's very bad."

"I can't leave her!" Hannah cried.

Vilan turned to look at the sun, then back to her. "I'm leaving," he said. "You can come with me or not, but I'm leaving now."

"No!" Hannah reached out, but he avoided her paw with a quick dodge and began walking quickly along the fence.

Vanessa hadn't moved throughout the exchange, making small groans as she rocked back and forth. Hannah pulled at her wrists. "Please, please!" she begged, but Vanessa's paws remained pinned to her ears and she did not move. Hannah turned; Vilan was almost out of sight around the curve of the fence. She pulled one more time and could not budge Vanessa. With a sob, she left her friend and ran after the trader.

"Good," Vilan said when she caught up to him. "We have to hurry. My boat is just ten minutes' walk along this path."

He did not mention Vanessa, but Hannah could not stop seeing her friend in pain from the voice of the angel, or whatever it was. Angels were

"A shape emerged from behind the wings"

supposed to be kind; angels were supposed to help you. They weren't supposed to scream so loudly that you were paralyzed. They weren't supposed to force you into doing what she was coming to suspect was not exactly the will of the benevolent God whose praises she had sung in church all her life.

"Just through here—" Vilan stopped.

Hannah had been watching her feet through the dirty ground, but when Vilan stopped dead, she looked up. A small boat bobbed in the water, and in front of it, a tall otter stepped forward amid the whirr of her white dress drying itself. Streaks of green ran down Angeline's dress and a small plant hung over one ear, but Hannah's companion took no notice. She stared at Hannah and Hannah knew her companion was trying to talk to her through the device she had ripped out and left back at her house.

"Hannah," she said, "you will come back with me immediately."

"I—" Hannah thought of her dream-self's forceful argument again. The presence of Vilan, unmoving beside her, lent her extra strength. "I will not," she said. "I am going with this trader and you cannot stop me."

"Hannah," Vilan said softly, warningly.

"You said if I went willingly—"

"Come here this instant." Angeline's voice rang out over the water. Insects buzzed around Hannah's ears. "This is your last chance."

Vilan whispered, so softly Hannah could barely hear him. "Do you still have that perfume?"

She nodded very shortly. He'd told her to bring it and so she had it in her pocket, not in the bundle slung over her shoulder. She dropped her paw, holding the cool glass of the bottle against her fingers as she took a step forward.

"Hannah," Vilan said when she was halfway to Angeline.

She turned. He tapped his nose and smiled. "I hope you have a wonderful life."

"Stop talking to her," Angeline said sharply.

Hannah's nerves jangled with every step. The buzzing of the insects around her ears reached a fever pitch. She gripped the bottle so tightly her paw ached by the time she reached her companion.

Angeline seized her arm above the elbow. "How dare you?" She brought her muzzle close to Hannah's, her brow wrinkled and fangs showing, as angry as Hannah had ever seen her. "You think to run away from God and you expect me to allow you to damn yourself to eternal torment? I tried to spare you from Vanessa's fate, but now there is no more I can do. We will not let your soul be lost so easily. What are you doing?"

This last was because Hannah had worked the perfume bottle out of her dress pocket. "I got you a present," she said, and before Angeline could respond, she sprayed the perfume into her companion's nose.

Angeline recoiled and began to speak, but then her muzzle froze in that position. Her eyes stared fixedly ahead and her body, even her tail, slowed and stopped.

"Come!" Vilan was beside her in an instant, grasping her paw. The perfume fell to the ground as he pulled, and Hannah jumped to keep up with his long-legged stride.

They scrambled aboard the boat, over the wooden plank before Hannah had a chance to be afraid of its shaky balance. Vilan dropped down into the pilot's seat and Hannah sat behind him. "Just a moment," the red wolf said, bending forward.

A loud report sounded at the back of the boat. "What was that?" Hannah clamped her mouth shut as soon as she spoke. Her voice sounded so high.

"Not good news." Vilan straightened, hesitated, and then stood up in the seat. As he turned to look behind him, a beam of light crossed the boat to strike him in the eye.

He made a guttural noise in his throat and fell back against the wheel, then slowly, slowly, slid down, so that Hannah had all the time in the world to see the smoking cavity in his skull where his left eye had been, to see the blackened flesh and fur around it, to see a flash of sunlit leaves through the other end of the hole *through his head*, before it was obscured by smoke. His body jerked and spasmed as it fell, a stain appearing on his pants as he came to rest, and only then did Hannah scream.

She kept screaming as the boat rocked, as strong hands pulled her from the seat, as she was pushed across the plank and fell to the ground, as Nephaline bent over her and told her to stop that noise. Hannah could not stop, and it was no longer only the memory of Vilan's death that made her scream, but all of her anguish coming out in the only voice she could give it.

Nephaline said more words, but they were lost, meaningless, and Hannah scrambled for the water only to be pulled back by a foot like a kit. She thrashed and yelled, and cried out when a needle pain stabbed her in the behind. And then her muscles grew heavy, hard as taffy, and she turned to look at Nephaline with open eyes.

"When you can hear the angels…" Nephaline's words faded as the world dimmed, "…then you will be at peace…"

Chapter 44

I woke with my throat raw, my whole body protesting and stiff as I jerked upright in bed. I was yelling too, as Hannah had been, and I could see just as vividly in my mind the gaping scorch mark where that laser—laser?—had gouged out the red wolf's brain. My last—Hannah's last chance, because surely now she was going to be taken off and fitted with a box in her head, a voice that would talk directly into her brain and tell her what she should do as a good, *happy* little girl.

The next time I dreamed, would I hear the voice too? Would I wake with the impetus to call Athos and apologize? Or call my parents and move back home, find a male otter to marry, go to church, start a family? Already I couldn't draw, couldn't have sex, couldn't even keep a relationship going, and now I'd be terrified to sleep?

I had the phone in my paw, my finger stabbing at the number. I didn't remember picking it up, but I knew I had to talk to someone. Then I had to wipe my paws on my shirt because they were damp. Under my fur, my skin still burned; under my skin, my heart still raced.

He answered, voice rough with sleep. "Meg?"

"I'm sorry to call so late, but she's fucked, she's completely fucked, and it's my fault."

Sol made a gruff noise and then whispered, "Hang on."

Clicks and clatters reached me through the phone as he moved around, and only then did the silence in my room sink in. No light came in through my window, and no sounds of construction reached my ears. I rolled off the futon and ran to the window, pushing the blinds aside; the site was still and dark. Nobody moved there, and the great machines stood stark and still amid the upright girders and concrete platforms.

"Who's fucked?" Sol, in my ear.

"Hannah. The girl—the otter—I was dreaming about."

"Ugh." He exhaled. "Did she die?"

"No, but..." I told him quickly what had happened.

"Ah, shit." He breathed quietly for a few moments. "I'm really sorry. I mean, for her, but also that you had to go through that. What happened to me with Niki—it wasn't fun. At least you didn't have to feel her die."

For once, I didn't mind him mentioning his dream fox. "No. But she lost her whole future. And she was dreaming about me."

"Wait, what?"

"Didn't I tell you? She dreams about me, about things in my life. I'm like, I inspired her to be lesbian or something. Or at least to give in when her best friend put the moves on her. And I was talking with Athos last night and he was being kind of a prick, and—"

"Whoa, slow down. What happened with Athos?"

"It's not important. He doesn't want me to move up anymore because I told him about being asexual. But the thing is, I was going to say—"

"What? You slept with him already, right? What else does he want?"

"We didn't get into that. That's not the point, anyway. The point is that I was thinking of Hannah and I was being aggressive and standing up for myself, and that's what got her into trouble."

"What a douchebag."

I frowned. "Who? Hannah?"

"Athos! Alexei said you guys were all boyfriend-girlfriend and now he's like, what, let's not bother to work this out, let's just call it the fuck off?"

"No, it—"

"Fuck him. Fuck him! If I didn't have class tomorrow, I'd go up to Port City and kick his tail."

"Settle down, Punisher." As misplaced as Sol's anger was, it was at least calming me down. "We're still talking. I was pissed at him, too, but I'm handling it. Can we talk about the dream again?"

"Sorry," he growled. "Just pisses me off."

"Well, my sexuality is different and it took him by surprise."

"You're making excuses for him?"

"I'm making excuses for you. I'm pissed at him too, believe me, but right now I'm a little more worried about the girl I'm dreaming about who just had her friend lasered through the head and is about to get a box shoved into her skull that repeats the Word of the fucking Lord twenty-four-seven, the box that turned her best friend into a Stepford otter. What do I do when I go back? How can I help her?"

He exhaled. "I don't know that you can. I wanted to save Niki, but... he's gone, you know? I was watching a show that had already happened. Like trying to change the ending of a book you're reading."

"Wait. Wait." I pressed a paw to my head and started pacing the room. "But this hasn't already happened. It's in the future, right?"

"Uh...didn't you say you went to the lake where it happened?"

"Yeah, but—no, where it's *going* to happen. They have androids and lasers and shit. And the South is its own fucked up country with God laws and subjugated wives."

"Sounds about current," he said.

"The point is, it hasn't happened. Maybe I can change it. Maybe I can make her dream something else."

"Or go into her world," Sol said.

I stopped in the center of the room and stared at the faint outline of my door. "Yeah, I wasn't in your 'Spirit Travel' class in high school, remember?"

"Niki did it. When I needed him most. Maybe he saw something terrible happen to me and went back to change it. Time is weird that way. We don't really know how it works."

"It goes forward," I said. "But in this case, maybe I'm looking ahead at things that might happen."

"Maybe."

"So how do I do it? How do I help her?"

He snorted into the phone. "Ask Niki. I have no idea."

I ignored the bitterness that had crept into his voice. This time the mention of his dream-fox was nostalgic. "Great. Thanks for the advice."

"Meg…"

"What?"

He was silent for a moment. "You're in the middle of something now. So if you do get to talk to him…"

"I know, I know, I'll tell him you say, 'Nothing compares 2 U.' "

"Just…just say thanks."

That was surprising. Was Sol getting over his obsession? Maybe having sex had done it. Or having sex with a girl? "Yeah, I'll do that."

"And Meg?"

"What?" Having thought of what I was going to do, I was now itching to do it, even if I didn't have a clue how.

"Remember when I was going to go dream of Niki…of him dying?"

I snorted. "Don't go all drama-queen on me again, wolfy."

"I'm not! Just remember you told me to be careful. You even dropped the sarcastocynical act to say it."

"Did I? That doesn't sound like me."

"Thhbt." He blew a raspberry. "Be careful, okay?"

"I will."

"And text me when it's over."

"I *will*. Jesus. Go crawl back into bed with your coyote gal."

He made a choked noise. "I'm not—she's not—oh, fuck you."

Which is what I was after, so I said, "Fuck you too," and hung up.

Go into Hannah's world, right? So easy to say, and even though I'd been joking about the 'Spirit Travels' class, one would've come in handy right about then. What was I going to do? I could try to do the ghost sum-moning thing in reverse, maybe, but I didn't have anything of Hannah's to use, and those rituals were going to be bullshit anyway. I needed something *I* believed in. When Sol had wanted to go into the dream, he'd drunk the absinthe we'd gotten from Athos, but I didn't have...

Oh.

Ah, shit. Shit.

Go get the pills, Meg. You know where they are.

I dropped the phone by the futon and walked out to the kitchen.

∽

The front of the label had a cluster of blackberries on it above the words "Blackberry Flavored Brandy." I turned the bottle over, and the room felt colder as I revealed the picture of an angel in black robes, black feathery wings stretched out behind her, holding a cocktail glass in which a purple drink shone. "Black Angel," read the recipe.

We'd gotten drunk on this sweet, sharp liqueur that night by my pool. I'd looked at the back of the bottle and that was what I'd seen—at least, the silhouette of it—at the bottom of my pool.

The seal still circled the cap, unbroken. I'd taken it three years ago when my mom had bought a replacement, counting on her to forget she'd bought it when she went looking and found it missing, which was exactly what happened.

My claw traced the plastic over the lip of the glass bottle, found the perforation. I hesitated and then punched down, ripping the plastic off. Theoretically, of course, I had decades before whatever I'd dreamed about would come to pass, but it didn't feel like I did.

The cap crackled as I twisted it off, and thick, sweet blackberry rose to my nostrils. I flashed back to that night, sitting on my bedroom floor, Margie saying, "Blackberry?" and me saying that all my mom had was fruity alcohol, not saying that I thought the picture on the back was cool.

I hadn't taken a drink of this—or anything blackberry-flavored, for that matter—since that night. I tipped the bottle up, and then thought, well, if I'm going to do the Black Angel, I better do it right.

The recipe was simple enough: club soda and a dash of lime. My paws only shook slightly as I mixed up the drink and then lifted the glass. I did wish Sol was here with me, or that Alexei was awake, or even that Athos was here, but I would have to do this myself. "Bottoms up," I whispered, and drank.

The club soda and lime did a lot to cut the sweetness of the blackberry; at least, it wasn't as sweet as my four-year-old memory would have it. Wasn't bad, if you didn't have the associations I did.

I finished it off, set the glass on the counter, and re-capped the bottle. The angel on the back kept holding out the drink to me. "I'm good," I said.

Halfway to my room, I stopped and looked at Alexei's door. Sol had said, "Talk to Niki," and as idiotic as that sounded, I felt like this thing was dicey enough that I needed all the help I could get. It was worth waking up Alexei, which I hadn't wanted to do, but the alternative was to try to sneak into a fox's room, and that was sure to end badly.

I knocked twice, and then as I raised my fist for a third time, there was a sleepy, "Mwuh?"

"Alexei," I called. "I need to come in for a second."

"Why is it so quiet?" he murmured as he opened the door a moment later.

"Construction guys have the night off? I dunno. They've been getting a ton done." I stepped past him.

He yawned and scratched down his bare side. He wore only a pair of boxer shorts and his tail and fur were all disheveled. More trim and muscular than Athos, I noticed, without any stirring of desire. "What do you need?"

"This is gonna sound weird." I stopped opposite Sol's bed and stared up at the painting.

Alexei came to stand next to me. "You have seen Niki?" His ears were up, his voice sharper now. "Or wish to?"

"Wish to. Or...need his help, maybe."

"Hah." He nudged me. "You have changed your opinion much."

"Yeah, well. I guess when you have fucked-up dreams for a while..." I stared at the painting. The fox was getting up, looking back. *Follow me*, he seemed to be saying.

"What do you wish to ask him?" Alexei asked.

Do you know how to ask?

"How can I help her?" I whispered.

The room remained silent and still. Niki didn't move from the painting, didn't gesture, didn't speak into my head.

"Did he answer?" Alexei whispered, also staring ahead at the painting.

"No." I turned to meet his eyes. "Completely unexpected, I know."

"Tch." He flicked his ears. "Perhaps he is Sol's ghost only. He may not wish to speak to you."

"Or," I said, "it's just a fucking painting and it has nothing to do with what I'm going through."

I turned to leave the room, and Alexei grabbed my arm. I flinched, the memory of Angeline seizing Hannah's arm fresh in my memory. But he just looked at me and said, "Are you in trouble?"

I started to shake my head and then said, "Maybe. I don't know."

"Can I help?"

"No."

He released my arm. "You will be careful?"

"Hey," I said. "It's not like any of this is real, right?"

His brow creased and then he laughed. "I suppose, if you look at it that way…"

"I'll be fine, fox-boy. Sorry to wake you."

It wasn't until I was at the door that he spoke again. "Meg?" I turned. He was watching me with a half-smile, but intently, ears up, tail still. "I will come check on you before I leave for work."

"You don't have to—"

He held up a paw. "I have already lost one sister," he said, and the smile was gone.

"That's not fair," I said. He frowned, not understanding. "I mean, distracting me from my own troubles by making me feel sorry for you."

"I did not—"

"Also by calling me a sister for the first time."

Then he smiled again. "We have different tails but not so different spirits."

"Your spirit," I pointed at him, "is an old Siberian soldier. Mine is an old voodoo weasel. Or else a young muskrat. Or a future otter. I'm not really sure. Maybe all of them."

"You know what I mean." He folded his arms over his bare chest.

"Yeah. Thanks." I waved. "I'll be okay. I promise."

"You had better be."

I took one more look at him, my friend, my—brother? Yeah, maybe brother fit best of anything. He and Sol both, brothers, best friends, a better family than I'd ever known or thought I deserved.

There would be time to think about that. For the moment, I had an otter to rescue. I walked back to my room, tasted the blackberry in my muzzle, and thought about Drowned William.

Maybe you're right, I told him. *Maybe I will die alone. But that doesn't mean Hannah has to. So help me out here, whatever you were, or whatever's been sending me these dreams. This hasn't happened yet. We can change it.*

Like Drowned William would give a shit about that. But I didn't know who else to talk to, and it seemed important for me to talk to him, to talk back after all these years.

Chapter 45

"How far are we going?" Vanessa clambered over a root as high as her waist. "And why can't we swim there?"

I knew this part of the dream. I felt a little exultation that at least this part of it had worked. But... what now?

"It's on land." Hannah stopped to look around. The high cypress that was the church's steeple lay between them and the afternoon sun, as Vilan had told her, and so they should be coming to the cemetery soon. Surely it had been a mile already. They had taken half an hour to get to the church without swimming, and it had been at least another hour since then. Hannah's fur felt dry and itched, and bugs kept flying into her eyes. She hadn't realized until this trek how much she hated walking, but the hardship would be worth it.

"Nothing is this far on land around here." Vanessa followed Hannah along the surface of a thick root onto a clump of sedge grass. "Look, there's water just through those bushes." She stopped to wave. "Hallo!"

"Hannah!" Nothing. No sound.

"Shh!" Hannah's heart skipped a beat. She grabbed Vanessa's paw. "Come on!"

"But why don't we want them to see us? We're just on the way to your surprise." She paused again. "It isn't a surprise I will be unhappy with, is it?"

Those pauses always reminded Hannah of the box, and her fingers curled despite herself. "You'll be very happy," she promised.

Vanessa's muzzle relaxed into a smile. "Good."

"Hey! Hurry up!" I tried waving my arms, but neither of them seemed to notice. How could I be so invisible in my own dream?

"I can't wait for you to see it," Hannah said.

I followed them along the trail, trying to jump in front of them, yelling, trying to move branches, but nothing worked. Was I back in the dream only to relive the whole experience again? No. No. There had to be some way I could change it.

They pushed through a large bush some fifteen minutes later, and aging wrought-iron fencing rose before them, each rail looking as though it had sprung from the thick growth of white-rimmed green ivy that clustered around the fencing. Vanessa stopped and stared, and only after a moment noticed the marble slabs and mausoleums beyond.

"Oh, no," she said. "We can't go in there."

Even the insects had grown silent and the wind dropped to a dead calm. Vanessa's words sank into the ivy and left the clearing and the small hill as silent as before. Hannah suppressed a shiver of her own. "We won't stay," she said. "And we'll be out before dark."

"It's wrong," Vanessa insisted.

"That's the angel talking," Hannah said.

And that's what gave me the idea. I focused in really closely on Vanessa's head. I imagined seeing Hannah through her eyes. I thought about the box Hannah had seen.

"**...into the cemetery. You cannot go into the cemetery. You have to turn around and go home right now.**"

The voice surrounded me, honeyed, flowing, pleasant and compelling. I wanted to do what it said. I had to do what it said—no! "Follow Hannah," I said, and this time I felt a response.

Vanessa lurched forward. Hannah stared at her.

"**Stop where you are!**"

I yelled as loudly as I could over the voice. "Go! Go with Hannah! Go now or you will both die!"

"I don't want to die," Vanessa whispered. She looked at Hannah with wide, fearful eyes.

"We're not going to die." Hannah grasped her friend's paw and pulled.

I watched through Vanessa's eyes as we stumbled forward. The voice wouldn't stay quiet for long, I knew, so I had to shut it up somehow. I felt around for the box—well, mentally felt around, not like I had fingers, and I wouldn't go poking around someone else's head even if I did—while holding on to the memory of what Hannah had seen.

"**Do not listen to the other voice. It is the devil. He wishes you to abandon God's path.**"

"I'm not the devil. I'm—I'm a true angel." I visualized the box. "God wants you to be happy. He doesn't want a voice in your head telling you what to do. This whole country is founded by—" What was some good biblical shit? "False prophets."

Vanessa clapped her free paw to her ear. "The angels," she gasped.

"**We are the true angels, the messengers of the Lord! There are no others—**"

I pictured the box's electronics scrambling, but that didn't do anything. "Shut up," I said. I imagined my paw reaching into the box, my fingers tightening around the voice, squeezing.

"**—who speak—urk—**"

Silence.

Holy shit, it worked.

Vanessa opened her eyes, letting the paw fall away from her ear as she straightened. "Hannah?" she whispered.

"I'm here," Hannah said. "Just a little farther."

"It's so quiet." Vanessa smiled, tentatively. "So quiet."

I focused on keeping my fist around the voice, and I didn't want to ruin Vanessa's peace by talking, but I was going to have to soon. I watched as Vilan came down to join them, watched both girls hurry along behind him.

"Tell Hannah to have her perfume ready," I said. "Tell her to spray it in Angeline's nose."

Vanessa shook her head. Hannah saw it. "Are you okay? Are the voices back?"

"Do you have...perfume?" Vanessa asked. Hannah nodded. "The angel—the other angel—said for you to keep it ready and spray it into Angeline's face."

Vilan's big ears flicked back. "One of your companions is coming?"

"That's what the angel said." Vanessa looked between the two of them, eyes wide.

"The angel said that?"

"Another angel. She made the other one be quiet." Vanessa swallowed, and squeezed Hannah's paw. "You rescued me."

"Not yet." Vilan's voice grated with tension. "There's still the boat to get to, and then—"

And that was when Angeline came along the trail after them, gliding all in white through the brush. "The perfume!" Vanessa whispered, but Hannah had already brought the bottle out into her paw.

The three of them stood staring at the companion, and Angeline did not move except to extend her arm and beckon to Hannah. "Hannah and Vanessa. Come here now," she said.

Hannah took a breath and then ran forward. "Oh, Angeline! I was so scared!" she cried.

The companion had no time to react before Hannah was upon her, hugging her, resting her head against Angeline's shoulder. The companion closed her arms lightly around Hannah, and that was when Hannah lifted the small bottle and sprayed her in the face.

"Pick up the perfume," I said when Hannah dropped it.

Vanessa bent down and picked up the little bottle and then hurried after Hannah and Vilan.

I could feel her excitement—or maybe it was my own excitement—as she followed them across the plank and onto the boat. But her excitement was at the prospect of escape, at being free from the "angel's" voice. Mine was mixed with tension, because I knew that Nephaline was in the water, either coming for them or waiting for them. And I didn't know what else was out there.

"Go to the back of the boat," I told her when she climbed aboard. "Watch the water. Have the perfume ready."

"What are you doing? Sit down," Hannah said.

"I have to watch the water behind the boat." Vanessa gripped the perfume bottle in one paw and spread herself out on the wooden deck.

The quick obedience gave me a rush and disgusted me at the same time. How horrible was it that Vanessa, even in my dream, obeyed me without question? And what would I do if I could control any number of people like that? Would I get over the horror of it and enjoy the power? If I could make Bellie leave me alone; if I could tell Athos to be happy without sex; if I could...

Nothing stirred the surface of the water. Vanessa kept her eyes sharp for the silhouette of a swimming otter breaking the surface.

But I was looking for shadows in the water, for Drowned William or Baron La Croix or any of the other threats that couldn't be seen until it was too late, and I saw the shadow, arms spread like wings. "Look down!"

Startled, Vanessa focused below the surface. The black shape in the murky water approached faster than she would have thought possible. "What is it?"

"Nephaline!"

"Nephaline?" Vanessa leaned over the boat. "Nephaline!"

The shadow pulled to a stop two feet from the boat. Now it was recognizable as an otter, the tight grey dress clinging to her form. She raised her head and broke the surface, small ears rising over wet fur. "Vanessa."

Behind her, Hannah urged Vilan to get the boat moving. Vanessa inched closer to the rail around the boat, remaining flat on her stomach, the perfume bottle hidden in her paw. She situated her thumb, and her heart pounded. She could do this.

"What are you doing there?"

I tried to think of what to say, but Vanessa beat me to it.

"The angel told me to," Vanessa said, and brought her open paw out, just as the boat's engine purred to life, vibrating below her.

"No!" Nephaline turned to the engine, raising a paw.

"She'll destroy the boat!" The words came out without me thinking about them.

Vanessa could only think of one thing that would stop her companion. She pulled herself over the railing and yelled, "Help! Help!"

Water closed over her. Nephaline's arm remained frozen; she was still conditioned to respond to Vanessa's cries, but an otter falling into the water wasn't an emergency. The boat began to slide backwards, but Vanessa was no longer on it.

Her hesitation gave Vanessa enough time to raise her paw. "I'm sorry," she said as she released a spray of the perfume into Nephaline's nose, and then another to be sure.

"Van—" The companion froze and then tilted gently onto her side, bobbing in the water as the boat continued to slide by her.

Vanessa watched for a moment and then turned her eyes up to the side of the boat, where a long brown arm reached down to her. She grasped Hannah's paw and climbed up the side of the boat.

"Still a few miles to the river," Vilan said, accelerating, "but I'm thinking we can handle whatever comes. You both okay there?"

The warmth of their bodies against each other with the rocking of the boat made both girls smile. "We're fine," Hannah said.

I didn't know how long I would stay in the dream, or how long I could keep Vanessa's voice at bay. "Tell them to sedate you."

"Please sedate me." She looked startled as she said it.

"What? Why?" Hannah pressed her muzzle against her friend's. "Don't be afraid."

"I'm not." Vanessa gripped Hannah's paw. "I don't know why. But maybe the angel—the other angel, the one that wants me to stay—will come back."

"I've got a couple pills in the kit should knock you out." Vilan indicated a compartment in the console. While Hannah opened it, he kept most of his attention on the water, now steering the boat through widening channels with only swamp on either side. "Good plan, keep you under 'til we can get that infernal box out. Can't be easy fighting it."

"Which pills?" Hannah stared down at the bewildering assortment of small white packages with various colors of lettering.

"Should be blue letters, says 'Sleep' on it."

She pulled a small package out and read the instructions, then opened it. "It says one pill is enough."

"Give her two," Vilan advised. "Won't hurt and will keep her asleep until we get to the highway."

"Do you have a coach?" Vanessa asked as Hannah held two pills out to her. She took them and swallowed them easily.

"Somethin' like that." Vilan grinned. "Don't you girls worry. We'll be in Cansez by nightfall, assumin' your police aren't better trackers than I think they are. Now we're in the boat, all your electronic stuff is shielded. They can't find that box."

"Thank you," Vanessa whispered. Her head was very heavy, lolling back, and the thick grey clouds filled her vision. But beyond them she knew there were angels, the good kind, the ones who had helped her. "Thank you," she whispered again.

Chapter 46

Light streamed in through the window. I lay in my futon, arms spread at my side. My mind spun, still back in the southern swamp on a boat a hundred years in the future, coming slowly back to the present.

Sounds filtered through to me: traffic, light murmurs of conversation, wind. The world went on as it always did, regardless of how my dreams had gone. I felt, for the moment, peaceful.

That lasted about fifteen minutes, until there was a rapping at my door. "Meg?" came Alexei's voice.

I waited a moment for reality to coalesce around me a little bit more. The moment Alexei started to knock again, I said, "Yeah, I'm okay."

"May I come in?"

"Sure." I sat up and straightened my t-shirt.

The door swung open slowly. Alexei walked in, ears half-down, tail curled around one leg. "Did you dream?"

"Yeah."

He waited. I rubbed my paws, still damp with sweat, but at least I wasn't shaking or terrified anymore. "I changed it. I went ahead and changed it. She's going to be okay—well, maybe not, but she's at least going to have a chance to be okay. A hundred years from now." I looked up and snorted. "You should see your expression."

He grinned and his ears came up. "I am glad the dream has worked out." He sat cross-legged on the floor, tail swishing until it came to rest around his legs. One paw pressed briefly on the carpet and he looked down, then back up at me. "And what of you?"

"What of me?"

He waved a paw. "You can draw now. You will be able to make rent perhaps?"

I chuckled. "Yeah, if I can find someone magically willing to pay me four hundred bucks for a drawing. That's something that happens, right?"

"How much does a drawing cost usually?"

"I'd do them for a hundred fifty." I sighed. "But I don't actually know who's going to be willing to pay me. I've burned a lot of my customers in the last couple weeks and it takes time to find new ones. And even if I do, then what?"

We sat quietly for a moment, and then I said, "You know, when Sol's story ended, he felt better. He got over that stupid fucking rapist sheep, and his eyes got brighter, and he was a lot more chill. Until he started dating. And when you were finished, you were dealing with your sister better."

"Yes?"

I clasped my paws together in front of me. "So what do I get?"

"Ah." He looked down briefly and picked up the white tip of his tail in his black fingers, flicking it back and forth. "What did you need?"

"What?"

He smiled. "Sol needed confidence. I needed family. What did you need?"

"Shit, I dunno. I need someone to explain to me how to get through this fucking life, you know? I figured out I'm asexual, but I did that on my own with the Internet. How to not piss off people and how to keep friends would be helpful. I dunno."

Alexei's phone buzzed. He reached into his pocket and turned it off. "My alarm," he said. "I can shower, or we can go get coffee."

The bed was comfortable, and I didn't really want to move, but my head was much less comfortable. "Let's get coffee."

It was a nice walk, even though the wind had picked up and the day smelled like rain. I felt drained by the night and I kept replaying the dream in my head. I still felt the reality of it in the way it lingered more clearly than any other dream, and I'd never been an active participant in my dreams the way I had with Vanessa. It was more like playing a video game, only it had all been in my head.

Alexei wanted to hear about it, but all I told him were sketchy details about possessing someone in my dream—or in reality, a hundred years from now, who the hell knew? Don't get me wrong, I was glad that Hannah would escape, whether she would one day be real or only ever exist in my subconscious. But all the way to the coffee shop and back, the question I'd asked Alexei nagged at the back of my mind: what happens to me now? Or, less selfishly, what was this all supposed to mean?

He insisted on hugging me before he left for work, and I didn't even mind it so much, though I grumbled at him and told him this was a special occasion, and he told me Sol would be mad if he didn't. And when he was gone, I took out some paper and sat down to draw, just to see if I could.

My paw kept control of the pencil. I sketched out a boar and a cougar, the figures I should've been drawing a week ago. They looked fine, and in a few days they could become pictures I could charge rent money for. Athos and I were going to keep talking, Alexei and I would keep being roommates, and Sol and I would keep being friends. I wouldn't have to go back to Dr. Wallace if things stayed stable. My life could go on just as it had been.

I could have finished the cougar, maybe offered it to the original commissioners at a discount (no way in hell I'd go back to Chet), but it didn't inspire me. So I went back to the closet and retrieved the comic of Marie-Belle. My decision, not hers.

The pictures were as rough as you'd think from being whipped out in record time, something like fifty pages over the course of fifteen hours. But they weren't bad, all in all. I went back to the first one, Marie-Belle in the swamp. With a little work…

My phone buzzed some time later. I'd added lots of detail and finished linework on a page and a half, and it felt really good. I stretched my fingers and looked down.

The phone showed a message from Athos. It started with "Sorry about how…"

I sighed. At least he was apologizing. I didn't have any illusions that he was going to change his mind about me moving, and to be honest, in the light of day, I wasn't that excited about moving up there anyway. So I thumbed the message and read it.

Sorry about how things ended last night. I still want to be your boyfriend and talk about stuff. In the meantime, I did some digging and found something you might be interested in.

Another message came in while I was reading it, also from him. I went on to the second one.

There's a listing for a Marie-Belle Guignac outside New Kestle. Phone number disconnected but might be worth a visit. I'll buy your ticket, meet you there?

On the paper in front of me, Marie-Belle was climbing out of the swamp. I'd never thought specifically about whether she was real, but had lumped her in with Hannah. If she had been real, she'd be old now, like a hundred or something. No, wait; she'd been sixteen or thereabouts in 1915, so…a hundred and thirteen now? I picked up the pencil and traced a line on her face.

Did I want to go all the way to New Kestle to chase a dream? What if I got there and this Marie-Belle was a rabbit or a fox and she had no idea what I was talking about?

The Marie-Belle on my page looked earnestly up at me.

What do you want?

Maybe two weeks ago I would've laughed it off, wouldn't have wanted to know anything more about it. That someone in the world had the same name as a story I'd made up? Coincidence. I'd seen it when reading the New Kestle phone book or something, right? I'd have still been clinging to what I knew (or thought I knew) was real. But what exactly did I have to hold onto now? A thin thread of hope with Athos, and he would be coming to New Kestle with me. He was reaching out to me here, trying to make amends. I still didn't know if what we had was real or a product of his and my imaginations and hopes, but I wasn't going to figure that out sitting on my futon.

And hey, maybe Marie-Belle would turn out to be a 113-year-old muskrat.

I picked up the phone and typed to Athos:

I guess I don't have anything better to do.

Chapter 47

Turned out that when Athos said "ticket," he meant "bus ticket," so I guess there was still some caution in his reaching out. But the bus trip was fine with me because it gave me time to do a little more linework on the comic. Busses aren't great for that, but on the freeway it was pretty smooth.

I'd gotten a few more pages done on Wednesday after he texted. I felt like I should go back to the Café La Croix and apologize to people there, but it did start to rain around lunchtime and for once the fucking apartment was temperate, so I drew in the kitchen. Now that the comic was done, it had lost the power to entrance me. I still loved the art enough to work on it, and the echo of Marie-Belle surfaced at odd times, making me pause. But her story had been told, and these were now just drawings on a page.

I did send an e-mail back to Eve in the early afternoon letting her know I was all right and that I was going out of town for a few days, that I'd come by when I got back. I asked her to apologize to Geoffrey for me and told her I was under a lot of stress because my new boyfriend wanted me to move in with him and we'd had a fight about it. I wrote more than I'd intended to; picturing Eve's sympathetic eyes in the light blue raccoon mask helped everything spill out.

I had dinner with Alexei, and he was way more excited than I was about the prospect of meeting Marie-Belle in person. "I wish I could go with you," he said, "but I cannot miss a day of work."

"This is going to take two," I said, "and Athos is flying in Saturday morning. I should be back Monday. So really it would be four." Four days in which I could avoid worrying about the rest of my life.

"Call me," he said. "And call Sol. He will want to know."

"I will," I promised.

"Call when you arrive."

"I will!"

He grinned and patted me on the shoulder. "Maybe you needed to understand that people can care about you and that is okay."

"I knew that. They're still annoying about it."

That made him laugh, and we watched a couple TV shows on my computer that night before bed. Neither of us mentioned that the rent was due on Monday.

For the first leg of the bus trip, I got stuck next to an old wolf who smelled like he didn't know there was a bathroom at the back of the bus. I changed seats at the first rest stop and sat next to a skunk, which was an improvement. Pretty much everyone kept to themselves, but the mouse behind me noticed my drawings and kept asking me about them despite my best one-word conversation-killers.

Then the way she was talking, I got a little bit excited that maybe she was some kind of art collector or teacher and she was going to invite me to do something for her personally. What could I charge four hundred dollars for, I wondered? But when we stopped at a little town called Possum Springs on the state border, the mouse said, "It's been very nice talking to you," and walked off the bus without asking my last name or contact information or anything, and she didn't get back on.

A couple other people asked me about my art, but mostly in polite "hey, we're on a bus together for fourteen hours and I'm bored" ways. I fell asleep for a few hours and woke up when the bus jolted to a stop and my bladder complained at me that I had to get up.

The sun hung low in the sky above layers of clouds that glimmered with streaks of pink. Fluffy green trees lined the horizon as far as I could see, except for a patch to the left of the sunset where water reflected the bright orange ball and where the highway we were on rose to a long bridge. I looked around and breathed in the thick, warm air and the smell of swamp and bus exhaust.

Outside the rest stop, a small sandwich stand with wood so weathered it might have been from Marie-Belle's time had attracted half our bus. My stomach growled enough for me to go stand in line behind them. Waiting there, I must have read the sign about six times: Pearl River Po'boys. I'd been wondering what a "po'boy" was, trying to remember where I'd seen the name before, and then the rest of it clicked with me.

"Hey," I said to the person in front of me, another otter I was pretty sure had been on our bus. "What happens if we miss the bus?"

"I dunno," he said. "I guess you don't get to go to New Kestle."

A marten two people behind me in a pink sundress spoke up. "You can get on the next one. Longest you'll have to wait is twenty-four hours."

"Can you?" the otter asked.

There ensued a fairly boring conversation about the marten's friend who had fallen asleep in the restroom or something and who'd caught the next bus. "But you won't miss the bus," the otter assured me. "We'll make him wait. What do you have to do?"

"I might be a while," I said. "I'm probably better off getting the next one."

I'd checked my phone while they were talking, and there was the address Athos had texted me: Powers Lane, Pearl River.

"How far is Pearl River?" I asked the muskrat making the sandwiches when I got there and had ordered a catfish po-boy.

"Bout six mile." The words came out lazily, in contrast to his quick, efficient motions. "Mile" became "mahl," a long slow drift on the water. He jerked a thumb and went back to the sandwiches.

"You know any way I could get there from here?"

At that, he grinned. "You got legs, aintcha?"

I squinted at him. "Okay, uh, so just walk…that way?" I pointed approximately the way his thumb had jerked. "For, what, two hours?"

He laughed and handed me my sandwich. "If y'wait couple hours, y'can ride back with me. I close up at nine."

It was seven-twenty, according to my phone. I squinted at him, but he looked casual, not all that interested. I didn't think he was hoping to get me alone on a dark country road to assault me. "You know where Powers Road is?"

"Ayup." He scratched his ear and took the order of the person behind me, but waved for me to stand there. "Whyfor you goin' there?"

"I got…family. Um. Great-aunt lives there."

He frowned. "What's her name?"

"Guignac. Marie-Belle…or Marie…"

"Huh." His eyes brightened. "Oh! The ol' Guignac place on Powers. Oh, you goin' on a tour of haunted houses?"

"Uh, no. I was hoping to see Marie-Belle."

He laughed again and handed the sandwich to the next customer. The marten stepped up to the counter and ordered a catfish po'boy, same as me. As the muskrat made it, he kept talking. "Headed to the right place, then. They say she still walks 'round there at night."

"So she's…"

"Ayup." He nodded. "Four-five years ago. Tried t'sell the place two-three times, but ghosts and stuff…"

"So it's sitting there empty?"

He nodded again. The marten took her sandwich and said to me, "We're leaving in five minutes. You coming?"

I shook my head. "I'll catch the next one. I'm gonna check out this haunted house."

The marten looked skeptically at the muskrat behind the counter. "Give me your name and phone number," she said. "Both of you. I'll give you mine." She reached into her pocket and pulled out a wallet, and then a business card. I took it and read "Alison Deland," then "Freelance" with a phone number. "If I don't hear from you in twenty-four hours, I'll call the police." She looked at me as she said it, but spoke loudly enough that the muskrat definitely heard her.

I thanked her, and the muskrat laughed. "Y'ain't got nothin' to worry about. Old Tom's happily married."

I wouldn't normally trust random guys, but I liked the way he said it. Also the sandwich was pretty darn good.

☎

"Sorry about your great-aunt," Old Tom said as I climbed into his rusty green pickup and tossed my bag into the footwell. "Thought the Guignacs were muskrats though?"

"Oh, yeah." I'd called Alexei and he'd insisted on coming up with an explanation in case this Marie-Belle turned out to be the old muskrat he was convinced she was. "She wasn't blood family, but she grew up with my great-grandmother or great-great- or something."

It worked. Tom just nodded and pulled out onto the road. The sun had set, and while my side of the road was dark, his was lit with orange and purple glows. Both his window and mine had been rolled down, and even over the noise of the truck I could hear the silence of the world outside. I leaned an arm out of the window to feel the rush of warm air and looked back at Tom. He adjusted his hat. "Lot of people grew up here and moved off soon's they could."

He didn't seem to be particularly angry at my fictitious great-great-whatever grandmother for leaving the area, so I relaxed. "You always ran the sandwich stand?"

"Po'boys." He grinned. "What'd you think of it?"

"Tasty. I licked my fingers." I wiggled my fingers.

"Best in the state." He sat up straighter at the wheel. "Bought it off Rozelle Parkins ten year'go. Rebuilt t'whole thing."

I thought back to the ancient stand. "Looks great."

He laughed again. "I used old wood. Ain't nobody gonna buy po'boys from a brand-new po'boy stand."

"It works." I leaned back and tried to adjust to the truck's bounces as the road got worse. "So what can you tell me about Marie-Belle Guignac? I only met her a...a while ago."

He shrugged. "Kept t'herself. My ma was her great-nephew's cousin or somethin', but we never had much t'do with 'em."

"What about her family?"

He shook his head slowly. "Ain't never seen no other Guignacs here. Couple down Slidwell way, but they never come visit."

"That's...sad." I was thinking more of Alexei and his family, because I couldn't give a shit about being visited. Being left alone by my family was like my best-case scenario—but I knew I wasn't the typical case. "I, uh, thought she was married. I mean, my great-great had pictures..."

"Mighta done." Tom shook his head again. "Ain't never seen."

I thought about what might have happened to Marie-Belle—or if, perhaps, the wedding I'd seen had been an alternate reality. Had someone from a hundred years before her changed that event in her life the way I'd changed Hannah and Vanessa's? At least, in my dream. Or maybe the Marie-Belle here wasn't the one I'd been drawing. I glanced down at the backpack with the sheaf of comic pages in it. How crazy was it that I was here in some backwoods town heading for the house of someone who'd been dead almost five years because I'd had an idea for a story back in...

Back in ninth grade. Almost five years ago.

I was numb to the possibilities of spirits in my life at this point. Either it was coincidence or it wasn't, and when I got to the house I would figure it out.

What do you want?

An empty house. An old muskrat's spirit. Answers, in any case, about what had happened to me and what might happen to me. And what that meant I should do about Alexei, about Athos, about Dr. Wallace?

"Here's Powers," Tom said as we pulled around a corner onto a pitted dirt road that was the worst we'd been on yet. "Guignac house is up a mile."

"Thanks." I strained to see past his headlights through the pitch darkness ahead of us. The glimmers of sunset light had almost completely faded.

"Hey," Tom said, and cleared his throat. "You got a way to get home? You want me to wait?"

I took a look at him. He smelled like fried oysters and fish, but he smelled basically honest. Not that I had any basis for knowing. "Um, I think I'll call a..." I pulled my phone out. No signal.

He chuckled. "Not too many folks in Pearl River to call. I'll wait around."

"I don't want to keep you. Why don't you come back in...an hour?"

"Huh." He nodded. "Could do that. You sure you'll be okay?"

We hadn't stopped moving through darkness. "I'll either be freaked out or really bored. But unless you've got murderers and rapists wandering around, I'll be alive."

"Pearl River's a quiet little town. Don't you worry none. I'll go home'n freshen up."

"Hey, thanks," I said. "I really appreciate it."

"Ah, ain't nothin'. Glad to help a pretty lady."

"You were doing well. Don't ruin it."

He laughed as we rolled to a stop outside a house that was no more than an outline in the darkness. "Here we are," he said. "You sure 'bout this?"

"Yeah. I guess." I popped the door open. "I came all this way. What else am I gonna do?"

"Got a light?"

"Uh…" I shook my head. "That would've been good, huh?" I took out my phone and experimented with the little flashlight setting. It felt weak and inadequate.

"Here." He reached into the pocket of his shirt and pulled out a lighter. "Should have enough to last you an hour. Or maybe you can find a fireplace. Don't burn the house down." As my fingers closed around the lighter, he said, "See, I can trust you, too."

"Thanks. I won't set the house on fire." I grabbed my pack and slid out of the truck, pulling my tail with me. It didn't feel like it had laid in anything particularly grungy in the back.

"Seeya in an hour."

I slammed the truck door before I could change my mind. Tom drove off and left me in pitch blackness.

Chapter 48

After a few minutes, my eyes adjusted to the light from the moon and stars. So many stars—I'd thought I'd seen a lot from Midland, but here they were like glowing grains of sand in the sky. The half-moon shed enough light that when the afterimage of the truck's headlights had faded, I could make out a small porch in front of a little two-story house with a gabled roof and brick chimney. The chimney looked ragged at the top, but I could only tell that because of the uneven silhouette against the stars. It was definitely not the Guignac house from my comic.

If there had been a walkway to the house, it was buried below a miniature jungle of knee-high weeds. But there was a post at the side of the road that had maybe once held a mailbox, approximately opposite what I thought were the porch steps, so I pushed forward through the growth.

My paws crushed plants but also felt bricks beneath them. I hurried up the porch steps, which creaked under my weight but did not give, and then I stopped in front of the door. A small plaque to the left of the door probably read "Guignac"; I took out the lighter to be sure.

The flame revealed a stone square in which had been carved a pair of angels, a small one standing in front of a larger one. The larger one's arms circled protectively over the small one, and while the large one was in relief, the smaller one was inset into the body of the larger. The whole plaque was pitted and worn, and in the flickering flame, it appeared to be cracked.

I touched it with one finger. Grit and dust came away. Nothing else happened.

Okay. Deep breath. I'd come here to go inside and that's what I was going to do.

I would've thought I'd be a little more nervous about walking into an empty, supposedly haunted house in the middle of a backwoods town at night. But it didn't even occur to me that the door might be locked. I reached out, grasped the door handle, then wiped off the spiderwebs and grasped it again, and it opened easily. I held the lighter in front of me and walked inside.

It certainly smelled like a house that had been empty for five years. Mice and rats and maybe other things had lived in it, done their business in it, and died in it. Some of them might still be there, to judge by the quick scurrying sounds as I walked into the first room, but there weren't many. After that first rush, the house remained quiet except for my footsteps.

Tom had been right about her family, or the absence of them. The sideboard drawers were open and empty of small, easily stolen things, but the sideboard itself, a cloth-covered table, and four chairs remained. One of the chairs had been knocked over, but the other three sat neatly around the table. I picked up the fallen one and set it back upright.

The chairs were all very plain, solid wood without any real designs. I lifted one edge of the cloth; the lighter revealed plain varnished wood. A serviceable, sturdy table. I held the lighter back and let the cloth fall.

On the walls, several old portraits of muskrats hung between discolored spots that probably marked where more desirable-to-looters paintings had hung. I looked more closely at the portraits to see if any of them looked familiar.

Most of them didn't, but as I moved to another room in which the large furniture was covered with dusty ghost-white sheets, I did find a portrait of a young muskrat whose features reminded me of my drawings. I took out one of the comic pages to compare it, but couldn't really tell in the flickering light, so I took a photo of the portrait with my phone to look at later.

By the time I got to the upstairs, I wasn't feeling nervous so much as bored and frustrated. Marie-Belle was dead, and the house was empty save for furniture and piles of newspaper in the corners, and now I had another day and a half to think about how the comic had all been in my head. Then Athos would arrive in New Kestle expecting a ghost story and would get a crazy almost-girlfriend, so *that* would be fun to navigate. Not to mention that walking through an empty house at night was creepy and smelly, and bugs were chittering outside as nighthawks shrieked, and the house looked depressingly normal, abandoned and alone.

But what the hell, I had another forty-five minutes before Tom came back, so I might as well scout around the rest of the house. Maybe she'd left a book that hadn't been stolen.

I did find a bookshelf, but the only books left on it were some old pocket-sized mystery books and one cookbook that looked to be from before the war—World War II, that is. And then I reached the bedroom, where a large plain bed lay just as dust-covered as the rest of the house.

By this time, I'd put the lighter away unless I wanted to read something, because enough light came in through the windows for me to see, and all the flame did was throw everything outside into darkness. But on the other side of the bedroom, a painting hung covered by a sheet, and all around it were shelves that held bottles and pictures, postcards and animal figurines, skulls and bones, just the kind of artistic garbage collage I'd imagined for Toutou's cottage.

And on a small table in front of the painting there sat a white candle and a glass, and a deep black figurine, about ten inches high, of a grinning weasel in a top hat.

The table, unlike the rest of the room, was covered in neither a sheet nor dust. The weasel figurine gleamed in the moonlight, sparkles around the collar and cuffs of his jacket, a cigarette in his mouth, but he did not move nor talk to me. The glass seemed out of place, and then I noticed that it was full of water.

Well, that shouldn't be possible. Not unless someone had come in here in the last day or so and dusted the table and set out the water. But who would have done that? Who knew I was coming?

Maybe Tom was wrong and Marie-Belle did have family, one old family member or friend who came in once a week to clean off the table and put out the water and candle. Weird, anyway.

And what picture was hidden by the sheet? I picked up the candle, but as I held the lighter close to it, I saw it was brand-new, hadn't ever been lit. What if it was something that was put in here as part of a ritual? I set it back down on the table and flicked the lighter off.

The cloth over the painting was just as dusty as everything else. I rubbed it between my fingers. Now I was spooked, unsettled by the incongruous water and weasel figurine (Baron La Croix for sure) and clean table, even though the house was as silent as before. What if the painting was the Baron, leering at me? What if he'd laid a trap for me here in this old house?

Right. Because he needed me to get Marie-Belle's address and come all the fuck the way down to Backwoods Swamp, Middle of Nowhere. If he was a real thing, he could get me just as easily in Vidalia as anywhere else. In a quick motion, I lifted the cloth and looked under it.

Glass covered the painting, reflecting moonlight back at me. I tried to flick the lighter on, but the cloth slipped from my fingers and fell to the floor, and then I saw what it had been covering: a large mirror in a painted, elaborate frame carved to resemble a giant serpent.

Weird. I brought the lighter up to it, revealing small people of many species embracing the snake, worshipping it. The paint had chipped but the cloth had kept it dust-free and very bright: vibrant reds and yellows. Then glittering in the mirror brought my attention to my reflection. In the dark, my piercings shimmered with reflected fire, and my whiskers flickered into and out of view. My expression was the same as it always was, neutral and maybe a bit more worried than usual.

"A shadow moved behind me"

Then a shadow moved behind me.

I spun around, brandishing the lighter and backing into the table so hard that water sloshed out of the glass, the weasel scooted an inch back, and the candle fell over. "Who's there?"

Nothing in the room moved. I waved the lighter back and forth, then put it out even though that left me blind for a couple seconds. The room remained still.

My breathing returned to normal. I turned cautiously and held the lighter to the mirror. The flame flickered with my paw; I stilled the trembling.

Again, I saw a shadow behind me, and this time I heard a faint voice. *Light the candle, dear.*

I dropped the lighter with a clunk. "What?" Again I whirled, again the room confronted me with silence.

I bent to retrieve the lighter, and picked up the white candle. Looking into the mirror, I flicked the lighter on and brought the flame to the wick.

The candle caught after a few seconds. I slipped the lighter back in my pocket, holding the candle up. If I held it in front of my muzzle, I couldn't see anything but the flame. So I held it back behind my head, and then the shadow that I'd seen twice grew more distinct, and the candle's light outlined the fur of a round, thick head: a muskrat.

More calmly, I turned, and still the room was empty. But the muskrat was there in the mirror, no doubt now. Her eyes glittered in the candlelight and I could see not only the texture of her fur, but the patches of grey on it and up on her ears. She looked about a hundred years old.

Her teeth shone as she spoke. "Hello, dear," she said with a smile. "I've been looking forward to this."

"Marie-Belle?" I whispered.

"Ordinarily, of course, you should never uncover mirrors in a house where someone has died, not for a year and a day at least, or longer if the spirit is restless." She brushed her paws down the blue flannel nightdress she appeared to be wearing. "As I suppose I am, sadly."

"How—why—" I shook my head, the questions coming too fast and thick.

"I do ask that you forgive me for the impositions I have made on you this past month or so—years, I suppose, but it is really mostly the last month." She lowered her eyes. "But first, let me tell you why, and second, let me tell you why I had to wait to talk to you directly until you were here, and third, I will answer any of your questions. And three is enough to be going on with, for now."

"No," I snapped.

She had gotten herself all primly set to say her piece, and now stared at me. "I beg your pardon?"

"I'm sorry," I said, "actually, I'm not. But you've fucked up my life, basically left me with no way to make a living, and that's not to mention whatever is happening with the guy in the coffee shop and those dreams—"

"I don't know what coffee shop you are referring to." Her voice had taken on a chill. "I have not been sitting listening to your life like a radio program."

"Whatever, you..." I waved the candle at her. "I come all the way here, sixteen goddamn hours on a bus next to the cast of "Stink It Up" eating shitty roadside food and you're sitting in the mirror..." I turned around to check that the room was indeed still empty, "giving me your grandmother's one-two-three line and I've got a guy coming back for me in like fifteen minutes. I don't care why you had to make someone draw your story. I want to know why it was me. I think you owe it to me."

"You think your life has been ruined?" Her eyes narrowed. "Try losing your six-month-old cub. Try losing your husband in a war across an ocean, never having his body to mourn, his spirit lost to you. Beg for help from two families and have both turn their backs on you. Survive for eighty years on the sufferance of others. This house and everything in it was given to me, willed to me by those close to me when they died, but out of respect, not of love. Everywhere I look, I see a dead spirit."

The weasel statue grinned up at me in the candlelight. "Your husband died? So you did go back to the Baron."

"No!" She cried it out, her face twisted in anguish. "I loved my daughter! I wrote to Pierre of her death. He wrote back and said we would have many more cubs. That was the last letter I ever got from him."

"That sucks," I said, trying to sustain my anger. "So why didn't I get that part of the story? Why did you leave it at the wedding? And more importantly, let's go back to why did I get the story at all?"

Her eyebrows pinched together. "Believe me, I wish it had not been you. But I knew your great-grandmother Adelaide, and she had some connection to the spirit world."

"Adelaide Lowry."

"Yes. She and her family were very kind to me when...when others were not. And then you crossed close to the boundary, and you retained a connection to the spirit world." She talked in short, almost petulant bursts. "When I crossed over, I felt you nearby and tried to tell you then, but your mind was muffled, muted. Recently, that muting lifted, and you contacted spirits, so I knew you would be receptive. Two weeks ago you were feeling lonely—"

"Hold up," I said, lifting a paw. "I contacted spirits? When I went off the pills?"

"How else did you think your friends met spirits?" Her eyes narrowed. "You believe that anyone might contact the deceased?"

"No, I thought they were all hallucinating. Still not sure about that, to be honest."

She drew herself up. "You do not believe in my reality?"

"Hey," I said. "It's not about you. It's about me. I've seen some pretty fucked-up things."

"You talk like a whore."

"All right, all right." I moved the candle around to get a better look at her. Was this my future? Lonely ghost haranguing people from a mirror? Wax dripped on my fingers. "If I called the spirits before, can I call them now? Will, say, Niki come if I call?"

"You are imagining all this, are you not? Do what you will." Marie-Belle gave a disgusted sigh and closed her eyes, pressing her fingers between them.

So I focused on my memory of the painting of Niki. "Niki," I said. "I have a message for you."

No response, nothing except whispered muttering from Marie-Belle. "I guess I can't," I said, but then I caught sight of a ragged-eared silhouette, a fox behind the muskrat. The ears shifted, and green eyes flashed at me.

I caught my breath. I wasn't sure what I'd expected, but seeing Sol's dream fox, even just as an apparition in the mirror, shocked me into silence. Those green eyes, so like the ones now in Sol's black muzzle, and the quiet air with which he waited for me to talk all made me reluctant to speak.

"Well?" Marie-Belle's sharp words broke my hesitation. "You wanted to speak to him, here he is."

"Niki?" I said cautiously, and the ears nodded forward. "Uh. Thank you for what you did for Sol."

Then I heard a voice, a soft whisper with a Siberian or maybe Gallic accent. "I am pleased to have helped him."

Unlike Marie-Belle's fairly normal voice, Niki's *felt* as though it was coming from beyond the grave. I shook off the shivers. "Look, I want to ask you a favor. You have this connection to Sol or whatever. Can't you visit him in a dream or something, let him know you're watching him and everything's okay? He's kinda obsessed with you and I think it's affecting his life."

Niki remained back in shadow. "I do not wish to interfere overmuch."

"You've already interfered. And it did him some good, to be honest."

Again, the ears dipped forward. "I know he misses me. But it is important that he find his own way. Henri says the same."

"Yeah, he needs to grow up," I said. "But it really wouldn't hurt him to know that he has a friend looking out for him. Especially one he has a crush on."

The ear flicked to the side and the green eyes vanished momentarily. Niki didn't speak, but his silhouette began to fade.

Marie-Belle said, "Very well, you've said your piece."

"Please," I added, looking directly back at Niki. I wiped wax off my paw.

A ghostly voice said, "I will try," and then the ears and bright green eyes were gone.

"How about that," I said. "Is Alexei's old bum back there too? Because—"

No sooner had I pictured the old Siberian soldier than his face swam into view. Unlike Niki, he came into the light of the candle, abreast with Marie-Belle, who looked even more annoyed.

"Yes," he said. "I am here." Medals glinted on his chest; candlelight played across his muzzle everywhere but in the darkness of his eyes.

"See," I said, "now I know I'm dreaming or hallucinating or whatever. Because why would it be this easy to call up spirits?"

"Because you are already familiar with him, and because you are in a temple of vodou, stupid girl. Some of the spirits are eager to talk. It is lonely beyond." Marie-Belle didn't acknowledge the old soldier, but his ears did flick at her sharp remark.

"Well," I said to the fox, "if this is real, then I'm sorry for disturbing your rest."

He smirked and made a small half-bow. "The experience was…educational. I enjoyed meeting Alexei. My regrets lie much farther back in my life."

"Oh, I just meant right now. Konstantin," I said, remembering.

"Yes." I caught the flash of his medals and the shine of his eyes and, as his silhouette faded further into the shadow, the hint of a crescent smile.

Marie-Belle gathered herself up. "Have you quite finished toying with the dead?"

"Almost. Why couldn't you come to me in dreams, like Konstantin did to Alexei? Why did you send me those dreams of Hannah?"

She glared at me. "Your dreams were closed to me, and I know nobody named Hannah."

"I'd expect my hallucination to know all about my dreams."

"Probably it was all those drugs you took," Marie-Belle went on with a sniff. "But it did not matter. The story I gave you was what I wanted you to know, that you may wish to be alone but it is not bad to become part of a family."

"That's why you ended it with the wedding. When you were almost happy." I thought about Athos and all the reservations I'd had about our relationship. Marie-Belle wanted to lie to me, to tell me that it was okay to end up in a relationship, but everyone she'd loved had died, many of them because of her. She'd ended up alone anyway. Could I do that to Athos?

"The Guignacs were good to me. Once I saw what resulted from my selfishness, I accepted my position."

"It sounds like they weren't too nice to you after Pierre died." She remained silent, but I saw the shift in her eyes and followed it to the voodoo temple. "They blamed you, didn't they?"

"Yes." The word was dragged out of her.

"And you became a voodoo priestess…to prove them right?"

"Because there were no other roads open to me!" Her eyes blazed again.

"Sounds familiar," I said. "Like when you took over my life to make me draw your story. When you ruined my livelihood, putting pressure on my relationship." I waved the candle, making the shadows grow and shrink around our reflections.

"I never intended to take over your art—"

I almost missed the last word because I became aware of a mechanical noise outside, the growl of an engine and the thunk of something moving over ragged earth. For a moment I felt I was back in our apartment and the construction machines had come to life again, but operating in the dark without the large klieg lights. "My ride's here," I said.

"Old Tom," Marie-Belle said. "He's a good soul."

That was good to hear, and I took it as an olive branch from her. "Well, thank you for at least explaining a few things to me, if not the dreams about Hannah."

"I told you, I don't know who this Hannah is. I'm sorry you came all the way here and didn't get answers to *all* your questions about life." Marie-Belle now looked like one of the portraits of her aged relatives, severe and humorless. "You can rest assured I shan't bother you again."

"For what it's worth." I set the candle down on the nightstand. "I'm sorry. About your life. I'll draw your story and show it to people."

It was harder to see her with the light down below the mirror. I could only make out the outline of her rounded jaw and whiskers, and the little ears above them. "I hope it has made a difference," she said.

The truck's engine died, but the reflections of the headlights remained. I had to leave soon and I still didn't know the answer to the most important question. "Is this real?" I asked.

She shook her head at me, not in answer, but in reproach.

So I dropped the cover back over the mirror and blew out the candle. The house fell silent again, and I made my way out.

The truck sat outside with the lights on, and Tom's shadow hunched over the wheel in the front seat, a cigarette glowing in front of his muzzle. I hurried up, thinking that I'd been pretty clever but still feeling empty from the encounter.

The smell of fish and Cajun spices permeated the cab along with the tobacco smoke. "Been a few hours since that po'boy, so I brought you dinner," Tom said, starting up the truck as I slammed the passenger door shut. He indicated a wrapped package on the console between the front seats.

"Thanks." I grabbed the package. "I'm pretty hungry."

I expected a sandwich, but the paper fell back to reveal a big fried pastry shell stuffed with white fish meat, dripping with red sauce. I nibbled at it, trying to keep my fingers clean, and Tom looked over with a wide grin.

"Don't lick at the edges. Get right in there, take a big bite, let the juice run down your fur. That's how to do it."

"Uh, okay. It's your truck, I guess." I opened my mouth wide, but as I was bringing the pastry up to it, we hit a rut in the road and my paw slammed upward into my muzzle.

Fish and sauce and okra and other things filled my mouth, splashed all over my whiskers and fingers and down into my lap. The pastry broke in half as I brought my other paw up to keep hold of it.

I chewed, gulped, swallowed. "God, I'm sorry," I said, but Tom was laughing. "All right, all right. You got a napkin?"

"Ah, probably." He grinned. "You okay?"

"I'm fine, just messy." There were splashes of sauce and crumbs all over the seat. "See, this is what I was afraid of."

"Of what? Of getting right in there and eating?"

He was watching the road now, not me, still with that amused smile. "No," I said slowly, "of making a mess of your seat."

"Ah, if you don't make a mess then you ain't really having fun, right?"

"I guess not," I said slowly. I lowered the pastry. "Hey, thanks for driving me all around. Very friendly of you."

"Well, anyone who comes all this way to see a ghost must be on pretty important business. You get to see her?"

"For a bit." We were still bouncing down a dark, unlit road, and I realized I had no idea how to tell if Tom was really taking me back to the highway. "She said she knows you. I guess she thought you're okay, or she wouldn't have let me get back in the truck."

He laughed again at that and slowed to take a turn in the road. Off to the right, some house lights glowed, and our headlights briefly caught a sign that read: "I-10 4mi" before we bounced past it. "Course Old Tom's okay," he said. "Old Tom wouldn't hurt you."

I'd lifted the pastry to take another bite, but the way he said that made my whiskers tingle. I stared at his muskrat's face, the pleasant expression traced in the blue glow of the truck's console and the yellow gleams of the reflected headlights and his cigarette. He looked perfectly normal, even when he turned to me with a broad smile that showed two missing teeth. "But Old Tom ain't driving right now."

"Shit." I said it out loud and then stared down at the pastry. I guess there was no reason you couldn't put roofies in spicy, saucy food. Fuck.

"Don't worry about the food," he said. "Jolene made the food. It's perfectly fine."

"Why the hell should I believe you?" I was hungry enough to want to, and hell, if he'd poisoned me or drugged me, I might as well have a full stomach.

He shrugged. "Don't matter if you do or if you don't, but it's good food and I hate to see good food go to waste."

"You're him, aren't you? The Baron."

His grin widened and he raised his eyebrows. "You're a smart gal. Sometimes."

I took another bite of the pastry, partly to show him I wasn't afraid, and partly because what the hell was I going to do? Jump out of a moving truck? It still tasted good; if there was poison in it, it was a tasty one. "So all this shit happening to me *is* real."

The pleasant expression evaporated; his muzzle twisted in disgust. "Blood and bones, jus' listen to you!" he exploded. "You talk to spirits from beyond and all you can think about is yourself. 'Oh, oh, you fucked up my life, oh, oh, is it real?' Maybe if you looked *out* rather'n in once in a while, you wouldn't be here in a swamp being lectured to. You'd be out living life!"

I gaped at him and then snapped my jaw shut. "I'm sorry, but it seemed kind of important to know whether I was seeing real ghosts or going crazy."

"And what difference does it make?" He turned toward me. "Huh?"

The truck bounced along, hitting ruts and rocks. We were going at least thirty. "You wanna keep watching the road?"

He shrugged and did so. "Answer the question."

"It's a stupid question. If I'm crazy, then there's pills I can take."

"To stop yourself seeing the ghosts and things."

"Well…yeah. If they're not real."

He smacked the steering wheel. "Is your life more interesting with them?"

"That's not the point." I groped for words. How do you argue with a crazy person who might, I reminded myself, exist entirely in my own head? "I have to be able to live with other people and if I'm seeing fucking ghosts everywhere, that tends to make things difficult."

"Lots of people do it."

"Yeah, and Sol and Alexei haven't exactly been models of sanity."

"People believe that ghosts bless their babies, that ghosts sanctify their marriage, that ghosts eat milk and cookies left out on a particular night of the year, that ghosts will possess them if they do a ritual and dance a certain way."

I felt calm enough to finish one of the halves of the pastry in my paw. "Oh, cool, we're doing the 'religion as superstition' argument. Look, I don't buy into any of that shit either."

"I'm not asking you to."

"Mom and Dad loved all that. 'The universe has a plan.' You know how many fucking times I heard that, growing up? Second only to 'all you need is love.' So don't tell me about what people believe in. Trust me, I had a front-row seat."

"Heh." The disgust had melted back into good humor. As he took another turn, I saw a green sign flash by, but was too distracted to read it. "So what do you believe in?"

"Whatever I can touch. This dinner." I licked my fingers and took a bite of the half I held in the other paw. "It's really good, by the way."

"Jolene's a good cook." He shot me an amused smile. "So what'ya think is happening now? You think Old Tom's having you on?"

"I don't know," I said. "You know what I said to Marie-Belle, so either you parked the truck a ways away, snuck back to eavesdrop, then ran to get the truck and came to pick me up, or you're a dream I'm having in my head. Or…or there really is a Baron La Croix and you're fucking with me the same way you've been fucking with me since…" I lowered the pastry. "Was that you, you fucker?"

"Was what me?"

"You know goddamn well." My voice got higher, unsteady. "Drowned Fucking William! When I saw him in the water and he told me to go get the pills and I went and did it! All that bullshit I read about hallucinations bypassing our logic filters, the voice coming from inside our own head—"

"Ain't bullshit," he said mildly. "You sayin' you don't believe in science neither?"

My paws trembled. I wrapped the free one around the other. "*Was it you?*"

"You still ain't listening." His voice had gotten colder. We weren't bouncing on the road as much, but we continued to plow through darkness with no light outside.

"I'm listening. You're not answering."

He turned to me again. "What difference does it make?"

"What, if my own brain is trying to kill me versus some voodoo spirit? I think it makes a lot of fucking difference."

"Guardian of the Crossroads, thank you." He was still staring at me.

"Hey," I said, "Whatever you call yourself, watch the fucking road."

He didn't look back at the road, just reached over with the paw that wasn't on the steering wheel and turned the headlights off.

My heart slammed against my ribs. "Okay, okay, fine, it doesn't make a difference, whatever you want me to say, just turn the lights on and drive." I squeezed my eyes shut.

"Does the darkness scare you less if you can't see it?"

"It's not the dark that scares me. It's the driving at thirty miles an hour and not being able to see trees and other shit. Would you turn the damn headlights on?" Fuck, my heart wanted to jump out of my chest and every second I expected to feel an impact, see a bright flash—what was a car accident like? I knew people who'd experienced trauma often lost the memories from right before the trauma, so more likely I would just wake up in a hospital. Or everything would just…end.

"What do you really want?"

I chanced a look, but no, we were still careening through the night. "Turn on the fucking headlights!"

"Why?"

My voice echoed around the cab. "Because I don't want us to die!"

"Old Tom won't die. Tom has his seatbelt on."

I dropped the rest of the pastry right away and scrabbled for the seatbelt. Tom—the Baron—laughed as my paws scratched at the door and closed around the buckle. "We won't crash unless I want us to crash."

The seatbelt stuck and then came loose in my paw. I wasn't sure if it was still connected, but I felt around for the place to lock it anyway. "That doesn't make me feel better. You didn't think anything of killing Pierre."

"Who? Oh, that old muskrat." He laughed. "That was a centenary ago and, well, not so far away, come to think on't. But she summoned me, wanted her life changed. Favors come with a cost."

I slammed the buckle into place. Then I forced myself to open my eyes. Featureless night still stared back at me. "So what did I do? I didn't summon you."

"No," he said, and wrenched the wheel to the right. I let out a cry as we went around a corner, but the road stayed under our wheels as if we were on a track. "Let me put it this way. You're an artist. Y'ever see someone sitting in your coffin shop drawing but they ain't putting the work in to get any better? And you want to tell them, look, do it right or don't do it at all? Shit or get off the pot?"

"What?" My paws gripped the seat. "Yeah, a couple girls in my art class maybe, but what the hell?"

The cigarette hung from his lips, smoldering. "Answer me this: why don't you want to die?"

"What the fuck kind of question is that? Who wants to die?"

He was still guiding the truck with one paw and watching me, smiling faintly, not paying any attention to the road. If I imagined we were on an amusement park ride, that trees weren't whipping by us on either side, then I could get my breathing under control. "Seriously," I said. "Who else have you asked that to? Does anyone ever want to die?"

When he still didn't answer, I said, "It *was* you."

"Maybe it was and maybe it wasn't." He gestured with a spread paw, the one that wasn't on the wheel. "If it wasn't, then I sure admire your mind for coming up with it, because it was a great trick."

"It was shitty!" I yelled. "You told me my life was worthless!"

"I told you, it might've not been me. Anyway, Baron Samedi ain't nothing to be afraid of. Death's just another adventure. Even so, I wouldn't push nobody 'cross the roads 'less their time come. Or 'less they hangin' around too long and won't go one way or another." He narrowed his eyes at me.

"You told me to kill myself!"

He shook his head again and turned his attention to the road. With a flick of his fingers, he turned the lights on and I could see the intersection coming up. The truck slowed. "What was your life like, then?"

"Shit, I dunno, I was fifteen, I was confused and lonely…"

"You were shuttin' yourself off from life, weren't you?"

"How the hell do you know that?" I leaned forward toward him.

"There ain't much mystery about it. It's pretty clear in your head even now, missy. The point is, you already had them thoughts in your head. You was born so you can't taste one of the great joys of life, an' that's a shame, no doubt about it. But there's people who can't abide cayenne pepper, who get sick from rum, who got no ear for music. You know what? There's other joys. But you didn't want to hear none of that."

"My parents—"

He waved a paw with a snort that brought me to a halt. "Your parents filled your head with love nonsense. Love is great if you got it, but you don't need it. All them other people, they're no better. They can't even understand you, so how do they know what you need? What you need is joy, you hear me, and if you don't want joy, then what are you doing?"

I didn't have an answer, and he turned away from the road again, his eyes dark and impenetrable. "But anyway, you weren't done with life, were you?"

"No thanks to you." I folded my arms, though my self-righteous demeanor was somewhat broken when I put my foot into the cold remains of my dinner. "I ate enough pills, but they found me in time to pump my stomach."

"Uh-huh. And why did they find you in time?"

My mom crying in the hospital, telling me, *I walked into the bedroom and thought you were dead.* "Because—because their movie ended and they came back to the bedroom."

"And why did you stay in the bedroom?" The road curved; even though he was staring at me, he turned the wheel and we stayed unerringly on it.

"I—I don't know. I don't remember anything after finding the bottle of pills." Not strictly true. I remembered opening it and the compulsion to pour them all into my paw.

"Why didn't you go back to your own room? Why not just slide yourself into the pool? Blood and bones, you about as thick as oak. You never thought of this."

I swallowed. "I took the pills. I—I didn't think—"

"You changed your future. You knew when that movie was gonna end, right, that movie they'd seen a hundred times? You wanted them to find you. You wanted to punish them for all that lovey talk, for all the shit they say and you couldn't feel. And you wanted to live to see it."

I stared blankly ahead. "What do you mean, I changed my future?"

"You coulda gone on like you was, but you didn't want to. You coulda ended it, but you didn't want to. Whatever happened that night, whether it was a spirit or all in your head, it forced you to choose, and you chose life." He hammered me with the words, not raising his voice but focusing it. "You came close, but you chose to live. So I ask you again: what difference does it make which one it was?"

"It's all my fault," I whispered.

"Ah, don't go relievin' your Creator of the responsibility of makin' you the way you are." He flashed me a fierce grin. "But yeah, mostly it's your own fault. You chose life and then you weren't doin' nothin' with it. Can't stand about at the crossroads, y'know. I like company, but guests and fish stink after a while. So I nudged you a bit. And look what you did! You came down here, you told off that old muskrat, you're on your way back to life. So this is just a li'l *na wè* and thanks for the fun times, because I thought you needed a little pick-you-up after that miserable muskrat."

Fun. Jesus Christ. I was going to yell at him for that, but then he barreled through a stop sign at an empty intersection and we emerged from a small stand of trees to see the hazy glow of lights ahead: the rest stop and the highway. "What about Hannah?" I asked quickly.

"Heh. She needed a li'l nudge too. And you did real fine by her." The truck accelerated and the Baron leaned back.

"She's real?" I caught myself as he turned an eye on me. " I mean, that future is going to exist?"

"Maybe." He stared through the windshield, speeding up as the truck lurched onto the paved road. The world brightened around us. "Way people around here are forgettin' what spirits look after'm, it's more and more likely."

"So I was seeing something that might happen a hundred years from now? And I changed it? That's—that's not possible."

"Of course it ain't *possible*," he said as though explaining math to a four-year-old, "but that don't mean it didn't *happen*."

"What's that supposed to mean?" I asked, but he didn't answer, and when we pulled into the rest stop, Old Tom's expression had changed.

"Here ya go," he said, and then his eyes widened and his whiskers splayed as he looked at me, a real fuckin' mess in the stark overhead lights. "Ah, shoot, I'm sorry about that. Jolene warned me a truck weren't no place for a pirogue and I said it warn't so bad."

"I can clean up in the restroom there. Tell Jolene it was delicious, and thank her. And thank you, Tom." I looked in his eyes—brown, not black—and saw an honest smile there, the fur creased around his eyes and bunched up at the corners of his mouth.

"You're right welcome. Come back and see us again. And tell folks about the sandwiches!"

"I sure will." I grabbed my pack. "Hey…what's 'na we' mean?"

His honest face registered only puzzlement. "Sounds Creole. Sorry, I don't speak it."

"Okay. Thanks again," I said, and hopped down from the truck.

After a quick clean-up in the restroom, I looked at the chairs. I could sleep there, for sure. I didn't really want to stay around here, but maybe I should. I could catch the next bus tomorrow and still be in time to meet Athos in New Kestle.

Athos, my grey fox friend. Boyfriend, maybe. Marie-Belle's story had almost convinced me to cut ties with him, let him go find someone he could be happier with. But I'd just survived a crazy truck ride through a pitch-black swamp and been yelled at to "shit or get off the pot." Maybe it was time I stopped worrying about what *might* happen, whether the feelings between us were real or imagined. If we felt them, what difference did it make?

There were still a few cars going by on the highway, so I walked over to the ramp and stuck out my thumb.

Chapter 49

Athos's plane was twenty minutes late. It didn't make much difference to me; I hung out at the shitty airport café with a book and nursed the same two-dollar cup of coffee for two hours until he appeared in the terminal with his bag.

"Thanks for meeting me," he said.

"Thanks for sending me hotel and food money for two days," I countered. "Not that sleeping outside the gas station wouldn't have been fun and all."

He noticed the book I was carrying. "You're into legal thrillers now?"

"I grabbed it off the shelf of a coffee shop yesterday."

His ears flicked back and then forward. "Only in New Kestle three days and already turned to a life of crime. You could've bought a book with the money I sent."

"I did buy a book. I finished that one and traded it at the coffee shop for this one. It's not terrible." I riffled the pages with my thumb. "No ghosts in it, anyway."

Athos's grey and orange muzzle bobbed from side to side, checking out the crowd, but we were isolated in one of those little pockets of privacy you can get in a mass of people. "Tired of ghosts?"

"Kind of. I'll tell you about it later. Hope you like the hotel. The food's killer."

"It's New Kestle." He lifted his nose. "Even the airport smells good."

"Wait until we get to the swamp."

We walked along the carpeted airport corridor in silence, his tail swishing back and forth so that it brushed mine. That was unexpected, and unexpectedly nice. Announcements blared overhead for people arriving, people leaving, people delayed on their trips. We followed the signs and the crowd toward the exit, through baggage claim and out to the lobby. "It's good to see you," he said finally. "And I'm sorry. I know I said that already, but I wanted to say it in person."

"I know." I walked a little closer. "I'm sorry too. I can be kind of a bitch sometimes—"

"I knew that going in," he said with a smile.

"But that doesn't mean I have to be." I returned his smile. "I've been thinking about a lot of stuff the last couple days. Some of it to do with you."

"I'm glad." He gave it a bit of a sarcastic tone, but gentle and joking.

"Hey, a lot of shit happened."

"I know, I know. I've been thinking about you, too. If you want to move up, then…then we'll make it work."

He met my eyes as he held the door leading out to the pickup island. I walked through and nodded. "Well, that's one of the things I thought about. I think I want to stay in Vidalia for now. But I'll come up and visit. Meet your friends, see your neighborhood."

"Yeah, okay." He hitched his bag up on his shoulder, and though his ears went down for a moment, they came back up again. "I'd like that."

∾

In the rental car, he finally asked about Marie-Belle. "Do you want to go back out to her house?"

I shuddered. "No. She's an old bitch."

He laughed, and pulled up to the exit with his rental agreement in paw. A moment later we were navigating the access roads to the highway. "You'd said the conversation with her was frustrating. What happened?"

So I told him a little about that. I didn't mention Konstantin or Niki's appearance, only that Marie-Belle had other ghosts with her. "She was pushing me to draw her story because she wanted me to tell it."

"Well, I get that," he said. "Why else would she do it?"

"And then she wanted to tell me about her shitty life."

"Ghosts remain behind because they're unsatisfied." Athos patted my knee, guiding the car with one paw, which reminded me unsettlingly of my drive back from Pearl River with Tom. "If she was lonely, then it stands to reason she would want to talk to someone."

"That's fine, but she didn't have to fuck up my whole art business."

"Oh, speaking of that, I have a bit of a surprise for you." I waited, and he flashed me a quick look, beaming. "I showed a friend of mine your work—well, he's a friend of a friend, really—anyway, he's crowdfunding this game and I asked if he'd like some art for it, and he said your art looked good. So you might have a real, professional gig. If you want it."

"Friend of a friend, huh?" I was about to ask more, but in the look I got from Athos, the whole chain of events became clear. "Yeah, put me in touch. I'll send him a portfolio."

His tail wagged so hard I could hear it swishing against the seat backs. "Cool. So you saw a ghost in person. For real."

At least he stopped himself from saying, "Again," which was nice of him not to bring up the whole bit from when Alexei was attacked. "Maybe," I said.

"Maybe?" He snapped his head around. "But you talked to her—"

"Watch the road," I said, and his muzzle jerked back.

"I thought…" He trailed off.

"Take this exit, then right at the bottom of the ramp," I told him. "Yeah, I talked to a ghost, but whether it's real or not…you know, I had to think about this for a couple days. The book I bought had a thing, a point, about how we can come up with any number of stories to explain the world we live in, and no one story is better than any other. I mean, yeah, some stories are bullshit, but if the people believe them…anyway, we're always coming up with new stories to explain the world. So I just have to figure out what my story is."

"All right." His tail had stopped wagging and he was driving with one paw again while the other hung in the air like he was waiting to catch a ball. "But. But what about…what about the other people? Don't you all have to agree on a story?"

"I don't think so. I mean, I hope not. You know, it would be neat if all this were real, if some ghost really did save Sol and help Alexei and bitch at me in an old house. But Sol might just have had some weird dreams and a rare genetic condition that changes his eye color, or stress or whatever. Alexei might have had similar dreams and decided that this old bum was an ancient soldier."

"But I saw—"

"You saw what you wanted real badly to see."

He shook his head once. "Okay, but all three of you having hallucinations? That's hard to explain."

I settled back in the seat. "Turn left up here and the hotel will be on the right. Twin Flowers Lodge. Did you know there was a Superfund cleanup site outside of Midland? Big factory dumped chemicals all over the fucking place. Know what they made? Pharmaceuticals."

"I—I didn't know that." He swallowed. "But just the three of you…?"

"Hell, I don't know. We lit out of there the minute the school year ended. Maybe other kids are having hallucinations too."

He thought about that for a moment, paused at a red light. "We could verify that. Go back to town, ask around, see what other evidence there is."

"No," I sighed. "That's not the point. Besides, I made that up about the Superfund site."

"What?"

"But there could be a factory that isn't cleaned up. Or government testing of biological weapons, or something."

"Twin Flowers?" He pointed at the sign as it came into view.

"Yeah, that's it. The point is, Sol came out of his experience more chill, more confident. Alexei came out of his with—I dunno, he said 'family' and I guess it has to do with him staying in touch with his roots and dealing with Kat's death. You got a sense of wonder about the world. And that's what's important: what we get out of them."

He swung the car into a parking space and stopped, but didn't get out. His eyes met mine. "What did you get, then?"

I bit back all the sarcastic responses. "I'm still sorta trying to figure that out. But I think I got a future."

He cocked his head, ears perked. "Is that something you can explain in a few minutes in the car, or should it wait until we're in the room?"

"I think it's gonna take longer than that, even. But I'll try tonight maybe."

I walked him upstairs and noticed his slight disappointment when he saw the room had two beds, mostly because I was watching for it. But he didn't say anything as he crossed to the made-up bed and dropped his bag on it. "The view's shitty," I said, "so I kept the curtains closed."

He nodded and lifted his nose. "What smells so good?"

"There's some grillade and grits left over from breakfast in the refrigerator." I indicated a styrofoam container on the dresser. "Also maybe the beignets from yesterday. Maybe some of the pralines? I got them as a thank-you for you, which I know is cheesy because I used your money, and also I tried one because they looked so good, and they were, so I ate another one, but…" I found the candy store box on the dresser and brought it over to him.

He took it, frowned down at it, then at the dresser, and then over to me. "You're throwing yourself into the local cuisine."

"Yeah. I figured, when am I going to get back here? And some of this shit is really good."

His tail twitched. "This from the 'let's go to the burger place, it's cheap and solid' girl? What did that ghost do to you?"

"This isn't from Marie-Belle. This is…" I paused. I could tell him about the Baron, but that conversation felt more personal and intimate, and I wasn't ready to share it yet. Besides, the shame of yelling at Geoffrey in the coffee shop still echoed in my head—even though, in retrospect, I was not sure I'd been wrong about him. "I don't have any habits here, and everyone keeps recommending places to eat."

"All right. I am kinda hungry. Are you?"

I walked over to the bed and sat next to him. "I am, but I wanted to say something to you first."

He didn't tense up or anything, but he didn't relax against me, and his tail flicked away from me on the bed. I felt bad about that. "I'm sorry," I said, and when he flicked his ears, I went on. "I should've told you more about what was going on with me. But I don't want you thinking that your first time wasn't special because I didn't enjoy it. It was special because it was with you."

For another few seconds, he remained silent. "Hey," I reached for his arm, and then I saw the corners of his mouth twitch. "What?"

"Ahem. Well." He turned, and now I could see the whole smile, stretching across his long muzzle, lifting his whiskers and lips so I could see the points of his teeth. "Next time you ask Alexei to write you a romantic speech, at least try to make it sound like something you might actually say."

"I—" I stared, and then smacked him on the shoulder. He gave an exaggerated wince and laughed. "I made that up myself! Mostly. Well, I modeled it off these movies—don't laugh at me, fucker!"

"There's the Meg I know." He intercepted my attempt to smack him again. "I appreciate the thought, I really do. But I know you. I've known you for four years. Look, I came here intending to apologize, too. I know I was pressuring you, but I didn't really understand why you were resisting. And yes, I thought it would be nice for my first time to be special, and to find out that you didn't enjoy it—maybe can't ever really enjoy it the way I do, well…" He took my paw. "I'm really sorry. Not that you're the way you are, but that I put all that onto you."

His paws were warm and the thought to pull away never even entered my mind. "Fair enough," I said, "but I still initiated sex under false pretenses and I was using it more to—more because it was something I thought you wanted. I should've just told you from the start that there might be something wrong with me."

He held up a paw to interrupt me. "I did a little research on asexuality too. It's not something wrong with you. It's something different about you."

There, believe it or not, was the first moment I could really understand what the Baron meant. Because my first thought was, *Does he really believe that or is he just saying it because he thinks it's what I want to hear?* And I heard that old muskrat say, *What difference does it make?* And I saw it there, I really did. Athos was trying to show me that he cared about me, and it made me feel good, and that was what mattered in this moment. "Yeah. Thanks. Anyway, I'm sorry about that. And I didn't know it was your first time. I'm sorry your first time wasn't fireworks and little floaty hearts."

"First times suck," he said, making me blink. "But you know, I thought about it. I'd rather have had my first time be with you than anyone else, even someone who might've actually enjoyed it." He coughed and flattened his ears. "Is that selfish?"

"Sure." I grinned, feeling lighter. "But it's okay. Be selfish when it comes to sex. I'm not saying I'll do it a lot, but maybe I'll enjoy it more because I get to watch you make those stupid faces and noises you make, and then I can laugh at you about them."

He twisted up his muzzle and stuck his tongue out at me. "If you want to watch 'Disprovers' while we have sex, you can. Also, did you just agree to have sex again?"

"Provisionally." I squeezed his paw. "I mean, I don't want to step backward, and we've already done it a couple times."

"You know, there are asexuals with sexual partners." His ears flicked, and he grinned. "There's things both of us can try to do."

"You suggesting some kind of experimental trials?"

"Purely scientific," he said. "I don't know much about asexuality."

"I don't know much more," I admitted.

He leaned forward, nose close to mine, and waited for me to object. When I didn't, he kissed me lightly on the lips. "I'm still hungry," he said. "Should we go out or should I eat leftovers?"

I considered. "Let's go try something new."

So we ended up at a touristy place because it was close to the hotel. "They say the etoufee is great here," Athos said, putting away his phone as we sat down.

"Sounds good to me." I picked up the menu and scanned the drink side. "Oh. Hm."

"What?"

"Nothing."

The waiter came by to get our drink order. Athos ordered a glass of wine and then looked at me with that look that meant he was going to try to order for me. Instead, I tapped the drink list. "The Black Angel...you guys make a good one here?"

Our waiter, a porcupine, spoke with a drawl that reminded me of Old Tom, but without quite so many consonants drifting together. "Bartender's finest in the Quarter. He'll make a good whatever. Never had that one myself. Don't like sweet drinks so much, but lots of people like it."

"I'll have that, then."

"Sure. See your IDs?"

I showed him the one I give the liquor store guy and he scanned it briefly, then gave it back to me. "I'll get those right up."

Athos raised an eyebrow when the waiter was gone. "Mixed drinks?"

"One specific one." I held up a finger. "Don't worry, I'll limit myself to that one."

"Special drink?"

I nodded. "I'll tell you about that night sometime, but it's a long story, and…" I looked around at the chattering tourists. "Not here."

"All right." He smiled, and we both looked back at the menu.

A moment later, my phone buzzed. "Sorry," I said, taking it out. "I told Alexei and Sol you were coming and I forgot to call them."

He waved for me to go ahead, but when I picked up the phone, it was my mother. "Hi," I said. "Athos got in okay, we're at lunch now."

"Oh, good. I'm sorry to bother you, honey. You're doing okay?"

"I'm fine, yeah."

"And what are you two going to be doing there again?"

I rolled my eyes theatrically at Athos, a wasted gesture because he was examining the menu. "Just some sightseeing. There's some really nice cypress swamps here."

"You're going to draw them? Did you talk to him about that school?"

"Not yet, but I will."

"All right. Is there good swimming there? Don't swim in the river, it's filthy."

The waiter brought our drinks. I waited for him to leave again before going on. "The hotel has a pool. And I'll let you know when I can come back to visit."

I'd dispelled most of her wariness on my previous call, but there was a little bit of it left when I talked about visiting. "Before I forget, Dr. Wallace called. He wanted to know if you're okay. He doesn't have your number."

"Ah, shit. I forgot to cancel the appointment. Yeah, I'm fine, I just don't want to go back to him."

Athos looked up at that as my mom said, "Do you want us to look for another doctor?"

"No," I said. "I'll find one."

We said a few more pleasantries and then she said, "I'll let you get back to your lunch. Say hi to Athos for me."

I hung up the phone and slid it back into my pocket. "Mom says hi."

He lifted his glass of wine, and I picked up my cocktail, which was a very nice shade of purple. Blackberry scent overwhelmed my nose as we clinked, and the fruit brandy and club soda rolled over my tongue, leaving behind the tang of lime.

"How is it?" Athos asked.

"It's not bad. If this is good, then I mean, mine was pretty good, too." I swirled the drink. "Maybe I could be a bartender."

Athos's ears flattened a bit. "What, in two years?"

"You only have to be eighteen to serve drinks."

"Really?" He shook his head, getting back to his point. "Don't give up on the art. Now that you don't have the comic to do…"

"Oh, I'm not." I sipped the cocktail again. "In fact, I wanted to ask you something."

His ears came up again, with the corners of his mouth. "What's that?"

"Well, there's this pretty good art school up near Port City. Bateman Academy, maybe you know it? Anyway, it's in, uh…I forget the town."

"I can look it up." His smile stretched a bit wider. "So you want to go to Bateman?"

"At least it's worth seeing what it takes to get in. My mom said they'll help with the tuition and there's scholarships and shit, and I have like a year to figure it out." I traced a claw on the tablecloth.

"It's a plan," he agreed. He took a sip of his wine and licked his lips clean. "Uh. What if, you know…what if things don't work out with us? Would you still want to go there?"

I snorted. "I'm not doing this for you."

"I know, but—"

"Nah, I know what you mean." I rested my elbows on the table. With my drink in one paw, I felt very grown up. "There's no good art school in Vidalia, so I have to think about my future. I mean, Sol went off for college, but he'll come back. And I think—I hope—that even if things 'don't work out,'" I used air quotes, "we'll still be friends and I can hang out with you once in a while. And we can talk about ghosts." I hid a small twinge of trepidation. If I had a connection to the spirit world, or at least believed I did, I'd have to be very careful about trying to call up ghosts from now on.

"If you're up for it," Athos said, and sipped his wine.

"Speaking of which," I went on as the waiter ambled back to the table, pad out, "I should call Alexei and Sol when we're done with lunch here."

The porcupine looked down at me and gestured with a claw at my glass. "Enjoying the drink?"

"It's pretty good, yeah." I glanced at the menu to remind myself what I'd intended to order.

"Good." He leaned down so I could smell the tobacco on his breath. "It's important to enjoy things, you know. That's why I let that fake ID slide."

My fur prickled. Across from me, Athos's ears flattened. I looked back up into the waiter's eyes. "I don't know what you're talking about," I said coolly.

He laughed. "You got nothin' to worry about. I'm glad to see ya in here." With a rustle as he shook his quills, he straightened up. "If you want the best lunch, I recommend the BBQ shrimp. Ain't like the barbecue you're thinkin'. It's been described as 'sinful.'"

Athos and I exchanged looks, and he looked how I felt: wary and a little confused, but also interested. "Sure," he said. "We'll each have one."

"While I appreciate your gustatory dedication," the waiter said, "I'd recommend you li'l folks share a single order. Comes with a big basket of bread. If you're hungry after, we've got plenty of dessert, as this fellow well knows." He patted his own round stomach.

Then it clicked, the way he talked about himself in third person, the stress he'd put on "enjoying" the drink. "Right," I said, and searched for something I could say in front of Athos. "We'll share, and thank you very much for the advice. Sometimes it's hard to make a decision, you know? There's so many good choices, it feels like you're at a crossroads."

"Oh, I know." He winked. "That's where I step in."

"Well, we gotta order something. Or get off the pot." I smiled. "And I don't feel like getting up just yet."

"Um." Athos gave me a look. "Anything else you'd recommend?"

The porcupine's grin stretched wider. "Go out here, down to Rue Chevre and turn left, then right at the second alley. There's a blue door about halfway down. Madame Zaqui will take good care of you."

The grey fox's ears folded down and he coughed. "On the menu, I mean."

"Oh. The fried okra." The eye that was turned toward me winked again.

"I'll try that, then."

The porcupine scribbled notes on his pad. "Very good. But don't forget Madame Zaqui, either." He put his fingers to his lips in the French gesture for 'delicious.'

"Hey," I said before he could go, and he turned my way. "What's 'na we' mean?"

He put a finger to the side of his muzzle as if thinking. "You folk might say, 'See you soon.'" He smiled widely and walked away.

"Wow," Athos said, leaning across the table at me. "Talk about inappropriate. I wonder how many tourists come in here asking him where to find a brothel. And the thing with your ID?" He lowered his voice. "I was afraid we were going to go to jail for a minute there."

The 'we' in that sentence was touching. I watched the porcupine walk, turn the corner, and lose the confidence in his stride. He stopped, looked down at the pad in his paw, then shook his head and kept walking. "Yeah," I said. I hoped that "see you soon" was nothing more than an expression, but Marie-Belle's story left me wondering how easy it was to shake the spirit world once you'd stepped in—and people with hallucinations often had them recur. "Would you believe me if I told you that that might've been a spirit who knows me?"

Athos gaped, and then narrowed his eyes. "Is this a hypothetical, like that Superfund site in Midland?"

I smiled back. "Does it matter?"

"Of course," he said, and then, because he's smarter than me, he actually stopped and considered the question. "Well…I'll have to think about that."

The porcupine returned with a basket of bread. He set it down and scratched his head. "Uh…you guys ordered the BBQ shrimp?"

"That's right," Athos said.

"Okay. Just making sure." He wandered away again.

We looked at each other and grinned. Athos took a piece of bread and sniffed it. "Oooh. Warm. And crunchy."

I took one too, and inhaled the fresh scent of bread. "Yep," I said. "There's a lot of joy in the world, if you know how to listen for it."

Chapter 50

Three more things that happened, real quick before I wrap up.

∞

I got back to the bus station at like four in the morning and Alexei was there to meet me. I wouldn't have bothered him, but I guess Athos texted him with my arrival time. And damn, I was glad to see him.

"I wasn't going to walk home alone," I reassured him. "I would've slept in the bus station until five or whenever the city bus comes."

"It is not as luxurious as it looks." He grinned. "Trust me. I do not mind."

"Well, thank you."

He held the door for me as I left the station. "You had a good trip?"

I nodded. "It was freaky in some parts. I had a guy driving a truck without headlights in the middle of the night through a swamp at one point. And I broke into a house and talked to a mirror that might or might not have had a ghost in it."

"Might?"

I met his eyes as we passed under a streetlight. Up and down the mostly empty street, the earliest risers went about their business. "Yeah. It's complicated. I'd, uh." I smoothed down my whiskers because they felt awkward after the long bus ride. "I'd like to talk to you about it. You know, sometime."

"Of course." His tail swished, and he flashed me a smile. "By the way, I know you have not mentioned that rent is due today."

"Right. I got some money from Athos—"

He held up a paw. "I found someone willing to pay you four hundred dollars for a commission."

At first I thought I hadn't heard him properly. "What?"

His long muzzle turned to face me, lips stretching back into a smile. "I would like you to draw Konstantin and Cat for me."

We crossed a street and I took the time to look around the neighborhood, at the glimmers of dawn in the sky, at the bright crescent moon overhead. "You know how hard it is to draw without a reference? I mean, I'm going to have to be checking back with you constantly."

"Yes." He nodded. "This is why I think it is worth four hundred."

"But—where did you get four hundred dollars?"

He smiled again so that his whiskers lifted and flared out. "I did not steal from anyone."

"No, I know, but—"

"It is my money and I would like to pay you to do this picture for me."

When I stopped fighting it internally, I felt much lighter. I didn't have to worry about rent for a month, and in that time I could get more commissions, maybe follow up on that bartender idea. School was back in session at the college downtown and there were lots of bars there that would need help, and maybe there'd be a couple at Riverwalk.

"All right," I told Alexei. "But I'm going to do a hell of a job on it for you."

His wagging tail brushed mine. "I know you will."

∞

Walking into the Café La Croix two mornings later, when I'd caught up on my sleep, still gave me a shiver. Sure, I'd e-mailed Eve and I was pretty sure she and I would be cool, but I didn't know about anyone else in the place.

It was nice just to be there, though, with the smells of coffee and pastry and the sun coming in through the window, warming the air. People sat around at tables, with books and laptops and tails curled up off the floor, with the low murmur of conversation and the clink of cups and spoons. I stepped onto the tile floor and scraped my claws across it as I passed the first couple tables.

Sherine was the first one I saw, clearing a table near the entrance when I walked in. She met my eyes and then threw a few coffee cups into her plastic bin and walked off. On the way, she stopped by a table and said something, and Bellie looked up from her book.

I'd planned to get coffee first and then deal with those two, but my gut fluttered and I figured, hell, I'd best just do it. So I walked over to Bellie's table and tried to remember what Eve had advised me to say. In the end, none of those words came to mind, and I said, "Hey."

"Hey." She kept reading her book at first, then seemed to think that that was weak, because she looked up, challenging me with her eyes.

"Look, I'm sorry." She didn't respond, and her eyes didn't get less hard, but at least she didn't jump down my throat. "I really do like you and I'm just really confused—I was really confused about shit. You tried to help me out and I was shitty about it, but I was scared, too. I know that doesn't make up for it."

"No," she said, but now I saw the softening of her expression. "You were shitty."

"I'm sorry," I said again, and bit back a lot of the other things I wanted to say because they wouldn't be useful right now.

She shook her head. "All right, just fuck off, okay?"

The words were meaner than the way she said them, and as she buried her nose in her book, her shoulders relaxed and her tail uncurled.

"I guess that's about all I'll get out of her for now," I said to Eve as I ordered my coffee.

The taller raccoon smiled at me, her mask freshly tinted blue. "Did you say what I told you?"

"Ah, well." I coughed. "I sorta winged it, I guess. But she told me to fuck off."

"Oh, that's promising." She slid my coffee across the counter.

"I think so. And I hope Sherine will be okay, too." I breathed in the fresh smell. "You know, you guys make the best coffee. Seriously."

"I know." Eve fluttered her eyes at me. "Don't stay away so long. Where did you go?"

"New Kestle." I slid to the side to let the person behind me step up and order. "I had to go take care of some stuff."

"And it's taken care of?"

"Yeah." I breathed in the coffee, which was still boiling hot. "It's done. I mean, it's about as done as it's gonna get, I guess. And, uh…" I glanced around the café. "Is Geoffrey going to be in today?"

"I already told him you were sorry." Eve held up a finger and took the next order. When she turned back, she said, "Geoffrey said he understood."

"I'd still like to apologize in person." And maybe, maybe see his eyes when I talked to him. "And, uh. I wanted to ask you something, too."

She nodded, but I waited until the customers were away from the counter. "Do you know of any psychiatrists, therapists, anyone like that, who's, you know, open to alternate sexualities?"

Her eyebrows rose, widening her mask. "I can ask around."

"And it would help if they could be really cheap, too, y'know?"

That got a smile out of her. "Understood. I know a few people who work on a sliding scale based on what your income is."

"I can get a little help from my parents, too, I think. If I tell them it's for a doctor, anyway."

Eve nodded as another customer came up to the counter. "Are you sure you want to see someone?"

"No," I said. "But at least I gotta try, don't I?"

The office smelled like Neutra-Scent, like nothing. I'd been waiting fifteen minutes in a small private waiting room, drinking water from the cooler. The office was a few blocks from the center of Riverwalk, in a scruffier neighborhood, but despite the cracked sidewalk and many closed buildings, the street was clean and I didn't feel unsafe.

An arctic fox in her blue summer coat and a white blouse opened the door. "Meg?"

I stood up and she extended a paw. "Dr. Cooper?" I asked as I followed her back into the hallway.

She was about my height, with a warm smile and light amber eyes. "Nope, just Joselle. I'm a therapist, so I can't prescribe drugs. But if we decide you want to try some, I can write you a referral."

"That makes me feel better." The office had a small desk and a plush chair as well as a couch, and there wasn't room for much more. "Where should I sit?"

"You pick." She walked behind the desk and opened her laptop.

"Is this a test?" I looked between the different places.

She smiled. "You know, if you're worried about giving away something about yourself, asking me that question also does that."

I paused, and she laughed. "Meg, all I'm saying is that you can be suspicious if you want, but let's focus on the problem you came here for. Okay? Sit wherever you're comfortable."

I picked the plush chair and curled my tail around to one side, settling in. "This is good. So...what now?"

"Why don't you tell me why you're here?"

I thought about that one. "First off, are you open to weird experiences about how the world works?"

She raised an eyebrow. "Like what?"

"Well..." I took a breath. "Like things that might technically get me qualified as insane if I talked about them to too many people."

"I promise you, nothing you say will leave this office without your consent." She tapped the laptop. "I might not be a doctor, but these sessions are confidential."

I stared at the back of the laptop and then up at her muzzle. "All right," I said. "Here goes."

She waited patiently. "I'm nineteen," I said, "and I'm fucked up."

The inadequate words hung there. Her expression didn't change, and that calmed me. "But," I went on, "I'm trying to get better."

Epilogue

Sol had a long weekend in the middle of October, a Monday-Tuesday fall break that his school stubbornly called Columbus Day despite student protests, and since we were going to be having Thanksgiving with our families, he suggested we could have a kind of pre-Thanksgiving, just him, me, Alexei, and our significant others.

Athos was glad for the chance to come down again, and of course Mike was happy to join us. I couldn't get Saturday night off work, so we decided we'd do our pre-Thanksgiving meal on Sunday.

Sol was scheduled to come back Friday night and Athos was going to come in Saturday morning. I'd warned him that I had to work and he said he'd come to the bar and hang out if that was okay. Xora never minded when Alexei came in, as long as I didn't serve him alcohol, and Eve, Alain, and Sherine dropped in all the time, so I said that was fine.

I got home Friday night at like three-thirty in the morning and had to go get Athos from the airport at seven—fucking real jobs with actual hours—and so it wasn't until Athos and I got back around nine that I met Bret.

The dingo stood right away when we opened the door, while Sol and Alexei remained sitting at the table. "Hi," he said, and even in that one word, his Oceanian accent came through. He stuck out a paw. "You must be the artist-slash-bartender."

I shook. "I hope you're basing that on what Sol's told you and not on my clothes. I'd hate to think I look like a type."

He laughed. "Nah, nah. And this is your fox?"

"As opposed to that one, yeah." I gestured at Alexei, who grinned back at me.

"Athos," Athos introduced himself.

Bret shook Athos's paw, and I said, "So you're the famous Bret."

"An' I hope you're basing that on what Sol's told you, and not the newspapers, because they lie."

"Yeah, I figured that story about the dingo who swam here from Oceania around Tierra del Fuego was a lie."

"Least you know my species." He laughed, and his tail wagged. "Even with the accent, some people think I'm a wolf that dyed my fur blond."

I feigned surprise. "Wait, you didn't?"

Sol had stood by this point and walked over to rest a paw on Bret's arm. "Told you," he said.

"Oh, what?" I looked between the two of them. "That I'm a funny, upbeat otter?"

"Yah," Bret said, "but not in those words."

The kitchen table really only had room for four, so we pulled the chairs over near the sofa and sat around, all five of us. Sol and Bret talked about college, and Alexei laughed and said, "You almost make me want to go." They asked how my portfolio was coming for the Bateman School, and I told them it was slow going.

"Are you still doing commissions?" Sol asked.

"A couple, here and there." I glanced at Alexei and smiled. "But mostly it's because this can't just be, y'know, a bunch of fantasy drawings I did for people. Everyone says your portfolio is stronger if you have a message, like, something you're trying to say with your art."

"I don't think I've ever known you not to have something to say," Athos said.

"Amen," Sol added.

"Anyway," I glared at them both, "it's making me try some new stuff. I've got another three and a half months to work it out, and Athos found a couple other schools in the Port City area that are pretty good too. So Bret, was Sol really awkward and uncomfortable the first time he asked you out, or had he rehearsed?"

The dingo laughed and put an arm around Sol. "Totally awkward."

Sol elbowed him as the rest of us laughed. "But nah," Bret went on, "I'm glad he did. The rest of the LGBT crowd at Charleton are either shoppers or dreamers."

"Shoppers?" Alexei asked.

"Just looking to hook up," Sol said. "And the dreamers are the ones who want everyone to go march on Potomac and run around door to door getting support for marriage and shit."

"Not that that ain't worthwhile." Bret stretched his legs out in front of him, at which point I was sure he was wearing shorts to show off how nice those legs were. "But take a break once in a while."

"Funny," I said to Sol, "I would've thought you'd be more into shopping."

He glared at me, and Bret laughed. "Bit like a cub in a candy store, he was, but he settled down some."

"Baseball helps," Sol said. "No time for much else."

"But time for me, right?" Bret stuck his muzzle into Sol's neck, and the wolf giggled and hugged him, more open and relaxed than I'd seen Sol—well, ever. "Yeah, thought so."

When Mike showed up, we all walked down to Riverwalk to have lunch, and for me to show off the café to the guys who hadn't seen it. Sol contrived to get me alone on the walk down, as Athos and Alexei were talking, and Bret and Mike had fallen into a music discussion.

"Hey," the wolf said in a low voice. "I told Alexei last night...I dreamed of Niki last week."

"Really."

He stuck his paws in his shorts pockets and wagged his tail. "Yeah. I mean, I don't remember a lot of it, but he was smiling and I felt good. I mean, I know he's still around and watching me, and that's just...that's cool."

"Okay." I remembered now that I'd asked Niki to look in on him. But that had been a month and a half ago, and wasn't Sol likely to have dreamed about his fox sometime anyway? I found that I didn't really care whether this proved anything or not. "I noticed you stopped asking about his picture."

"Yeah." He kicked at a branch, sending it skittering across the bricks. "I got a little busy, and I have the image on my phone and everything. Seemed silly to fixate on the painting. I know you guys will keep him safe. And," he said, holding up a paw, "I know he's not *in* the painting, too."

I grinned back at him. "Well, good. Hey, if you keep going on like this, I won't have anything to tease you about. So are you really taking Bret home for Thanksgiving?"

His ears folded back and he stared down at the bricks. "Hope to. I talked to Mom about it and she sounded okay. I mean, she said she'd have to think about it."

"You can always tell your folks that he's got nowhere to go. Anyway, they don't celebrate Thanksgiving in Oceania, do they?"

He shook his head. "Nah. And he wants to have a real one."

"There you go. He's a friend who wants to have Thanksgiving."

"I could do that." His tail stilled. "I don't wanna, though. I'm gonna call Natty next week and ask him, too, but I want to bring him as my boyfriend."

"Well, good for you." I patted him on the shoulder. "And when your folks kick you out, you can come down the hill to my place and have tofurkey and organically farmed sweet potatoes."

He stuck his tongue out. "God dammit." He slowed even more, as everyone else had stopped a half block ahead of us to wait. "How's it going with Dr. Cooper?"

"Joselle. She's not a doctor. It's good, you know. She listens, she doesn't judge. She looked up asexuals and gives me advice on my—with Athos."

"You told her about the other stuff?"

I nodded. "She referred me to a doctor who wanted to prescribe an anti-psychotic at first. I talked her out of that, and since nothing's really happened since then, she's backed off."

"But you are back on anti-depressants, you said."

"Not the same ones, and a way lower dose. Just something…" I put both paws out, palms down, flat. "Stabilizing rather than muting, you know? The doctor looked at what Wallace was giving me and said it was 'criminal.'" I'd felt super-smug when she said that and yet had resisted throwing it in my mom's face. I hadn't actually told anyone but Athos.

"I haven't really noticed much difference, except you're freaking out less."

"That's the idea."

We caught up to the rest of the group then, and joined in the music discussion the rest of the way to the café.

"Whoa," Alain said as I walked in. "Meg, your harem gets bigger every week."

"Think we can all sit somewhere?" I grinned.

He looked around, tail swishing. "Let me clear this table, then you can push it next to that one. If you don't mind squeezing together."

"Not at all." Alexei took Mike's hand.

I followed Alain's look and waved toward Bret and Sol. "Those two are together too."

He rolled his eyes and flicked his dishtowel at me. "I'm not on the prowl all the time, dear."

"Just thought you'd appreciate the information."

"Go get your coffee. I'll have this ready when you come back."

So we all swarmed up to the counter, chattering and laughing, and Eve took our order with a smile to Athos. "Good to see you again," she said.

"Likewise." He lifted his nose. "I've missed the coffee here."

"Even up in Port City?"

"You'd be surprised." He gave her a smile.

"Hey," Sol said behind us. He pointed to the wall. "That's one of your drawings."

Everyone turned to look at the framed picture, a pencil rendering of the river and the bridge I'd finished a couple weeks ago. "Surprise," I said. "Geoffrey wants to start hanging art here, and he asked if I'd do a piece for him."

"It's good." Bret padded over to look. "Two hundred fifty?"

"It'll sell," Eve said. "People keep going over to look at it."

"That is what you were working on!" Alexei shook his head. "I thought perhaps you were doing another comic."

"Nope. I only told Athos."

"I didn't tell anyone," Athos said proudly.

I slipped an arm around his shoulders and hugged him. "I knew you wouldn't."

We crowded around the table with our coffees, talking while we waited for Alain to bring us sandwiches. At one point, Mike asked whose idea this pre-Thanksgiving had been, and Sol and I looked at each other. "Don't remember," I said.

"Yeah, it just kind of happened." Sol shook his head. "Few weeks ago, we were talking on the phone about getting together."

"Well, I like it." Mike had his arm around Alexei's shoulders. "Thanksgiving's a family thing, but we can be thankful for more than just family."

"I do think this is a family, too," Alexei said with smiles for me and Sol.

"For sure," Sol chimed in.

Mike hurried to say, "I didn't mean it wasn't. I mean, more than just blood family, I guess."

"Oh." Alexei grinned at him. "I thought you said we can be thankful for more than one family."

"You know," Mike said, "I like that one better. Let's just say I said that, if everyone's okay with it."

"Sure," we said, and Bret added, "That's what I heard, far as you know."

Athos didn't say anything, but he smiled, and I reached over to take his paw in mine. "I'm thankful for all of you," I said.

"Hear, hear." Sol raised his cup, and all six of us drank.

The warmth of Athos's paw reminded me of how unlikely this all was. I'd lived a life where emotions were either suppressed or terrifying, coped with being asexual, dealt with a hallucination and a suicide attempt. He was a nerd fascinated with the supernatural, more comfortable reading Wikipedia than talking to people, and despite being very heterosexual, had maybe less visceral understanding of sex than I did. And yet here we were with a table of friends, our fingers twined not because the movies said we should be holding paws, but because we wanted to and it felt good to both of us. It just didn't seem possible.

But you know, that don't mean it can't *happen*.

Vodou vs. Voodoo

There is a distinction between vodou and voodoo that is not explicitly drawn in this book, but is worth mentioning.

Vodou is the Haitian-based religion born among the slaves brought from Africa, deliberately plucked from many different regions so they would not have a language in common. Vodou became the commonality in that community and played a key part in the revolution and eventual emancipation of those slaves.

Voodoo is the Louisiana practice that has been popularized as well as mischaracterized and denigrated in American popular culture. The two are related, of course; voodoo arose in New Orleans not only from African immigrants but also from Haitians following the Haitian revolution and diaspora.

Many of the gods and spirits described in *Black Angel* derive from Haitian vodou, while the *gris-gris* and the tradition of "voodoo priestesses" are more closely tied to Louisiana voodoo. I envisioned Marie-Belle's grandmother tracing her ancestry back to emigrants from Haiti, who over the years melded their religion into the traditions of their new home; thus, she dispenses amulets and charms, but does not forget the old gods.

If you're interested in further reading, Wikipedia is of course a great place to start ("Louisiana Voodoo" and "Haitian Vodou" are the two primary articles). I also referred to *A New Orleans Voudou Priestess: The Legend and Reality of Marie Laveau*, by Carolyn Morrow Long, and I took Bloody Mary's Haunted New Orleans tour, which included a visit to a voodoo temple and a talk with a voodoo priestess. Convincing details in this book are thanks to them; any inaccuracies are all my own invention. Baron La Croix, in particular, has little written about him apart from some physical descriptions, and the top-hatted weasel in this book springs largely from my imagination.

Acknowledgments

Several people have helped to make this book and series special. My thanks to Kougo for his help with the Russian elements of *Red Devil*, to the aforementioned Bloody Mary for opening her temple and answering my questions during the tour, to Lyda Morehouse for reassuring me that Meg's exploration of her sexuality at least bore some resemblance to reality, and to a very patient asexual acquaintance who spent a couple hours talking to me about their life and feelings.

Jay Maxwell has done a terrific job bringing the audiobooks to life. He auditioned for *Green Fairy* and I gave him first option on the other books because he read them so well.

Jasmine Stairs, Becky Wright, Kevin Frane, Malcolm Cross, Ryan Campbell, David Cowan, and Watts Martin all at one time or another provided very helpful feedback for one or all the books in this series. *Black Angel* specifically was workshopped with Kij Johnson and Barbara Webb at the Center for the Study of Science Fiction's novel workshop, and great thanks are due to them (especially Barbara for her critique of the final manuscript a year later), as to my fellow workshoppers Dayna Smith, Elizabeth Bourne, Marcy Arlin, Kevin O'Neill, Dominic D'Aunno, Jennifer Campbell-Hicks, and Watts Martin again.

I would be remiss if I didn't mention Furry Weekend Atlanta and its staff, who invited me to be a guest of honor at their convention for which the theme was the Moulin Rouge. Because they didn't have a con book for me to write a short story in, I decided to write a novella, which became *Green Fairy* and led to the rest of this series.

And of course, my co-GOH for that convention was Rukis, the talented artist whose work has enhanced all three books. No slouch in the writing department herself, she has contributed feedback and enthusiasm and made these books better in many ways.

As always, thanks to my husband Kit, who is always supportive when I say I want to try something new and weird, even a supernatural YA/New Adult book series. He grew to love this series as much as I did, which is as much reason for me to have written them as anything else.

And lastly, thanks to my mother, who first introduced me to the beauty of language and writing, and who left us at far too young an age. I suspect that if not for her, I would not be quite so interested in stories of talking to ghosts.

About the Author

Kyell Gold has won twelve Ursa Major awards for his stories and novels, and his acclaimed novel "Out of Position" co-won the Rainbow Award for Best Gay Novel of 2009. His novel "Green Fairy" was nominated for inclusion in the ALA's "Over the Rainbow" list for 2012. He helped create RAWR, the first residential furry writing workshop, and was one of the instructors at its first session in 2016.

He was not born in California, but now considers it his home. He loves to travel and dine out with his husband Kit Silver, and can be seen at furry conventions around the world. More information about him and his books is available at http://www.kyellgold.com.

About the Artist

Rukis is a freelance illustrator and writer who grew up in the Appalachian region, working with animals and on farms from a young age. After earning a Bachelors in Traditional Animation, she started a career in freelance art, writing and illustrating a small collection of comics and novels in the Anthropomorphic fandom. You can see more of her work at *www.furaffinity.net/user/rukis*.

ABOUT SOFAWOLF PRESS

Sofawolf Press was founded in 1999 to provide a venue to showcase great writers of anthropomorphic fiction and to promote the genre to a wider audience.

Since the debut of its flagship publication, Anthrolations, a literary anthology of short stories, the Press has added to its lineup other magazine-length anthologies, novels, shared-world anthologies, and other novel-length collections, comics and graphic novels, artists' sketchbooks, and calendars. The Press continues to seek out new and creative ways of expanding its offerings of printed creations. Sofawolf's publications have won twenty Ursa Major awards, and in 2012, Ursula Vernon's *Digger* gave Sofawolf Press its first Hugo Award.

Please visit their website at *www.sofawolf.com* for a full list of titles available from Sofawolf Press. Thanks for reading!